The dragon sho...
tering the adven...
a claw swipe on h...
backward. Uldane managed to step to the side as the dragon flew past, but at the last moment its tail snaked out to deliver a glancing blow to the halfling even as the tail's rounded, scale-covered tip slammed into Shara's chest and knocked her off her feet.

Jarren rolled with the blow that had hit his shield and jumped to his feet just as Borojon began rapidly firing arrows at the swooping dragon. Most bounced off the green scales, but a couple pierced the creature's tough hide.

Vestapalk soared in a great, wide arc, landing beyond the clearing at the river's edge. Jarren couldn't see the rushing water. The bank must have been higher than the level of the river at this point. He looked around wildly for his companions, but only Borojon remained on his feet, firing arrow after arrow as he moved toward the dragon.

Borojon fired another pair of arrows, and then he tossed his bow aside and drew two blades from their sheaths. "You'll kill no more farmers, monster!" Borojon shouted. "We shall destroy you for the harm and damage you have caused in the Nentir Vale."

"Is that what you call this insignificant depression in the earth, human?" the green dragon asked in a rasping, alien voice. It spoke the Common tongue, which sounded strange emerging from the green dragon's deadly maw. "This one calls it Vestapalk's hunting ground. This one shall take what Vestapalk wants and kill what Vestapalk pleases. This one shall start with you and yours, human. Is that your spawn this one smells lying in the grass behind you? Will her blood taste like yours, this one wonders? Will her guts show this one the sign he seeks?"

THE ABYSSAL PLAGUE

From the darkness of a ruined universe
comes the source of a new evil . . .
Follow the story from its very beginning with
The Gates of Madness,
a five-part prelude novella by James Wyatt

Part one is included in
FORGOTTEN REALMS®
The Ghost King
R.A. Salvatore.

Part two is included in
DUNGEONS & DRAGONS®
The Mark of Nerath
Bill Slavicsek

Part three is included in
DARK SUN®
City Under the Sand
Jeff Mariotte
October 2010

Part four is included in
FORGOTTEN REALMS
Whisper of Venom
Richard Lee Beyers
November 2010

Part five is included in
EBERRON®
Lady Ruin
Tim Waggoner
December 2010

**Bear witness to the worlds-spanning
DUNGEONS & DRAGONS event
beginning in March 2011 with**

DUNGEONS & DRAGONS
The Temple of Yellow Skulls
Don Bassingthwaite

DUNGEONS & DRAGONS®

BILL SLAVICSEK

THE MARK OF
NERATH

Dungeons & Dragons
The Mark of Nerath

©2010 Wizards of the Coast LLC

All characters in this book are fictitious. Any resemblance to actual persons, living or dead, is purely coincidental.

This book is protected under the copyright laws of the United States of America. Any reproduction or unauthorized use of the material or artwork contained herein is prohibited without the express written permission of Wizards of the Coast LLC.

Published by Wizards of the Coast LLC

DUNGEONS & DRAGONS, FORGOTTEN REALMS, EBERRON, DARK SUN, WIZARDS OF THE COAST, and their respective logos are trademarks of Wizards of the Coast LLC in the U.S.A. and other countries.

Printed in the U.S.A.

Cover art by Wayne Reynolds
Map by Rob Lazzaretti

First Printing: August 2010

9 8 7 6 5 4 3 2 1

ISBN: 978-0-7869-5622-7
ISBN: 978-0-7869-5762-0 (e-book)
620-24741000-001-EN

The sale of this book without its cover has not been authorized by the publisher. If you purchased this book without a cover, you should be aware that neither the author nor the publisher has received payment for this "stripped book."

U.S., CANADA,
ASIA, PACIFIC, & LATIN AMERICA
Wizards of the Coast LLC
P.O. Box 707
Renton, WA 98057-0707
+1-800-324-6496

EUROPEAN HEADQUARTERS
Hasbro UK Ltd
Caswell Way
Newport, Gwent NP9 0YH
GREAT BRITAIN
Save this address for your records.

Visit our web site at www.wizards.com

For my sister, who encouraged my imagination.

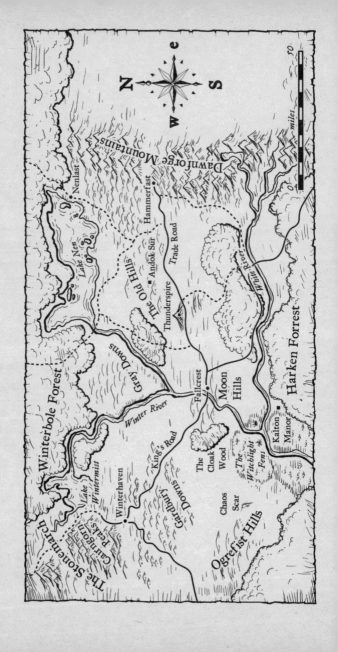

An ancient time, an ancient place . . . when magic fills the world and terrible monsters roam the wilderness . . . it is a time of heroes, of legends, of dungeons and dragons . . .

PROLOGUE
THE CAIRNGORM PEAKS, MIDDAY

Jarren followed Borojon through the thick-packed trees, watching for any signs of their quarry. The dwarf paladin Cliffside, strong and confident, strode a few paces back, an axe in his strong right hand.

"Any sign of that thrice-cursed dragon?" Cliffside called as he pushed through a thorn-covered bush, his shield in front of him to part the branches.

Jarren would have smiled if the situation didn't have him sweating beneath his scale armor. They had been following the green dragon for five days, tracking its course from the farms around Winterhaven and into the mountains beyond. Five days of travel, and they hadn't seen the beast in more than two days. They saw signs of its passing, though. Lots of signs.

"Care to shout a little louder, dwarf?" Borojon whispered loud enough for all of them to hear. "I don't think the orcs on the other side of the mountain heard you when you bellowed."

"I never bellow," Cliffside said, sounding hurt. "I just have a bit of gruffness to my voice."

"Never mind that," Borojon said, "I'd really like us to try to be stealthy right about now, if you please."

Jarren paused and stepped to the side of the path, letting the dwarf paladin pass by so that he could confer with Borojon. He waited, leaning against a tree, as the final members of their adventuring party appeared out of the forest.

The rogue Uldane slinked into sight, looking as though he was having the time of his life. Uldane was a halfling, one of the small folk. He stood about four feet tall, with a lean, athletic build and brown hair that hung loose and a little wild. Jarren liked the halfling. He couldn't help it. Uldane's curiosity and fun-loving nature were contagious. Uldane walked over to Jarren, smiled, winked, and held out a large platinum coin that Jarren recognized all too well.

Now a smile did cross the fighter's face. "Did I drop that again, Uldane?" Jarren asked. The platinum coin was Jarren's lucky charm, he supposed. It was an ancient Nerathi Imperial Crown, a coin of the old realm that Jarren's father had given to him when he left home to fight in the border wars five years ago. Lucky or not, the coin had remained with him through two years of battles with gnolls and hobgoblins and bandit gangs, one year of aimless travel, and for the two years that he had been part of Borojon's band. Except, that was, when Uldane practiced his sleight of hand by deftly slipping the coin into and out of Jarren's pocket.

"Must have slipped right out," Uldane laughed. "Lucky for you I spotted it on the path back there. I do have excellent perception, you know."

"So you keep telling me," Jarren said, gently closing the halfling's fingers around the coin. "Since I seem to keep losing that, why don't you hold on to it for me? You can return it after we've put an end to this dragon."

"Dragon? Is that what we're hunting this time?" said the tall woman with the long red hair. It was the same shade of red as Borojon's, except without the added gray that was rapidly filling the older man's hair and beard. She smirked boldly at Jarren, hands on her hips, her greatsword slung across her back.

"Must you take this threat so lightly, Shara?" Jarren asked, returning the female warrior's look with equal boldness.

"If I didn't take it so lightly, dear Jarren, I would probably run screaming back to the Vale and then you'd never see me again."

"Lightly. She learned that from me," Uldane proclaimed proudly.

"Well, that would be a terrible event, indeed," Jarren said in mock seriousness. "If I wasn't able to see you, to gaze into your intense blue eyes, to look upon your supple. . . . "

"Careful now," she warned, her red lips full of mirth.

"Anyway, you must stay close or I would be lost, dear Shara, so continue to mock our foe as much as you care to."

Uldane's expression turned serious, as though an important thought had just occurred to him. "This dragon is pretty smart, though. And mean. Did you see the way it played with that family of farmers before it slaughtered them?" Uldane shivered. Then the sensation seemed to pass as quickly as it had come, and he beamed happily. "Do you think it will breathe fire at us when we catch it?" he asked excitedly.

"Poison gas, Uldane," Borojon corrected as he appeared at the head of the path. "It's a green dragon, and they breathe poison gas. Not fire."

"Oh," the halfling said, a little disappointed. "Gross."

"Yes, well if you youngsters are done with your nap time, can we get back to the business at hand?"

"Of course, Borojon," Jarren said. "We're ready to take on three green dragons."

"One is more than enough for me," Shara declared. "Besides, this one insulted us, and for that it must pay."

"It killed twelve farmers and seven head of cattle and gods know what else," Borojon said. "That's why we're here. Don't forget that, girl."

"Never, Old Man."

That was the only term of endearment Jarren ever heard Shara use when she spoke to her father. But for all their bluster, he knew that they loved each other.

"Then let's get this over with," Borojon said, and he turned and led the group deeper into the forest.

Jarren and the others had walked for almost another hour when Borojon, in the lead, stopped. He studied the area for signs of the creature's passage, any telltale hint that would confirm that they were still on the dragon's trail. Borojon was a big man, robust despite his age. He wore two blades at his belt and a bow and quiver of arrows across his back. Borojon had been the leader of their band since before Jarren had joined them. He had trained them all in teamwork and hunting, and his daughter, Shara, had inherited all of the older man's skill and determination.

"Smart," Borojon murmured, "this beast's damn smart."

Cliffside moved closer. "I've been thinking about what we found at the first two farms," the paladin said, "before the dragon realized that we were following it."

"Spit it out, Cliffside," Borojon said as his eyes roamed across the path ahead, seeing everything but finding nothing. Jarren knew that the older man sensed something, however, and Jarren had grown to trust Borojon's instincts in their time together.

Shara moved up, giving Jarren's arm a gentle squeeze as she came to stand beside her father and the dwarf.

"The way the farmer and his family had been torn apart," the paladin explained, "gutted and their insides pulled out for all the world to see. The dragon was looking for something."

"Like that shaman we met a few months back? The one that read the future in a rabbit's intestines?" asked Uldane, his eyes bright with excitement.

"That's what it reminded me of," Cliffside agreed.

Jarren and Shara both noticed Borojon cock his head to the side, suddenly listening intently.

"What is it, Old Man?" Shara asked, her hand reaching for the pommel of her greatsword.

Borojon shook his head. "Just a feeling," he said. "The same feeling I had when we entered the Connal farmstead and found the bodies . . . a feeling that something terrible was nearby. Something that savors the fear in its victims."

"We are not afraid!" Cliffside rumbled, slamming his axe and shield together.

Jarren sighed. "And if the dragon didn't know where we were, I'm sure it does now."

"Let it come!" Cliffside demanded. "We can't kill it if it isn't here."

Shara smiled, as she always did when the male warriors had this kind of discussion. She leaned against a tree and planted her great-sword blade into the soil so that she could use both hands to extract her waterskin. She drank deeply, letting her eyes scan the area before they settled on Jarren. She had that gleam in her eyes that reminded him that Shara enjoyed her life. She relished the battles, the challenges. They were a lot alike, although she certainly found more fun in combat than he did. He was good at fighting and killing, and he appreciated the skill and prowess he had honed, but he always felt a little sad after a battle. Shara, however, reveled in the excitement and loved to feel her heart pumping and her blood rushing and the sweat dripping down her face. He loved her for who she was, and he believed that the feeling was mutual. Perhaps after this hunt, once the dragon was dispatched and they were back in Winterhaven, perhaps then she would finally agree to marry him as he had asked.

"Why rush?" she had said. "We have all the time in the world."

Jarren wished that that was so, but he had a bad feeling about this hunt. A very bad feeling.

Uldane whispered from his place a few paces back, "If we're taking a break, could Borojon make it official? I've got a fire apple I've been waiting to bite into all day."

"No break," Borojon said. "Shara, take up your sword and get back into position. Something is out of place up ahead, and until I figure out what, I want everyone on alert and ready for anything."

"I'm always ready for anything," Shara whispered to Jarren as she brushed past him. "Anything."

Jarren smiled and returned the whisper, "Later." When she was back in her place, he let his smile fade. He hoped they were going to have a later. But this dragon . . . it was unlike any creature they had faced before. Jarren hated to admit it to himself, but he was worried. This hunt felt more dangerous, somehow, than any of their previous missions.

The group pressed on. Borojon led the way, moving almost as silently as Uldane through the trees ahead. After a time, Borojon paused. "There's a river up ahead," he said. "It sounds fast and deep."

Jarren heard the rushing water, but there was another sound as well. And a smell. "There's something else in the clearing," he whispered, trying to keep his voice steady despite the sudden tension that filled his body.

Borojon crept forward, carefully parting the branches so that they could look into the clearing. The green dragon was there, leaning over the splayed corpse of a draft horse. The dragon had slit the horse open from neck to belly and was examining the animal's insides as they steamed in the cool afternoon air.

"The sign," the dragon growled as it poked and prodded with one extended claw. "Show Vestapalk the sign."

Vestapalk, Jarren thought as his stomach tried to turn over, *the dragon has a name.*

"It's an abomination," Cliffside grumbled, tightening the grip on his battleaxe. "Look at what the dragon's doing."

Vestapalk pulled a tangle of intestines out of the gaping wound and peered carefully at the mess. "The Eye has looked upon the land and the way has been opened," the dragon proclaimed, almost in a trancelike state. "An emissary has been sent, a harbinger of things to come. Vestapalk must find this Herald. This one must offer the Herald aid."

"What is it jabbering on about?" Borojon asked.

"Who cares?" Cliffside countered. "We must attack now, while it is otherwise occupied."

The dwarf paladin was moving then, rushing into the clearing and charging straight for the dragon.

Jarren saw a green blur as the dragon exploded into action. It was up and moving to meet the charging dwarf, swordlike talons slicing through the air. Cliffside screamed in pain as talons shredded armor and flesh, sending the dwarf spinning. The dragon never slowed, never roared. It rose into the air on powerful wings, disappearing into the cover of the trees just as Jarren and the others emerged into the clearing.

Borojon strode toward the wounded paladin, glancing once in the direction that the dragon had flown. "Maybe the beast has fled again," he said, bending down to examine Cliffside.

Maybe, but Jarren didn't think so. Not this time. They had interrupted something important. Something the dragon cared about.

And Jarren didn't think it was as fearful of them as Borojon believed it to be. The fighter listened to the rushing water that was ahead of them, beyond the clearing. The sounds seemed strange in this part of the forest, as though the river had somehow spun around and was now behind them. Growing louder. Getting closer. No, Jarren realized, it wasn't the river.

"Dragon!" he shouted, spinning in place as he raised his shield and drew his sword.

The others were moving, reacting to Jarren's warning. Shara dove to the side, while Uldane spun around to challenge the fast-moving creature. Borojon, meanwhile, leaned across the fallen paladin, meaning to protect his companion from another attack.

The dragon shot out of the trees like a massive green arrow, scattering the adventurers like leaves in a hurricane wind. Jarren caught a claw swipe on his shield, but the force of the blow sent him sailing backward. Uldane managed to step to the side as the dragon flew past, but at the last moment its tail snaked out to deliver a glancing blow to the halfling even as the tail's rounded, scale-covered tip slammed into Shara's chest and knocked her off her feet.

Jarren rolled with the blow that had hit his shield and jumped to his feet just as Borojon began rapidly firing arrows at the swooping dragon. Most bounced off the green scales, but a couple pierced the creature's tough hide.

Vestapalk soared in a great, wide arc, landing beyond the clearing at the river's edge. Jarren couldn't see the rushing water. The bank must have been higher than the level of the river at this point. He looked around wildly for his companions, but only Borojon remained on his feet, firing arrow after arrow as he moved toward the dragon.

Borojon fired another pair of arrows, and then he tossed his bow aside and drew two blades from their sheaths. "You'll kill no more farmers, monster!" Borojon shouted. "We shall destroy you for the harm and damage you have caused in the Nentir Vale."

"Is that what you call this insignificant depression in the earth, human?" the green dragon asked in a rasping, alien voice. It spoke the Common tongue, which sounded strange emerging from the green dragon's deadly maw. "This one calls it Vestapalk's hunting ground. This one shall take what Vestapalk wants and kill what Vestapalk pleases. This one shall start with you and yours, human. Is that your spawn this one smells lying in the grass behind you? Will her blood taste like yours, this one wonders? Will her guts show this one the sign he seeks?"

"We are not farmers that shall cower and die without a fight, dragon!" Borojon said, moving slowly yet purposefully toward Vestapalk.

"No," Vestapalk laughed. It was a terrible, frightening sound. "No, you are adventurers. Do you know how many adventurers Vestapalk has faced and killed in his time, human? This many!"

The green dragon turned its left forelimb so that Borojon and Jarren could see the inner scales. There were hash marks scratched in straight, even lines, starting at the wrist and working toward the elbow. Nine deep slashes, as though each was made with the swipe of a single claw.

"Before this day ends," the dragon proclaimed, "Vestapalk shall add five more marks to his scales."

"Never!" Borojon shouted. He began to charge the dragon, his twin blades glistening in the sun.

"Borojon! No! Wait for the rest of us!" Jarren called, but his leader wasn't listening. He was charging ahead, ready to face the green dragon by himself at the river's edge.

Jarren was sure that the dragon was smiling.

Vestapalk roared, and a blast of green gas exploded from its open maw. The gas struck Borojon, its noxious vapors boiling his flesh and filling his lungs with poison. Borojon tried to ignore the pain, but Jarren could see that he was moving slower because of the effects of the deadly gas. Borojon stumbled to one knee, and the dragon was upon him, clamping its powerful jaws onto his left shoulder and biting hard. Sharp teeth tore through leather armor, flesh, and bone, and Borojon wailed in agony.

Jarren was moving then, watching the blade fall from Borojon's left hand even as the younger fighter charged the dragon's left side. His shield raised high, Jarren delivered a mighty blow with his long sword, striking Vestapalk in the left shoulder. He found the spurt of blood to be extremely satisfying. But the green dragon never released Borojon. Instead, it fixed its intense gaze on Jarren, showing a terrible hatred even as it crunched down harder on the older man.

Borojon refused to scream again, but Jarren could see the gush of blood welling out of the older man's mouth. Borojon wasn't finished yet, however. He slashed upward with all his might, letting his right arm swing back like a pendulum to scrape along the scales that covered the top of the dragon's forelimb.

Vestapalk tossed the ravaged Borojon away like a well-gnawed piece of meat, and the old human slammed into a nearby tree with bone-crunching force. Jarren wasn't sure that even Cliffside's healing power would be enough to deal with Borojon's injuries—if the paladin was even still alive to use them. He hadn't recovered yet from the dragon's initial attack, and that wasn't a good sign. Jarren leaped to the side, preparing to make another attack when a dagger flew out of the woods and buried itself in Vestapalk's right nostril.

"Yes," said Uldane in an excited tone, "a bull's eye! Or a dragon's eye, maybe. That sounds good. A dragon's eye! I think the next one will find a nice home in the dragon's left eye socket."

Jarren saw that Shara was moving up to join him, her greatsword held across her body in preparation for her first strike against the dragon. "You'll pay for the injuries that the Old Man has suffered," she said, her voice cold and hard.

"Old?" Vestapalk asked in disbelief. "Old? This one shall never understand how the lesser creatures measure time."

Shara ignored the dragon's words. She swung her greatsword in a powerful arc, cutting through scale and biting into flesh as the blade traced a bloody slash across Vestapalk's neck. Jarren struck at almost the same moment, his sword piercing the green dragon's upper left forearm.

"By Moradin's holy hammer!" Cliffside shouted as he stumbled forward, holding his shield with the symbol of his god Moradin high enough for the dragon to see. The symbol was an anvil that burned with blue flame, superimposed on the head of a dwarven hammer. The shield glowed with power, and a lance of holy light flew from the symbol to smash into the dragon with unbelievable force. Suddenly the battlefield had changed, and Jarren could see that the dragon recognized the paladin as the obvious threat. It launched itself into the air with a single beat of its wings, landing atop the dwarf with terrible force. The dragon's claws pierced Cliffside's chest, driving him down and pinning him to the ground.

"You dare call upon another god in Vestapalk's presence?" the dragon roared. "When Vestapalk is here, there are no other gods!"

The green dragon pulled to each side, ripping the dwarf apart with a sickening tearing sound. Jarren couldn't believe how powerful the creature was, or how poorly his companions were working together. "Shara, Uldane, to me!" Jarren called, working out a new plan of attack even as the dragon turned back toward him.

Jarren stood tall, his weapon and shield at the ready. Uldane was to his left, nearer to the tree line. Shara was to his right, near the river's edge. The dragon watched them all, but its eyes were fixed on Jarren. It didn't see Borojon, battered, bloody, poisoned-ravaged

Borojon, lift himself up and stagger toward the dragon's exposed back, holding his remaining blade and preparing to strike. Before Jarren could call out an order, Shara was moving.

Shara rushed the dragon, attracting its attention and giving her father time to make his attack. Borojon made the most of the opportunity, slashing at the collection of muscles and tendons where the right wing connected to the dragon's body. With an audible effort, Borojon sunk his blade into the spot, coaxing a cry of pain from the dragon, even as it spun and bashed its body into Borojon's terribly wounded left side.

Shara never stopped moving, but before she was close enough to bring her greatsword to bear, Vestapalk's chest swelled up as it prepared to breathe poison again. Jarren realized that both he and Shara were in range of the dragon's breath. He brought his shield up, hoping to avoid the brunt of the blast, but there was nothing between Shara and the dragon.

With a mighty roar, Vestapalk released the cloud of caustic green gas. As Jarren ducked behind his shield, he saw Uldane leap past him. The halfling collided with Shara, and the two of them went sailing over the edge of the river and out of reach of the poison cloud. "Well done, rogue," Jarren whispered, as the cloudburst roiled around his shield and harmlessly dissipated. "Now it's my turn."

But Jarren realized that something was wrong. Shara and Uldane hadn't splashed into the river. He leaped over to the edge and saw that it was actually a dizzyingly high cliff. The rushing river was far below, its sound amplified by the high, rocky walls. Jarren locked gazes with Shara, who was falling toward the rushing water. He knew she was watching as Vestapalk towered over him. He knew she could see as he spun to face the creature. She could just watch as Vestapalk struck twice with its powerful claws and blood exploded from Jarren's freshly opened wounds.

Jarren hoped that Shara was now too far away to see him fall to his knees. To see the dragon triumphantly swipe its claw across its foreleg three times. To see it open its maw and bite as the life finally flowed out of Jarren in a single, powerful gush of blood and viscera.

As pain and darkness overtook him, Jarren's last thoughts went to Shara. "I love you," he whispered, glad that Shara, at least, had escaped the dragon's claws.

PART
ONE

1 DARANI, IN THE SHADOWFELL, TWILIGHT

Kalaban marched through the streets of Darani, head held high and eyes straight ahead. He realized long ago that this was the last remnant of the ancient empire of Nerath, the human-ruled utopia that once covered most of the known world. The familiar buildings, with architecture that borrowed freely from elf, dwarf, dragonborn, and tiefling, somehow remained uniquely human in design. The cobbled streets. Even the smells. It all combined to create an illusion of a time that had come and gone. And sometimes Kalaban felt as though he was the only person in the whole place who realized it. If not for his duty, he would have tried to find a way out of this weary existence long ago. He sighed and tried to ignore the insignificant and sorry peasants who scurried around him as they performed tasks out of habit. They were shadows, echoes of lives lost long ago.

Just like him.

Few others in the city might understand the truth of their existence, but Kalaban knew. He imagined that this knowledge was in some way tied to the hell he had been consigned to. Because Kalaban, knight-commander of Nerath and captain of the Imperial Guard, was dead, as was every other entity that inhabited poor, lost Darani. Or, to be more accurate, they were all undead.

Time had lost all meaning for Kalaban, but he remembered the day he had failed in his duty. That was the one blemish on an otherwise spotless record that had resulted in this unending nightmare from which there was no way to awaken. It had been a day like most other days for the Imperial Guard, which was charged with protecting Emperor Magroth: boring and glorious . . .

Kalaban stood beside his brother, Krondor, on the steps outside the Imperial Palace in Darani. Each of Nerath's imperial cities had a palace set aside for the emperor's use, in case Magroth was traveling. Magroth traveled often, and the members of his most-trusted Imperial Guard were always by his side. He was not a sit-in-his-castle ruler, not Magroth. The emperor enjoyed surveying his vast holdings almost as much as he enjoyed conquering neighboring lands and squelching rebellion. Kalaban sometimes wondered if the insults whispered by the crowds were true. They called Magroth "insane" and "mad." They likened him to a tyrant, and a few called him "demon." Kalaban knew that Magroth ruled with an iron fist, but the rest? His duty didn't allow him to question the methods or the orders of his emperor, so he tried not to think about such things.

The crowd this day seemed more nervous than usual. Rumors were rampant that the emperor had tracked a group of political malcontents to the walls of Darani, and now Magroth and his Imperial Guard were going to punish the entire city because of the supposed actions of a few. As usual, Kalaban had no idea what his emperor had in mind for today, but he knew that cruel punishment was not beyond Magroth's repertoire. He glanced over at Krondor, who was younger than Kalaban by two years, and noticed that his brother had a haunted, distant look in his eyes.

"Something bothering you, brother?" Kalaban asked.

Krondor continued to stare over the crowd, not turning to face his brother as he said, "What could possibly bother me on this fine day, Kalaban? Why, look at all the potential victims that have dutifully gathered before the palace for Magroth's amusement."

Anger flared in Kalaban. His little brother was very good at making him angry. "Lose the attitude, Krondor, and act like the Imperial Guard you're supposed to be."

"I've earned my post, Kalaban," Krondor said, "just as you have. Now leave me be so I can perform the duties assigned to me. Isn't that your credo? Duty above all?"

Before Kalaban could reply, the palace doors began to swing open. He glared briefly at his brother, and then stepped to the side to flank the stairs in anticipation of the emperor's appearance.

The usual swarm of advisers and attendants were absent today. Emperor Magroth strode out of the darkness of the palace entry into the daylight, walking alone, wearing his robes of office and carrying the staff that hinted at the arcane power he possessed. Sometimes Kalaban wondered why the emperor even kept the Imperial Guard. He never really seemed to need the protection. Kalaban had seen the emperor in action, and Magroth was a deadly foe. He easily tossed spells around that devastated single enemies and attacking armies alike. Kalaban had even seen Magroth survive wounds that would have killed any other man ten times over. The knight-commander had never determined if it was the wizardry or the emperor's own stubborn determination that allowed him to shrug off sword wounds or arrow or spear piercings, but Kalaban had seen the emperor survive such attacks with his own eyes. Sometimes the powers demonstrated by his emperor frightened him, and on those occasions he felt a bit closer to the common folk of the empire. But Kalaban couldn't dwell on such thoughts, and he forcibly turned his attention back to the emperor.

Approaching his fiftieth year, Magroth was hearty and robust. Tall and thin, his gaunt features were sharp and his eyes blazed with intelligence and—yes, Kalaban had to admit it to himself—a touch of madness that sometimes chilled the knight-commander to his core. The emperor took a few steps and stopped so that he stood directly between the two brothers who were his most trusted Imperial Guard. Magroth nodded at Kalaban, and then he turned to survey the crowd. The corners of his thin lips turned upward, and Magroth seemed to breathe deeply of the fear that rose from each man and woman gathered at the base of the palace steps.

Kalaban scanned the faces arranged before them, watching for any signs of treachery or danger. All he saw, though, was fear. It was etched into the expressions of the humans, dwarves, scattered elves, and halflings, and the few solitary dragonborn and tieflings in the crowd. They were afraid of their emperor. And Magroth relished that fear.

"People of Darani," Magroth said, his voice strong and loud, "a terrible danger to your emperor and to Nerath itself festers in the shadows of your fair city."

Muttered expressions of disbelief and denial reverberated through the crowd. Magroth allowed the people a few moments before he tapped his staff three times on the stone step, signaling them to fall silent.

"How hard it is to see the truth," Magroth said, "but that is why your emperor has come. I shall help you eliminate this danger. I shall help you become better citizens of this great empire." He paused, letting his words sink in, and his thin smile pulled back ever farther across his sharp, narrow features. "Though only a handful of malcontents hide within Darani's walls, you are all guilty of not seeing the signs. Of not taking action. Of forcing my own hand in these matters. For that, each family must sacrifice one of its own. Fathers and mothers, bring forth one child each. I want to see this square painted red in their innocent blood before the sun sets this very day, for their innocence is the price of your guilt!"

The crowd let out a shocked gasp. Kalaban reached for his weapon, certain that this announcement would elicit some kind of hostile response. If not for his own duty, Kalaban himself might have reacted as the crowd was to this unexpected punishment from Emperor Magroth. From the corner of his eye, Kalaban saw that Krondor was also drawing his blade. Suddenly, Kalaban's senses were screaming at him. Something was wrong! He turned to face his brother, his sword slipping free of its scabbard in one swift motion. But he was too late.

Krondor's dagger flashed once, twice, three times. The final time, Krondor left the bloody weapon sticking in the emperor's back. An expression of surprise replaced the smile on Magroth's face, as blood began to trickle from the corner of his mouth.

"This . . . is . . . not . . . possible . . . " Magroth sputtered, spraying crimson droplets with every hard-fought word. "No natural power . . . can . . . harm me . . . "

"I am no longer natural," Krondor spat, "and your reign of evil ends today!" He began to pull his sword free as Magroth dropped to both knees and blood stains spread across the back of his robes.

Kalaban struck then, driving the blade of his sword deep into Krondor's flesh, finding the exposed portion at his side where the armor didn't completely cover him. Krondor had assassinated the emperor, and Kalaban had killed his brother.

At the instant that Krondor fell, at the instant that the emperor simultaneously sank to the cold, blood-soaked steps, dark clouds covered the sky and blotted out the light of the sun. Thick mist began to rise from the cobbled streets, making it hard to see more than a few dozen feet in any direction. Kalaban tried to make sense out of what was happening. It seemed as though the entire city of Darani was sliding away, carrying them all with it as the dark clouds and thick mist consumed it. Even as the crowds screamed and wailed and prayed, even as Krondor's life slipped away, Kalaban could feel his own heart come to a sudden stop. The familiar beat was gone, but somehow Kalaban remained standing. Panic threatened to overwhelm him when he heard the strong, steady voice of his emperor at his side.

"Yes, Kalaban, we're dead," Magroth said. "Get over it and help me up." And then the emperor laughed. It was a crazed laugh, full of both sorrow and madness.

Now they were all trapped here, in a dread domain deep within the Shadowfell. The natural world has reflections, parallel planes of existence that have different laws and house different creatures. The Shadowfell, a dark echo of the world, was a place of the dead and the undead, as well as things of shadow and darkness. Not wholly evil, but certainly a place with a sinister side. Kalaban wasn't sure how much of this knowledge he had learned in the centuries since Darani slid into the Shadowfell and how much of it was just in his head as part of this afterlife punishment he believed he was suffering. No matter. He had the knowledge, and it was his particular burden to bear.

His and that of his emperor.

Which brought Kalaban back to the present. Emperor Magroth had sent for him, and he was already late in answering that summons. Kalaban picked up his pace. When he reached the palace steps, he mounted them two at a time. Images of his brother's body falling after his own sword struck flashed briefly before his eyes as he climbed the steps, but Kalaban refused to acknowledge them. He sometimes wondered why, of all of them, death had only truly claimed Krondor. But mostly he cursed his brother for bringing this disaster upon them and then having the good fortune of finding a way to escape from it while the rest of them had been trapped.

At the top of the steps, Kalaban ignored the guards stationed there and entered the palace. As always, it was cold inside. Cold like a grave, he realized.

Kalaban slowed his pace as he approached the emperor's audience chamber. There were voices inside. One was clearly Magroth, but Kalaban did not recognize the second voice participating in the conversation. It was a woman's voice, but it wasn't the voice of any woman in Darani. How could that be? In all the centuries that had passed since Darani had abandoned the natural world and taken up residence in the Shadowfell, it had been a closed domain. No one ever visited Darani. And worse, no one could ever leave. They were all trapped in this shadow city, punishment for the wrongs they had perpetrated in life. Or, at least, that was what Kalaban believed. Now there was a new voice in the palace, and Kalaban was both excited and afraid.

He paused outside the door to the audience chamber to listen, trying to determine if the newness of the strange voice was just a trick of his imagination.

"You must complete three tasks in return for your freedom," the woman said, her voice exotic and soft, but with an undertone that Kalaban couldn't identify.

"And these tasks? Do I get to know what they are before I sign in blood?" That was Magroth's voice. Kalaban could recognize that the emperor was attempting to disguise his rising excitement.

"Of course," the woman continued, "Lord Orcus would never require anyone to agree to a deal that was not fully understood by all sides."

"No, of course not," Magroth replied sarcastically. "So, these tasks?"

"First, you must locate the Necropolis Stone," the woman explained. "Called kelonite or dead glass, it is a fragment of crystal as black as a starless night, shaped into a triangular pendant encased in a gold frame. It resides in the tower of the wizard Moorin, in the town of Fallcrest. With the amulet, you will be able to track down Sareth, a creature who has turned away from Lord Orcus and abandoned its responsibilities. Take possession of the amulet and destroy Sareth. Do this, and your first task shall be complete."

"The second task must be performed within the lost Necropolis of Andok Sur. The Necropolis Stone shall guide you to this lost city of the dead. When you arrive, you shall perform a special ritual. I shall provide you with a scroll describing the ritual."

"Sounds easy enough," Magroth said. "And the last task?"

The woman paused. Kalaban contemplated entering the chamber, but before he could take a single step, he heard the next words the woman uttered. "The third task requires you to eliminate the remaining members of Nerath's royal bloodline," she said. "You must slay your remaining descendents."

"That's all?" Magroth responded. "And here I thought that the demon prince Orcus was going to ask for something difficult and disturbing."

Kalaban decided that he had heard enough. He entered the audience chamber and said, "You called for me, my emperor?"

Magroth turned to his knight-commander and a hint of annoyance played across his gaunt features. "Took your time, Kalaban," the emperor said. "This is Barana Strenk, a death priest of Orcus, the Demon Prince of Undeath. She has come a long way to see me this day."

Kalaban bowed before the woman. She was tall, shapely, and dressed in crimson robes. A streak of silver highlighted her otherwise black hair. Kalaban noticed two other things about the woman.

First, she wore a small, pearl skull around her neck, its mouth open as though in a scream. He assumed this was the symbol of her office as a death priest of Orcus. The second was that she was alive, and the warmth emanating from her was like a bonfire blazing within the death-cold of the palace. He was drawn to her warmth, her life, in a way that he had not experienced in countless centuries. It was all he could do not to rush over and bask in the life-heat that radiated from her.

Kalaban forced himself to say, "My lady." Then he took his usual position beside the emperor.

Barana glanced briefly at Kalaban, then she ignored him and turned back to Magroth. "Do we have a deal, Emperor Magroth?" she asked, but to Kalaban's ears it sounded more like a demand delivered in a soft, silky voice. Not unlike a sharp dagger hidden within a velvet glove.

Magroth rose from his throne, using his arcane staff to support his tall, gaunt frame. He had lost much of his vitality in death. His hair was totally white now, and his flesh was sunken and gray, stretched tight across his sharp-boned features. The handle of Krondor's dagger still jutted from Magroth's back. Try as they might, neither the emperor nor his knight-commander had ever been able to remove the weapon that had forged this Shadowfell domain.

Magroth's eyes were milky white, but they still shone with the intelligence and madness that Kalaban was familiar with. What was the term? Lich? Yes, that's what Magroth had become. A lich. And Kalaban had become a death knight.

The emperor faced the priest of Orcus. "The deal is struck."

"Very well," Barana nodded, "You have your freedom from this place . . . for a year and a day. Complete your tasks, and your freedom is forever. Fail and you shall be drawn back into this domain of dread as a moth is drawn to a flame."

Magroth laughed. "A year and a day? A year and a day? Does that sound like a fair amount of time to you, knight-commander?" The emperor suddenly turned serious as he faced the death priest. "And if that isn't enough time to do these tasks you require of me?"

"It must be," Barana said, "for that is all the time there is."

2 NENLAST, FALON'S HOME, DAY

Falon came awake to the sound of his mother's voice.

"Falon," she called from the doorway. "Did Cleric Basku declare a special holiday and I just didn't hear about it?"

"What?" Falon stammered, rubbing the sleep from his eyes. "No. Not that I know of. What are you talking about, Mother?"

His mother laughed. He loved the sound of her laughter, especially because he didn't often have occasion to hear it. She wasn't a sad woman, but she rarely laughed. He was sure it had something to do with his father's death, even though that was a long time ago. Or perhaps the more recent death of his grandfather had made her more reserved. But here she was, laughing at something he said, and he had no idea why.

"Come, my favorite son," she urged. "I've made the morning meal and if you don't eat it and get moving, you're going to be late. Cleric Basku has never been known as a patient and forgiving master."

"Favorite? I'm your only son. I'll be right out," Falon said, giving his mother the look that said "a little privacy, please."

She smiled, nodded, and stepped out of the doorway. "Don't take too long," she called back. "I have a feeling that you're in for a busy day."

Young Falon, fast approaching his seventeenth birthday, hopped out of bed and reached for his clothes. As Cleric Basku's only apprentice at the small shrine dedicated to Erathis, the god of civilization, Falon was never without either work or studies to occupy his time. He was a diligent student, an enthusiastic worker, and totally devoted to the teachings of Erathis. He had always felt a connection to the small shrine and the stories and parables that Basku shared with those who worshiped there, and when he turned thirteen he had asked his mother for permission to seek out an apprenticeship with the old cleric. His mother, just a little reluctantly, agreed.

He stepped into the kitchen, where the smell of fresh-baked bread and fried eggs made him realize just how hungry he was this morning. He sat at the large table, a plate already piled high and waiting for him. As he began to shovel the delicious food into his mouth, he noticed that there was an unusual amount of activity happening outside the house. People where talking animatedly and hurrying toward the outskirts of the village.

"What's going on?" Falon asked, his mouth full of warm, buttered bread.

"I'm surprised you were able to sleep through all of the noise," his mother said, placing a mug of fire apple juice beside his plate. "It started more than an hour ago. The caravan arrived this morning, and the dwarves are setting up a market just outside the village."

"The Hammerfast caravan? Isn't it a little early for that to be passing through?"

"Maybe a bit, but it never follows an exact schedule. When the dwarves have filled their wagons and are ready to make their biannual trek south, they always take the time to come up here and engage in a little trade with us and the tribes of the Winterbole Forest."

Falon sighed. "I guess you're right about the day being busy. Cleric Basku will want to bless the caravan, and we're sure to get at least a few extra bodies at this afternoon's and evening's ceremonies. I better get going."

Falon finished the last of the eggs and bread, then washed it down by draining his mug of juice. He made sure he had his mace, which he wore more for show than any need to protect himself here in the village.

"Will you be heading over to the caravan market?" he asked as he reached the door.

"Certainly," his mother said, a hint of excitement in her voice. "You never know what the dwarven merchants have with them, and many of the best things disappear quickly. You know how Old Lady Hagger always tries to grab all the cave mushrooms before any of the rest of us can get any."

"I'm sure you can move faster than Old Lady Hagger," Falon smiled. "Just don't knock her over on your way to the mushroom tent."

Falon and his mother exchanged good-byes, and then the young cleric headed for the Erathis shrine. He pushed his way through the crowd of people heading toward the hastily constructed caravan market. Everyone from the village and the surrounding farms would be crawling all over the place by the time the sun was high in the sky. Falon almost considered heading in that direction himself, but then he remembered the chores waiting for him at the shrine. He had responsibilities, and there was no room in his day for browsing the market stalls or talking with the caravan dwarves. He sighed and turned toward the path that led to the shrine.

Falon took a single step, when suddenly a tightness clutched at his chest. Something was wrong. He slowly turned back to scan the crowd. Nothing seemed out of the ordinary, other than the excitement instigated by the arrival of the dwarves. Still, for a moment it had seemed like something terrible was about to happen. The feeling was gone now, fading away like a bad dream. Had he imagined it? He looked around again. He saw plenty of faces he recognized, people from the village or the surrounding countryside, a few Winterbole barbarians, and more dwarves than he had ever seen in one place.

Falon shook his head. Whatever it was, it seemed to be gone now. Maybe he'd mention it to Cleric Basku and see what his master thought. But Falon would forget by the time he reached the shrine and was given the extra duties that Cleric Basku had decided needed to be done that day.

Besides, he never actually saw the two tall figures, their hoods drawn tight and their cloaks covering their gaunt forms, as they passed through the crowd across the way.

3 WINTERHAVEN, GRAVEYARD, TWILIGHT

Erak awoke in absolute darkness. He lay completely still, feeling the cold, hard stone beneath his back. Where was he? Why was he here? After long moments of listening to the deep silence, he sat up. Pain blazed through him as his forehead smashed into something hard barely a foot above him. Erak fell back, stunned. He tried to think, to remember how he had gotten to this place. He knew that his name was Erak, and he remembered only fleeting images of which he could barely make sense. And pain. He remembered pain. He remembered dying and pain and darkness. And he remembered the woman's voice as it followed him from the depths of sleep.

Arise, my champion, the woman's voice had said, *You have work to do.*

Erak couldn't see at all as he gingerly reached upward. He placed his hands on cold stone pressing down on him from above. He reached to the sides and found the same cold stone. He was inside a stone box of some sort. No, that wasn't right. He knew where he was. He was in a coffin. Buried.

Erak reached up again, setting his hands on the stone slab. He pushed. Nothing happened. Fear began to well up within him, threatening to drive him into a panic that would surely be the end of him. Instead of allowing that to happen, Erak channeled the fear into strength, and he pushed again with all of his might.

At first, the stone slab above him remained securely in place. Then, ever so slowly, it began to move. Erak continued to apply pressure, despite the pain, and the effort paid off. The stone slab slowly grinded open, revealing a sliver of moonlight that eventually widened enough for Erak to squeeze his way out of . . . what was this? A sarcophagus? Another memory surfaced, again in the woman's voice.

The living have need of the dead this day, my champion, the woman had said.

Erak stumbled out of the sarcophagus and tried to get his bearings. He appeared to be in a small, stone building. A window high on the wall showed the deepening darkness beyond and let in the light of the rising moon as it hovered above the tree line. The headstone at the top of the stone coffin bore no name or date, just a carved symbol of a bird's head. No, more than just a bird, Erak thought. A raven.

The symbol of the Raven Queen, the god of winter and fate. The god of death.

Erak shivered. Was this his tomb? Was he dead?

The word "revenant" suddenly surfaced in his thoughts.

"I was dead," Erak said aloud, and his own voice sounded loud and alien in this otherwise silent chamber.

He remembered the darkness, the quiet. He remembered the lady's presence. The Raven Queen? He couldn't be certain, but that felt right to him somehow. Why had she cast him out? Why was he back in the world of pain and anguish?

Arise, my champion.

Her words echoed in his mind.

You have work to do.

Erak shuddered. He was cold, and his chest felt heavy and empty. At the same time, his thoughts were a confused jumble of images and half-formed sensations. Perhaps they would sort themselves out in time. Perhaps not. No matter. He had work to do.

After a quick examination of the tiny mausoleum, he found a wrapped package at the foot of the sarcophagus. It was sealed with a wax casting of a raven's head. Erak broke the seal and examined the contents of the package. There was a long sword with an exotic and cruel blade, all elegant curves and terrible serrations, with hints of crimson within the folded steel. The pommel featured a raven's head, one crimson eye set on each side.

"Hellsteel," Erak said, touching the blade as he remembered the word. Tiefling crafted, he knew, whatever that meant.

He set the weapon aside to examine the armor. It was padded leather, with lots of straps and buckles, dyed as black as the inside of Erak's coffin. It fit perfectly. He donned the accompanying leather jacket colored a blue as deep as darkest twilight. The armor and jacket felt right as he fastened the buttons.

Erak picked up the long sword and headed for the mausoleum's stone door without glancing back at the sarcophagus he had emerged from. The door was heavy, but it was equipped with hinges that allowed it to swing open easily. It certainly required a lot less effort than moving the stone slab that had covered his tomb. With the door opened, he stepped out into the night. It was time to leave this place of the dead behind him. It was time to do his work.

Erak took a couple of steps and paused. Had he heard something? He listened intently, trying to determine if he had heard a noise or if his thoughts and scattered memories were playing tricks on him. He turned slowly, examining the deep shadows clumped around the mausoleum he had just emerged from.

Nothing moved. No sounds broke the stillness of the night. Erak sensed danger in the darkness, however, and he drew the hellsteel blade from its sheath. The first creature appeared then, slipping out of the shadows to crouch atop the edge of the mausoleum's roof. It was humanoid in form, but its flesh was ashen gray and its mouth was nearly bursting with large, oversized teeth. Erak recognized the creature as a ghoul, and it hadn't come alone. There were at least five of the undead scavengers sliding out of the shadows around Erak's one-time tomb.

"It looks edible, don't it, you flesh-eaters?" the first ghoul growled around its mouth full of pointed teeth.

"Hungry," moaned two of the ghouls.

"Edible, edible," sang the other two as they danced from side to side. One of them was gnawing the last bits of meat off a long bone as it sang.

Erak took the measure of these filthy creatures, noting their long, talonlike nails, their hunched posture, and the stink that perfumed the air around them. By the Lady of Fate, he hoped he didn't smell like that.

The first ghoul leaped down from the roof of the mausoleum, landing lightly on the path between the tomb's door and where Erak stood. "There's no honor among the dead," the ghoul sneered, "at least not in this graveyard. Our graveyard, really. To us, you're just more meat."

"A little more ambulatory than most," another ghoul called.

"That just makes it interestin'," a third ghoul said as it laughed.

Erak returned their smiles, but it was a hard, humorless smile, and it caused the lead ghoul just a moment of pause.

"Your call," Erak said, his eyes locked on the ghoul that had stopped a few paces back along the path.

The lead ghoul hesitated. It seemed to weigh its options, glancing back once to gauge the mood of its companions. Then it made its decision and hurled itself forward, its talonlike nails cutting through the air toward Erak's face. But before the ghoul could strike, Erak was in motion. He easily dodged the ghoul's lunging attack, following through with a single sweep of the hellsteel blade he had found in the tomb. It was a fine weapon, and it seemed to have been specifically crafted just for him. The curved blade cut deep, drawing forth a howl of pain from the ghoul. Before it could react, however, Erak stepped into the ghoul's shadow—and disappeared.

The ghouls fell silent, collectively disoriented by the behavior of their supposed dinner. Erak stepped out of the shadow of one of the other ghouls and plunged his sword into the foul creature's back. The curved tip briefly emerged from the ghoul's chest before Erak drew it back out and then turned the motion into a slice that lopped off the creature's head. He turned to face the one beside it.

The ghoul flew into a rage and leaped toward Erak. As it moved closer, Erak gathered the shadows around him and seemed to fade. The ghoul passed right through Erak's now shadowy form and smashed headlong into the stone wall of the mausoleum with bone-breaking force. It fell to the cold ground, stunned by the impact.

Erak never paused. He stepped away from the two fallen ghouls as his body began to shift back into solid form. Before the shadows completely faded away, he scooped a handful out of the air and hurled them. The shadows became a volley of black darts that streaked toward the lead ghoul. The ghoul started to break to the left, but the shadow darts struck in rapid succession. The lead ghoul collapsed even as Erak strode back to stand over its body. He turned to face the remaining undead.

"Well?" he asked, the hellsteel blade held ready in his right hand.

"Hungry," one of the ghouls repeated.

"Not that hungry," the other said.

"No, not tonight."

Without another word, the ghouls slipped back into the shadows and were gone, leaving Erak alone in the graveyard. He sheathed the hellsteel blade, turned, and walked out into the night.

4 FALLCREST, MOORIN'S TOWER, NIGHT

The wizard Moorin drew his robes around him. The cold and the damp bothered him more these days than he cared to admit, and the recent rain made his bones ache. If not for the fact that it was expected of him, he'd close up the tower and move everything into a warm and comfortable manor house. Maybe when he retired and turned over his spellbooks and library to his apprentice, Albanon. Maybe then he could find a home that wasn't always chilly. Speaking of the young eladrin, Moorin wondered where his apprentice was and what he was doing.

"Albanon?" Moorin called. "I'm preparing to seal the tower for the night."

"Your lazy, good-for-nothing apprentice is down in his room, getting ready to go gallivanting around town," purred the small creature sitting on the arm of one overstuffed chair. She was a tiny dragon, about the size of a house cat, covered in scintillating scales that reflected the light from the fireplace she sat in front of.

Moorin smiled at the psuedodragon and rubbed under her jaw. "Now, Splendid," Moorin said as the tiny dragon cooed, "you know perfectly well that Albanon is neither lazy nor good for nothing. He does feed you every day, doesn't he?"

Splendid seemed to consider this for a moment. "Yes, but he doesn't do it well. The bowl he uses could certainly hold more than he ever puts in it."

Moorin chuckled. "Well, I'll certainly have to have a talk with him about that."

"See that you do," Splendid said as she closed her eyes and immediately fell asleep in front of the fire.

The old wizard sighed. If only he could fall asleep that easily. He almost envied the tiny dragon. Years of aches and pains, combined with memories that never truly grew quiet, made the long hours before dawn particularly difficult for the old man. He tipped his staff, pointing it toward the burning fire. With a whispered word of power, the fire in the hearth went out.

"Hey!" snarled Splendid, opening one eye to stare at the wizard. "I'm sleeping here!"

"Upstairs," Moorin said quietly. "Your perch awaits."

Splendid grumbled, but the words were too soft for Moorin's old ears to pick up. The psuedodragon took flight, winging her way to the upper levels of the tower.

Moorin slowly followed, walking toward the stairs that were set against the outer wall. The stone steps led up to his library and work space or down to the two sleeping chambers below ground. Using his wizard's staff to support his weight and help him maneuver, he began to work his way downstairs.

As Moorin took the stairs slowly, one at a time, he could feel his left hand and arm begin to shake. The episodes were coming upon him with increasing regularity. He knew that his time as a fully functioning master wizard was almost at an end. If he was honest with himself, he knew that he hadn't been fully functioning for more than a year. The old wizard was dying. He just wasn't ready to admit it to the world. Not yet. There was still so much to do.

And it started with Albanon.

Moorin paused in the doorway to Albanon's sleeping chamber and watched the young eladrin as he critically examined a set of robes and a mantle that hung more like a jacket when worn. Albanon was about six feet tall and slim, with fine silver hair and long, pointed ears. He had been with Moorin since his eleventh birthday. It was sometimes hard for Moorin to believe that seven years had passed. It seemed like only yesterday that the eladrin had come to his tower to study.

"I'd go with the mantle," Moorin said. "The cut looks good on you and the blue brings out the color of your eyes."

Albanon turned to look at the older wizard, showing the opalescent blue orbs of his eyes. As with all eladrin, the close cousins of elves who hailed from the Feywild instead of the natural world, Albanon's eyes were solid orbs of color that glowed softly in the dim light of the chamber.

"If it's all right with you, master," Albanon began, "I thought I'd go out for a little while this evening."

"Back to the Blue Moon?" Moorin chuckled. "Who is it this time? Are Valenae and her father back in town?"

"No, no. I heard that a couple of adventurers were passing through and I wanted to listen to their stories. If that's all right."

The old wizard nodded. He had much to discuss with his apprentice, much he still had to prepare him for. But it could wait until tomorrow. It was good to see that Albanon was trying to fit in. Most eladrin projected a detachment that could make them seem distant and intimidating. But Albanon had come to the natural world specifically to engage in new experiences, as well as to learn the arcane arts from Moorin. The old wizard was proud of how far the young eladrin had come.

"Of course, Albanon," Moorin said. "Have fun. I'll set the wards around the tower, but I'll leave the inside wards dormant until you return."

"Thank you, master!" Albanon burst out. His time in the natural world had made him more expressive than other eladrin that Moorin had known, including Albanon's father. "I won't be very late."

As the young eladrin started for the stairs, Moorin cleared his throat. "What are you forgetting, my apprentice?"

Albanon froze in place, took a deep breath, and slowly turned to examine his room. His gaze finally came to rest on a slender, tapered piece of wood on the dressing table. "My wand," he said, looking embarrassed.

"Your wand," Moorin agreed.

Albanon snatched it and ran up the stairs. "See you later, master!" he called from above. Moorin heard the heavy tower door open and shut.

The old wizard sighed and sat down heavily on Albanon's bed. He watched as his left hand shook uncontrollably. Time catches up with us all, Moorin thought. Even wizards. He tried to begin cataloging all the things he had to explain to Albanon in the morning, but there was so much that came to mind. The kelonite, for one. The glass cylinder and the Order of Vigilance, for another. And whenever Moorin thought about the Order, he remembered his old friend Kri. He hadn't seen Kri in more than ten years, but Moorin knew that the cleric was still out there, fighting the good fight and keeping an eye out for any signs that the invaders had returned.

Why had his ancient mind suddenly coughed up these particular memories, Moorin wondered? He looked at his left hand, with its gnarled fingers and the scars from battles fought long ago, and he tried to make the shaking stop. It didn't. He slowly rose and stepped from Albanon's room to his own chamber across the hall. He was tired tonight, very tired. Maybe sleep would come more easily this night. He set his staff against the headboard and stretched out on his bed.

And with thoughts of things he had to tell Albanon and memories of old companions, Moorin drifted off into a fitful sleep.

5 NENLAST, THE DRUNKEN GOBLIN TAVERN, NIGHT

Darrum sat with his back to the wall, nursing a tankard of ale. Darrum was a dwarf ranger, about four and a half feet tall and built solid and broad of shoulder. He wore intricately detailed leather armor that must have been impressive in its day. But the armor's day, like Darrum himself, had been long ago. Now it was scuffed and stained and repaired more times than the old dwarf could count. He had lost his right eye in a battle long ago, and the leather patch that covered it appeared as weathered as the rest of the dwarf. Only his gray hair and beard, long and braided, hinted at the pride that Darrum still possessed somewhere deep within his soul.

It was a crowded night in the Drunken Goblin, a small tavern in the small village of Nenlast, the last plot of settled land in the northeastern corner of the Nentir Vale. Nenlast sat on the eastern shore of Lake Nen, where its mostly human population earned a living by fishing and trading with the barbarian tribes of the Winterbole Forest. It was a quiet spot, a great place to pass some time in utter obscurity, which was just the way Darrum preferred to spend his time these days. Unfortunately, the usual quiet that filled Nenlast was replaced with the bustling activity that always accompanied the arrival of a trading caravan—especially a large caravan on its way to distant towns and villages far to the south. Twice a year, such a caravan diverted from its usual route to visit Nenlast. It was just Darrum's luck that he happened to arrive in the village only a few days before the caravan.

The trading caravan hailed from the dwarven town of Hammerfast, laden with dwarven goods of all descriptions, including weapons, armor, tools, jewelry, and raw materials pulled from the mines of the Dawnforge Mountains. The carts and wagons probably also contained various goods and foodstuffs from the nearby settlements of Fallcrest, Harkenwold, the Seven-Pillared Hall, and Winterhaven, since it made more sense to combine the cargo of several merchants into one easier-to-protect caravan than to let the small-time traders fend for themselves. It was just good business, and the dwarves—especially the dwarves of Hammerfast—were all about good business. Darrum should know. He grew up in Hammerfast. But that was a very long time ago, in another life.

Darrum scanned the tavern's common room with his one good eye. Just yesterday he was one of a handful of dwarves in Nenlast. Now he was one of dozens. That didn't make Darrum feel less conspicuous. On the contrary, he felt as though he had suddenly been thrust into the center of attention, though he couldn't quite understand how that could be. The old ranger was quickly coming to realize that his short time in Nenlast was nearing its end. It was time to pack up his few belongings and move on. Again. Something felt wrong in the small village. It was a sense that had started building with the arrival of the trade caravan and had become more intense as the day slid into evening. Darrum trusted his instincts, and he wasn't about to break his long habits of caution and vigilance after they had served him so well for almost one hundred and twenty-five years.

Darrum sipped his ale. He was old, especially by human standards. But for a dwarf, he still had a few years left before he was ready to take on the mantle of "venerable" or—gods forbid—"ancient." How he hated that word. Ancient was a term that should be applied to the ruins of the long-dissolved kingdoms that dotted the landscape, places with names such as Bael Turath and Arkhosia. It could also be used to describe forests and mountains, artifacts and relics. But it should never be applied to a person, whether he or she be human, dwarf, elf, or dragonborn. And Darrum, no matter how old and battered he lived to be, would never willingly allow the term to be applied to him. At least not as long as there was enough strength left in his arms to swing his twin hammers, *Dawnfire* and *Nightstorm*. He sipped again, smiling at the thought of himself as a decrepit old man trying to heft warhammers that were larger and heavier than he was. Then he paused in mid-sip, trying to figure out why such a depressing thought held even the slightest bit of humor.

Darrum shook his head and turned his attention back to the common hall. There was the usual collection of locals, grumbling about the weather or the current influx of strangers. Off-duty caravan guards crowded around the bar, drinking their way through various contests they used to amuse and test themselves as they approached heavy inebriation. Merchants and clerks and a handful of travelers filled the tables scattered throughout the chamber, pouring wine, telling stories, and even conducting a small amount of business while they passed the hours in front of the fire.

One old dwarf was staring at Darrum from a nearby table. His eyes were heavy with drink, but he had a look of intense concentration despite his obvious state of drunkenness. The old dwarf stood, spilling beer from the cantered tankard he held tightly in one thick-fingered hand. He stumbled toward Darrum, his expression never faltering.

"I know you," the drunken old dwarf muttered, spraying foam with every word. "You're one of those Imperial Shields bastards, so high and mighty. . . ."

"Leave me be," Darrum said, trying to sink deeper into his corner of the tavern. "Imperial Shields haven't been seen in the land since the fall of the Empire of Nerath, and that was a long time ago."

"Where were you, oh high and mighty Shield, when the empire was crumbling?" the drunken old dwarf demanded, his voice growing louder as his anger built up a head of steam. "Where were you when poor old Emperor Aldoran was slaughtered? Why didn't you do your duty and save him?" The old drunk fell to his knees then, wracking sobs overtaking him, and his words slurred into blubbering incoherency.

Darrum stared at the older dwarf, unsure what to do. The drunk's words had struck home, however, because those were the same questions that Darrum had asked himself every night for the past century. *What more could I have done? Why did I survive when so many of my comrades had fallen along with the empire?* And, just like every night for the past century, Darrum had no answers.

One of the barmaids gently laid her hands on the old dwarf and whispered, "It's all right, Togon, it's all right." She gave Darrum an apologetic smile and led the drunken dwarf closer to the fire. "Leave the poor man be and let's get you to someplace more comfortable," she said as he allowed her to lead him away.

Darrum took a long pull on his tankard, letting the bitter ale calm his rattled thoughts. The old drunk had recognized him, somehow, and his words had pierced him like arrows from a gnoll's bow. He turned away from the barmaid and the old dwarf, and that's when he noticed the two strangers near the door.

They were tall and lean, hidden beneath dark hoods drawn tight and dark cloaks that fell almost all the way to the floor. Humans? Elves? Might even be tieflings under there, Darrum thought. The way they held themselves. The way their cloaks hung. The way the shadows seemed to drape around them. Darrum's instincts warned him to be wary of these two. They were dangerous, of that he had no doubt. But there was something else about them that Darrum couldn't quite identify. Not yet. At least they didn't seem to be paying any attention to him or the brief drama that had taken place between him and the drunk. No, the two hooded figures seemed to be looking for someone else in the crowd. And the way they were concentrating their attention on the taller folk in the place, Darrum was confident that they weren't looking for a one-eyed dwarf or a prancing halfling.

After a few moments, the pair slipped out into the night. Darrum drained the last of the ale in his tankard, dropped a couple of copper pieces on the table, and followed the hooded figures out of the crowded tavern.

I might be getting old, Darrum thought, *but I'm not dead yet.*

6 NENLAST, THE SHRINE OF ERATHIS, NIGHT

Falon collected the flowers and other offerings left at the foot of the altar in the small shrine dedicated to Erathis, the god of civilization and laws. He dropped the flowers into the large wicker basket that hung around his neck. The shrine was a simple affair, little more than four stone pillars that formed a square within the small park. The altar, a stone block inscribed with the half-circle symbol of Erathis, a rising sun within a gear, was placed at one end of the square, and the pillars that rose above it held a stone crossbeam that served as a small roof over the shrine. The rest of the square was open, though the garden beyond created a curtain of flowers and bushes that gave the place a serene privacy that the young man loved. The solitude was even more pronounced at this time of night, when most of the business of the village had slowed to a crawl. He enjoyed working in the evening, in the crisp night air, when Cleric Basku had already retired and Falon had the place to himself.

As Falon worked, he let his mind wander. Though he was content studying to be a cleric of Erathis in the out-of-the-way community of Nenlast, he sometimes dreamed about what life was like in one of the larger settlements, such as Winterhaven or even Fallcrest. He sometimes even imagined himself on a grand adventure, as a heroic cleric, striking out to bring the light of Erathis to the untamed darkness of the world. They were fine dreams, and they helped pass the time as he completed his chores while the rest of the shrine was quiet and empty at the end of the day.

Young Falon had never stepped beyond the borders of the tiny village. His family had lived in Nenlast since, well, since forever, at least according to the stories his grandfather used to tell him. Falon missed his grandfather. He didn't remember his father, whom he had been told had died in the gnoll raids shortly after Falon was born. His mother raised him, and his grandfather had always been a stabilizing force in his life. His grandfather had died last winter after catching an illness from which he had never recovered. He had often filled Falon's head with stories of adventurers, of distant places, of lost treasures and heroic deeds. Maybe that was why Falon had tried so hard to become apprentice to Cleric Basku here at the shrine in Nenlast. "A good cleric always has a place in an adventuring party," Falon's grandfather had told him on more than one occasion. Falon smiled at the memory. Whatever had driven him to a religious life, Falon knew one thing. He had heard the call of Erathis, and he had answered it with all his heart and soul.

The young cleric set aside thoughts of his grandfather and adventure and got back to his chores. Basku could get extremely unpleasant when Falon failed to keep the small shrine tidy. Luckily, a small shrine meant that there was never a terrible mess to clean up, though the garden around the shrine constantly needed tending. Falon was almost finished when he heard the familiar voice of his friend Gamun, strong and loud in the small courtyard, call a greeting.

"Why did I know I was going to find you here, friend Falon?" Gamun said, his deep voice resonating.

"Because this is where I always am?" Falon replied. "You know that Cleric Basku works me as though I was his slave instead of his apprentice."

"Ah, my friend, my heart bleeds for you and your terrible woes," Gamun said as he laughed and strode into the center of the shrine's square.

Gamun was one of the goliaths of the barbarian tribes of the Winterbole Forest, though he regularly visited Nenlast with his father to engage in trade. The two young men were about the same age, but Gamun was much taller and more powerfully built than the young human. They had met six years earlier, on one of the first trips in which Gamun had accompanied his father to the village, and their friendship had grown stronger with each passing year.

"Why aren't you out and about, mingling with the visiting dwarves or exploring the market camp set up around the caravan outside the village?" Gamun asked. "It's like you have no adventure in you, no curiosity."

"I have responsibilities, Gamun," Falon said. "We can't all be carefree wanderers."

Gamun frowned. "That's true. You would not make a very good carefree wanderer."

"Oh? And why not?"

"Because you care too much, my smallish friend," the goliath said, laughing.

Gamun's laugh was infectious, and Falon couldn't help but join in. He laughed hard, spilling some of the flowers he had collected from the wicker basket hanging around his neck. He reached down, letting his left sleeve slide up to reveal the birthmark on his wrist. It was an unusual mark, and Falon usually took great pains to keep it covered. The mark was shaped like a crown, with three small star-shaped dots arced above it. He quickly pulled his sleeve down. He didn't know why he tried to hide it, but it had become almost a reflex to do so.

"Let me help with that," Gamun said, moving forward and bending to gather the fallen flowers.

As the goliath stepped in front of the young cleric, Falon heard something whistle out of the darkness. There was a sound of fabric and flesh being pierced, and a metal shaft buried itself into Gamun's shoulder. With a small grunt of pain, Gamun shoved Falon to the ground just as a second bolt whizzed past them and ricocheted off the altar.

"Crossbows," Falon whispered as he tossed aside the wicker basket and pulled the mace from his belt.

"But who would attack a holy shrine, and why?" Gamun asked, drawing his own sword. He was forced to use his left hand, since the wound to his right shoulder made that appendage unusable.

"Let's figure that out after the fighting is finished," Falon said, getting back to his feet as he scanned the area for their unknown attackers.

"There," Gamun grunted, gesturing toward the path that led through the garden away from the shrine. Two figures stood in the shadows, tall and lean, with long cloaks billowing around them. They discarded their crossbows, letting them fall beside the path as they drew long swords from sheathes hanging at their waists.

The two figures separated, moving through the garden from each side as they rushed toward the shrine. They moved with supernatural speed, Falon thought, and there was something else about the pair that made the hairs on the back of his neck stand on end. Before he could work out what it was, one of the attackers was on him. Falon brought his mace up quickly, but even so he barely managed to deflect his attacker's blade as it blurred through the air.

From the sound of metal clanging on metal, Falon knew that Gamun had engaged the second attacker in combat. "Be careful, Falon," the goliath called, "these aren't your ordinary sort of bandits or brigands."

Falon used every bit of skill and luck he could muster to keep his attacker's sword from finding flesh. He parried with his mace, though every strike of the sword reverberated through his arms and made his hands ache. The tall figure was fast and strong, and the young cleric knew that it was only a matter of time before the attacker found a way through his meager defenses. He dodged and side stepped, swinging his mace hard to try to land a blow of his own, but to no avail. The tall figure easily deflected the mace and intensified its own assault.

As they fought, Falon instinctively uttered a prayer to Erathis. The words came naturally to the young cleric, and they were pure and heartfelt. As the divine energy gathered, Falon's mace glowed with power. His attacker hesitated before the building light, taking a step back as though trying to assess the extent of this potential danger. Then the light flashed, releasing a searing burst that rolled into and through the attacker. As the light burned away, the cloaked figure collapsed to the ground.

Falon turned to see how Gamun was doing and his heart skipped a beat. The second attacker had managed to disarm the goliath, who had been forced to use his weaker hand to hold his sword. The second attacker was about to plunge its weapon into Gamun's exposed chest when suddenly a new figure leaped out of the garden's shadows. It took Falon only a moment to recognize the new figure as a dwarf, compact and powerfully built, with a gray beard that contained only hints of black and a patch over his right eye. He swung two warhammers that appeared to be exact opposites. One was bright as a sunny morning, its head a brilliant gold. The other was as dark as the deepest night, its head a deep gray that was almost black. The dwarf dispatched the second attacker without a word, striking it over and over with his warhammers. The weapons flashed each time they struck the cloaked assailant, hinting that they were enchanted in some way.

Falon was so captivated by the dwarf's spinning weapons that he failed to notice a third attacker slip out of the dark garden surrounding the shrine. "Your blood for Orcus!" the attacker cried, driving its sword toward the young cleric. Falon managed to raise his left arm protectively, and the sword slashed him from bicep to elbow. Falon staggered back, trying to call upon a prayer or to bring his mace up, but the attacker was too close, too fast.

"No more blood for your master this night," the dwarf declared, hurling his golden hammer. It spun through the space between dwarf and attacker, glowing like a miniature sun. When it struck the third attacker squarely in the chest, its light exploded in a burst that forced Falon to avert his eyes. As his vision cleared, he noticed that Gamun was examining the attacker that Falon had defeated.

"I think you killed this one, Falon," Gamun said, sounding surprisingly impressed.

The dwarf shook his head. "You may have defeated it," the dwarf said, ripping Falon's sleeve so that he could examine the wound on his arm, "but these three were already dead when they attacked you."

The dwarf turned Falon's arm, studying the birthmark on his wrist. Falon pulled his arm away. "I'm fine," he stammered, feeling uncomfortable at the look of recognition that seemed to pass before the dwarf's good eye at the sight of his birthmark. "Let me tend to Gamun's wound."

The dwarf let Falon go, and he turned to stare into the dark garden.

Falon removed the bolt from Gamun's shoulder and muttered a word of healing. The wound instantly closed.

"Thanks," Gamun said, flexing the fingers of his right hand.

"It's not over," the dwarf said, still staring into the darkness. "There's another one out there, and I think it's after you, young cleric."

Falon swallowed hard, because the same thought had already occurred to him.

7 WINTERHAVEN, WRAFTON'S INN, NIGHT

Uldane Forden was miserable, and that was extremely unusual for the halfling rogue. He prided himself on his happy-go-lucky nature, his optimism, and his unshakable lust for life and all of the wonderful experiences that waited to be . . . well, experienced. Encounter a closed door? Uldane was always the first to run up and open it. He couldn't wait to see what was behind it, to see where it led.

But that was the old Uldane.

The Uldane who hadn't lost three of his friends to the green dragon, Vestapalk.

The Uldane who hadn't fallen hundreds of feet into a rushing river.

The Uldane who didn't have to sit in Wrafton's Inn, sipping wine and watching his one remaining friend, Shara, drink herself into oblivion while also picking fights with anyone stupid enough to get within earshot.

The halfling fingered the platinum coin in his pocket. Jarren's lucky coin. It didn't feel so lucky now, Uldane thought. At least, it wasn't lucky for Jarren, because Jarren didn't have the coin when the dragon attacked. Uldane had it, and Uldane had survived. If he hadn't borrowed the coin from out of Jarren's belt pouch, if Jarren hadn't told him to carry it for safekeeping, then maybe its luck would have protected the fighter.

Instead, Uldane and Shara had survived the battle and the plunge into the river. Uldane. Not Jarren. Not his other friends.

Uldane watched as Shara downed another mug of strong dwarven ale. She hadn't spoken a civil word to him since they had dragged themselves out of the river and made their way back to the site of the terrible battle with the dragon. They had worked silently to gather the bodies of their companions, secure them to their horses, and bring them back to Winterhaven for a proper burial. When the necessary preparations had been completed, Shara turned and marched into Wrafton's Inn. That was three days ago. She was still here, drinking and brooding.

Uldane wished that she would grieve. She hadn't cried for her friend. She hadn't cried for her lover. She hadn't even shed a tear for her father, Borojon. But she was angry. Uldane recognized that look in her eyes, the tension in her muscles. Shara wanted to fight something, anything. That had always been the best way for her to work through her feelings. The halfling was certain, however, that as soon as she started, she wouldn't stop until either she had been killed or everyone around her had fallen to the sharp blade of her greatsword.

And then how would she feel? Even worse, Uldane was sure.

The halfling rogue noticed that Shara's gaze had shifted. She was staring intently at a large human who was sitting at the bar and eyeing her with a sneer.

"What are you looking at, troll spit?" Shara asked, motioning for a serving girl to refill her mug.

"I was just trying to figure that out," the human said, smiling more broadly. "I was trying to decide if you were a bog hag who had wandered out of the marsh or an owlbear who was trying to pass an egg. Either way, I figured that if you wanted to have a go of it, I'd be happy to provide the coin for one of this fine establishment's upper rooms."

Oh gods, Uldane thought, *this fool is going to give Shara exactly what she's been looking for.*

Shara stood up, rising to her full height of six feet and showing off her curves and supple muscles. She was as strong as she was beautiful, although her pent up grief and three days of near-constant drinking had turned her usually pretty features into a mask of pain and rage. She stepped toward the human, a stranger who was passing through Winterhaven on the way to who knew where. When this was all over, Uldane imagined that the man was going to regret his brief stop in the village. If he survived the next few minutes, of course.

"I would sooner lay down with a lame orc," Shara said, her voice surprisingly light despite her words. "But even that comparison makes you sound more handsome than you actually are."

She moved very close to the man, so close that they were almost touching. Uldane saw a cold smile creep across Shara's full lips, and he knew that she was about to explode into violence.

"You are a mushroom growing on the tentacle of a carrion crawler," Shara said, as light as could be but with an undercurrent of sheer loathing that Uldane recognized was as much for herself as it was for the man at the bar.

"No, what am I saying? You'll have to excuse me, as I'm obviously extremely intoxicated at the moment," Shara said.

"Well," the man said, apparently confused.

"Please," Shara said, "let me finish."

The man sat back, obviously expecting an apology of some sort.

Here it comes, thought Uldane, and he exchanged a quick glance with Salvana Wrafton, the proprietor of the inn.

"Referring to you as a fungus is an insult to fungi everywhere," Shara continued. "You are the excrement in which the fungi grow. You are the sweat that stinks in the armpit of a mangy bugbear. You are . . . not worth my time."

Shara started to turn away then, as Uldane knew she would. And the man, his face registering confusion and then anger, stood up, balled his hand into a fist, and did exactly what Shara had been waiting for.

He hit her.

Uldane was impressed. It was a solid punch, and it actually knocked Shara back a step. Unfortunately, the attack was the opening that Shara had been goading him to give her.

She turned, her smile never wavering. "My turn."

Before Shara could return the blow, Salvana Wrafton stepped between her and the man at the bar. Salvana was nowhere near as tall as either of the two she had placed herself between, but when it came to defending her inn, no one could match her ferocity or passion.

"Is this how you honor the memory of Borojon, Shara?" Salvana asked. "Of Jarren? Did that dragon take your senses as well as your family out there in the mountains?"

Shara's smile faded, but the expression that replaced it seemed much, much worse to Uldane. He quickly got up and gently laid a hand on her arm before she could strike out at the innkeeper.

"Time to go, Shara," Uldane said, nodding to Salvana. "They'll be no more trouble here tonight."

"Crazy b—," the man started to say, but Uldane silenced him with a stern look and a raised finger.

"It's over," Uldane said quietly, "let it go."

The man hesitated, then nodded and sat back down.

Uldane led Shara outside, into the cool night air.

"You're right, Uldane," Shara said.

"Of course I am," Uldane agreed. Then he thought about it some more. "I am? About what?" he asked.

"It's time to go. Tomorrow, my friend, the hunt resumes."

Great, Uldane thought, *why do I always have to be right?*

8 FALLCREST, IN THE SHADOW OF MOORIN'S TOWER, NIGHT

The town of Fallcrest stood near the intersection of two roads and the Nentir River, in the center of the region known as the Nentir Vale. The last time that Kalaban had passed through this land, all that had been in the area was a scattering of human hill tribes, a few elven settlements, and a number of outposts dating back to the dwarven kingdom of Shatterstone. Giants, orcs, goblins, and kobolds plagued the area, and the growing empire of Nerath, to the south, was eyeing this northern realm as prime territory for expansion. From the looks of the buildings and the makeup of the citizens, Kalaban assumed that the area had eventually been subsumed into the expanding empire. It was what the empire did, after all.

Kalaban stood beside Magroth, relishing the feel of the night air on his undead skin. They had both walked out of the dread domain of

Darani, out of the Shadowfell, and back into the natural world. The new sense of freedom was exhilarating, and Kalaban never wanted it to end. Which meant, of course, that Kalaban had to help Magroth complete the three tasks the death priest of Orcus had given to him. Magroth stood nearby, his cloaked hood hiding his features, resting on his staff and studying the tower that seemed to glow in the pale moonlight. The tower was three stories high, built atop the bluff overlooking the Moonwash Falls. The emperor had been silent since they reached this spot, so Kalaban scanned the area around them and waited for his master's next order.

"The tower is wrapped in arcane defenses," Magroth finally said, his low voice sounding loud in the stillness of the night. This part of the town was quiet. The inns and alehouses were beyond the bluffs, in the lower portion of the town nearer the Nentir River. "You will need to proceed with caution, my knight-commander."

"As always, my liege," Kalaban replied.

"The first task starts in that tower," Magroth continued. "Find a black crystal of unusual design, formed into a triangular amulet encased in a golden frame. Find the amulet and retrieve it, as I command. But do not stare into its black depths. I understand that a crystal such as this has a powerful effect on those who look too deeply."

Kalaban bowed and moved off into the darkness toward the silent tower. He traveled only a dozen paces or so and dropped to one knee to study the approach to the tower. After a moment, he heard Magroth speaking to someone. Kalaban remained quiet and listened, waiting to see if his master needed his help before he moved on.

"You must tell me how you manage to suddenly appear like that one of these days," Magroth said dryly.

"I bring news, Magroth," said the female voice that Kalaban recognized as Barana Strenk, the death priest of Orcus.

"Well, spit it out," Magroth said, "It's not like I have all the time in the world."

"We have located one of your descendents, one of the royal blood of Nerath," Barana said, "in an insignificant collection of huts called Nenlast."

"And?"

"And my agents were . . . overeager," Barana said with something like contrition in her voice. "They attempted to take the youth, but they were . . . unsuccessful. One of my agents remains close, following the boy. Now the boy is alert to danger, and he has gained an ally to help him against us."

"Wonderful," Magroth said. "And I assume that these agents are what Orcus considers to be his best?"

"I considered them to be up to the task," Barana replied.

"From now on, death priest," Magroth warned, "leave my kin to me."

"As you wish," the woman said, and then the area behind Kalaban grew deathly still.

A few moments passed, and then Kalaban heard Magroth mutter, "She's gone, knight-commander. Get on with your work."

Chagrined that Magroth knew he was within earshot, but not surprised, Kalaban resumed his march toward the tower, shifting his concentration to the task at hand.

9 FALLCREST, THE KNIGHT'S GATE, NIGHT

Nu Alin slipped through the bars of the lowered portcullis and moved into the dark streets of the town beyond. No guards currently walked the walls of the town, and no one was posted in the locked gatehouse. As was typical of the soft creatures of this world, the people of Fallcrest were less than vigilant in the protection of their town. And that, Nu Alin understood, would be why this world would fall.

Nu Alin kept to the deepest shadows as he searched. Not only did he prefer the darkness, he also knew that he had to stay out of sight of the local inhabitants of the town. The body he currently occupied was rapidly deteriorating, and if anyone saw Nu Alin's vessel in its current state an alarm would be raised. Nu Alin believed that, at this point in his mission, stealth and secrecy were necessary. Anything that made either tactic unavailable was best avoided.

Nu Alin needed to take on a new form before he advanced to the next stage of his mission. The creatures of this world were so fragile, and so far none of the bodies he had taken had been able to contain Nu Alin's essence for more than a few days. But at least the current body had been able to carry Nu Alin to Fallcrest, where the item he sought waited to be collected. All Nu Alin needed was a new body to control, a new form to wear. A new vessel.

The form that Nu Alin currently wore, that of a human boy, had barely lasted two days. The boy's eyes had already become dry and clouded, and his flesh was beginning to wither with every stirring of the wind. Cracks in the skin around the eyes and mouth let Nu Alin's true form peek through, a glowing crimson substance that filled these cracks. It was like liquid crystal, with veins of metallic silver and flecks of gold swimming within the viscous substance.

Nu Alin squinted and strained to look through the boy's eyes to examine the hand he controlled. It was a gnarled thing, the digits more like claws than fingers. Nu Alin strained to flex the tightening joints, and the pain was excruciating. Nu Alin forced the deteriorating body to move. He stayed close to the buildings, in the deep shadows, scanning the night for a creature, any creature, to take control of. He preferred to nest within intelligent hosts, but Nu Alin could occupy any living form if the need was great enough. And at this moment, Nu Alin's need was exceedingly great.

Nu Alin sensed the nearby creature before his host body's eyes were able to focus on it. The creature, a large rat, was noisily digging through a trash pile at the side of one of the buildings. Another wave of pain welled up within Nu Alin's vessel, threatening to drive Nu Alin out before the demonic essence was ready to depart. He steadied himself, resting against the building, when the form's failing ears picked up a new sound nearby.

Nu Alin strained to see the young halfling woman emerge from the back door of the structure. She was carrying a bucket as she made her way toward the refuse pile where the rat was busy scavenging for scraps. She walked bravely toward the pile of trash, calling out to frighten off the rat.

"Shoo," she shouted, "flee before my magical bucket of puke." The young woman laughed as the rat scurried away, but Nu Alin failed to comprehend the humor in her statement.

Nu Alin watched the young woman approach the refuse pile and toss the bucket's contents. She appeared to be strong and healthy, at least by the standards of others of her kind that he had encountered since winning his freedom. He had been trapped for too long, locked away and separated from the Voidharrow. Now he was free, and all he needed was to take possession of a new, healthy vessel and recover the Voidharrow. Then he could complete what he and the others had started all those centuries ago.

Nu Alin looked up, toward the southeast, finally resting his failing gaze on the glowing tower that had drawn him to this place. The Voidharrow would wait a few more moments, Nu Alin was certain, while he replaced the body he wore with a fresh vessel. With an effort, Nu Alin ignored the pain and shrugged off his current vessel, discarding the failing flesh as so many tattered rags. The shell that was the human boy collapsed, as though whatever strings had been holding it up were suddenly sliced away, and the crimson substance that was Nu Alin slid free.

In his true form, Nu Alin slithered silently across the open space between himself and the halfling woman. As silent as Nu Alin was, however, some sense of danger alerted the young halfling to his presence. Her eyes went wide and she slipped a dagger from her belt as she turned to face the approaching danger. She had only a moment to register confusion before Nu Alin was upon her. Fear exploded within her mind at the touch of Nu Alin's true form, but still she struggled, still she resisted.

For a time.

Nu Alin feasted on the halfling woman's fear as he slipped into her body. The demonic presence had exchanged a set of tattered rags for an elegant new suit, and Nu Alin was very pleased.

Yes, Nu Alin confirmed, taking total control of the halfling. *This form will do.*

10 FALLCREST, MOORIN'S TOWER, NIGHT

The wizard's tower was quiet and still. Kalaban had easily bypassed the protective wards that guarded the door and first floor of the tower, using skills and techniques taught to him by Magroth over the ages. The knight-commander had to admit that his emperor was a good teacher. Perhaps he should have asked to learn a bit of true magic to go along with his other skills. Of course, that could have been a dangerous path to pursue. Magroth had always been extremely protective of his arcane talents, and he might have misinterpreted any interest in such pursuits by Kalaban.

And when it came to Emperor Magroth—the Mad Emperor, as some called him—you did not want your intentions to be misinterpreted.

The first level of the tower was divided into two chambers. The first chamber looked more like a sitting room in any well-to-do household than the entryway to a wizard's lair. Overstuffed chairs were arranged neatly before a fireplace situated along the curved wall. The fireplace was still warm, but the fire had been extinguished for the evening. A few tables held thick books and assorted sheets of parchment, and a map of the Nentir Vale hung on the wall beside the fireplace. The town of Fallcrest was positioned prominently at the center of the map.

The second chamber contained a kitchen, complete with cooking fire, work tables, pots and pans, a water trough, and a side pantry full of foodstuffs. The kitchen had a small door that opened on to an herb garden, but it and the entry chamber both appeared to be empty. Wherever the wizard was, he wasn't on this level.

Kalaban touched nothing, but his eyes examined everything within the two chambers. He looked for signs of recent activity, for arcane symbols, for hidden panels. He also kept his eyes open for the relic he had come to retrieve, but there were no amulets of stone as black as a starless night. No stones or gems at all, at least not on this level of the tower. Confident that there was nothing of interest or danger in either chamber, Kalaban headed for the stairs.

The knight-commander scanned the stone steps that led up and down into darkness. He saw nothing that gave him pause. Was the wizard Moorin so confident in his first line of defenses that the rest of the path through the tower had been left unprotected? Perhaps he didn't want to inadvertently stumble into a ward in the middle of the night. Or, more likely, he didn't want a pet or an apprentice setting off an alarm inside the tower. Even the best wizards make mistakes, Kalaban knew. If it made his job easier, why should he complain about the lapse in judgment?

The stairs down most likely led to sleeping chambers, Kalaban determined, remembering his visits to places such as this in the past.

One of the higher levels, then, the knight-commander decided.

Kalaban took the steps up one at a time, carefully checking for any signs of wards he might have missed. He reached the second level of the tower without incident. Here, the space was filled with shelves of ancient tomes and ornate scroll cases, along with a well-used desk of heavy wood that was covered in sheets of parchment, quills, and bottles of ink. A strange stone sat atop the desk, but the color was all wrong. It appeared to be filled with fire, though it was only barely warm to the touch. Interesting, the knight-commander thought, but ultimately unimportant. It was not the stone he sought. With a final gaze around the room, Kalaban made his way to the stairs that led up to the final level of the tower.

On the third level, Kalaban immediately noticed the many windows that opened in the circular wall of the tower. These windows held no glass, exposing the tower room to the cool night air. Curtains were rolled up at the top of each window. With a quick pull of a cord, the curtains could be lowered to cover the openings. Thanks to the height of the tower and the bluff on which it was situated, Kalaban could look in any direction and see the town of Fallcrest as it spread out around the tower. The large chamber at the top of the tower included a couple of long tables covered with a variety of alchemical instruments such as mortars and pestles, beakers, jars, needles, and scalpels. Three spyglasses set on tripods were positioned at different windows, two pointed toward distant landmarks and one pointed toward the night sky. There was also a tall set of shelves set against the wall between two of the open windows. The shelves held more books and scrolls, as well as an assortment of unusual items that immediately piqued Kalaban's curiosity.

Before he could step closer to examine the items in the cabinet, Kalaban heard a tiny snore. His eyes quickly darted to a domed cage that sat on the floor beside a tall pedestal. Kalaban noticed that there was something curled up atop the pedestal. A cat, perhaps? He moved with a supernatural silence that was as much born of practice and skill as it was his own undead abilities. As Kalaban stepped closer to the pedestal, the moonlight seeping through the windows illuminated the creature's scintillating scales, sharp, pointed tail, and tiny, almost translucent wings. A pseudodragon, the knight-commander realized. An apropos pet for a wizard's tower, he thought.

Kalaban quietly raised the domed cage, which he saw was shaped to perfectly fit atop the pedestal should the wizard desire to secure the cat-sized dragon for any reason. Kalaban carefully lowered the dome over the little creature, making sure not to disturb its rest as he did so.

Rest well, Kalaban thought, smiling slightly at the sleeping creature. With the pseudodragon sealed away, Kalaban stepped over to examine the items on the shelves against the wall.

There was a trio of skulls, one human, one some kind of small bird, and one that took up an entire shelf and had to have come from a relatively small black dragon.

There was the mummified claw of a small humanoid creature, perhaps a kobold, the withered flesh decorated with arcane symbols that Kalaban did not recognize.

There was a collection of small, geometrically shaped pieces of bone, including pyramids, squares, and hexagons. Each flat side was inscribed with a draconic rune.

There was a strange compass that pointed to runic shapes instead of toward the cardinal directions.

And there were two other items, alone on a shelf set about half way up the wall. One was a cylinder of glass, about three inches long and three quarters of an inch wide. It was capped at both ends by gold seals, and a golden chain was strung through a hook at one end. Inside the glass vial, an unusual crimson substance with silver strands and flecks of gold swirled through it filled about half the available space. It was a crystalline substance of some sort, like lique-fied honey that was a translucent red instead of amber, and it pulsed with an inner light. Kalaban found himself drawn to the vial and its interesting contents. It was almost . . . alien, and looking at the slick crimson-silver substance made Kalaban's head swim. As he watched, the strange liquid rippled. His hand reached out, almost of its own volition, and the liquid crystal flowed up the side of the glass to meet him. He wrapped his fingers around the vial, feeling the coolness of the glass as well as the heat of the substance within. Without really thinking about it, he slipped the vial into his belt pouch.

Then Kalaban turned to examine the other item on the shelf.

It was a triangular shard of black stone, about the size of Kalaban's palm. The shard was so dark that the knight-commander had almost missed it. It was sitting within a small frame made of gold from which another chain was strung. This was kelonite—dead glass—fabled to come from a place far beyond the shores of the natural world and deep within the confines of the Shadowfell. It was almost as if he could see . . . *things* . . . floating in the depths of the shard's flat surface. The knight-commander shook off the sensation and averted his eyes, remembering that Magroth had warned him about looking too deeply into the black stone. He drew a strip of cloth from a pocket, draped it over the amulet, and gently lifted it from the shelf.

"You have a rather regal bearing for a common thief," said the voice coming from the entryway to the chamber.

Kalaban turned to see a man he assumed must be the wizard Moorin. The man was of average height, slightly round as befits a wizard who was more scholar than adventurer. He appeared to be in his sixties, but when it came to magic-users, who could really tell such things? A ball of arcane light floated beside the wizard's head, illuminating the tower room with an otherworldly glow. The wizard held an ornate staff, not unlike the one that Magroth carried.

Kalaban could also see that the wizard's left arm was shaking. He was apparently unwell.

"I assure you, mage," Kalaban said, slipping the cloth-wrapped shard into a second pouch on his belt, "there is nothing common about me."

Before the wizard could act, Kalaban dashed across the room. He knocked the wizard's staff aside and hurled a powerful punch toward the wizard's head. The blow, augmented by Kalaban's supernatural strength, knocked Moorin senseless. Kalaban caught the wizard as the man's knees buckled. He gently lowered the wizard to the floor, making sure not to let his head strike anything on the way down.

"Nerath must rise again," Kalaban whispered as his hand reached into his pouch to find the cloth-wrapped stone. "Perhaps you'll understand that one day."

As silently as he arrived, Kalaban slipped out of the tower. He had recovered the Necropolis Stone for his emperor and something for himself as well. He knew that they still had much to do before their time in this world ran out, but the knight-commander couldn't stop thinking about the unusual substance in the glass vial or about the strange black stone.

11 FALLCREST, THE BLUE MOON ALEHOUSE, NIGHT

The young eladrin named Albanon sat at a table in the Blue Moon Alehouse, hoisting a tankard as he listened to the tales of the travelers sitting across from him. Albanon was a wizard-in-training apprenticed to the great mage Moorin of the Glowing Tower. He had studied with Moorin for nearly seven years. At times he felt like he was ready to strike out on his own, but at other times he felt he still had so much more to learn. Moorin was a fair master, kind and wise, and he permitted Albanon a good amount of freedom when there were no chores to do and no experiments to watch over. Now, for instance, Albanon had walked down into town, wandered into the Blue Moon, and struck up a conversation with the two travelers.

The first was one of the humanoid dragonkin known as the dragonborn. He was tall, well above six feet, and powerfully built. He called himself Roghar and resembled a humanoid dragon covered in bronze scales. He claimed to be a paladin of Bahamut, the god of justice and honor. He did wear the symbol of the Platinum Dragon on his shield, so Albanon was willing to take him at his word. But each story that Roghar and his companion told seemed more fantastic than the last. And the pair seemed awfully young to have taken part in so many amazing adventures. In fact, they seemed only a few years older than Albanon himself.

"So, elf," Roghar said, "that was the way that Tempest and I escaped from the death trap known as the Pyramid of Shadows."

"Eladrin," Albanon corrected for the twelfth or thirteenth time this evening.

"What's that, friend?" Roghar asked, motioning for another round of drinks for the table.

"Eladrin, not elf," Albanon said. "I'm an eladrin, and my name is Albanon."

"Elf, eladrin, drow. What's the real difference, I ask you? None, as far as I can see," Roghar said.

"Well, the difference is . . . oh, never mind," Albanon said, draining his mug before the fresh one arrived. Something poked at his side and he reached into his robe. He removed his wand and placed it on the table beside his mug.

The tiefling female, a warlock named Tempest, leaned close and whispered to her companion. "The Pyramid of Shadows?" Like other tieflings, Tempest's appearance testified to her infernal heritage. Her skin was a subtle shade of red, and sweeping horns curved out from just above her red eyes to frame her head. She wore her dark-red hair long, and her thick tail constantly moved behind her as she sat and talked with them.

She assumed that Albanon couldn't hear her above the noise in the rest of the alehouse, but she was wrong. His pointed ears were extremely well-suited for hearing the faintest of noises, as Moorin was fond of mentioning whenever he caught his apprentice eavesdropping on a conversation.

"You know," Roghar replied quietly, "the place those braggarts were going on and on about in the Seven-Pillared Hall. What was that fighter's name? Brakis? Boregard? Something like that?"

"Belkas," Tempest said, rolling her eyes, "I believe he called himself Belkas. And the other one, the loud and obnoxious one, that was Goren."

Albanon smiled. So what if they probably hadn't accomplished half or even a quarter of what they claimed? The stories of adventure and excitement that Roghar spun were intriguing. Fascinating, even. And the duo certainly had an adventurous spirit that Albanon found infectious. He sipped from the fresh tankard and made a face. He always found the ale here in the Blue Moon to be just a little too bitter for his taste. Albanon noticed that the tiefling was leaning close to him, her red eyes mischievous and her red lips turned in a friendly smile.

"So, my eladrin friend," Tempest began.

"Elf," Roghar corrected, incorrectly.

Tempest ignored the dragonborn. "So, my eladrin friend, what do you want to be when you grow up?"

Albanon stared at her over the top of his tankard of ale. He was grateful that neither Tempest nor Roghar seemed at all uncomfortable around him. That wasn't always the case when the other races interacted with an eladrin. Anyway, the question that Tempest posed was the very one that had been bouncing around in his head when he had left the tower earlier this evening. Well, not when he grew up. Not exactly. More like what was he going to do when his apprenticeship had ended. Did he want to be a sage or a scholar, locked away in a tower of his own with nothing but books and spells for company? Or did he want to join up with people like Roghar and Tempest and use his arcane talents to battle monsters and gather treasures from dank dungeons and ancient ruins? Or maybe, just maybe, he should go back to his family's estate in the Feywild and forget all about the pursuit of arcane magic. He was young. There was still time to start over. All he had to do was figure out what it was he really wanted to do with his life.

"Don't tease the elf, Tempest," Roghar chided. "Not everyone is cut out for a life of adventure."

How true, thought Albanon as he stood up from the table. "It was a pleasure meeting the both of you," the eladrin said, trying not to slur his words. He couldn't remember the last time he had three mugs of ale in one sitting. "Good luck to you both."

"Going so soon?" Roghar asked, but Albanon had gathered his mantle around himself and was already heading toward the door.

Tempest laughed, "Stop teasing the boy, Roghar. I'm sure he has to get up early in the morning to take care of his chores."

Albanon could hear them laughing as he stepped out into the chill night air. His mind was full of Roghar's stories of adventure and his own doubts about his future as he started the long walk back up to Moorin's tower.

12 FALLCREST, MOORIN'S TOWER, NIGHT

Moorin blinked, trying to clear his head. *That was a death knight,* the wizard thought. *A death knight in my tower. Of all the audacity!*

The old wizard sat up and peered into the darkness of the tower chamber. His arcane light had gone out when he lost consciousness, but some inner sense told him it wasn't yet time to recall it. He had survived a meeting with a death knight. More to the point, the death knight had easily overcome him and yet, here he was, still among the living. The death knight had left him alive, and that confused the old wizard more than he cared to admit.

Moorin stood up, stretched, and touched the bruise on the side of his jaw. He shook his head, but the feeling that something was wrong inside the tower persisted. He found his staff and started to move around the outer wall of the tower, toward the pedestal where the pseudodragon was perched. He had noticed that Splendid was awake and growing agitated. She never liked it when the domed cage was placed over her. She would start wailing soon, and Moorin didn't want that to happen.

Splendid reached out her tiny claws, gripping the bars of the cage tightly. She strained against the bars, but the metal wouldn't give, wouldn't budge at all. The pseudodragon prepared to call out when Moorin's gentle finger reached through the bars and patted her on the top of her head.

"Stay quiet, my little friend," Moorin whispered as he draped a cloth over the dome of the cage. "Stay out of sight and be safe."

He watched as Splendid began to fade away, drawing her invisibility around herself as Moorin might slip on his traveling cloak. Then he let the cloth fall completely over the dome, hiding it and the pseudodragon from sight.

A strange sensation ran down Moorin's spine. It was fear, definitely fear. But it was something stronger than ordinary fear, more primal. The old wizard was afraid to his very core. Something *alien* had entered the tower chamber. Moorin couldn't see it yet, but he could sense it. It was powerful, and it didn't belong here. Not just here in the tower. It didn't belong in this world.

Moorin stepped away from Splendid's cage and moved across

the chamber. He wanted to draw the strange presence away from where the pseudodragon crouched, cloaked in invisibility of her own creation. He hurt all over, and he knew that he was well and truly past his prime. His left arm had never stopped shaking, and the death knight had been on him before he was even able to call up a simple spell let alone a spell of amazingly destructive power.

He turned to the far window. He sensed that the new intruder was there, hidden in the darkness. The old wizard let arcane energy flow through his staff, and the tower chamber filled with soft light.

The light revealed a female halfling standing before the window. She appeared to be a scullery maid, probably from one of the inns or alehouses in the town below. Appearances, as Moorin well knew, were often deceiving. She had a strange look about her, at once fierce and distant, as though she was totally focused on him and yet totally detached from this moment in time. Her look was unsettling. Cracks radiated from the corners of her eyes, forming spider webs of glowing red that fanned out around the side of her head. The cracks in her skin were filled with a crimson ooze that ululated like a liquid but that had a crystalline sheen that reflected the light of Moorin's staff. The old wizard immediately knew who and what he was facing.

For the first time that he could remember, certainly for the first time since he had passed his tests and had taken on the mantle of wizard, Moorin of the Glowing Tower was unsure if he was up to the task before him.

13 FALLCREST, MOORIN'S TOWER, NIGHT

Nu Alin stood before the wizard, wearing the borrowed form of the halfling woman he had acquired in the town below the tower. He stretched out his senses, detecting the faint tingle deep within his true form that told him that the substance he sought was nearby.

The sensation was weak, however, and it was beginning to fade. Had the wizard detected his approach? Had he sent the Voidharrow away?

Nu Alin forced the halfling woman's vocal cords to operate, pushing air through them as the woman's mouth formed the words that he borrowed from her mind. "Will you challenge me, wizard?" Nu Alin asked in the strange speech of this land, ignoring the weak sound that emerged from his host. "Or will you stand aside and allow me to retrieve that which I have traveled very far to obtain?"

The wizard stood tall, staff in hand, its tip glowing with arcane energy. "You are the second thief to disturb my tower this night," Moorin said, "and it is time to remind the world of the power of Moorin of the Glowing Tower."

Arcane fire erupted from Moorin's staff, washing over the space where Nu Alin had stood. Before any of the licking flames could touch his host's form, however, Nu Alin made a powerful leap. It carried him clear of the wizard's initial attack and on to the ceiling of the tower chamber. Nu Alin made the halfling form hang there, upside down, like some kind of gigantic insect. He made the head spin at an unnatural angle, made the eyes bore into the wizard with hatred and anger.

"I almost feel sorry for you, mage," Nu Alin said through the halfling woman's mouth. "Almost."

Nu Alin saw that the old wizard recognized him somehow, or at least recognized the threat that he represented. He also saw that the old wizard wasn't exactly healthy. His left hand and arm shook with an intensity that must have made the delicate art of spellcasting difficult. Maybe even impossible, at least with the subtlety and precision that a master wizard preferred to work. Nu Alin had nothing to fear from this old man. Nothing at all.

But Moorin hadn't lived as long as he had to go down without putting up some kind of fight. He forced the fingers of his left hand to open wide—even though the look of pain that crossed his face seemed to be excruciating—and uttered a word of power. Small bolts of arcane energy flew from the wizard's shaking fingers and pounded into Nu Alin's host form with amazing accuracy. The halfling's grip on the ceiling failed, and the borrowed body crashed on to one of the long tables in the tower room.

"I don't know how you managed to free yourself, demon," the wizard said as the air around him crackled and hummed with power. "But I won't allow you to leave this tower. Forgive me, young woman. I know that none of this is your fault."

Before the wizard could complete the complicated gestures needed to focus and unleash the power he had gathered, the shaking in his left arm spread out so that his entire body was caught in the convulsions. His concentration wavered, and the gathered power dissipated like dust in the wind.

"You are ill, old man," Nu Alin said through the halfling's mouth. "Perhaps your threats meant something once, but not now."

Fear filled the old wizard's eyes, but he refused to give up just yet. He struggled to calm his shaking form, but that only seemed to make the shaking worse. Still, he managed to point his staff at Nu Alin and force the words of power from his suddenly dry lips.

Silvery missiles exploded from the tip of the staff and streaked across the tower room. The missiles struck Nu Alin over and over again with staggering force, each one driving the borrowed body back a half step as it hit.

The effort obviously took a lot out of the old wizard. He went down on both knees, barely able to keep himself upright by clutching tightly to his staff.

"Enough of this," Nu Alin said.

And then Nu Alin leaped again, carrying his host form directly at the wizard. The halfling's body landed right in front of the old man, her eyes just about at the right height to look into his as he struggled to get back up.

Nu Alin smiled inwardly, giving himself over to the destructive nature he mostly held in check. He relished these moments of pure freedom.

Of carnage.

Of blood.

The old wizard never had a chance.

14 FALLCREST, MOORIN'S TOWER, NIGHT

Albanon hurried up the stairs and into his master's chamber at the top of the tower. The wards that usually guarded the entrance to the tower had been broken, and the apprentice was worried about what that could mean. In all his time serving under Moorin, the wards had never failed or been removed, and they had never been expertly dismantled as his cursory examination had seemed to indicate. He hadn't waited to analyze the magic that had been used against the wards. If an intruder had stormed the tower, then Moorin could need his help.

At the top of the stairs, Albanon paused before rushing into the upper chamber. The room was dark except for the faint light of the moon that spilled in through the many windows. He saw familiar shapes outlined in the faint glow, shapes that were now askew and out of place in the silent chamber. A pedestal had been knocked over, the one where the pseudodragon Splendid usually spent her nights, as had a stool, a chair, and a small table. There was a metallic smell in the air, as well as the lingering scent of arcane fire. Albanon tried to keep his emotions in check as he stepped into the chamber.

"Master?" Albanon inquired, keeping his voice uncharacteristically low as he moved cautiously into the darkness.

The eladrin's boot touched something wet and sticky puddled on the floor. He drew it back, struggling to keep the fear that was growing inside him at bay. He whispered a word of power and called forth his will. Instantly, a small ball of light appeared beside his head. It illuminated the chamber in a soft, arcane glow.

Albanon almost wished that he had left the chamber in darkness. There was blood everywhere. It covered the floor. It decorated the walls. It even speckled the ceiling like some kind of insane art. Albanon forced the ale he had consumed at the Blue Moon to stay down, though it turned to acid as soon as he saw all the blood and it definitely wanted to vacate his stomach. The apprentice shook his head and took a couple of deep breaths, steadying himself, and then he looked over the scene again. He spotted ancient Moorin, the wizard who had been his teacher and his mentor these past six and a half years (nearly seven, really), sprawled against the far wall. His once-stern eyes, usually filled with a spark of intelligence that was equally fascinating and disturbing, were glazed and vacant. His usually immaculate robes were torn and bloody. Worse, the front of Moorin's body had been ripped open and more or less emptied of its contents.

"Moorin?" Albanon tried to say, but all that emerged was a pained squeak.

Then the apprentice doubled over, the contents of his own stomach spilling out in uncontrolled heaves and gasps.

"What could have done this?" Albanon whispered, wiping his mouth on the sleeve of his robe. Moorin was the most skilled and powerful wizard that Albanon had ever met, even counting the court wizards of his father's estate back in the Feywild. Of course, Moorin had been growing weaker these last couple of years, and Albanon had noticed how his hand and arm would shake at times. He should not have had to defend himself. This was his tower, damn it! Who would do this? And why?

"Apprentice!" a high-pitched voice called from the shadows beyond the reach of Albanon's arcane light. "Defend yourself! The danger is not yet gone!"

Splendid, Moorin's pseudodragon, launched herself out of the darkness. Her wings spread wide and her scales glistening in the arcane light of the floating ball of energy, Splendid roared with surprising power as she flew over Albanon's head toward the chamber entryway. Albanon strained to see what had startled the pseudodragon, and he noticed a figure standing at the door.

The figure ducked, letting the pseudodragon fly by and raising open hands to show that it was unarmed. The figure stepped forward, into the light of Albanon's spell. The light revealed Tempest, the tiefling adventurer from the Blue Moon Alehouse.

"I'm a friend," she said softly, her eyes scanning the bloody chamber before finally coming to rest on Albanon. "I'm so sorry."

Albanon nodded, noticing that Tempest had his wand stuck within her belt. He had forgotten it. Again. And she had followed after him to return it.

He bent down beside his fallen master. Splendid landed beside him, still watching the tiefling with undisguised mistrust. "There's another one," she hissed, indicating the second figure that came to stand behind Tempest.

Roghar, the dragonborn paladin, looked almost as stricken as Albanon felt. "What did this?" he managed to say as he made a reflexive gesture of blessing.

"It killed him," the little dragon said.

And then Splendid wailed for the dead wizard, and her sorrow poured forth in such waves that Albanon could scarcely believe the little form had contained it. He wanted to join her, but not yet. He had something to do before he could give in to his grief.

15 WINTERHAVEN, THE KING'S ROAD, DAY

Uldane rode beside Shara as their horses pounded down the King's Road. They were riding southeast, away from the village of Winterhaven. To each side of the road, the hills of the Gardbury Downs rolled into the distance. It was a clear day, the kind of day that Uldane usually enjoyed. But he hadn't felt very much joy since the battle with the green dragon, Vestapalk. Since three of his best friends had died and the life and happiness had fled from Shara, leaving her hollow. No, not hollow. She was filled with anger. Anger and pain.

The woman warrior rarely spoke to Uldane anymore. She brooded. She drank. She remembered. But she hadn't cried. Not yet. And that lack of tears frightened Uldane more than he knew. He was worried about his friend and companion. It wasn't healthy for her to hold back her grief.

"Shara," Uldane began, trying to think of some way to start up a conversation.

"Not now," Shara said, cutting him off.

And so they rode on, in silence.

As they crested the next rise, Uldane spotted a wagon being pulled by a pair of draft horses. Two figures sat in the wagon, both cloaked. The taller figure wore a straw hat and held the reins. The smaller figure had a pitchfork nestled across its lap. Most of the back of the wagon was covered by tarps, but Uldane noticed a few sacks poking out from beneath the coverings.

Farmers, the halfling thought, *probably a farmer and his son.*

A small band of short reptilian humanoids surrounded the farmers, maybe six or eight, but it was hard to count them as they ran this way and that around the wagon. They carried javelins and spears, and they were whooping and hollering and having a grand old time terrorizing the poor farmers.

"Kobolds," Shara said, a note of excitement creeping into her voice.

Uldane sighed. *Well, maybe a little violence will help her sort out her feelings,* he thought as he reached for his weapons.

Without waiting to confer about tactics or even to check to see that Uldane was with her (she knew that he would be), Shara kicked her horse and charged toward the band of kobolds. It took the marauders a moment to notice the large warhorse bearing down on them, and another moment to realize that the tall woman atop the horse was dressed for battle and carrying a massive greatsword.

The kobold closest to the charging horse called out a warning as he threw his javelin at Shara. She easily batted the shaft of wood out of the air with her sword, never slowing her horse or changing direction. The warhorse ran over the kobold, hooves bashing the creature to death as it scattered the rest of the band.

Shara was already leaping off her horse so that she could deal with the remaining kobolds in a more personal manner. Uldane followed behind her, watching for any signs of unexpected trouble from the marauders. The halfling reached into his pocket and rubbed the ancient coin nestled there for luck. He glanced at the farmer and his son, thinking not only to check on them but to reassure them as well, when he noticed a curious thing.

The farmer had thrown off his cloak and straw hat, revealing two kobolds beneath the disguise. One stood atop the other's shoulders to attain the height necessary to pull off the deception. And the one on top wore a horned skull of some sort as a headdress, and a variety of feathers and smaller skulls adorned his spear like tribal fetishes. The third kobold atop the wagon, the one that Uldane had mistaken for a farmer's son, had also shrugged off his cloak and was preparing to hurl the pitchfork at Shara's exposed back. The woman warrior was engaged in battle with the other kobolds and had not bothered to protect herself from the "people" in the wagon.

Uldane spurred his horse to gallop faster. He threw a pair of daggers in quick succession and then leaped from the horse toward the wagon. He heard grunts of pain as both daggers found their mark, and the tossed pitchfork landed wide of Shara, who still hadn't noticed the danger from the wagon. The halfling landed on one of the draft horses, grabbing the reins that the farmer had discarded when it revealed itself to be a pair of kobolds.

"Shara, there's more of them," Uldane shouted, drawing his sword and watching the kobold that wore the horned skull. That had to be a wyrmpriest, Uldane decided, and from the size of his sneer, probably a powerful one at that.

The wyrmpriest tapped the blunt end of his spear against the wagon's floorboard. At the prearranged signal, the tarp was thrown off and more kobolds poured out of the back of the wagon. Among the emerging kobolds were two that carried short swords and shields—the dreaded dragonshield warriors that had recently appeared among the marauding bands that were causing trouble all around Winterhaven.

"Mighty Vestapalk sends his greetings," the wyrmpriest sneered. "He ordered me to relate how sweet the flesh of your companions tasted. I was honored to be allowed to partake after Vestapalk had had his fill."

Shara spun to face the wyrmpriest, four dead kobolds sprawled at her feet. The remaining three had stepped back, out of reach of her greatsword, and they were now being joined by the gang that had been hiding in the wagon.

"There're a lot of them, Shara," Uldane noted, "including two dragonshields and a wyrmpriest."

"They're working for that damned dragon," Shara said, focusing all of her attention on the wyrmpriest.

"Working for Vestapalk?" the wyrmpriest asked in genuine surprise. "We are not common laborers! Vestapalk is our god, and

I am his high priest! Our god has demanded your blood this day. Make them bleed!"

1 6 WINTERHAVEN, THE KING'S ROAD, DAY

Erak had been walking since leaving the graveyard. He didn't know where he was or where he was going, but he knew he had to leave that place of the dead. The sun was high in the sky, and the rolling hills he had been traversing seemed to go on forever. He still couldn't remember anything from before he woke up in the sarcophagus, nothing but fragments, images really.

Arise, my champion, the woman's voice had said, *You have work to do.*

He thought that the woman's voice had belonged to the Raven Queen, the god of death and fate. But as to who he was or what he was supposed to do, those were still mysteries to him.

He walked on, listening to the gallop of hooves off to his left. There must be a road in that direction, he thought. It sounded like a pair of horses, riding side by side across a well-paved road. They had come from the same direction as he had, probably from the village near the graveyard. He wondered where they were going, but then dismissed the thought. He had his own things to deal with.

After another few moments, Erak heard the horses break into a faster run. Something was going on over the rise. He contemplated ignoring the sounds, just walking on and letting whatever it was happen without him. He thought about it, but stopped to listen anyway. He heard the pounding of hooves, the clang of steel. A battle, then, by the sounds.

A shout echoed from that direction, bouncing around the low hills. "Shara, there're more of them!"

The one who had shouted was male. He sounded concerned but

not the least bit afraid. Erak was suddenly interested in the noises and the one who called the warning.

"They're working for that damned dragon," another voice said. It was a female voice, full of pain and anguish. Erak knew that he had to help this female, whoever she was.

He drew his hellsteel blade and started to run toward the distant hill and whatever was happening beyond it.

17 WINTERHAVEN, THE KING'S ROAD, DAY

Shara swung her greatsword with all the force she could muster, smashing it against the shield that appeared to have been crafted from the scales of a green dragon. The blow knocked the smaller kobold back, but the dragonshield charged at her again, and the second dragonshield circled wide to come at her from the other side.

"This one is worthy of a quick death," the second dragonshield said, obviously impressed by Shara's combat prowess.

"Then make it quicker, brother," the first dragonshield said, catching another mighty blow on his shield, "the human has already killed six of our kin."

Shara didn't want to be caught between the two, and she certainly didn't want the other six kobolds—definitely less competent than the dragonshields but potentially deadly in these numbers—to surround her. She hopped to one side, trying to get her back against the wagon. As she did so, the second dragonshield darted toward her, and she had to bring her greatsword around to deflect the thrust of his short sword.

This provided the first dragonshield with a small opening, and he rushed to take it. He slashed wildly, slicing through the leather covering her right arm and drawing a line of crimson. Jarren had often chided her for not wearing a full suit of armor, but she hated to be totally covered in metal. It was too confining, and she felt slow and clumsy in plate mail. Instead, she preferred to wear a mix of scale mail and leather. She was good, and opponents rarely scored direct hits against her. But since the deaths of Borojon and Jarren, she seemed to have lost a bit of herself. She hated to admit it, but she might have taken on more than she and Uldane could deal with in her current state of mind.

Suddenly remembering the halfling, she glanced behind her to see how he was faring. Uldane was locked in battle with the wyrmpriest and his minion, working hard to keep the cleric off balance and unable to complete any prayers.

"Are those phoenix feathers?" Uldane asked the wyrmpriest, badgering the kobold with an endless stream of questions that were designed to make him too mad to concentrate on unleashing any deadly wyrmpriest powers. "They look a bit raggedy if they are. You should really take better care of them. If the phoenix knew how you were treating them I'm sure it would take umbrage. And is that a dragon skull on your head? Can I try it on? Please?"

Shara turned back to the dragonshields, confident that Uldane was at least holding his own against the wyrmpriest. He would have to. She couldn't help him if she wanted to. Not until these armored kobolds were dealt with.

The dragonshields approached Shara cautiously, spread apart and moving in from each side. At the same time, the gang of javelin-wielding kobolds pressed forward, creating a wedge between the armored kobolds. Shara had her back to the wagon, but the arc in front of her was swarming with kobolds.

And the kobolds were smiling.

"No," Shara shouted, "I will not be beaten by the likes of you."

Shara had to win this battle. She had to survive. She promised herself that the dragon would pay for the deaths of Borojon, Cliffside, and Jarren, and for that promise to come to fruition she had to get out of this situation in one piece.

The second dragonshield clanged his sword against his shield. "You have my respect, warrior," he said earnestly.

"Enough," the first dragonshield said. "We are here to kill her, not exchange pleasantries. Mighty Vestapalk commands it!"

"Yes," Shara smiled, "Let's get on with this. I'm already late for my afternoon ale."

The dragonshields darted in then, shields raised and swords at the ready. Shara dodged the sword thrust of the first dragonshield with a quick step to the left. At the same time, she brought her greatsword up to deflect the second dragonshield's strike.

The gang of kobolds prepared to join the fray, when they suddenly turned as one to look to the west. Shara didn't know what had distracted them, and frankly she didn't care. If she just had to deal with the two dragonshields for the moment, she would make the most of the more or less even battle.

Shara followed her deflection of the second dragonshield's attack with an attack of her own. She bashed her elbow into the kobold's shield, using her greater weight to knock the smaller creature back. Then she swung her greatsword in a powerful arc, bringing it down to hack into and through the armor at his right shoulder. The weight of the sword cut deep and drove the kobold to the ground.

The first dragonshield jabbed again with his short sword, but Shara moved so that the blade harmlessly glanced off her scale breastplate. She brought her sword up in another arc, coming up from beneath the kobold's extended stance and cutting him nearly in two. She followed that up with a second jab, running her blade through the dragonshield and finishing him off.

Shara could hear the gang of kobolds. Someone else had joined the battle, and the kobolds were clearly occupied and fighting for their lives. She turned back to the remaining dragonshield. Though he was wounded, he still seemed ready to continue the fight. The wyrmpriest was also saying something up in the wagon behind her. He must have managed to fend off Uldane long enough to utter a prayer, for she could see that the wound she had inflicted on the dragonshield had begun to heal a bit.

"Have faith, my followers!" the wyrmpriest shouted, inciting the kobolds to muster their courage and fight on. "Vestapalk shall reward us this day, regardless of the outcome!"

She heard the crackle of energy, and Uldane shouted out in pain. Before she could turn to check on her friend, the dragonshield leaped forward.

"For Vestapalk!" the armored kobold shouted, his shield extended and his sword poised to strike.

Once again, Shara deflected the dragonshield's sword thrust with her own blade. She let the smaller creature's blade fly back from the shock of the impact even as she swept her weapon forward to meet the leaping kobold in midair. The blade caught the dragonshield across the chest, crumbling his scale armor and knocking the air out of him. He landed hard, stunned by the two quick blows. Shara stepped toward him, raising her greatsword one last time.

"You fought bravely," she said, driving the blade down and ending the second dragonshield's life.

As she pulled her sword free, Uldane slipped up beside her.

"The wyrmpriest fled," the halfling said, his tone apologetic. "He caught me flatfooted with some kind of poison blast, and while I was trying not to breathe in too much of it, he took off over the hill."

"Hmm," Shara grunted, but she really couldn't blame Uldane. Neither of them had been prepared to deal with a magic-wielding kobold today.

"Who's your friend?" Uldane asked, motioning toward the figure in black leather who was putting sword to the last kobold standing.

"Jarren?" Shara whispered, reminded of her fallen lover as she watched the figure move among the defeated kobolds. He had the same general build as Jarren, though he wasn't quite as tall and his shoulders weren't exactly as broad as the fighter's had been. He moved with the grace and confidence of Jarren, the same swagger that said that he knew how to fight and he wasn't afraid.

The figure turned to face them, swinging the crenulated blade he carried to fling off the kobold blood. It was a man, that much was clear, with dark, wild hair and gray, ashen skin. He wore a long leather jacket over leather armor that was cinched closed with numerous buckles and straps.

Shara stared as he approached. Why she imagined that this . . . *creature* . . . could have been Jarren she had no idea, but it was obvious now that he wasn't. She raised her greatsword, pointing the blade directly at him.

The figure stopped, standing just beyond the reach of Shara's blade.

"What manner of foul creature are you," Shara asked, "and why did you help us?"

1 8 NENLAST, FALON'S HOME, DAY

Falon paced around the kitchen of his mother's home, trying to make sense of the events of the previous twelve hours. He had been minding his own business, cleaning up at the shrine after the evening prayers had been held, just as he did every night since becoming an acolyte in service to Erathis, the god of civilization. But last night something terrible occurred. It was right out of the stories his grandfather used to tell him, the stories about adventurers and monsters and hidden treasures.

"No," Falon repeated again, as he had been repeating since Darrum had first mentioned the idea last night. "I am not of royal blood. I am not the heir to some long-dead kingdom. I'm not anybody!"

Darrum grunted, sitting back in the chair by the table and reaching for another chunk of cheese.

Falon was glad that the old dwarf had appeared in the garden and had helped them deal with the brigands that had tried to kill him and Gamun last night. He was glad that none of them, except for the brigands, had been seriously injured. At least, none of them had received any wounds that Falon wasn't able to heal. Except those hadn't been brigands, at least not ordinary brigands. They were undead.

Falon was tired. He wasn't used to fighting for his life one moment and arguing with the old dwarf about things he just knew couldn't be true the next. He was tired and confused.

"No, no. I'm just a novice cleric in service to a tiny shrine in the middle of nowhere. Look around you! Would the royal family, even in exile, live in a place like this? I'm nobody special!"

Darrum made a harrumph sound. "Then why did those undead creatures try to kill you?" he asked, speaking around a mouthful of bread and cheese.

Falon wanted to scream, but he had no real explanation for what had happened last night.

"Maybe it was all just a big mistake," he said, slumping down into the chair across from Darrum.

"Falon, listen well to what I say," Darrum said quietly. "I was an Imperial Shield. Protecting those of royal blood was one of my primary duties back in the day."

"Great job," Falon laughed, but there was little humor in his voice. "Look how that turned out. Nerath fell, the royal family died out, and now you're here trying to find lost glory in an insignificant village by hooking up with an insignificant nobody."

Darrum tried to restrain his anger, but his hand dropped to the dark hammer resting at his side. "The birthmark is clear," the dwarf said in a clipped tone.

"My father was a farmer," Falon continued, ignoring the warning signs that he might have pushed the old dwarf a bit too far. "My grandfather before him was a farmer, too. I come from a long line of farmers, and we're so far from the center of civilization out here that your story doesn't even make any sense. Think about it! If I was an heir to the throne of Nerath, what would I be doing way out here in the borderlands?"

"You would be hiding," Falon's mother said as she entered the room. After she had welcomed them and fed them, she had disappeared into one of the back rooms and left her son and the dwarf to their discussion. Now she had returned, and she was carrying a long object wrapped in oilcloth. She placed the wrapped object reverently on to the table, between Falon and Darrum.

"Mother?" Falon asked, his eyes wide. "What are you saying?"

She ignored his question, slowing unwrapping the oilcloth from around the long object. As the cloth fell away, Falon could see a soft glow emanating from the object within.

"By Moradin's anvil!" Darrum proclaimed, obviously recognizing the object as something important.

It was a sword, sleek and well-honed. The hilt was fashioned with the holy symbol of Erathis, the same one that Falon wore on his tabard and on a chain that hung around his neck. Moreover, there was something etched into the blade itself, just above the hilt. It was a crown, and three small stars floated above it in a graceful arc.

The etching looked just like the mark on Falon's left wrist.

His birthmark.

Darrum suddenly dropped to one knee and bent his head before Falon's mother. "My lady," he said solemnly, "I am yours to command."

The woman smiled. "Arise, good dwarf, there is no need for ceremony here."

She turned to Falon, gently placing a hand on the side of her son's face.

"The time has come for you to hear the truth, my son."

19 THE MOON HILLS, DAY

Tempest rode her horse across the Moon Hills, a stretch of land that rolled away from Fallcrest to the south. Albanon rode behind her. The young wizard hadn't said more than a few words since they started this journey. She felt sympathy for the eladrin, and she wanted to help him get whoever or whatever had ripped apart his mentor. Her own anger and need for vengeance had risen since she and Roghar had entered the dead wizard's tower and seen what had happened there. She just wished there were more than the three of them. Well, four, if you counted the annoying psuedodragon that was draped across Albanon's shoulder. Tempest didn't count her, so they were back down to three.

Tempest followed behind Roghar, keeping her eyes locked on his broad back. As they rode, she remembered how the dragonborn paladin had found her in the Warrens, a rundown section of the city of Nera. That was three years ago. She had been barely sixteen then, on her own and trying to stay alive on the streets of the decadent city.

She had bumped into the dragonborn early in the day in the Market Ward, using the distraction and her disarming smile to deftly lift the coin pouch from his belt. She remembered how distraught Roghar had been, thinking that his clumsiness had caused her injury. He kept apologizing even as she tried to disengage and slip away among the crowd before he noticed that his money had been taken.

It took longer than she had hoped, but she eventually got away from the good-hearted dragonborn. As she made her way back to the Warrens, she passed by the ruins of the Old City, where the ancient palace had fallen into the earth on the day the empire collapsed. Not far from the ruins, Tempest happened upon another mark that she couldn't resist. The human examining the wares at a small stall situated at the back corner of a narrow street, far from the other traders, was dressed all in black. He had a sinister air about him, from the skull clasp at the neck of his black cloak to the infernal pattern etched into the left side of his hard, sharp face. He was arguing softly with the merchant, obviously hoping to strike a better deal for whatever arcane trinket he had his eye on. Tempest casually strolled by, reached into the pack resting on the ground at his feet, and walked away with a small, hard item that she hoped she'd be able to sell to one of the brokers in the Warrens.

She turned the corner, made sure she was no longer within the man's line of sight, and she started to run. *What a day!* she remembered thinking. She might have earned enough to rent a room for a couple of nights, to get a couple of hot meals for a change. Maybe even pay off The Jolly Man, the always-smiling halfling who ran the Rogues' Guild and who was as mean and deadly a predator as any monster running around the Underdark. It all depended on what she had retrieved from the sinister man's pack.

She found a spot to rest, a place where she could put her back against a wall and duck down out of sight from any passer's by. Only then did she uncurl her fingers and look at the item she had taken from the man's pack. It was a small onyx statue, no longer than the length of her palm. The statue depicted a shapely woman with long, flowing hair. She was in a seated position, her knees drawn up to her ample chest and her slender arms wrapped around them. The woman wasn't exactly human, however. Great bat wings extended from her back and were pulled tight around her, like a cloak. As Tempest looked at the small statue, its eyes sparked with crimson light. The tiefling let out a startled squeal as the statue changed. It no longer had the shape of a woman, but instead resembled a powerfully built male tiefling. It sat in the same pose, the same bat wings draped around it.

"I believe you have something that belongs to me," said the deep, menacing voice that startled Tempest even more than the shape-changing statue did.

Tempest looked up to see the sinister man in black standing over her. He had a sharp-bladed dagger in his hand, and he was pointing it in her general direction. She quickly slipped the small statue into a pouch she wore on her belt and turned her head up to give the man her most dazzling smile.

"Don't try that on me, girl," the sinister man warned, "I've been seduced by creatures much more practiced at the art than you."

"Like your devil?" Tempest said, letting the words slip out before she had really thought about it. Speaking before she thought was part of her problem. That and the fact that she was poor, hungry, and all alone in the big, bad, partially ruined city of Nera.

The sinister man's eyes narrowed and a darkness seemed to spread across his sharp features. "Is a tiefling going to lecture me on the ways of devils?" he asked, pointing the dagger at her face. "Return my property to me and maybe I'll let you live."

Before Tempest could come up with a proper retort or decide on a course of action that didn't end with her getting cut, a third participant entered the narrow Warren street. It was the dragonborn she had robed earlier. She must have been losing her touch that both of her marks had been able to track her down so quickly.

"There's no need to make threats," the dragonborn said calmly. "Put away your weapon and let's work our way through this obvious misunderstanding."

"Back off, dragonborn," the sinister man said, "or I shall deal with you after I punish the tiefling thief."

The dragonborn placed a hand on the human's arm, gently but forcibly lowering it until the dagger was no longer pointing directly into Tempest's face. Rage twisted across the sinister man's features, and he spat a curse that surrounded the dragonborn with a dark aura. Then he raised his other hand and a ribbon of twisting darkness burrowed into the dragonborn's chest. The dragonborn fell back, clutching at his heart as the twisting darkness continued to flow into him.

Tempest, horrified by the sinister man's attack on the dragonborn, leaped up and barreled into the man. She heard a satisfying cry of pain as her horns slammed into his chest. He was still holding the dagger, however, and he sliced at her with its sharp blade. A line of red appeared on her face, tracing the path of the dagger as it cut across her cheek and barely missed her right eye.

"Now, little thief," the sinister man said, a spark of anticipation in his eyes, "now you die."

Before he could plunge the dagger into Tempest, the dragonborn's clear, powerful voice filled the narrow alleyway. "May the light of Bahamut stay your hand, foul warlock," the dragonborn shouted from where he had fallen, "on pain of death!" Radiant light flooded the cramped space and the sinister man screamed in terrible pain. He tried to attack Tempest, but more pain seemed to overtake him as he approached her, and the dagger fell from his spasming hand.

Tempest didn't wait to see what was going to happen next. She caught the dagger before it hit the ground, turned the blade, and plunged it into the sinister man's neck.

She remembered how she had cried after that. How Roghar had embraced her and held her tight until the wracking sobs had finally abated. Since that chance meeting and fateful day, they had been the best of friends. He had taught her how to fight, providing her with more training than she had gotten on the streets of Nera. She had accompanied him on numerous quests, sometimes on their own, sometimes by teaming up with other adventurers. He had shown concern when she had taken up the mantle of warlock, but he had never turned away from her.

"We fight for what's good and right," he told her. "Never forget that and I will always be there for you."

She had promised him. And she had kept that promise, even when the devil statue offered her the things she had always dreamed about. Roghar was her friend and her rock. As long as they were together, she knew that she would do what was good and what was right.

"Look at those tracks, there in the soft earth," Roghar said, drawing Tempest out of her memories. "Whatever we're chasing is obviously on foot."

Tempest swung down off her horse to examine the tracks. "How can someone on foot stay so far ahead of us? And look at the size of those tracks. They're small. Are we chasing a child? A halfling?"

Roghar shook his head. "You saw what it did in the tower," the dragonborn said. "By Bahamut's platinum scales, we're chasing some kind of demon."

Tempest climbed back on to her mount, giving Albanon a smile of encouragement. But she could feel the tension rolling off of Roghar. The paladin was confused, uncertain. And that made Tempest more than a little afraid.

20 KALTON MANOR, ON THE EDGE OF THE WITCHLIGHT FENS, DAY

Kalaban stood among the ruins of the ancient manor. He stared into the darkness within, looking back the way they had come for any sign of the thing that was following them. He had one hand in the pouch on his belt, holding the smooth glass vial so that he could feel the strange warmth that emanated from it. The knight-commander had given the dead glass to his emperor, Magroth, but he had thus far failed to tell his master about the vial of crimson liquid that was run through with streaks of silver and flecks of gold. It was a strange substance, an important substance, and it was all his. He didn't feel the need to share it with his master.

He and Magroth had departed Fallcrest by the south road to reach one of the borderland outposts that had been established when Nerath's soldiers first began to explore the Nentir Vale. The outpost they had in mind had been established during Magroth's original reign, and it was only about twenty-five miles from Fallcrest.

"If the outpost still exists," Magroth explained, "then perhaps the teleportation circle still exists as well. I need to reach the grand palace as fast as possible, and a travel portal is the fastest means I know. We don't have much time, and there are tools that I have been without for far too long."

They had traveled across the Moon Hills, moving at the supernatural speed granted them by their undead status and Magroth's magic. Kalaban began to sense a presence behind them as they traveled. It was strong and unnatural, and it made the knight-commander more than a little uncomfortable. It was fast, but Kalaban and Magroth had maintained a steady pace and had managed to reach their destination well ahead of whatever the thing was.

"Could the wizard have sent something to track us?" he asked Magroth.

The Mad Emperor studied the horizon, reaching out with arcane senses that were even more sensitive in many ways than Kalaban's own. He closed his eyes, whispering words of power that Kalaban didn't understand.

"No, not the wizard," Magroth said, his eyes snapping open. "I don't know what that is. It almost appears to be demonic in nature, but it isn't like any demon I have ever encountered. Come. Let's head inside and find that magic circle."

The outpost was located on a patch of open land just beyond the White River, nestled between the Witchlight Fens to the west and the Harken Forest to the east. Kalaban studied the place with a practiced eye. It was no longer a small outpost, but it was obviously deserted.

A half-finished keep occupied the spot where the outpost once stood. The builders never completed the keep, and from the looks of things they had abandoned the place some time ago. The unfinished keep was little more than a ruin, empty of lords or knights, servants or tenants. The place felt unfinished. Two words were carved into the keystone of the keep in the Common letters: Kalton Manor.

Magroth willed light to glow atop his staff as he boldly strode deeper into the ruined structure.

"This way, Kalaban, this way," Magroth urged. He wore the dead glass amulet around his neck, and Kalaban couldn't help but notice how often the emperor's hand reached up to stroke the smooth stone.

Reluctantly, the knight-commander drew his own hand out of his belt pouch, leaving the glass vial hidden inside. He needed to be ready to defend Magroth in case the ruin wasn't as deserted as it appeared or if the demon-thing finally caught up to them.

"If my sodden descendent who allowed my empire to fall into ruin had any wits at all—and that is still in question, mind you—then there should be an inscribed circle in the chamber ahead," Magroth said as Kalaban ran to catch up to him.

The emperor never slowed. He walked into the ruined chamber, moving directly toward the magic circle that was inscribed in the flagstone floor, just where it was supposed to be. Kalaban studied the rest of the half-finished room, noting the cracks in the walls, the partially completed roof, and the scattered pieces of armor spread across the rubble-littered floor. The knight-commander stepped toward his master, but then he paused. Something wasn't quite right.

Kalaban glanced back at a dented helmet near the doorway. As he watched, glowing embers sparked within the helmet, appearing to be flaming eyes. The helmet slowly floated off the ground, as did other pieces of armor. The pieces of armor drew together, each clanging into place and held there by a fiery red glow that infused the entire form. Kalaban scanned the room, noticing that three such animated suits of armor had assembled themselves. They each wielded a flaming greatsword, and they moved into a battle formation that appeared every bit as formidable as any the knight-commander had ever devised.

Kalaban drew his own weapon, a long sword with a gem-encrusted pommel that had been a gift from Magroth many centuries ago. It held its own enchantments and had become a soulsword when Kalaban had died, and the death knight was well-practiced in its use.

"Helmed horrors, my liege," Kalaban warned, placing himself between his emperor and two of the three animated constructs.

Magroth laughed. "Worry not, Kalaban," the emperor said, "these ancient guardians know who I am."

The emperor examined the third animated suit of armor and rapped his knuckles on the ancient metal. He nodded his approval.

A sound toward the front of the ruined keep made Kalaban spin around, and Magroth laughed again.

"Whatever is out there has made my knight-commander as nervous as a chicken on its way to the farm-wife's cook pot," the emperor chuckled. "Protect the door. Let nothing in."

At the emperor's words, the three helmed horrors levitated into the air and floated through the doorway into the darkness beyond.

Kalaban watched them go as Magroth returned to the inscribed circle. It was about ten feet wide, etched into the flagstone floor. The arcane symbols formed a pattern that, Kalaban knew, could be used as the focus of a teleportation spell that would open a portal between this circle and a similar circle in another part of the empire.

Magroth began to perform the ritual that would activate the portal. First, the arcane symbols began to glow. Then the line of the circle itself pulsed with intense light. The light was dancing now, leaping from symbol to symbol and coalescing in the center of the circle.

As Magroth continued to cast the spell, the first sounds of battle echoed from the dark doorway through which the helmed horrors had passed. Kalaban stepped closer to his master, listening to the clang of metal and the scrape of steel on stone.

A massive crash as armor rained down on the stone floor. The first helmed horror had fallen.

A second crash. Metal bounced off the half-completed wall in the chamber beyond. The second helmed horror had been defeated.

Kalaban raised his sword. It would only be another moment or two before whatever had followed them from the wizard's tower in Fallcrest came rushing through the doorway. The knight-commander truly had no clue about whether or not he could deal with the thing that Magroth had said was almost a demon. He wasn't sure if that uncertainty frightened him or excited him.

A terrible rending sound, followed by another crash. The third helmed horror was no more.

"Time to go, Kalaban," Magroth said, stepping into the glowing circle.

Kalaban hesitated, his eyes fixed on the darkened doorway. A small hand reached through, illuminated now by only the light of the magic circle. The hand was ripped and bleeding, and Kalaban could see exposed bone peeking through the torn flesh. He desperately wanted to know what was following them, but he couldn't delay any longer. He stepped into the circle, just as the magical energy began to fade.

As Kalaban was whisked from the ruined keep, he tried to comprehend what he saw in the fading light of the circle.

It was a female halfling, torn and misshapen, with crimson-silver liquid oozing from her wounds as well as bright-red blood.

21 THE MOON HILLS, TWILIGHT

Albanon followed Moorin's murderer south, across the rising and falling landscape of the Moon Hills. He rode on the back of Tempest's horse, a chestnut mare with a mane of white hair, right behind the tiefling. To his left rode Roghar, seated atop a massive black stallion with a shock of white at its throat. Splendid sat across his neck, her head resting on his shoulder. She was going on and on about how he shouldn't trust these two so-called adventurers.

"The tiefling smells of pact magic," Splendid said, "and the dragonborn reeks of stale ale and overspiced mead. I'm sure they're in league with the creature that murdered the greatest wizard who ever lived. I'm sure of it."

Tempest sighed. "I know that the events of last night have been hard on the both of you, but if you don't stop talking about me like I wasn't here, I'm going to turn you into a belt pouch!"

They had been riding since just before dawn. After the initial shock of discovering the murdered wizard, Albanon decided that he had to go after the murderer and recover the dead glass that had been taken from the tower. He gathered his spellbook and staff, packed a few personal items into a backpack, and sealed the tower with the warding spells he had learned from Moorin. Splendid decided that she would accompany the apprentice, to make sure he didn't get into too much trouble. Roghar and Tempest conferred briefly, and then they offered to help Albanon avenge his mentor's death. The young wizard, relieved by the offer of help, readily agreed.

The pseudodragon complained and warned him against trusting the two adventurers, but Albanon ignored the little creature. They were experienced in matters such as these. At least, they had more experience than he did. He needed them if he was going to succeed in this dangerous quest. After all, the murderer had been able to kill the mighty Moorin. What chance did an apprentice wizard have? Still, Albanon had to try.

Now, just a little more than six hours later, the four companions had covered almost twenty-five miles of countryside and they were exhausted. They were irritable, and the constant complaining and accusations of the pseudodragon weren't helping anyone's mood. As they approached the banks of the White River, Roghar called a halt to their travels.

"We need to rest," the dragonborn paladin said, "or we won't be of any use when we finally catch up with the murderer."

He hadn't said it, but Albanon knew that they were all thinking it: What kind of murderer can outrun horses? Probably the same kind that can kill powerful wizards in their own towers, Albanon imagined grimly. It made no sense, and that made all of them more than a little nervous about what they were facing.

Tempest broke out a waterskin and began to pass it around while Roghar pulled a few pieces of dried meat from his saddlebag. Albanon, suddenly overwhelmed by sheer exhaustion, slumped against a tree that grew beside the river bank. He looked across the river and down into the clearing between the dense trees of the Harken Forest and the swamp known as the Witchlight Fens. The ruins of Kalton Manor sat in the clearing, as quiet and empty as they had been for more than one hundred years.

"Bahamut, bless this quest and give us the strength we need to succeed," Roghar prayed as he gave each of the companions a piece of the dried meat.

Albanon gratefully accepted the waterskin from Tempest, who smiled at him as he drank deeply. Albanon, meanwhile, couldn't take his eyes off the ruined structure in the distance. A soft glow emanated from inside the half-finished keep, and he thought he heard sounds coming from the structure as well. He strained to listen, absently placing a gentle hand atop the pseudodragon that had curled up beside him. There was a sound, like crashing metal, coming from within the keep. It was followed by a second, similar sound.

As though someone had knocked over an empty suit of armor.

"Something's happening down there," Albanon said.

22 THE IMPERIAL PALACE, IN THE RUINED CITY OF NERA, NIGHT

As the intense glow of the inscribed circle faded, Kalaban found himself standing beside Magroth in the ruins of what was once a grand palace. The palace chamber was slanted, the floor at an angle and the walls askew; the place was riddled with cracks and even gaping holes in some places. Still, despite the destruction and disrepair, Kalaban recognized where they were.

"The Imperial Palace in Nera," the knight-commander whispered.

"Of course," Magroth replied. "Where else did you think we would wind up? But look at this place. Look what has become of my once-grand palace. Time is never kind. And it seems as though there was an earthquake or other disaster, for I believe that the entire building has fallen into the earth. Such a bother."

The emperor forced his will into his staff, causing the tip to glow with arcane light. The light from Magroth's staff illuminated the cantered chamber, revealing grand columns and intricate carvings that were still impressive despite the damage the place had sustained. Kalaban looked around, seeing things he remembered as well as new touches that had been added after he and Magroth had died and been drawn into the Shadowfell. There were sounds within the ruins as well. Water dripped from the cracked ceiling, and the stones overhead creaked and groaned with age and the misplaced weight of the slanted chamber. It could all come down on their heads at any moment, he thought.

"Really, Kalaban, you worry too much," Magroth said, following Kalaban's gaze to the ceiling. "The place has been like this for a long, long time, I'd wager. The chances of it deciding to collapse on top of us at this exact moment are . . . well, pretty good, actually." Magroth laughed.

In the darkness beyond one of the open doorways, Kalaban heard something large slither across the bare stone.

"The light, my liege," Kalaban said, "it attracts whatever haunts this place."

"That's why I brought you along, knight-commander," Magroth snorted. "It certainly wasn't for your witty conversation skills or your constant moaning. Deal with it, Kalaban. I have other things to do."

Kalaban watched as Magroth headed toward the far wall, searching for the secret entrance to his hidden workshop. "If it still survives," he whispered, warily turning back toward the shadowy doorway. Kalaban glanced briefly at the inscribed circle, but it was now dark and inactive. He was glad for that. He didn't relish trying to deal with the demon-thing that had so easily dispatched three helmed horrors back in Kalton Manor. He was still trying to make sense of the crimson-silver substance that oozed from the halfling-thing's horrific wounds. Wounds that didn't appear to bother it. And crimson-silver reminded him of the substance inside the glass vial hidden in his belt pouch. What was that creature and how did the crimson substance fit in? Was it simply coincidence? Kalaban didn't think so, and he certainly didn't believe in coincidences when it came to matters of life and death.

"Ah, here it is," Magroth said gleefully as he manipulated concealed switches hidden among the carvings on the wall.

Kalaban turned as the wall slid open, revealing a secret passage beyond. That was when the scavenger in the outer hall, attracted by the sounds and the light, rushed into the chamber. The large, worm-like creature plowed into Kalaban, knocking the knight-commander to the floor. As Kalaban smashed into the stone tiles, his sword bounced from his hand and clattered away.

"It's just a carrion crawler," Magroth called as he entered the passageway. "Deal with it, Kalaban."

Easier said than done, the knight-commander thought gravely. Without his soulsword, he could already feel the weakness come upon him, slowing his reaction time and stealing the strength from his limbs. He had to retrieve his weapon quickly, before the crawler struck again.

Kalaban cursed as the large crawler reared up, exposing a maw of sharp teeth and thick, serrated mandibles, as well as a nest of writhing tentacles growing from beneath the crawler's maw. Before the knight-commander could react, the tentacles shot out, striking him over and over with their poisonous tips.

Kalaban cursed again as the crawler began to bite.

23 GARDBURY DOWNS, NEAR THE VILLAGE OF WINTERHAVEN, NIGHT

Shara sat before the roaring campfire, acutely aware of the . . . *creature* . . . watching her from the shadows. Uldane was curled up inside a blanket beside the fire, snoring softly. Shara had decided to take the first watch, wary that the wyrmpriest might return or that he might have a way to summon the green dragon, and she didn't want to be caught sleeping if that occurred. She was also concerned about the *thing* that called itself Erak.

Erak had helped them against the kobolds, fighting alongside them to overcome the ambush that she had walked right into. She could kick herself for falling for such an amateur ploy. It was because of the anger and the pain. She wasn't thinking straight, and her inattention had almost cost Uldane and her their lives.

Erak came to her rescue, just as Jarren had so many times before. She had even thought that it might have been Jarren, at least for a moment. After they had defeated the kobolds and the wyrmpriest had escaped, Erak had introduced himself and asked if he could accompany them.

"I have work to do," Erak had said, and the words chilled Shara to the bone.

She ordered the creature to leave, and Erak had departed. But he didn't go very far, and Shara and Uldane had both noticed him trailing them from a distance astride one of the draft horses the kobolds had used. Not willing to let the creature follow them back into Winterhaven, Shara decided to set up camp and use the night to figure out what she wanted to do.

She had heard rumors of creatures such as Erak. Revenants, she believed they were called. When the living had left undone tasks behind at the moment of death, they were sometimes sent back to complete those tasks. The followers of the Raven Queen, the god of fate and death, often preached about such creatures, sent back to the world of the living by their mistress to finish whatever had been left undone. They returned with few, if any, memories of who and what they had been, and they often returned wearing completely different forms. But they returned with a compulsion to complete whatever compelled them back to life.

I have work to do.

What if Shara had been correct the first time she saw him? What if Erak was Jarren, returned in a new body to help her destroy the green dragon but without any of his true memories? Was that possible?

Her beloved.

Shara felt tears begin to well up at the corners of her eyes.

What if it was Jarren?

What if?

She stirred the fire, letting her tears flow and her thoughts go where they may.

Shara sat like that for a long time, remembering the past, imagining the future.

She looked past the fire to where Erak was sitting in the shadows, against a large tree. So still, but so attentive, as though he was guarding them, keeping them safe.

As he had done on the road earlier today. As Jarren had done on every quest they had undertaken.

"Uldane," Shara said, waking the halfling from his sleep.

Uldane sat up and reached for his sword. "Trouble?" he asked, pushing the blanket away.

"No, no trouble."

"Then what? Why'd you wake me up?"

"Please, Uldane," she said, her voice quiet. "Invite our . . . *friend* . . . to join us. The night is too cool not to share our fire."

Falon sat on a bench near the dock, waiting for Darrum to finish making the arrangements so that they could board the merchant ship *Hammerfast's Boon*. He cradled the sword his mother had given him across his lap, once again wrapped tight in oilcloth and hidden from prying eyes. He replayed what his mother had told him in his mind, going over it for the hundredth time as he tried to come to grips with the revelation.

"My grandfather was just a boy, younger than you are now, when the empire began to crumble," she had explained. "Well, as I understand it, the empire had been falling apart for years. But it was the events of a century ago that finally spelled the doom of glorious Nerath. The emperor, my grandfather's father, had sent his son away. Names were changed. New identities were forged. It had to be that way. The royal blood had to survive."

She wiped tears away as she spoke, talking directly to Falon even though she knew that Darrum was listening. "There may be others out there. Probably are. Cousins and the like. But you, Falon, my son, you are the direct descendent of the last emperor of Nerath. You are the heir to the throne."

"And this," she said, holding up the sword, "is *Arande*, the holy sword of Nerath. Take it, use it. It will not fail you."

She had hugged him tightly then, holding him close. "Accompany the Shield," she said, nodding toward Darrum. She turned to address the dwarf directly. "They know that the heir of Nerath is here, so you must take him elsewhere. Perhaps to Argent, or to the Temple of Erathis in Fallcrest. Somewhere safe."

They had said their farewells, and now Falon was preparing to travel with the old dwarf to who knew where, trying to make sense of everything his mother had told him. He didn't understand what any of it could really mean. Even if he was the heir to the throne of Nerath, there was no throne to ascend to. The empire was gone, and there was no overarching force governing the Nentir Vale or the lands beyond. That time was done, and Falon had no desire to rule in any event. So why did someone want him dead?

Darrum strolled over, interrupting Falon's internal conversation.

"Water travel always makes me queasy," Darrum complained. "Never liked it. But I got us passage on the dwarven merchant ship. They'll take us across the lake and down the Nentir River, to Fallcrest. Hopefully, by that time I'll have figured out what we're going to do next."

Falon nodded and rose, hefting his pack and the oilcloth-wrapped sword.

"Don't look so glum," the old dwarf said, "it'll be an adventure."

Yeah, thought Falon, remembering the tales his grandfather used to regale him with. *That's what I'm afraid of.*

25 THE IMPERIAL PALACE, IN THE RUINED CITY OF NERA, NIGHT

Kalaban wedged his armor-encased left arm in the carrion crawler's maw, hoping that the plate mail would withstand the sharp teeth and crushing pressure the creature was bringing to bear long enough for the knight-commander to determine his next move. Obviously, he had to retrieve his weapon. But first he had to get out from under the giant worm before it found something meaty to chew on.

The giant scavenger seemed slightly confused about why Kalaban was still putting up a fight. It had raked him repeatedly with its poisonous tendrils, and the creature expected its prey to start slowing down or even stop moving altogether at this point in the battle. The knight-commander, however, wasn't the beast's normal fare. Kalaban was no longer truly alive. He was undead, and his immortal state offered him a number of benefits that most living creatures didn't possess.

Including immunity to poison.

He wasn't sorry to disappoint the carrion crawler. In fact, he was about to make its day even more miserable.

As the crawler continued to gnaw on Kalaban's left arm, crushing the metal and tearing at the leather straps, the knight-commander reached for the dagger hanging on his belt. The beast undulated as it bit at him, so he had a bit of room to maneuver between the motions of the creature. He gripped the dagger, drew it free, and then plunged it upward to meet the crawler's next downward motion.

Even in his weakened state, Kalaban's aim was true and the dagger struck deep. The beast wailed in pain. It was a strange, disturbing sound that Kalaban never wanted to hear again. The touch of the dagger was only the first wound he planned to visit on the creature, however. As the crawler reared up, trying to escape the stinging blade, Kalaban rolled away and scurried to his feet. He picked up his sword, feeling the familiar energy of the weapon fill him as he gripped the handle. His was a soulsword, bound to him just as he was dependent on it. It was a part of his undead existence, and he was relieved to feel its heft in his hand. With it, he felt complete.

With sword in hand, the knight-commander spun to face the crawler, feeling the strength and vitality returning to him. "You should have looked elsewhere for a meal," he snarled, dropping into a combat stance as the crawler slithered toward him.

Kalaban waited, biding his time, gauging the power and deter-mination of his foe. The carrion crawler reared up, fixing the orbs on the end of its eyestalks on him as its tentacles lashed at him like living whips. He caught the attacks on his left arm, letting most of the tentacles whip harmlessly across the plate armor that was dented and slick with crawler spit but otherwise intact. He grabbed two of the writhing tentacles in his mailed glove and pulled them toward him. Then he slashed with his sword, cutting through the taut tendrils and soliciting another inhuman scream from the creature.

The knight-commander stood facing the beast, still holding the pair of severed tentacles in his left hand. "Are we done here?" he asked in a low voice, not willing to kill the creature if he didn't have to.

The carrion crawler regarded Kalaban for a long moment, breathing hard and grunting with the pain of its three wounds. Then, without further hesitation, the crawler slithered out of the chamber and disappeared into the darkness beyond the open doorway.

Kalaban watched for a few seconds, listening to the sounds of the departing scavenger. "May your next hunt be more fortuitous," he said, slipping his soulsword back into its sheath and tossing away the dripping tendrils.

"Are you done playing, Kalaban?" Magroth asked, emerging from the hidden passage. "My workshop is still here, though it has been used by others since last we visited the palace. The sword of Nerath isn't here, damn the luck, but I found something else that will be of service to our cause."

A large figure emerged from the secret door. It was so tall and so broad that it barely managed to squeeze out of the passage. It was a giant carved from blue-gray stone, standing nearly eight feet tall and easily twice as wide or more than Kalaban was, and Kalaban was not small by anyone's definition. It was humanoid in shape, standing on two solid legs of stone, but it was all chiseled lines and faceted contours. Its head was like a helmet, with no distinct features except for a visorlike slit where its eyes should be.

"A golem," Magroth cackled with glee, sounding like a child who had discovered an unexpected present beneath his bed. "It's one of the stoneguard, the golems specifically enchanted to protect the royal blood of Nerath and obey their commands."

"I remember," Kalaban said. "A powerful weapon."

"Yes," Magroth agreed. "Now we can face this creature, Sareth, and complete the next of my tasks."

26 KALTON MANOR, NIGHT

Nu Alin stood completely still, forcing the anger and frustration to calm from a raging storm of massive waves and biting wind to a choppy sea. The Voidharrow was within his reach, and then it wasn't. Another wizard, undead this time, had used a magic circle of some sort to vacate this ruined place before Nu Alin could take possession of that which he so desperately needed to find.

He slowed the vessel's breathing, tried to quiet its beating heart. So fragile, these bodies of flesh and blood, so easy to break. Nu Alin had had little trouble with the animated suits of armor, but his vessel had paid dearly for the effort he had exerted. The flesh cracked and split with every blow he had delivered against the animated armor. Bones shattered. Blood oozed. And more than blood. Nu Alin's own substance, his true form, spilled from the open wounds along with the halfling's blood. He would need to replace this form, and he would have to do it sooner than he had originally planned.

With his destructive impulses more or less in check, Nu Alin bent to study the circle inscribed on the stone floor of the ruined chamber. It was actually two circles, one inscribed within another, the lines perfectly etched into the cold, stone tiles that covered the floor. Framed between the two circles, runes that Nu Alin could not interpret were written into the hard stone as though it had been soft sand, circumventing the entire inner edge of the larger circle. He could feel the lingering tingle of arcane magic floating above the circle, but he was no closer to figuring out how to make the magic work than he was when he first approached the area. He had missed his opportunity by mere moments as he finished dealing with the animated suits of armor.

The anger threatened to cloud over him again, and part of him wanted to give in to the urge to rip the ruined building apart stone by stone. But that wouldn't solve his current problem. He had lost the trail, and the Voidharrow that he had sought to retrieve could be anywhere in this strange, soft world. Anywhere! The thought made him want to bash the body he wore into the hard wall over and over again until he spilled from it and took up his natural form. However, he knew he couldn't survive very long outside a vessel. Not yet, in any event.

And Nu Alin had to survive. He needed to find the Voidharrow. He needed to set it free.

Nu Alin stood there in the near-darkness, thinking, trying to control his anger in order to come up with a plan that would salvage the events of the past few hours, when he heard sounds approaching from the north. The same direction he had come from.

He moved to the half-finished wall at the front of the keep and peered out into the night. He saw them just as they were emerging from the river, riding a pair of horses up on the dry land. The small band was led by a large, armored figure atop a massive black horse. Nu Alin searched the memories of his host and pulled what he needed from the halfling's tattered mind. A dragonborn, that one was called, and it appeared to be a warrior of some sort. A second horse followed, smaller and of a lighter color than the first. It carried two figures on its back. The one controlling the beast was a female in riding leathers, and by the horns jutting from her head he determined that she was a tiefling. Seated behind her, holding a staff in one hand while his other grasped the tiefling's waist for support, was an eladrin in robes.

A wizard! Perhaps Nu Alin could still grasp victory this night.

"The murderer," the last member of the small band said, looking straight into the ruined building where Nu Alin was hiding, "the murderer is close." The creature wasn't like the other members of the band. It was tiny, carried aloft by delicate wings. Nu Alin remembered the creature. It had been in the wizard's tower, trying hard not to be noticed while he and the wizard had battled.

Pain suddenly wracked Nu Alin, radiating through his host form and reaching deep into his own substance. His true body oozed in and out of the many wounds that covered the vessel, some inflicted by the animated suits of armor but many more created as Nu Alin used the body to destroy the guardian constructs. Nu Alin would need to find a new host soon. Perhaps the dragonborn would suffice. He seemed large and powerfully built, hearty. The pain was making it hard for Nu Alin to concentrate, to think about what he needed to do.

The small band approached the ruins, pausing just outside the half-finished wall. Nu Alin scampered back into the shadows, moving deeper into the chamber with the circle inscribed on the floor.

The tiny winged creature landed on the eladrin's shoulder and crawled down so that only its head was peaking up from behind. "It killed the mighty and great wizard, Moorin," the tiny creature squeaked. "No offense, but what chance do the three of you have against it?"

The dragonborn, tiefling, and eladrin slowly made their way into the ruined keep. The eladrin wizard called forth light from the top of his staff, and Nu Alin drew farther back into the chamber. A new idea formed amid the pain that was threatening to set off his rage and his anger. This idea was good, but it required patience and diplomacy, not wanton destruction.

The tiefling stepped toward the inscribed circle, bending to examine it.

"A teleportation circle," she said, her hand outstretched above the engraved runes. "It's been used, and not very long ago."

"Maybe the thing we've been chasing got away," the dragonborn said, lowering its sword as though hoping for Nu Alin's absence was the same as Nu Alin being gone.

"No," the tiny winged creature warned, "the murderer is still here."

Nu Alin sprang out of the shadows, leaping the distance in a massive bound that brought his vessel within arm's reach of the tiefling. Before any of them could react, Nu Alin grabbed the tiefling and dug the female halfling's clawlike fingers into the tiefling's neck. He fixed the eladrin wizard with a steely gaze, looking through the failing eyes of his halfling vessel.

"Make the circle work," Nu Alin said through the halfling's cracked and bloody lips. "Make the circle work, or this one dies."

27 LAKE NEN, NIGHT

How are you feeling?" Falon asked as he handed the mug of tea to Darrum.

"Like a volcano about to erupt," the dwarf grumbled, taking a single sip of the hot liquid and then setting it aside. "I hate the sea and everything about it."

"Technically, we're traveling across a lake, not the sea."

"Technically, I might forget that you're under my protection and shove one of my hammers up your. . . . "

"Excuse me," one of the dwarf crew interrupted, "but the captain asked me to let you know that we're entering a bit of choppy water known as the Graveyard. A number of ships sank here during the Bloodspear orc uprising, and this stretch of the lake has always had some strange currents."

"Thanks for the information," Falon said.

"Yeah, now I have another reason for why my head is spinning and my guts are rolling," Darrum complained.

As the crew member departed, Falon decided to try to get the dwarf's mind on to other topics. "Darrum, if you don't mind me asking, where were you when the empire collapsed?"

The dwarf fixed his one good eye on Falon, studying him with a critical gaze. For a long moment, Falon assumed that Darrum wasn't going to answer him. Then the dwarf slumped back against the bench and sighed.

"I was an Imperial Shield, one of the elite knights charged with protecting the royal family," Darrum began, hesitant at first, but then he let the tale unfold. "My place was usually with the emperor's daughter, a young lass who was every bit as stubborn and determined as her father. But the emperor sent me away that day. I don't know what was going through his head, or what he had been hearing, but he called for me. We met alone, in his private chambers. He gave me a sealed letter and said that it had to reach the Baron of Therund immediately. Of course I agreed. I departed from the capital city within the hour, and I never saw my emperor or any of the royal family again."

"Until yesterday," Darrum finished, giving Falon a knowing glance.

"You weren't in Nera when the disaster struck?"

Darrum shook his head. "I'm not even really sure what happened that day. I've heard all of the stories, conflicting though they may be. Perhaps all of them are true. Perhaps none of them. But whether it was a natural earthquake or a powerful spell, marauding gnolls or assassins sent by the emperor's own brother, whatever happened that day, the royal family died and the empire fell apart. I was far away and on my own, and there was nothing I could do."

Falon was quiet for a time, thinking about the various stories he had heard growing up in Nenlast. "Did you deliver the letter?" he finally asked.

"Enough about those dark days," Darrum said, waving the question away. "Tell me, young Falon, why did you decide to take up the cleric's oath?"

"It wasn't so much a decision," Falon admitted, "as much as it was a calling. I always felt a connection to Erathis and the teachings of law and civilization. Erathis wants to bring light to the wilderness, and there's so much darkness in the land. I want to be part of the light."

Darrum studied Falon, searching his face for something he expected to find there. "You sound just like him," the old dwarf said. "Just like my emperor."

A commotion at the front of the ship caught the attention of Falon and Darrum. "By Moradin's flaming beard!" one of the crew members exclaimed.

"Moradin doesn't have a flaming beard, you oaf!" someone else shouted.

"You can take it up with the good man when you meet him," the ship's captain bellowed. "Now get to your stations, every one of you!"

Falon and Darrum moved to the ship's prow, approaching the captain. Captain Stonehome was a steady, reliable dwarf with a quiet demeanor until the situation warranted a more blusterous response. Then he could bellow and shout with the best of them. He was solid, commanding, and with a level head that made Falon feel good about having him at the helm. Right now, he was barking orders in a strange shorthand that Falon couldn't quite comprehend, even though the crew members seemed to understand him perfectly well.

"Captain," Darrum asked, his hands never far from the handles of his twin warhammers, "what has your ship in such an uproar?"

"Take a look, sir," Captain Stonehome said, pointing toward the dark waters of the lake ahead of them, "and tell me how you think we should behave in the face of this."

The merchant ship was sailing directly into a churning whirlpool. Wind whipped off the lake to blow fiercely across the deck of the vessel, and the churning water became more violent with each passing moment. As the crew struggled to keep the ship from entering the raging water, Darrum gripped the rail so that he could get a better look.

"We're not in the open ocean," Falon said, shouting to be heard above the rising wind. "How can the water be doing that?"

"Now do you see why I hate to travel over water? Anyway, there's nothing natural about this storm."

"Really? What was your first clue?"

Falon stared into the churning lake water. The storm or whatever it was wasn't like any weather he had ever experienced. For all the wind and whirling water, the night sky was crystal clear, and the moon and stars above shed pale light over the ship and the lake around them. Falon thought he had seen something in the water. Debris? Some kind of animal? Then he saw them, clearly illuminated by the light of the moon.

"Darrum, do you see?"

"I see them," the dwarf replied, drawing his twin warhammers from the harness around his waist.

Falon might not have believed it if he hadn't fought similar creatures just two nights before. Now he was watching as skeletal forms rose from beneath the churning water of Lake Nen. They were crawling up the sides of the ship, dressed in wet tatters that might once have been noble finery or the rags of a common servant. The skeletons climbed toward the deck of the ship, some carrying rusted swords and daggers, others unarmed but no less menacing. The first of the walking dead were stepping over the rail, cold lake water running down their exposed bones to puddle on the deck.

"Hold them off," Falon ordered Darrum, shouting over the biting wind. "Maybe I can drive them away."

Falon ran back to their bench and reached for the oilcloth-wrapped sword. He quickly pulled *Arande* free, letting its soft glow warm him against the unnatural wind. Falon began to pray, even as he kept one eye on Darrum and the dwarf crew members, many of whom were now engaged in battle against the skeleton boarding party.

Darrum waded in to attack the first skeletons climbing on to the deck at the ship's prow. He twirled his twin warhammers with amazing speed, shattering bone and scattering the initial boarders with relative ease. The golden warhammer's head was blunt on one side and beveled into a wedge on the other. The dark gray warhammer, meanwhile, was blunt on both ends, so dark as to be almost black in the pale light cast by the moon and the few lanterns blazing on the deck.

"Erathis, let your light fill the darkness and drive off this evil," Falon prayed, even as he noticed that the fractured bones of the skeletons that Darrum had dispatched were knitting back together.

"I'm slowing them down, nothing more," Darrum called back. "If you have something else, now would be a good time to use it!"

Falon thrust forth *Arande*, holding it out like some kind of talisman. It did incorporate the holy symbol of Erathis within its design, so maybe the allusion held more truth than hope. Suddenly, Falon's sword, the sword of Nerath, blazed like a miniature sun. Divine light radiated from the blade, spreading out in all directions. As the divine light sliced through the shadows, it touched the invading skeletons. Some of the undead creatures exploded at the touch, raining bits of bone and tattered rags across the deck. Others simply doubled over in agonizing pain, leaping away from the light and back into the churning water.

"That's got them! Well done, Falon!" Darrum exclaimed as he continued to smash the nearest skeletons into pieces.

Falon was about to return an excited exclamation of his own when he noticed something new in the water off the side of the ship. It was a skeletal skiff, like some old wreck returned to the surface in much the same way that the undead were. It streaked toward the ship, and riding atop it was a figure in dark red robes. The figure pointed directly at Falon, and a bolt of dark energy flew from its fingers and slammed into the young cleric. Falon tried to twist out of the way, but the dark bolt caught him in his shoulder and spun him around. He dropped to the deck of the ship, wracked by a horrible pain that was concentrated where the bolt hit but was radiating throughout the rest of his body.

Darrum didn't hesitate. He grabbed a line from one of the crew and leaped over the side of the ship. He landed atop the speeding skiff as it turned away from the merchant vessel. Falon couldn't hear what the two were saying because of the distance and the still-howling wind, but he watched as Darrum's hammers blocked one bolt of darkness, then another, and then the old dwarf brought both heads to bear. He struck the robed figure with two solid, simultaneous blows. The robed figure crumpled, and at the same time the few skeletons still in the battle crumpled as well.

"Darrum," Falon tried to call out, but he was still suffering from the effect of the bolt of dark energy. He could only watch as the ancient skiff began to fall apart beneath the old dwarf. At the same time, skeletal limbs reached out of the water, grabbing hold of the robed figure even as they wrapped around Darrum and pulled him under.

As fast as it began, the churning water stilled. The wind died away, and silence descended over the dark lake.

Except for a single, mournful cry.

"Darrum," Falon called, finally finding his voice as the pain from the dark bolt faded away.

28 THE WITCHLIGHT FENS, NIGHT

Kalaban stood on one side of Magroth while the golem held position on the other. They stood on the deck of a small air skiff, an ancient and magical conveyance that Magroth had recovered from the ruins of his imperial palace. The air skiff was about the size of a small row boat, though it was perfectly round, shaped more like a basket than a vessel designed to ride through the water. A single sail, a colorful triangle of cloth covered in magical runes, seemed to be what held them aloft and propelled them through the night sky at fantastic speed, but Kalaban didn't completely understand the intricacies of magic.

The confined space was made even smaller thanks to the presence of the golem stoneguard. It was a huge construct, and it barely left enough room in the air skiff for Kalaban and his master. Luckily, the golem only moved when commanded to. Otherwise, it remained unnaturally still. In many ways, it reminded Kalaban of the massive statues that had adorned the steps of the Imperial Palace in Nera. Come to think of it, perhaps what he had assumed had been statues were simply more of the stoneguard, protecting the emperor by hiding in plain sight.

Magroth stood before a narrow pedestal made from a dark, solid wood. He held the Necropolis Stone atop its flat surface, letting the chain attached to the amulet hang down so that it jangled against the pedestal. The noise didn't seem to bother either the golem or Magroth, but it was making Kalaban's skin crawl. He tried to ignore the sound, concentrating instead on what Magroth was up to.

The top of the pedestal was inscribed with a magic circle, a smaller version of the one that had transported them from Kalton Manor to

Nera, but it was obvious that it used a different type of magic. The emperor studied the dead glass, then looked out to see where they were flying. He constantly touched different parts of the runed inscription and whispered words of power that Kalaban couldn't understand.

"Interesting," Magroth said as he continued his work. "Orcus's priest was correct. I can use the dead glass to find the one she called Sareth. Apparently, this Sareth is hiding in the Witchlight Fens."

"Weren't we just there?" Kalaban asked ruefully.

"Mind your manners, knight-commander. You should follow the example of my golem and only speak when spoken to."

The golem turned to gaze on Kalaban with its helmetlike face. The knight-commander couldn't be sure, but it seemed like the golem was gloating.

The air skiff slowed as it descended into the fetid swamp. It came to rest a few paces from a circle of stones located deep within the Witchlight Fens. There were nine stones set within a circle, each about three feet wide and eight feet tall. In the darkness, Kalaban couldn't see any inscriptions on the standing stones, but he assumed that they were marked in some manner. The circle of stones stood beside a small rise in the earth, a more or less solid hill in the otherwise marshy fen. "The magic is gone, but the air skiff has served its purpose," Magroth said as he exited the basket and strode boldly into the center of the standing stones. The emperor examined the ancient site, studying each stone in turn as Kalaban and the golem stood guard.

"Ingenious, I must say," the Mad Emperor muttered, more to himself than to either Kalaban or the stoneguard.

Magroth held the Necropolis Stone high, letting the moonlight stream into its faceted depths. Light flashed within the dead glass, sending reflections back at five of the nine stones that formed the ancient circle. As the light struck each of the five stones in turn, intricate runes on each stone's weathered face momentarily resonated with an arcane glow. As the glow faded, the nearby rise rumbled, and an opening yawned wide in the small hill.

"I don't know what kind of creature this Sareth might be, Kalaban," Magroth said, his eyes sparkling with purpose and excitement, "but we must destroy it if Nerath is to rise again."

Kalaban followed Magroth as the dark sky began to brighten. Dawn was coming.

"Now, my knight-commander, we hunt."

29 KALTON MANOR, NIGHT

Albanon stood back, studying the female halfling who had leaped out of the shadows and grabbed Tempest around the neck. He tried to keep his mind calm, detached. He needed to approach the situation as though it were any of a hundred tests that Moorin had surprised him with over the years. If he remained in control, logical, he could find a solution to the problem at hand. He had to. If he couldn't, Tempest would die.

Just as Moorin of the Glowing Tower had.

The young wizard was certain that they weren't dealing with a halfling. At least, there was more going on here than appearances would indicate. First, the halfling had showed no signs of being able to use arcane magic. She showed no particular knowledge of such workings, either, as far as Albanon could tell, yet she had invaded a warded wizard's tower and had killed its master. Second, the halfling appeared gravely injured. There were strange cracks in the skin around her eyes. These cracks were filled with a red glow. She was also bleeding from a dozen different wounds, including several slashes on her hands and forearms that were open clear to the bone. Just looking at the gaping cuts was enough to make Albanon's stomach lurch, but the wounds seemed hardly to bother the halfling. In fact, she appeared supernaturally strong, as her hold on Tempest, who was easily two feet taller than she was, clearly indicated.

The halfling regarded the young wizard, peering at him through milky eyes that seemed to be having trouble focusing. "You are a wizard," the halfling said, though her words were clipped and hesitant, as though she were searching carefully for each word she uttered. "Make the circle work, or this one dies."

Roghar took a few measured steps to the left. He was trying hard not to be noticed, and he was failing spectacularly. The halfling snarled at him. It wasn't a sound that Albanon normally associated with the small folk—or with anything this side of the Stonemarch Mountains, for that matter. Roghar stopped, nodding his understanding to the strange and twisted creature.

"There's no reason to threaten anyone," Albanon said, sounding imminently braver than he felt. He stepped over to the magic circle inscribed in the stone tiles, briefly letting his eyes fall away from the halfling's unblinking gaze. He found her gaze to be very disconcerting.

"I killed your master," the halfling said, "and you followed me from the town. I believe we threaten one another, don't you?"

The circle was an ancient design, but Albanon recognized it for what it was. It was a permanent teleportation circle, probably dating back to the time of the empire of Nerath. Most major temples, many cities, and some towns—including Fallcrest—had permanent tele-portation circles, and Albanon had been schooled in the use of such magic. Travelers could step from one circle to the next, provided they knew the series of sigils that linked to a particular location. Albanon could make this one work, but he wasn't sure which sigils had been accessed when it was last operated.

The halfling, her hair hanging in tangles and crusted with drying blood and dirt, positioned herself so that she was holding Tempest between herself and Albanon. She had already apparently dismissed Roghar from her attention and was completely focused on the eladrin and what he was doing. "Open the portal," she said, speaking as though the words she was using were unfamiliar to her, although Albanon could detect no hint of an accent or other indication that she was from beyond the Nentir Vale.

Nothing, that is, other than the abnormal strength, the ability to ignore pain, and a general appearance of being half dead.

"Where do you want me to send you?" Albanon asked, noticing for the first time a strange crystalline substance oozing from the halfling's wounds. It looked very much like honey mixed with the halfling's blood, though instead of amber the substance was a translucent red that pulsed with a faint inner light. Streaks of silver and flecks of gold were suspended within the substance. It bubbled, thick and viscous, ululating in and out of the wounds in time with the halfling's breathing. The substance seemed familiar to the eladrin wizard, but he couldn't quite remember where he had seen anything like it before.

"Send me?" the halfling asked, a hint of suspicion rising in her voice. "I wish to follow the one who took the Voidharrow from the tower, the one who got to the Voidharrow before I did. I wish to go to where the thief and his master vanished to. That is where you will send me. Now. Or I will kill this one, take the dragonborn's form as my vessel, and then kill you."

Albanon had no idea what the halfling was talking about. Had someone else been in the tower last night? Who or what was the Voidharrow? Albanon wanted to scream. He wanted Moorin to appear to help him through this, to tell him what to do. But that wasn't going to happen. Moorin was dead. This thing had killed him. And if he didn't do something quickly, it was going to kill Tempest and probably the rest of them as well.

"Careful, apprentice," Splendid the pseudodragon cautioned from her hiding place in the shadows. "This murderer smells wrong. Alien. It doesn't belong in this world."

"Quiet, Splendid," Albanon said, trying to keep things from getting more out of control than they already were. He didn't need the pseudodragon, or Roghar, for that matter, making a move that was going to get Tempest's throat torn out.

The pseudodragon sighed loudly, but otherwise settled down and stopped talking. At least for the moment.

"Make it work now, wizard," the halfling said again, anger beginning to creep into her otherwise expressionless voice.

"I just need to pour the magic elixir into the circle to start the flow of magic," Albanon said, retrieving a waterskin from his pack.

The halfling continued to watch him, but she displayed no indication that he had just described a nonsensical procedure. His hunch was right. Whatever she was, she had no real knowledge of arcane magic or the spells and rituals performed by wizards. Perhaps his plan had a chance of working. Perhaps.

"Please get on with it, Albanon," Tempest said, her voice raw as she struggled to get the words out while the halfling continued to tightly hold her by the throat. "This foul creature smells rather terrible, and I'm afraid I may soon lose that wonderful meal we shared on the trip to this wonderful location."

Albanon wished he had known Tempest longer, or that this would all work out and he would get the chance to know her better. He had never met anyone like her, and he couldn't stand that she was in terrible danger. Of course, they all were, but Tempest was the one with the thing's hand around her throat. He concentrated, beginning the ritual that would open a portal to someplace else.

"I hope you know what you're doing," Roghar said, adjusting the grip on his sword.

"I've known young Albanon for many years," Splendid muttered from the shadows, "and I've never gotten that impression from him."

Albanon ignored both of them as he allowed his will to flow into the magic circle. The runed sigils flared in the sequence he had prescribed, and a glowing hole opened within the circle.

"There," the eladrin wizard declared, turning toward the halfling. "Let Tempest go and follow whoever used this before you. I don't care where you go or why, just let my friend go."

The halfling considered Albanon's words, tilting her head to the side as though trying to find their meaning. Then the halfling leaped, still gripping Tempest tightly, and bounded into the glowing portal.

"No!" Albanon screamed, diving toward the magic circle.

Roghar grabbed the young wizard around the waist, holding him back.

At the same time, Splendid flew out of the shadows and landed just outside the inscribed circle. She waved a paw over the runes and whispered a few words of power that she had learned in her service to the wizard Moorin.

With the spell disrupted, the portal winked out of existence.

"No," Albanon said again, this time his voice softer and full of defeat. "I sent them . . . away."

3 0 LAKE NEN, NIGHT

Falon stood at the railing of the merchant ship, looking for any sign of Darrum within the dark water. Just moments before, the water of Lake Nen had been churning like a whirlpool, but now a calm had settled over it with a suddenness that Falon found as disturbing as the skeletons that the lake had disgorged to attack *Hammerfast's Boon*. The ship was safe now, as far as Falon could tell. But Darrum, the old dwarf he was traveling with—the Imperial Shield, if the story that Darrum and Falon's mother had told him was true—had been dragged beneath the surface after he had defeated the robed figure who had apparently been controlling the undead.

"The old dwarf's line," a nearby member of the *Hammerfast's Boon's* crew said, catching Falon's attention. The crew member was powerfully built, even by dwarven standards, and he wore his beard in twin braids that fell neatly to his waist. "The line's gone taut. He's run out of rope."

"Line?" Falon asked, stepping over to where the crew member was examining a thick rope that was secured at one end to a stanchion jutting from the deck. The other end disappeared into the water, exactly where Darrum had gone under.

"Yes, young master," the crew member said, "he grabbed the line before he leaped out of the ship."

Hope rushed in at the crew member's words. Falon handed his sword, the one his mother named *Arande*, to the ship's captain, Stonehome. As he shrugged out of his chain mail shirt, he looked deep into the captain's eyes. "Take care of that for me," Falon said, slipping a sunrod from his pack. Amazing things, sunrods, he thought. It was a minor magic item, available in any well-stocked general store, that could be activated with a simple command. "Light," Falon said, activating the magic light as he held it in his left hand. Then, without another word, the young cleric climbed over the ship's railing, gulped a big breath of air, and dove into the water.

Lake Nen was cold and dark. Falon almost cried out as he splashed into the icy lake, barely managing to keep hold of the sunrod. He controlled himself, however, and quickly reached around to find the rope line as he let his dive carry him away from the surface. He had a momentary panic when he didn't immediately touch the line, but then his right hand found the rope. It was pulled tight, as though Darrum had gone as deep as the line would allow and was trying to go deeper still. Falon used the rope as a guide and followed it down into the bitter-cold water.

He took a small amount of comfort from the glow of the sunrod. He was just glad he hadn't made the dive in total darkness. Still, the light from the minor magic item did not penetrate very far into the darkness surrounding him, and all he could really see was the portion of the rope illuminated by the sunrod's light. It was kind of like a prestidigitation trick he had seen last summer at the traveling fair. The seer, who had about as much real arcane power as Falon's small toe, had somehow made a six-foot coil of rope float above the ground and stretch itself to its full length as it reached for the sky. That's how the rope line looked to Falon, or at least the section of it that he could see. It disappeared into the darkness beyond the circle of light cast by the sunrod so that all he could see was a ten-foot section of the rope, pulled tight by unseen forces somewhere above and below him.

Falon began to pray to Erathis, asking his god to protect him and see him and Darrum safely back to the surface. As always, Falon had no doubts about whether or not Erathis heard his prayer. He was just never certain as to the form the answer he received would take, or if he would even recognize it when it appeared.

Falon continued to follow the rope, and soon a dark shape began to emerge out of the darkness below him. As Falon and the light of the sunrod drew closer, the young cleric could make out the wrecked form of the skeletal skiff. The ancient boat was in terrible shape, as though whatever magic had returned it from its watery grave had been taken away. Darrum was caught within the wreck, struggling to free himself while holding on to the rope line with all of his might. Darrum had seen the light of Falon's sunrod, and he doubled his efforts to extract himself from the wreckage, though his efforts seemed to be to no avail.

Falon pushed hard, swimming down the final ten feet to reach Darrum and the remains of the skiff. The young cleric worked with the dwarf, breaking off pieces of the wood that had tangled around Darrum. It was only a moment's work, but already Falon's strength was fading. He kicked at a final chunk of wood, and the skeletal skiff fell away into the darkness.

He grabbed hold of the dwarf, but Darrum was too heavy. He couldn't swim back up the rope and drag Darrum behind him, and he could see that the old dwarf was as tired and straining for fresh air as he was. Falon wasn't going to get much more help from Darrum. Before Falon could attempt the massive effort to try to reach the surface with a dwarf who weighed at least twice as much as he did, the rope began to rise of its own accord.

Falon held on tight, one arm around the rope and the other around Darrum. He lost the sunrod somewhere along the way, and the two of them were rising through the water in total darkness. Just when Falon thought he was going to give in and take a reflexive breath that would have been the end for him, they broke the surface of the water and were being hauled up into *Hammerfast's Boon*.

Falon was pulled in and deposited on the deck on the ship. He was coughing, dripping wet, and very, very cold. Darrum was dropped beside him, in similar shape. The young cleric was glad to see that the old dwarf had somehow held on to his hammers. He believed that they were important to the dwarf. With another cough, Falon rolled over and tried to sit up.

"Rest a moment," Captain Stonehome said, handing a heavy blanket to Falon. When he saw the question appear in Falon's eyes, he laughed. "You saved my ship, so the least I could do was pull you out of the lake. Besides," he said, laying Falon's sword gently on the deck beside him, "I would never let someone of royal blood drown while in my charge. It's bad for business."

"Great," Darrum moaned, coughing up water as he wrapped his own blanket around himself. "I thought I told you not to draw attention to yourself."

"No problem," Falon said, shivering. Dawn was breaking on the horizon. He hoped the day would be warm and bright today. "Next time I won't jump in after you."

"See that you don't," the old dwarf grumbled, but Falon saw gratitude in Darrum's face, and maybe even something that looked a little bit like pride.

31 THE KING'S ROAD, DAY

Shara rode beside Erak along the ancient byway known as the King's Road. Uldane followed closely. The Nentir Vale hadn't had a king in untold centuries, but that was what the road was called, and who was Shara to argue semantics?

Uldane had been concerned about how the draft horse, unaccustomed to a rider, was going to take to Erak, especially with him being undead. But the leather-clad revenant had a way with the animal, and the three of them were on the road within an hour of breaking camp. Now they were riding at a good pace, heading southeast toward the town of Fallcrest.

"Why are we going in this direction again?" Uldane called as he rode up beside Shara. "The dragon hunts back the other way, around Winterhaven and into the Cairngorm Peaks. Are we abandoning our quest?"

Shara ignored Uldane's questions and kicked her horse, allowing the larger animal to pull ahead. They were the same questions that had been haunting her since they had started out this morning, but somehow she felt that this was the way they had to go—the way *she* had to go. She had talked with Erak long into the night, after

Uldane's eyes had grown heavy and he finally succumbed to sleep as the fire burned down.

"My quest leads that way," Erak had told her, pointing toward the southeast.

"Is it true?" Shara asked quietly. "Did the Lady of Fate send you back to the living world?"

Erak shrugged. "Was it the Raven Queen? I don't know. I remember only vague images and disembodied voices," he said. "Very little of it makes sense to me as yet, but I think it will become clear as time passes. I remember a woman's voice, strong and kind and very insistent. *Arise, my champion*, the voice said to me. *You have work to do.*"

"What kind of work? What quest has she sent you back to accomplish?"

"I don't know. All I know is that I was given this sword and this armor, and I felt compelled to head in that direction. When I heard the battle, your voice, I knew that I had to help you. Helping you feels right. It feels like part of the work I was sent back to do."

They had talked about the dragon she was chasing and about the land of the Nentir Vale. More precisely, Shara told Erak what she knew of the area. She hoped it would clear his memories, remind him of who he was and what he had come back to do. She wanted to believe that the revenant was Jarren, returned to her from the dead. She did believe it, and that's why she and Uldane were traveling with him toward Fallcrest.

"If that's Jarren," Uldane called, as though he had somehow been listening in on her thoughts, "then why are we going away from the dragon and not toward it?"

Before Shara could decide whether to keep ignoring Uldane or shout at him to shut up, she noticed something lying in the road ahead. Erak had noticed it, too, and he had his horse gallop ahead so that he reached the spot first.

Shara and Uldane followed. She now saw that there were two bodies lying in the road. From their simple garb and lack of armor, she assumed that they were travelers who had been walking along the road. Not an unusual sight this close to Fallcrest. Dead travelers, however? That was a different story.

"Bandits, you think?" Uldane asked, riding closer. "More kobolds, maybe?"

"This close to the town? Kobolds would be unlikely to venture into the area unless Vestapalk and the wyrmpriest have really riled them up," Shara said.

Shara watched as Erak leaped down from his horse and bent to examine the bodies.

"These men have been dead for some time," Erak said. "The flesh that remains is dry and sunken, and no smell of rot or decay is evident. But they do smell of fresh earth and old cloth. It's as though someone dug them up and left them here for us to find."

"I've been saying for years now that Fallcrest was falling apart," Uldane said, "hardly a proper town at all anymore. And now they're leaving their dead on the road for all to see. Disgraceful, really."

Erak leaned across the first dead man to examine the second. The second body appeared the same as the first, not a fresh corpse at all. As Erak moved toward him, the first dead man's hand shot up and grabbed Erak's wrist. The dead man's eyelids snapped open, revealing one empty socket and one milky white orb.

Shara began to draw her sword, but Erak raised his other hand to stop her. As she watched, the dead man's mouth fell open. A deathly moan began to issue from the open mouth, but soon the moan turned into words that she understood all too clearly.

"Your Lady has no power here," the dead voice said. "My lord commands that you turn back and abandon the quest you have been given. My lord commands this once, politely, and only once."

Uldane hurled one of his ever-present daggers. It sliced the dead thing's hand at the wrist, freeing Erak from its grip.

"Or what?" Uldane asked, not a hint of fear evident in his voice. If anything, he seemed curious and excited.

Suddenly, both bodies began to rise, and the severed hand crawled back to reattach itself to the dead man's wrist.

"You had to ask," Shara said, pulling her greatsword free of the sheath across her back.

Erak had his own weapon out, the blade made from the material he called hellsteel. He swung it with skill and power, slicing the dead thing's head from its body. Before the head hit the ground, however, the corpse exploded. Erak barely leaped back from the blast as parts of the dead thing flew in all directions.

"Ride!" Erak shouted, climbing on to the back of his mount. "Ride!"

Shara rode, with Uldane and Erak right behind her.

32 THE WITCHLIGHT FENS, DAY

Dawn had burst into the sky above the Witchlight Fens, but you couldn't tell as Kalaban made his way through the dark chambers beneath the circle of stones. He and Magroth and the golem had entered through the opening that appeared in the nearby hillside, but he was sure that the twists and turns they had followed as they descended had taken them under the standing stones.

The stone chambers beneath the hill and the patch of dry ground where the standing stones were raised were definitely ancient, and they had to have been placed here at great expense and with great effort. Magical effort, if the workmanship was any indication. Older than Nerath, certainly, with strange carvings all over the walls and ceiling that seemed to swim in and out of focus whenever Kalaban tried to examine them.

"Bael Turath," Magroth said, noticing Kalaban's interest. "This was obviously a holy place to the ancient tiefling empire. Let's make sure we don't accidentally call forth a devil while we're here. I've never been fond of devils."

Kalaban wished that his emperor would douse the light of his staff or at least remain silent as they moved through the ancient chambers. Not that it mattered much, the knight-commander supposed. The sound of the stone doors sliding open was enough to wake the dead, so whoever or whatever occupied this place surely knew that they were approaching.

"What do you suppose we shall meet down here, Kalaban?" Magroth asked, excitement evident in every word. The emperor was definitely enjoying this trip beyond the borders of the Shadowfell. "What kind of creature has the audacity to renege on a deal with Orcus, the Prince of Undeath? Other than us, I mean."

Kalaban stopped as soon as he stepped into the next chamber. The golem was right behind him, blocking Magroth, who had been bringing up the rear.

"We're not alone, my liege," Kalaban said, his sword already in his hand and his shield at the ready.

"Get out of my way," Magroth commanded, hammering the golem with his staff until the lumbering construct stepped aside.

Magroth huffed and moved to Kalaban's side, raising his staff high so that its light filled the chamber.

The creatures that had been lurking in the shadows hissed at the light, scurrying to the outer walls of the chamber. They were humanoid, dressed in tattered rags that exposed flesh that was pallid and grayish white. There were six of the creatures, their long fingers tipped with long nails that could have been claws. Kalaban noticed that they cast no shadows as the arcane light of Magroth's staff hit them, and as they opened their mouths to hiss, he saw the gleam of sharp, pointed fangs. More of the creatures had filled the passage behind them, surrounding the trio and cutting off any means of escape.

But escape was not their intention, Kalaban thought, formulating a plan of attack.

"Vampire spawn," Magroth said. "Our host must be a vampire. The dead glass has served me well. Now all we need to do is find the master of these vile creatures and dispatch it with all due haste."

Easier said than done, Kalaban thought as the first of the spawn leaped at them. His soulsword swung up in a powerful arc that caught the vampire spawn and sliced it in half before it could reach either Kalaban or Magroth with its claws or fangs. The knight-commander stepped in front of the emperor, hacking a path through the oncoming undead. While the vampire spawn had numbers, they were no match for Kalaban and his companions.

Behind him, the golem stoneguard was turning each spawn that leaped at it into paste with great fists the size of anvils. It hammered one into the ground and a second into the wall, dropping each with a single, powerful blow.

Magroth, meanwhile, not wanting to miss out on the fun, sent a handful of magic missiles streaking into the midst of the spawn in front of them. Each dagger of arcane energy unerringly flew from the emperor's hand to strike one of the vampires. With each explosive strike, another vampire spawn fell to the ground.

"The trouble with creatures such as these," Magroth said, "is that they are much too fragile for my taste. I prefer hearty minions, such as you, Kalaban, and the golem. Imagine how much work it would be for me if I had to replace you after every battle. Too much trouble, I say."

"Yes, my liege," Kalaban said, slicing two more of the spawn out from before them as he accepted Magroth's less-than-flattering praise, "thank you, my liege. It's good to know you consider me as valuable an aid as your golem."

"No, Kalaban, not as valuable as the stoneguard. But certainly more valuable than common vampire spawn such as these."

Magroth directed a fan of searing flames into the chamber ahead of them, roasting the remaining vampire spawn where they stood. At the same time, Kalaban turned and helped the golem dispatch the three vampire spawn still attacking from the rear. As fast as the battle began, it was over. Kalaban wiped thick blood from his blade, using the tattered garb of one of the fallen spawn.

"Careful, Kalaban," Magroth warned. "We are not done yet."

Kalaban watched as the shadows beyond Magroth's mage light began to flow and coalesce. It seemed as though a combination of shifting darkness and swirling mist were coming together to form a solid shape on the other side of the chamber. The shape, indistinct at first, soon took on the features of a handsome tiefling with curved horns and a deathlike complexion. His piercing eyes were full of anger. He wore dark leather armor of exquisite make. A spiked chain was wrapped around his right arm, its barbed end hanging down at his side. The chain wound around his back, and he held the other end in his left hand.

"You entered my home, uninvited and unbidden, but I ignored the insult out of respect for your station, lich," the undead tiefling said, his anger barely controlled. "But you simply strolled in and slaughtered my servants. This added insult cannot be ignored!"

"Sareth, I presume?" Magroth inquired innocently.

Sareth's eyes flared and his mouth twisted into an ugly grin. He was as regal as he was terrible, confident in his power and fueled by a fast-growing hatred for Magroth. Kalaban had seen that reaction often over the centuries. The emperor was a hard man to like. The knight-commander noticed the amulet hanging from a chain around Sareth's neck. It was the same as the medallion that Barana Strenk wore—the symbol of Orcus.

"I'm surprised you still wear that," Kalaban said, "seeing as how we've been told that you have betrayed your master."

"So," Sareth said with a bitter laugh, "the Demon Prince has sent you to punish me? You shall not fare any better than the last three mercenaries he sent this way. Sareth remains. Sareth always remains."

Magroth smiled. "Not this time."

Kalaban charged forward, hoping to end the battle as quickly as he could. His soulsword streaked toward the vampire lord, seeking to deliver a killing blow. But Sareth was fast. His spiked chain snaked out, wrapping around Kalaban's blade. He twisted his body and snapped his arm, and the soulsword flew out of Kalaban's hand and clattered into the darkness at the far end of the chamber. Still in motion, Sareth stepped toward the knight-commander and made a subtle movement with his left arm. The other end of the spiked chain flew out. Kalaban barely got his shield up in time, but even so the barbed chain wrapped around the back of his neck and cut deep into the exposed flesh there. The front of the chain, meanwhile, was blocked by the knight-commander's shield. With a strength Kalaban didn't expect, Sareth snapped the chain so that it unfurled from around Kalaban like the string on a child's top. The knight-commander was spun through the air.

Kalaban hit the stone wall with bone-crushing force. As he slid down the wall, he struggled to keep the darkness and the pain at the back of his eyes from rushing forward. He saw Sareth leap at Magroth as he crashed to the floor.

And then the darkness overtook him.

3 3 THE CAIRNGORM MOUNTAINS, DAY

Tiktag, wyrmpriest of the Greenscale tribe of kobolds, spread a layer of white sand in the clearing. Then he bowed to the mighty Vestapalk and stepped back to give the green dragon room. He watched as the mighty Vestapalk lifted the living deer over the patch of white sand and tore open the soft flesh of the animal's belly. The green dragon let the deer's insides spill out on the white sand, and then tossed the still-twitching carcass aside. Later, we shall feast on venison, Tiktag thought hungrily. But now he had to help his master interpret the signs provided by the blood and guts and sand.

"Examine them for yourself, wyrmpriest," Vestapalk commanded. "Tell us that which we have already seen a dozen times before."

Tiktag moved into position to examine the entrails, to see the pattern that had been created in the sand by the sacrifice of the deer. It was just as the green dragon had implied. The same pattern. Again. The consistency of the message sent a shiver down the kobold's spine.

"Tell us," Vestapalk commanded, "interpret the signs and tell us what they predict."

Tiktag swallowed hard, shaking the bones hanging from his spear so that they jangled over the steaming entrails. Symbols were appearing in the sand, forming as the blood flowed and spread of its own volition. The symbols appeared to be in the Draconic script, formed of blood and entrails snaked in the pure white sand.

"The Herald walks the land," Tiktag said, reading the signs and giving words to the omen. "It seeks something, a source of power, and together they shall usher in a new age. The age of the Elemental Eye." Tiktag fell back from the force of the vision, trying to contain the shivering that he suddenly couldn't control.

"Yes!" Vestapalk roared. "This one's vision is true! The end of the age is coming, and the next age shall belong to chaos and elementals!"

"Yes, my master," the wyrmpriest stammered, not quite sure why kobolds and dragons should see the rise of elementals as a good thing but also not willing to contradict the green dragon.

"And," Vestapalk said with a gleam in its eyes, "it shall belong to Vestapalk!"

The green dragon turned to the wyrmpriest. "We must find this emissary, this harbinger. It shall need Vestapalk's help, and in turn it will help Vestapalk . . . transform."

"Yes, my master," the wyrmpriest said, but he had long ago stopped trying to understand the green dragon. He only needed to serve Vestapalk, and hopefully live long enough to share in whatever rewards came the dragon's way. The kobold climbed atop the green dragon, settling in at the space where the dragon's neck connected to its body.

Tiktag held on tight as Vestapalk vaulted into the air.

They were following visions that Vestapalk believed came from the Elemental Eye. Tiktag wasn't sure what the source of the visions was, but the message couldn't be denied. The Herald walked the land.

And Vestapalk was determined to find it.

34 THE WITCHLIGHT FENS, DAY

Magroth fell back at Sareth's onslaught, barely calling forth a shield of arcane energy to protect him from the vicious attack. The spiked chain slashed against Magroth's invisible shield, sending up sparks as the powerful lashing managed to drive the lich back against the cool stone of the chamber's wall. The Mad Emperor smiled at the vampire lord, glancing quickly to see how Kalaban was faring. Dazed, certainly. Unconscious, more than likely. But he doubted that the knight-commander was more gravely injured than that.

"Well done, Sareth," Magroth said, a trace of laughter in his voice. "I take it that you're a vampire? Maybe even a vampire lord? But do you think you can really stand against both me and my golem?"

The stoneguard lumbered forth, each step shaking the ground as its foot slammed down. It balled its massive fists, preparing to hammer the vampire lord into a thick, red paste. It never got the chance.

Sareth danced back with impressive speed and grace, putting distance between himself and the golem's heavy fists. "This is my lair," Sareth said, his hand darting out to toggle a switch hidden among the carvings on the wall. The chamber shook as great, unseen gears twisted beneath the chamber, and the floor the stone golem stood on fell away, taking the golem with it.

"Well, that was unexpected," Magroth said, peering into the pit. He saw that the golem had landed hard about twenty feet beneath the level of this chamber. It would take the golem a few moments to climb out of the pit. Moments that Sareth would not waste.

The vampire lord locked his gaze onto Magroth's own, staring deep into the lich's eyes. "Your will is mine, lich," Sareth said, applying his considerable strength of will to overwhelm Magroth's own sense of self and purpose.

With an extreme effort, Magroth averted his gaze and broke the vampire's spell. "That may have worked on a lesser creature," the Mad Emperor said, swinging his staff around and gathering his own power, "but never on Magroth, emperor of Nerath!"

Lightning crackled from Magroth's staff and danced across Sareth's spiked chain and into the vampire lord's body. Sareth screamed in pain and rage as he tossed the spiked chain away before the lightning could destroy him. He reached for the sword at his side, but Magroth was unrelenting in his attack. The lich uttered a word of power, and a stream of darkness exploded out of his staff and hammered into the vampire lord. The waves of darkness drove

Sareth to the ground and slid him across the stone floor and into the chamber beyond.

With his line of sight broken, Magroth ended the flow of darkness. He followed Sareth through the open portal and into the next chamber. This room was lit by two flaming braziers, one on each side of the chamber. Numerous wooden coffins were stacked across the chamber's floor. These were probably the resting places for Sareth's vampire spawn, though none of the vile creatures remained to have any use for them. Where had the vampire lord gotten to, Magroth wondered? "Are you hiding from me, Sareth?" Magroth asked. "That's what I'd be doing if I were you."

Sareth exploded out of the shadows behind Magroth and slightly to his right. "You are certainly not me, lackey of Orcus!" Sareth screamed as he buried his sword into Magroth's back, not far from the dagger that still protruded from the wound that had killed the emperor so many centuries ago.

Magroth twirled away from Sareth, feeling the vampire lord's sword slide out of his body as easily as it had plunged in. As he whirled to the side, Magroth extended the fingers of his right hand and unleashed a spell at Sareth. Fire shot from his outstretched fingers, scorching the vampire lord and eliciting a howl of pain that brought a smile to Magroth's gaunt face.

Then, while the vampire lord was reeling, Magroth brought down his staff, gripped firmly in his left hand, and shouted the words of power that carried his next spell into existence. A clap of thunder erupted in the enclosed chamber as a wave of force slammed into Sareth and drove him into the stone wall. The vampire lord, dazed and disoriented by the twin attacks, slid down the wall and collapsed into a heap on the ground.

"Are we finished with this dance?" Magroth asked, madness sparkling in his milk-white eyes.

"Not yet," Sareth snarled. He launched himself at Magroth, who instinctively brought his staff up to protect himself.

No attack came, however. Instead, Magroth watched as a strange mist flowed around him and disappeared behind him.

Magroth turned, watching to see where the mist flowed. "Vampire trick," he muttered. "Why can't vampires play fair?"

The mist seeped into a crack in the far wall of the chamber, disappearing behind the thick stone wall. Magroth marched over to the wall, looking for anything that might serve as a switch or lever.

"You won't get away from me that easily, Sareth," Magroth said. The emperor knew that it was still daylight, so the vampire lord was not going to be able to get very far outside the ancient underground complex. He imagined that Sareth could flee to a remote location, but it was more likely that the vampire lord's personal coffin was just behind this wall.

Magroth found an indentation hidden among the decorative carvings near the top of the wall. He pressed the stone there, and the wall slowly retracted to reveal a small space beyond it. Inside the small space, a stone sarcophagus rested as it had for untold ages. "It probably isn't even yours," Magroth muttered as he strode to stand over the sarcophagus. "Just another thing you borrowed from those who were here before you."

Not nearly as physically strong as either Kalaban or the golem, it took Magroth no small amount of effort to slide the stone lid open. As he had suspected, the tiefling vampire was lying inside. Sareth had entered some kind of trancelike state, and Magroth could see the burns and cuts on the vampire lord's face already beginning to heal.

"Nice try," Magroth sneered, raising his staff over his head. He brought the butt of the staff down hard, piercing Sareth's chest and pinning him into the sarcophagus. The vampire lord's eyes snapped open, full of pain and outrage. "Guess who?" Magroth said, and then he unleashed more lightning through his staff and into Sareth's now-writhing form. The magic continued to flow, exhausting Magroth with the effort, but he didn't let up until Sareth was a charred husk.

"I could have simply decapitated him," Kalaban said, appearing next to the emperor and apparently none the worse for his injuries.

"I can do things myself," Magroth said.

The Mad Emperor stared into the stone coffin and examined the Orcus medallion. It bound those that wore it to Orcus's service, or at least it was supposed to. Sareth had overcome that particular hurdle. Magroth coveted the power that the medallion promised, however. The power of a vampire lord. He wanted to add that arsenal to his already considerable power as a lich and a master wizard.

He reached into the sarcophagus and snatched the Orcus medallion from around Sareth's lightning-scorched neck.

Suddenly Magroth was hunched over in grueling pain, screaming as he had never screamed before. It felt as though his blood was boiling inside his veins, as though every fiber of his being was on fire.

He waved off Kalaban's awkward effort to aid him and gritted his teeth against the intense pain. *No,* he decided, *this medallion will not get the better of me.* As the burning began to subside, Magroth placed the medallion around his neck, letting it fall to his chest to rest beside the Necropolis Stone he also wore.

"Master?" Kalaban asked, worry evident in his gaze.

Magroth, still too frazzled by the experience to form coherent words, dismissed the knight-commander with a wave of his hand. Kalaban stepped out of the small room and Magroth was about to follow when an idea came to him. He pulled a small, rectangular metal box from one of the many pockets within his robes and examined it with a practiced eye. The box was intact.

The small metal box was Magroth's phylactery, the magical receptacle that held his life force. All liches created such receptacles and used them to ensure that they could never be destroyed completely. At least not as long as the phylactery existed. All liches also kept the existence of their receptacles secret, so as not to reveal any weakness to their enemies. Not even Kalaban knew about Magroth's receptacle or what it meant to the emperor.

Magroth placed the small metal box, which measured six-inches on a side, into the pile of ash and bone that was once the vampire lord Sareth.

"Do me a favor, Sareth," Magroth managed to whisper as he slid the stone lid closed. "Keep that safe until I return."

3 5 FALLCREST, THE NENTIR INN, NIGHT

Falon was running. He was running through darkness. He couldn't see where he was running to or what he was running from, but he knew that it was close behind him. He was alone, having somehow lost the old dwarf Darrum who had been charged with protecting him. With keeping him safe. But Falon couldn't count on Darrum. He couldn't count on Erathis. He couldn't count on anyone. He just had to keep running, to stay ahead of whatever things were chasing him.

He ran, until he felt like his legs would cramp and his chest would burn and he wouldn't be able to run anymore, and then he ran on. Whatever was chasing him was closer now, nearly on him. He had lost the sword *Arante* somewhere in the darkness, and he was defenseless against whatever horror was about to catch up with him. He could hear water dripping from undead limbs. He could hear the sound of crossbow bolts whizzing past him in the darkness. And he could hear the screams in the distance, the screams of his mother, of Gamun, and of all the folk of Nenlast and the valley beyond. Somehow, the screaming was his fault. The screaming and the pain.

Falon saw a light in the distance. The dim glow revealed a tall, thin man in fine robes waiting up ahead for Falon to reach him. Falon slowed as he approached the man, whose wisps of white hair hung from his head in long, straight strands. Falon stood before the taller man, noticing for the first time that the light was coming from the man's ornate wooden staff. He also noticed that the man was dead. It didn't seem to impede the man very much, however, for as Falon watched, he rolled up the sleeve of his left arm to reveal a mark at his wrist. It was the same mark that Falon had been born with, a crown-shaped stain with three star-shaped stains arranged above it.

The mark of Nerath.

The dead man pointed at Falon.

"Soon," he said. "We will meet soon, my descendent. And then you will die."

Falon sat up in his bed, drenched in sweat, his heart racing. It was only a dream, he realized, a nightmare. But it had seemed so real. He shook his head, trying to clear it of the terrible image of the dead man with his birthmark. Of the terrible sound of his light-hearted but threatening words.

The young cleric got out of bed and stumbled toward the window. He needed some air. He and Darrum had reached the town of Fallcrest without further incident. *Hammerfast's Boon* had dropped them at the dock at the Upper Quays, and from there they had made their way to the Nentir Inn and secured a pair of rooms for the night. He opened the window and breathed in the cool night air. He was starting to feel better when the mark on his left wrist began to throb and burn. He looked down to examine the mark, to see if it looked as red as it suddenly felt, when he noticed the figure standing in the courtyard below his window.

He was a tall man, but not as tall as the man in his dream. He was also thin, but not as rail thin as the man he had imagined. He had wild, dark hair, and he was dressed in tight leather armor and a long leather jacket. He stared up at Falon with strange, crimson eyes.

Undead eyes.

Falon grabbed *Arante* from beside his bed and rushed out into the hall. He didn't bother with his boots or his armor. He wore only a simple tunic and a pair of pants, the same clothes he had worn under his armor when they had arrived at the inn. He bounded down the stairs to the inn's ground floor and stormed outside, the sword of Nerath gripped firmly in his hands.

The creature stood before him, arms at its sides and its weapon still in its sheath. It tilted its head in a quizzical manner, but Falon never hesitated. He whispered words of prayer to Erathis and the blade of his sword glowed with divine energy. Then he swung the weapon at the creature, meaning to make short work of it. He had had enough of undead monsters trying to kill him. The blade sliced right for the creature's neck.

Then it was swinging through the space where the creature had been, hitting nothing but the night air.

The creature had jumped back, easily avoiding the touch of the holy blade. Falon swung the weapon three more times in quick succession, advancing on the creature by a step or two with each attack. The blade missed each time, however. The leather-clad creature effortlessly ducked, dodged, and sidestepped each of Falon's attacks. Then the creature leaped back, increasing the distance between him and Falon.

Before Falon could decide whether to call on the power of Erathis or rush forward with blade in hand, the creature did an unexpected thing. It removed its strangely curved sword from the sheath at its waist and dropped it to the ground. Then, its gaze still locked on Falon's own, it dropped to its knees and spread its arms wide.

"What in the name of the Seventeen Anvils is going on out here?" Darrum demanded as he moved to stand beside Falon. The dwarf had his twin hammers in hand and seemed ready for a fight, but he was behaving in a much more controlled manner than Falon had seen him employ thus far in their time together. "Do you have any idea what time it is, boy?"

On Falon's other side, a tall woman in scale armor ran up to the group. She looked from the creature to Falon and back again, her greatsword at the ready.

"I am Erak," the creature said, clearly addressing Falon with its words. "I am a knight of the Raven Queen, returned to this world on a quest for the Lady of Fate and Death. I refuse to raise my weapon against the rightful heir of Nerath, but instead offer the heir my friendship and protection."

"How do you call this much attention to yourself," Darrum asked, speaking low so that only Falon could hear him.

"It's a gift, really," Falon replied, totally unsure about how to deal with the creature that called itself Erak.

36 AWAY

Tempest sat with her back against a cold, stone wall, listening intently to the darkness all around her. When the halfling that wasn't a halfling carried her through the portal that Albanon had opened, Tempest wasn't sure what to expect. They appeared within a circle much like the one they had just departed from, and by the slowly fading glow of the inscribed runes she was able to catch a glimpse of the worked stone around them. She saw a great statue of a noble minotaur, towering above them toward the impenetrable blackness above. She also noted a number of passages leading off this wide hall, and then the glow faded and the entire area was draped in total darkness.

The halfling-thing dragged her out of the circle until they reached a wall. Then it propped her against the hard stone and turned away. "Stay there," the halfling-thing said. Tempest decided to listen to it, at least for the time being.

Now she sat by herself, surrounded by darkness. She could hear the labored breathing of the halfling-thing. It was nearby, scouting the area, she assumed. She tried to figure out what the halfling really was. It was obvious to her that the poor woman had been possessed by something, but whether that something was a spirit, a demon, or something else entirely, Tempest had no way of telling. Her training as a warlock, if you could call it training, didn't include the more scholarly pursuits that she was sure Albanon had been taught during his apprenticeship to a wizard.

She knew that the halfling-thing was remarkably strong. Much stronger than she was, in fact, and probably stronger than Roghar. She imagined that the dragonborn paladin was extremely upset right about now. He had a habit of being overly protective of her, for some reason. She hoped that Roghar was working with Albanon to figure out how to help her and not beating the poor eladrin senseless for sending her away.

The halfling-thing was also hurt, though not so much that it seemed bothered by all the open, pulsating wounds. That told her something. She believed that whatever was in control of the halfling was wearing the halfling like a second skin. What frightened Tempest was that soon the thing inside would need a new skin to contain it, because it sounded like the halfling's condition was growing worse by the minute. She didn't want that thing to take over her body. She wouldn't allow that to happen. If she had a choice in the matter, that is.

Tempest tried to remember what the halfling-thing had said to Albanon. It was clear that it was trying to follow someone, another wizard, she guessed, who had taken something from Moorin's tower.

It wanted Albanon to send it after the wizard, who had apparently used the magic circle before they had arrived at Kalton Manor. She didn't think that this is where the fleeing wizard traveled to, however. Albanon wouldn't have known where to send the halfling-thing in any event. So he sent it here, where it would be out of the way. Who knew that it would have taken her with it? Well, actually, Tempest had suspected that was going to happen, but she had a bit more experience with lying monsters than Albanon had.

The halfling-thing was after something or someone it called "the Voidharrow." She had no idea what that could be. Or why the halfling-thing wanted it. It didn't matter, really. She just stored the information away so that she would remember it should the need arise. That was how Tempest approached most aspects of life. She noticed everything, remembered everything. And then, when the moment was right, she exploited what she knew to her benefit. She would get a chance to make a move against this foul creature, and when she did she would use everything she knew to make that move count.

Tempest imagined that they were in a large, underground space. The minotaur statue suggested that they were somewhere beneath Thunderspire Mountain, in the ruins of the ancient halls of Saruun Khel. That was just a guess on her part, but it felt right. She could practically feel the mountain pressing in on them from the darkness all around. Of course, Thunderspire Mountain was a big place. They could be anywhere within the ancient labyrinth that had been carved in the distant past from the living stone itself. If nothing else, however, she believed she knew more about where they were than the halfling-thing did.

Suddenly the halfling-thing's small, strong hand was once again wrapped around Tempest's slender throat. It pushed her head back against the stone, pressing so hard that she thought it meant to push her skull right through the solid wall.

"The wizard lied to me," the halfling-thing said, the words flowing out of the darkness like the lashes of a whip. "The Voidharrow is not here. The Voidharrow has never been here. I was deceived."

"Oops," Tempest said, managing to force the word out through her constricted throat.

"They cannot come for you," the halfling-thing said, ignoring Tempest's flippant response. "I have broken the magic circle. This vessel is failing, however. I need a new form."

The halfling-thing pressed its cracked lips to Tempest's ear. She shuddered at the touch as it whispered, "Your form will have to do."

Tempest tried to struggle, but the halfling-thing held her tight. She couldn't see in the darkness, but she felt something cold flow from the creature's hand and begin to crawl up her neck.

"No, please," Tempest said, trying to turn away or shake off the cold substance.

But the halfling-thing was relentless, and the cold substance continued to flow, climbing toward her mouth, her nose, her eyes.

That was when Tempest screamed.

TWO

37 THE WITCHLIGHT FENS, NIGHT

Kalaban entered the vaulted room beneath the circle of standing stones. The place had once served as the audience chamber for some infernal priest of Bael Turath, and it was decorated as was befitting of those who had long ago made a pact with devils. At the front of the chamber, set on a raised dais, was a throne fashioned of skulls and ornate stone. Magroth the Mad Emperor sat on the throne, holding the limp form of a goblin across his lap. He casually supped blood from a tear in the goblin's throat. The knight-commander had acquired the disgusting creature in the swamp above, just as his liege had ordered. Kalaban had hoped that Magroth would have finished while he was outside making one more sweep of the area, but he knew that the Mad Emperor preferred his meals to be slow and leisurely.

Apparently, that preference extended to the meals dictated by his newly acquired blood curse.

The stoneguard golem stood nearby, straight and silent, almost a part of the chambers of stone that had been built beneath the swamp. Kalaban marveled at the engineering and magic that was required to pull off this miracle of construction. The humans and tieflings of ancient Bael Turath were truly skilled. He was surprised that their empire eventually fell and made way for Nerath. Surprised, but not disappointed.

Magroth watched the knight-commander as he approached. With a long, lingering lick, the Mad Emperor gulped a final, congealing wad of dark fluid from the open wound at the goblin's neck. Then he tossed the body away as he might the gnawed core of a fire apple.

"Does my feeding disgust you, knight-commander?" Magroth asked, a cruel smile playing across his blood-coated lips. "It disgusts me. Having to settle for a lesser creature such as this to sustain my . . . hunger."

Kalaban refused to be drawn into this particular conversation, but he wished that Magroth would stop staring at him so intently. "What is our next move, my master?"

"Hmmph," Magroth grunted, eventually looking away from Kalaban. "We have two things we must accomplish before we seek the Necropolis of Andok Sur. I must first find out all that I can about the place, which means that we must find a repository of ancient documents. There must be something I can do to alter this one-sided deal I have struck with the Prince of Undeath. There must be!"

Magroth fell silent, as though lost deep in thought. Kalaban waited, counting to one hundred as he had been taught to do when he had first entered the service of the crown. Still Magroth remained quiet, staring into the distance. The knight-commander hated to interrupt, but he was even more afraid that Magroth wouldn't emerge from his contemplation any time soon. His liege was acting even more strangely than he was inclined to since he had donned the Orcus medallion. In addition to the blood hunger that had overcome Magroth, adding vampirism to his list of undead traits, he had grown meaner, more inclined to snap at Kalaban, and he easily drifted into these periods of disturbing silence.

"My lord?" Kalaban asked, "The second thing we must accomplish?"

Magroth blinked, turning his milky white eyes toward Kalaban. For a moment, he seemed almost surprised to see the knight-commander. Then his countenance became dark, angry. "Every time you interrupt me," Magroth said, his voice cold, "you hinder my ability to overcome this damned medallion and the hold it is trying to establish upon me. I should have seen it, but I was blinded by the promise of power that the medallion held. I have accepted that power, oh yes I have. But the power comes at a price, and I am trying very hard not to have to pay that price. Do you understand this, my impatient companion?"

Kalaban was at a loss as to how to respond to Magroth. He didn't know what he could say that wouldn't increase the emperor's anger and displeasure. Instead, he stood straight and still, letting one hand slip into the pouch at his belt to stroke the glass vial resting within. He could feel the strange substance within the vial as it shifted and flowed, reacting to the touch of his fingers along the sides of the cool glass. A part of him wanted to break the vial and feel the translucent red substance on his skin. That part of him wanted to do this very, very badly. But Kalaban refused to give that part of himself its freedom, at least for the moment. Instead, he contented himself with the feel of the glass and the nearness of the substance that seemed to him to be almost alive.

"I said, do you understand this?" Magroth asked again, this time with a threatening timbre in the tone that broke whatever daydream the knight-commander had fallen into.

"No, my lord," Kalaban stammered, coming back to himself and quickly withdrawing his hand from the pouch. "I didn't understand. But now I do. I shall not interrupt your thoughts again."

"Hmmph. Don't make promises we both know you can't keep. The second thing we must deal with? The thing you just had to know about right now? That's easy. I'm surprised you couldn't figure it out yourself. Well, no, not really surprised. You never were the brightest of my personal guard, were you, Kalaban?"

Magroth leaped from the throne and began pacing around the stone chamber. "Along the way, either before we complete our research into Andok Sur or immediately thereafter, we must find this troublesome descendent of mine. The one that Orcus and his priest are so adamant that I destroy. We must find him and see why he concerns them so. And then . . . I imagine that his blood shall taste far sweeter than the fare I have thus far been forced to sup on. Don't you agree, knight-commander?"

Kalaban swallowed hard. "I wouldn't know, my emperor."

Magroth laughed. "You wouldn't know!" The emperor laughed even harder, and the sound of it filled the stone chambers beneath the Fens. The sound was full of mirth, but there was also a strong undertone of madness that troubled Kalaban far more than any of the threats the emperor had made against him.

For if Magroth succumbed to his madness, what hope would Kalaban have of ending the undead curse that had plagued him since his brother had assassinated the emperor and he, in turn, had struck his own brother down?

38 FALLCREST, DAY

Albanon was exhausted by the time he and Roghar could see the walls of Fallcrest on the horizon ahead of them. Even Splendid was tuckered out. She was curled around his neck, her head resting on one shoulder, and she was snoring lightly in his ear. Only Roghar seemed unaffected by the two long rides—the first from Fallcrest across the Moon Hills to the ruins of Kalton Manor, the second back again. He rode straight and tall in his saddle, his eyes fixed on the town they were riding toward. Only the dragonborn's expression, a mix of anger and worry, reminded Albanon that the paladin cared for their missing friend at least as much as the young wizard did. And probably more, since Roghar and Tempest had been friends and adventuring companions for much longer than the day or so since he had met them at the Blue Moon Alehouse.

"Tell me again," Roghar said, his voice strong but with an undercurrent of anger that Albanon knew was at least partially directed at him. "Where did you send Tempest and that creature?"

Albanon sighed. "Roghar, we need to examine my master's library. We need to figure out what the creature is and how we can defeat it before we. . . . "

Roghar cut him off. "Tell me again!"

"I opened a portal to the Labyrinth beneath Thunderspire Mountain. I figured that the maze of tunnels and the various creatures that live down there would at least slow the halfling down and get it away from us."

"You sent Tempest into the Labyrinth?" Roghar asked, his voice low. "Alone?"

"No, I sent the creature," Albanon protested. "I didn't think. . . . "

"Ah, and so the apprentice reveals the true problem," Splendid purred, her eyes still closed as her head rested on Albanon's shoulder.

"Roghar, I'm sorry," Albanon said, promising himself for the hundredth time that he would find a way to make this right.

"I am not the one who requires an apology, elf."

"Eladrin," Albanon whispered.

As they approached the King's Gate, the southern entrance to Fallcrest, Albanon noticed that Sergeant Gerdrand of the Fallcrest Guard was stationed in the gate's one remaining tower. The other tower and much of the southern wall had been destroyed in the Bloodspear War, and only the most rudimentary repairs had been made in the ninety years since. Gerdrand had about a half dozen guards with him, which told Albanon that the town was on high alert.

Albanon took a deep breath, trying to clear the fuzziness from his exhausted brain. Although eladrin didn't sleep, they did need to enter a meditative state they called "the trance." It had been more than two days since Albanon had last spent time in the trance, and he could feel how his deprived body was reacting.

Albanon rode up to the King's Gate. "Hail, Sergeant Gerdrand," he called.

The usually quiet Gerdrand grunted as he watched Albanon and Roghar approach. "The Lord Warden is worried about you, apprentice," the sergeant said. "I suggest you head up to the Glowing Tower and present yourself. Now."

Albanon was only slightly surprised that the Lord Warden had already determined that something was amiss at the Glowing Tower. He didn't think that the town guard could get through the wards he had put in place when he and Roghar and Tempest had departed to track Moorin's murderer, but if Faren Markelhay, the Lord Warden of Fallcrest, had tried to communicate with Moorin and had received no answer at all from the tower, he would certainly be curious as to where Moorin and his apprentice had disappeared to without so much as a note of explanation.

Albanon and Roghar rode through the Lower Quay and across the small bridge that spanned the Moonwash, heading to the road that would take them up the bluffs and to the Glowing Tower. The people of Fallcrest stared at them from house porches and building windows as they rode by, an eladrin wizard and a dragonborn paladin. Albanon knew all of these people. He had lived among them for almost seven years. But today they seemed distant, nervous, perhaps even a little bit afraid. It was probably Albanon's imagination, along with his weariness, that was transferring his own feelings to the people around him. There's no way that anyone had gotten past the wards he put in place. They could have no idea about what had happened in the Glowing Tower.

Of course, that's probably what Moorin thought before the tower was invaded and he was killed.

"Relax, my friend," Roghar said. "You squirm as though you are guilty of some terrible crime."

Albanon looked into Roghar's eyes. "Aren't I?"

The dragonborn looked away, appearing slightly guilty himself. "No, Albanon, no. You made a mistake, and I'm angry about it and worried about Tempest. But a crime? No. Not that."

Roghar's words made Albanon feel a little better, but he still had to figure out how to make everything right. He had to figure out how to get Tempest away from the halfling-thing without getting them all killed.

At the top of the bluff, they turned their horses south and found the narrow road that led to the Glowing Tower. As Sergeant Gerdrand had indicated, the Lord Warden stood at the base of the tower with a squad of six of the Fallcrest Guard. Albanon also recognized the elderly human and the halfling huddled with the Lord Warden. Nimozaran the Green was an ancient human wizard who considered himself to be the High Septarch of Fallcrest. Tobolar Quickfoot was his apprentice. In his time as Moorin's apprentice, Albanon never saw his master treat the old wizard with anything less than respect. He also never saw Moorin acquiesce or bow to Nimozaran, either. He always had the impression that whereas Moorin had been an adventuring wizard before coming to settle in Fallcrest, Nimozaran had never been more than a sage and a scholar, spending most of his career locked away in the Septarch's Tower that rose atop the hill directly across from the Glowing Tower high on the bluff.

Albanon saw that the door to his master's tower was open. Nimozaran must have disabled the wards at the command of the Lord Warden. He brought Tempest's horse to a halt directly before the Lord Warden and the High Septarch, and then he slipped out of the saddle and leaped down to the ground.

"And so the apprentice returns to the scene of the crime," the old wizard said, straightening his crooked back as much as he could.

"Albanon," the Lord Warden said solemnly. "You are to surrender yourself to the Guard. You and the dragonborn."

"On what grounds?" Roghar demanded, still sitting tall atop his stallion.

"Murder," said Nimozaran.

39 FALLCREST, THE NENTIR INN, DAY

Falon and Darrum sat at a small table in the Nentir Inn's common room, finishing a meal of cold meat, cheese, bread, and wine. Falon had only picked at his food, but Darrum had attacked the simple fare with the enthusiasm of a starving rage drake.

"Slow down, Darrum," Falon said. "The food's neither so good nor so scarce that you need to wolf it down without so much as chewing it first."

"You'll learn to eat as much as you can whenever you can," the old dwarf said, with his mouth full of food. "When you're on the road, good meals can be few and far between."

Falon broke off another chunk of bread and went back to thinking about the people they had met the night before. Sitting at a table on the other side of the room was the undead revenant that called itself Erak, the woman warrior named Shara, and the halfling rogue Uldane. The revenant claimed to be a knight of the Raven Queen. Not exactly an evil god, but not a bright and shiny example of goodness, either. But then again, neither was Falon's god, Erathis. Moreover, the revenant had pledged himself to Falon, somehow recognizing the royal blood that Falon himself had only recently learned was flowing through his veins. It all made Falon's head hurt.

"So, old dwarf," Falon asked, taking a sip of wine, "what do you think about Erak and his claims?"

Darrum fixed his one good eye on Falon as he finished chewing a slice of cold beef. "I've heard about revenants," he said, keeping his voice low. "Even had the good fortune to work with one a few decades back. The Raven Queen is part of the natural order, for every life eventually leads to death. I think that this Erak is on a mission for the Lady of Fate, just as he said, and I think that mission has something to do with you—although I haven't figured out all the hows and whys of it just yet."

Falon nodded, even though he didn't want to. "Yeah, I've been coming around to the same conclusion."

"So what do you want to do, your majesty?" Darrum asked, a ridiculous smirk on his weathered old face.

"I want you to stop calling me that," Falon said, "and I want to find out what Erak has been sent back to do."

Falon got up and marched over to the table where Erak and his companions were seated. He nodded a respectful greeting to Shara and Uldane, and then he sat down in the empty chair beside the revenant.

"Can you tell me about your mission?" Falon asked the revenant.

Erak sat back, letting his gaze wander from Falon to Shara to Uldane and back again. He acknowledged the old dwarf as Darrum wandered over and pulled up a chair from another table. Then he tilted his head, as though trying to remember something important.

"*Arise, my champion,* the woman's voice said to me as I awoke within the stone coffin in a graveyard outside of the town of Winterhaven," Erak said in a far-away voice. "*You have work to do.*"

"He doesn't remember anything more than that," Shara said, putting her hand atop Erak's.

"I know that I am here to do something, and that it involves Shara and you," Erak added. "Beyond that, my memories are jumbled images, feelings of pain and death and a place of peace. I don't think I wanted to return to this world. But I don't think I had a choice in the matter."

Falon thought about what the revenant had said. "Darrum and I are on the run," he decided to tell them. "Undead creatures have tried to kill me twice in the space of just a few days. We think it has something to do with my bloodline, but I only just learned about my heritage so I'm a bit lost as to what to do or where to go next."

"Where does that leave us?" Shara asked.

"I think it leaves us in the revenant's hands," Falon said, looking hard into Erak's eyes. "I think we need to help you figure out what your mission is and then help you complete it. It's not like I have anything better to do at the moment."

Uldane looked around the table, an expression of sheer incredulity on his face. "And they call me impulsive," he said.

Falon ignored the halfling. "All right, Erak," he said. "What do we do next?"

40 FALLCREST, THE GLOWING TOWER, DAY

Albanon stared at the ancient wizard Nimozaran with an expression that was halfway between shock and horror. He knew that the old man was jealous of Moorin, but to accuse Moorin's apprentice of such a heinous act was beyond Albanon's comprehension.

"You think I killed my master?" Albanon asked, finally finding his voice.

"Let's not make this any more difficult than it needs to be," the

Lord Warden said, motioning for his guards to surround Albanon and Roghar.

"If I really killed Moorin," Albanon said, looking directly at Nimozaran, "really was able to defeat the greatest wizard in the Vale, what do you think you'll be able to accomplish with a handful of guards and a decrepit old mage?"

"Impetuous youngling!" Nimozaran said, stamping his wizard's staff on the ground. "If it must come to a battle arcane, know you that I am more than a match for your rudimentary skills."

"The apprentice didn't kill anyone," Splendid said, sounding rather annoyed that the commotion was interfering with her nap on Albanon's shoulder. "A foul creature from someplace else entered the Great Moorin's tower and slew the Great Moorin in a terrible battle that I was forced to watch from the inside of a cage."

Everyone turned to look at the pseudodragon that was draped around Albanon's neck. It appeared to be extremely tired, and its scales glistened in the afternoon sun.

Nimozaran's apprentice, the halfling Tobolar, peered from around his old master. "Of course the drake would say that," Tobolar said. "It makes sense that it would defend its master. It is his pet, after all."

"I am no one's pet," Splendid roared, making her voice louder than Albanon imagined possible. "And Albanon is no one's master."

"Even so, I saw the blood and poor Moorin's body with my own eyes," the Lord Warden said. "Until we can sort this out, I really think that you and your friend should come with us."

Roghar assessed the situation. Then he made a decision. "I shall not see another injustice done this day," the dragonborn shouted. Albanon noted that Roghar's voice was much, much louder than Splendid's. "Bahamut, aid your humble servant this day!"

Bright light burst from Roghar's sword, spreading out and blinding the Fallcrest Guard as well as the two wizards standing with them.

Roghar grabbed Albanon by the scruff of his mantle and tossed him on to Tempest's horse.

"Time to go, my friend," Roghar said. "We must be free if we are to save Tempest from the monster that killed your master."

Albanon nodded, and the two of them spurred their mounts into motion. Splendid took to the air, flying directly at Nimozaran and Tobolar. Both wizards dodged the tiny winged creature, dropping to the ground to avoid her slashing, stinger-tipped tail. The pseudodragon turned the attack run into an escape, flying wide around the close-packed trees surrounding the Glowing Tower to meet up with the horses as they pounded toward the eastern gate. The Wizard's Gate. It seemed fitting somehow that Albanon was going to leave Fallcrest, perhaps forever, by exiting through the Wizard's Gate.

"What a way to end my apprenticeship," he said, a hint of sadness in his voice.

"Better than spending the rest of our lives, however short those may be, in a jail cell," Roghar said.

In that regard, they were both in perfect agreement.

41 THE SEVEN-PILLARED HALL, DAY

The magic circle inscribed around the bronze minotaur statue glowed brightly as Kalaban, the golem, and his master Magroth appeared out of thin air. They appeared in a large natural cavern, atop a rise of rock that made this one of the highest points within the enclosed space. Stairs were carved into the rock, leading down from the circle to ground level. Kalaban noticed a river running through the center of the cavern, and a tower of stone was built into the rock wall directly across from where the outstretched arms of the minotaur statue were pointing.

"That is the Tower of Saruun," Magroth said, indicating the structure that Kalaban was already studying. "The documents I seek, if they exist at all, shall be found there."

Buildings made of stone and wood were laid out throughout the huge chamber. Some were freestanding, but others were built around the seven massive pillars that stretched from floor to ceiling, or into the walls of the cavern itself. The entire place was lit by hundreds of lanterns hung from the cavern walls and buildings. The light of the lanterns provided some illumination, but it did nothing to eradicate the crushing darkness of the place.

Magroth had consulted the many rituals in his spellbook back at the lair beneath the Witchlight Fens that had once belonged to the vampire Sareth. Eventually, he locked himself away and performed a ritual in secret while Kalaban and the golem waited in another chamber. When Magroth emerged, he had found a place to begin his search for information pertaining to the necropolis of Andok Sur. "We must travel to the Seven-Pillared Hall," Magroth said, visibly shaken from consulting with whatever entities his ritual had called up. "There, the Mages of Saruun shall aid me in my quest—or we shall destroy them and take what we need from their ruined tower."

And so Magroth opened a portal and they had all stepped through, into this town built within an underground cavern. Kalaban was about to lead the way down the stairs when a powerful looking ogre marched up the stone steps toward them. The ogre was followed by a handful of toughs, including a pair of humans, a dwarf, and a half-orc. They were all armed and clearly subordinate to the ogre. The ogre stood nearly ten feet tall. He wore a relatively clean tunic stitched together from a variety of hides, leather pants, and well-made boots. Unusually large, sharp teeth jutted from the ogre's lower jaw, and he wore seven silver rings in the lobe of his pointy right ear. A greatclub fashioned from what appeared to be the trunk of a small tree hung across his back. He looked remarkably bright, as far as ogres went, and that made Kalaban wary.

"Which one a youse wants ta tell me who ya is and why ya appeared in da Mages' circle?" the ogre asked in an almost bored tone.

Kalaban started to reach for his weapon, but Magroth stayed his hand with a gentle touch to his arm. "Now, now, Kalaban, there's no immediate need for bloodshed," Magroth said, favoring the large ogre with a friendly smile. "Good sir, we meant no harm. I am Magroth, a humble wizard, come to this place to seek the help and guidance of the Mages of Saruun."

"If he's a humble wizard then I'm the king of Hammerfast," said the dwarf. "They have the smell of undead about them, Brugg."

The ogre, who was apparently called Brugg, nodded. "Clearly, we got here a couple a zombies," Brugg growled. "The question is, are dey here to cause trouble? Maybe eat some of the townsfolk while dey sleep?"

Magroth laughed. It was a rich, jubilant sound that made Kalaban's undead skin crawl. It seemed to have a similar effect on Brugg and his enforcers.

"You are a clever ogre, aren't you?" Magroth said, drawing himself up to his full height. Brugg still towered over him, but the ogre seemed to draw back anyway. "We have not come to disrupt nor damage the fine people of this underground cesspool. We will bring this place down on your heads, if we need to, but that isn't our purpose in coming here. We have come to ask a favor of the Mages of Saruun, and neither you nor your associates will hinder us in that purpose."

Brugg swallowed hard, but to his credit his large hand never strayed toward the handle of his greatclub. He glanced briefly at Kalaban and the golem before his eyes quickly returned to Magroth. He studied the vampire-lich, sizing him up like he might any potential threat that wandered into the hall. "Maybe youse are as tough as youse say," Brugg said, keeping his composure in the face of what was clearly a superior force. "Maybe youse ain't. Brugg is nuttin' if not corgenial ta dose dat come ta visit, right guys?"

The dwarf, humans, and half-orc enforcers wholeheartedly agreed with their leader, nodding enthusiastically and adding their own words of praise about Brugg and his apparently legendary manners.

"I appreciate 'corgeniality,'" Magroth said, the smile never leaving his gaunt face. "I appreciate speed and decisiveness even more."

Brugg nodded. "If youse wait right here, I'll see if da Ordinator Arcanis has time ta see ya."

"Convince him to make time, please," Magroth said. "And quickly. We would rather not linger in this hall any longer than necessary, and I'm sure you'd like to see us leave sooner rather than later."

"Youse got dat right," Brugg muttered under his breath as he turned to go. The rest of the enforcers followed behind him without a passing glance at Kalaban or Magroth.

"That went well," Magroth said cheerfully.

"Yes, my liege," Kalaban replied automatically.

"Don't worry, knight-commander. Perhaps I'll still let you kill the ogre before we depart this squalor-filled cave."

"No need to call for blood on my account," Kalaban said, instantly regretting his choice of words.

"No," Magroth agreed, all humor fleeing from his voice. "Not on your account."

42 THE GRAY DOWNS, DAY

Tiktag gratefully slid from Vestapalk's neck to the grassy earth as soon as the green dragon touched down. The green dragon landed beside the cold, rushing water of the Winter River and immediately set to gulping great amounts of the clear liquid. The kobold wyrmpriest, meanwhile, carefully rubbed at his saddle sores. The long ride had not been very comfortable. He dreaded getting back atop the dragon, but he knew they still had a lot of flying ahead of them.

"Cast your bones, wyrmpriest," Vestapalk said, raising its dripping snout out of the river long enough to bark the command. Then the dragon went back to drinking.

Tiktag knew better than to complain, but he was certainly getting tired of serving as the green dragon's lackey. The wrympriest was used to being the one giving commands and having others serve him, and this situation with Vestapalk, while initially exciting and even spiritually uplifting, had grown wearisome. He almost wished that he and his tribe hadn't been singled out by the visionary dragon.

Almost.

The wyrmpriest drew a circle with the base of his staff as he began to chant. The circle was about two feet across, drawn in a relatively flat section of dirt near the river. He pulled a small pouch made of hyena fur from his belt, shook it so that the bone fragments within rattled loudly, and continued to chant in a singsong voice. Then he dumped the contents, letting the fragments fall toward the prepared piece of ground. Bone fragments bounced, spun, and came to rest within the circle he had drawn. The fragments were of different shapes—squares, triangles, rectangles, and bits that were irregularly shaped—each carved with a draconic symbol. How the fragments landed, both within the circle and in relation to each other, provided the wyrmpriest with clues and signs that he could interpret.

He noticed that the dragon was watching him with one large orb, making sure that the casting was true. Tiktag ignored the scrutiny. He shook the fetishes hanging from his staff and then struck the butt of the staff into the ground beside the drawn circle three times.

Tiktag bent down to examine the pattern of the bone fragments. Each fragment, with its carved draconic symbol, corresponded to a particular aspect of divination related to Tiamat, the evil god of greed, envy, and chromatic dragons. Since becoming a follower of Vestapalk, Tiktag was amazed at how relevant each divination he performed turned out to be. In the past, before coming under the wing of the green dragon, he sometimes had to adjust his interpretations of the signs to fit the questions he asked. But every question he asked at the behest of Vestapalk was answered with a clear, distinct, and totally relevant set of symbols and signs. It was uncanny, and this casting was no different.

"Great Vestapalk," Tiktag began, using the same tone he employed when preaching to the kobolds of the Greenscale tribe. "The Herald remains before us, along the path we have been following. Better still, this time the signs have shown me exactly where we can find the Herald."

The green dragon turned toward the wyrmpriest, its eyes wide with eager anticipation. "Tell Vestapalk what the signs have shown you, wyrmpriest."

Tiktag hammered the base of his staff into the solid-packed dirt, rattling the bones that hung among the fetishes at the top of the implement. "The Herald waits for you, Great Vestapalk. The Herald waits within the Old Hills, northeast of the mountain of storm and thunder."

The wyrmpriest pointed to the mountaintop rising above the forest that stretched across the horizon. A swirling thunderhead of black clouds and flashes of lightning obscured the peak of the mountain.

Vestapalk roared. "Then let Vestapalk take flight, little wyrmpriest," the green dragon said. "The Herald is close, and this one would like to see the Herald with this one's own eyes."

Tiktag quickly gathered up the casting bones, secured the fur pouch to his belt, and wearily climbed back atop the green dragon. He wasn't sure where all of this was going, and he was more than a little frightened by the implications he was seeing in the signs. But Tiktag was a survivor, and he would find a way to survive the coming changes.

The wyrmpriest believed that.

And he held on to that belief even as Vestapalk vaulted into the sky, Tiktag clinging to its neck, and winged toward Thunderspire Mountain.

4 3 FALLCREST, THE NENTIR INN, DAY

Shara found Erak at a table in the inn's common room. He was sitting quietly, his back to a wall. She sat down beside him and cleared her throat, waiting for the revenant to acknowledge her presence.

He came out of his reverie slowly, eventually turning his eyes toward her and offering her a slight smile. "Sorry," Erak said. "I was thinking."

"I've been thinking, too," Shara said. "Before this continues, before Uldane and I follow you to who knows where and back again, you have to tell me. Are you Jarren?"

Erak continued to look into Shara's eyes, but a profound sadness seemed to spread across his features. After a long moment, he finally said, "I don't know. I don't know who I was before the Raven Queen gathered me up and sent me back."

Shara sighed. She stood up from the table. "Then why am I following you? Why am I trusting you? I have my own things to take care of, my own dragon to kill. I don't have time for maybes."

She turned to go, disgusted with herself for letting her imagination and her sorrow take her away from who she really was and what she really should be doing. She was grateful that Erak had helped her and Uldane against the kobolds, and she hoped that the young cleric Falon would find whatever it was he was looking for, but as far as Shara was concerned, it was time to go back to Winterhaven.

"Later," Erak said suddenly.

Shara froze. That was the last word that Jarren had said to her before their battle with Vestapalk. "I'm always ready for anything," she whispered to herself, remembering the words she had said before Jarren had responded with that word. A single word, so full of promise and hope. She recovered her composure and turned back to the revenant.

"What did you say?"

"Shara, please. I can't confirm or deny what I don't know for sure. But I truly believe that you need to accompany me. Your own quest depends on it. And so much more depends on it as well. Trust me, at least for a little while longer."

The woman warrior stared hard at the revenant as she tried to sort through the conflicting emotions now raging inside her. She took a deep breath. Then another. Then she let out a long sigh.

"All right, Erak," Shara said at last. "I'll go with you. But if you've lied to me, if you've deceived me in any way, or if I find out that you're nothing more than a monster who is using us all for some foul purpose, I will destroy you. Do you understand that? Can you remember that?"

Erak nodded.

Shara turned away and started to stride out of the room. "I hope you don't disappoint me, Erak." And then she rushed away so that the revenant wouldn't see her tears.

44 THE TRADE ROAD, DAY

Albanon and Roghar had been riding east, away from Fallcrest, for more than an hour. No matter how many times Albanon craned his head back over his shoulder to look, he saw the same thing. Nothing but empty road behind them. No one was following them. No troop of militia was breathing down their necks. Not yet, in any event.

"If you fall off your horse because you keep looking where you have been and not where you are going," Roghar said, "I am going to leave you there. The Fallcrest Guard was willing to arrest us while we were within the walls of the town, but they have little interest in chasing after us or hunting us down."

"Really?" Albanon asked. "And how many towns have you been chased out of, Roghar?"

"More than I care to admit," the dragonborn paladin said wistfully. "Even the most noble and good-hearted adventurers are often feared and misunderstood by the common folk they seek to protect."

"I find it hard to believe that they didn't accept my good word regarding your innocence, apprentice," Splendid said. The pseudo-dragon was once again curled around Albanon's neck, comfortably dozing when she wasn't adding a snide comment or two to the conversation.

"You're a pseudodragon," Albanon said, letting his exhaustion and exasperation get the better of him. "Why would they believe you? And in case you hadn't noticed, I'm not an apprentice any more."

"Oh, really? And when did you pass your final tests, oh mighty wizard Albanon?"

"Leave the elf be, little dragon," Roghar said. "This is not the time to cut at each other with hurtful words and biting insults."

"Eladrin," Albanon said quietly. "I'm an eladrin, not an elf."

"Why not?" the pseudodragon asked. "Why is this time any different from any other time?"

"Because this time we're about to be attacked by a gang of bandits."

Albanon jerked his head to look toward the south where Roghar was pointing. There, rushing right at them, were nine horses, each carrying a human wearing either leather or hide armor. Seven of the riders were men, two were women. One of the humans was better equipped than the rest of the bandits. He wore chain mail and was armed with a two-handed sword. Two large gray wolves kept pace with Chain Mail's horse, running alongside it like some sort of feral honor guard.

The riders cut through the field and spread themselves across the road, effectively blocking Albanon and Roghar's path. The riders positioned themselves so that four of their number were set up to each side of Chain Mail, who stopped directly in the center of the road. The wolves stood one to each side and slightly ahead of Chain Mail's horse.

Albanon and Roghar pulled up their own mounts and stopped about a hundred feet or so from the line of bandits.

"We could be jumping to conclusions here," Albanon said. "Maybe these are nothing more than friendly travelers in need of directions."

"I am Sylish Kreed, leader of this band," Chain Mail called as the men and women to each side nocked arrows into bows or drew swords from scabbards. "The Trade Road east is temporarily closed to all travelers, but I might be inclined to open it just for you . . . provided you can meet the price."

"Bandits," Roghar said, drawing his own sword from its sheath. "Pretty sure of it."

"Maybe we should just pay them whatever they're asking," Albanon suggested, hoping to avoid any trouble.

"No," Roghar said, "not going to happen."

Four bows trained their arrows on Roghar, but none of them fired. Yet.

"Well," said Splendid, "this is becoming interesting."

Chain Mail put up a hand as he motioned his horse a few steps forward. "Believe me when I say this, dragonborn," the bandit leader called out with a smile, "but it would seriously upset this perfectly pleasant day I've been having if you force me to spill your blood all over the road. Let's just say that the toll you have to pay today is ten gold pieces each and we can all go on our merry ways."

"Ten gold seems like a perfectly fair price," Albanon said, though he barely had two gold pieces worth of coins jangling in the pockets of his robes.

"Listen to the eladrin," Chain Mail, who called himself Sylish Kreed, said. "Aren't your lives worth ten gold each?"

"I like to believe that my life is worth much more than that," Roghar said, letting his horse prance in place as he spoke. "What about you, Sir Kreed? What do you believe your life is worth today?"

"More than you can afford," Kreed said, casually waving a hand to remind the paladin about his armed associates. "You're outnumbered and, in my own humble opinion, outclassed. So pay the gold and we can both go back to whatever it was we were doing before we happened to meet on the road."

"Are you ready?" Roghar asked Albanon, keeping his voice low so that only the wizard and the pseudodragon could hear him.

"Ready? Ready for what?"

That's when Roghar gave his mount a swift kick and the horse catapulted forward, exploding toward the bandit leader as Roghar let out a battle roar. The paladin slashed two arrows out of the air as they sped toward him, twirling his long sword with a practiced hand.

"I wish you hadn't done that," Albanon muttered as Splendid launched herself into the air. Then he started to quickly run through the spells he had prepared as he decided how best to aid the fearless paladin.

"Fearless," Albanon said the word as though it were a curse, "just another way to say thick-headed . . . egotistical . . . stupid. . . ."

The two wolves snapped at Roghar's horse, causing the well-trained mount to turn to avoid their sharp teeth. This effectively ended Roghar's charge, giving Kreed the space he needed to draw his weapon and circle around to attack. One of the wolves leaped, sinking its fangs into the horse's neck. The animal screamed in pain, rearing up on its hind legs in an effort to dislodge the wolf. The wolf fell away, but Roghar also went flying. He crashed to the ground, apparently stunned by the fall.

Albanon rapidly proclaimed words of power, and missiles of arcane energy flew from his fingertips. They struck the two archers, knocking one from his horse and causing the other to drop her bow. He started to cast another spell as two of the riders pounded toward him.

The remaining four leaped from their mounts and surrounded Roghar, who still hadn't gotten back to his feet after falling from his horse. Sylish Kreed stayed on top of his mount, surveying the scene like a general inspecting his troops.

"I wish you would have just paid the fee," Kreed said with genuine sadness in his voice. "Ah, well. No sense dwelling on things that will not be. Kill them. And be quick about it."

45 FALLCREST, THE NENTIR INN, DAY

Erak stood in the shadows near the back of the inn's stable, watching as the others prepared the horses for travel. Shara and Uldane had secured mounts for Darrum and Falon, and now they were all busy checking straps and cinches and loading packs for the journey ahead. Erak was both excited and troubled by the events of the past few days. He was happy that things seemed to be coming together, that he felt that he was progressing in a mission that he didn't yet fully understand. He was also troubled by that lack of understanding, by the gaps in his memory, especially since the others had apparently decided that he should lead them. That hadn't been his goal when he went to Shara's aid or when he revealed himself to Falon. Was he capable of leading them when so much of his memory felt incomplete?

He felt that Shara was integral to the work he had been sent back to do, and he had felt compelled to seek out the young cleric named Falon. He somehow knew that Falon had the blood of Nerathi emperors flowing through his veins, and for some reason that was important to Erak. He felt a connection to the young noble, a commitment that seemed to clear away some of the dark spots in his memory so that he could almost see what he had forgotten. Almost, but not quite. Now they were all together, and Erak had no idea where they had to go next.

The revenant sensed the presence behind him a few moments before, but to this point he had ignored it. He didn't detect any immediate danger from the presence, but he also recognized that the presence wasn't a friend to either Erak or the Raven Queen. He casually drew his hellsteel blade and spun, letting the serrated edge come to rest just under the woman's chin.

She was a tall woman, with a streak of silver highlighting her otherwise black hair. She wore crimson robes, and a pearl skull hung from a chain around her neck. The skull's mouth hung open, as though it had been flayed clean and preserved while it had been screaming in terrible pain. She showed no indication of fear or distress of any kind in response to Erak's sudden action. As he examined her, his mind coughed up information he hadn't realized he possessed.

"What can I do for you, priest of Orcus?" Erak asked, somehow recognizing her as an agent of the Demon Prince of Undeath.

"I have been granted one last try to keep our paths from ending in bloodshed," the priest said.

"Really? The dead bodies we met on the road had indicated that they were our one and only opportunity to abandon our quest."

The woman smiled. It wasn't friendly.

"Lesser undead sometimes get too anxious in their efforts to impress our dark lord," she said.

"You aren't undead," Erak said, still holding his blade to her throat. "Why does a living human submit to the will of Orcus?"

"Why does an undead revenant not?" she countered, a touch of amusement in her voice. "I am Barana Strenk, and I must warn you that the Lady of Fate has sent you into a game that you have no hope of surviving. The blood of Nerath will die, and my master's plan will move forward. You can either get out of the way or be destroyed. The next agent of Orcus you meet shall not be as willing to avoid your destruction as I am."

"I guess I should thank you, Barana," Erak said. "But I can't help but wonder why you have come all this way just to warn me off. What are you afraid of? What do you and your master think I can do that you have decided to talk to me at all?"

Barana's eyes flashed with a hint of anger, but the smile on her face never wavered. "I have not acknowledged the insult you have shown me and continue to show me by holding a weapon in my face," she said. "I have tried to reason with you, to treat you in a manner that shows respect to you and your Lady, but I see that I am wasting my time. You shall go to the Seven-Pillared Hall and there is nothing I can say to convince you otherwise. So be it. Know this, though. You shall survive long enough to see the young cleric and the woman warrior fall. Only after they have been destroyed shall we remove you from the playing field."

"This isn't a game," Erak said, anger flowing into his voice.

"Oh, how little you truly know or understand, revenant. Of course this is a game. And it is played at the level of the gods, between Orcus and the Raven Queen and whichever other high and mighty beings decide to get involved. We are both just pieces in their cosmic struggle, pawns to be moved here and there in patterns of strike and counterstrike, until one side or the other gets the upper hand for a time. And then the game starts again."

Barana Strenk took a step back into the deeper shadows and disappeared, leaving Erak standing alone, his sword threatening nothing but empty space and the back wall of the stable.

Shara walked up a few moments later to find Erak still standing there, his blade outstretched. Concern wrinkled her brow as she put a hand on his arm. "What's the matter, Erak?" she asked. "Who were you talking to?"

Erak sighed and returned his blade to its sheath. "Nothing's wrong," he said. "And there's no one here but me. Come on, we have many miles to cover this day."

He turned back toward the yard where the others were finishing their preparations. The priest of Orcus had passed along a message, though he couldn't figure out why. She obviously wanted him to go to this Seven-Pillared Hall. Because he had no other lead about where to go next, it seemed as good a place as any to start. But Erak would be wary. This had all the markings of a trap, and he had decided to step right into it.

"Have you ever heard of a place called the Seven-Pillared Hall?" Erak asked her as they walked back to the others.

"Yes," Shara said, looking a bit disturbed by the question. "It's a trading town inside Thunderspire Mountain. Not a particularly friendly place to visit. Why do you ask?"

"We have to go there," Erak said. "We have to go there and we have to go there now."

46 THE SEVEN-PILLARED HALL, DAY

Kalaban leaned against the bronze minotaur statue and watched as the ogre Brugg led a black-robed figure toward the raised platform of stone on which the knight-commander and his master, Magroth, waited patiently. The black-roped figure seemed to float behind the ogre, but that could have been illusion perpetrated by the cut and flow of the deep-black cloth. The figure wore a golden mask that was carved to resemble an impassive, stylized human face. The rest of the enforcers were nowhere to be seen.

"The Ordinator Arcanis, I presume," Magroth said to Kalaban. "That outfit is as ostentatious as the title he goes by."

"Probably keeps the locals in line," Kalaban said.

"Undoubtedly," Magroth agreed.

Brugg stopped at the bottom of the stone steps that led up to the platform. "Da Ordinator Arcanis, magistrate of da Mages of Saruun, has agreed ta hear youse plea," the ogre said in what Kalaban assumed was a well-practiced voice of authority.

"Well, how fortune for us," Magroth replied.

The Ordinator Arcanis drifted up the stone steps until he was level with Kalaban and Magroth. It was hard to tell what the man beneath the mask—if it was indeed a man—was looking at, as the mask's eyes weren't holes but stylized orbs molded into the gold. Even so, Kalaban got the impression that the Ordinator glanced briefly at the stone golem before pausing a few feet from Magroth.

"Your kind is not welcome within this hall," the Ordinator said in a deep, resonate voice that was clearly augmented by magic. "State your business and be quick about it."

Magroth bowed his head ever so slightly as a smile began to creep up along his thin lips. "I will graciously ignore your impertinent tone and get right to the point. I am in need of ancient documents pertaining to a place once known as Andok Sur. I was told that the Mages of Saruun had the best library in the Nentir Vale, so I have come to ask permission to examine your scrolls and books. I shall pay handsomely for the use of your library, and then my companions and I shall be off."

The black-robed figure stood silently for a time. Then the deep voice said, "I must confer with my fellow Mages. In the meantime, you and your party can wait. . . ."

Energy crackled along the tip of Magroth's staff as he stepped close to the Ordinator and interrupted whatever proclamation he was about to make. Brugg began to advance up the steps, but Kalaban's soulsword was suddenly free of its sheath and its blade was pointed directly at the ogre. Brugg hesitated, waiting to see what the Ordinator was going to do.

"Save me your speeches and your threats and your shows of power," Magroth said in a low, threatening voice. "I can perform every trick in your repertoire and a whole lot more. You do not frighten me, and I am not some simple trader that you can bully into obedience. I am Magroth, undead emperor of mighty Nerath, and I will bring this mountain down upon your heads if I do not get a modicum of cooperation from you. Take me to your library, now, and you can still profit from my visit to this unsavory hole in the ground."

The Ordinator took a moment to regain his composure before he spoke. "The Mages of Saruun welcome so important a personage as yourself into our hall. You may visit the library within our tower, but your guards must remain here. None but masters of the arcane are permitted to walk the tower's corridors. I hope you understand."

Magroth's smile widened. "Of course," he said, allowing the energy around the tip of his staff to dissipate. "They can wait here. I assume I don't have to tell you what will happen if you or yours attempts anything . . . threatening to my person?"

"The Mages of Saruun follow the rules of hospitality," the Ordinator said.

"I would expect no less. Please, lead on."

The Ordinator floated over to the same magic circle that Magroth had used to teleport them into the hall. He made a few arcane gestures and chanted words of power until the inscribed circle glowed with crimson light. The Ordinator stepped into the glowing circle and disappeared.

"Don't wait up," Magroth said to Kalaban, and then he followed the Ordinator and vanished from sight.

"Wizards," Brugg spat, apparently happy to be rid of both the Ordinator and Magroth.

Kalaban knew just how he felt.

The knight-commander returned his sword to its scabbard and let his free hand wander into the depths of the pouch he wore on his belt. His fingers closed gently around the cylinder that rested there, feeling the contrasting sensations of cool glass and the radiant heat of the substance within.

As his fingers found the glass cylinder, it seemed as though the substance within awoke. He could feel the substance slosh against the sides of the glass, as though trying to reach out and touch his cold, undead skin. As Kalaban's fingers explored the glass cylinder, he looked toward the tower built into the side of the cavern wall to the northeast. That was where Magroth had gone. He wondered how long it would take for his emperor to find the information he sought, or if the information even existed. His eyes followed the rough curve of the cavern wall as it spread out to the west from the tower. About halfway along the wall, almost directly north of the bronze minotaur statue that loomed above Kalaban, the knight-commander noticed a dark archway. The keystone above the opening was decorated with a chiseled horizontal line with a vertical line carved into the stone beneath it.

Kalaban looked into that dark maw, and suddenly he felt compelled to see where the opening led to. It was the strangest sensation. A compulsion, really, a need that he felt he could ignore if he wanted to. But he didn't want to.

"Stay here and wait for the emperor," Kalaban told the stoneguard golem. He had no idea if it understood him, but it didn't move from its spot.

"Where da ya tink you're goin'?" Brugg demanded as Kalaban began to move toward the dark archway to the north.

He answered the ogre honestly.

"I have no idea."

And then Kalaban was off, running toward the dark archway and whatever waited beyond it.

47 THE TRADE ROAD, DAY

Falon had never ridden a horse before. Whenever he needed to get somewhere within the village of Nenlast, he simply walked there. Nothing was too far to walk to, and his family didn't own any horses even if he had wanted to ride. On the farm, he had sometimes ridden in a wagon drawn by an ox, but the wagon was usually used to transport dirt or harvested vegetables and rarely used as a way to get from place to place. So it was no wonder that he was having trouble on this ride out of Fallcrest. He could barely control the animal they had given him, and his bottom hurt more than he cared to admit.

"Is this usual?" he had asked Darrum when the two were more or less out of earshot of the rest of the group.

"Yup," the old dwarf had replied.

"Then why do people try to ride these foul beasts?"

"Same reason I have to keep getting on boats. It beats walking when you have to get someplace in a hurry."

About an hour after they had started out for Thunderspire Mountain, Falon found that he didn't like this method of travel any better. He looked around at his companions to see how they were faring. Erak, Shara, and Uldane seemed to be extremely good at this riding business. They each appeared to be totally in control of their mounts, comfortable in their saddles, and even happy to be pounding along the Trade Road atop the sweaty beasts. Darrum appeared to be as uncomfortable as he was, but he handled his animal with more confidence than Falon did. Falon hated them all at this particular moment in time. And he was sure that his horse was laughing at him.

Up ahead, Erak and Shara had reined in their mounts and were staring intently at the horizon. Uldane and Darrum pulled up beside them, and Falon joined them a few moments later. He could hear the clang of metal on metal and the whine of horses coming from just beyond the rise. There were howls as well. Was that a wolf? Falon gave Erak a questioning glance when suddenly a blossom of fire and smoke bloomed somewhere on the road ahead.

"Some kind of battle, that's for certain," Shara said.

"And someone has some potent magic at their disposal," Darrum added.

"Let's go see what's going on," Erak said, and he spurred his horse forward.

"I was hoping someone was going to say that," Uldane replied, beaming and moving to follow the revenant.

"Stay behind me," Darrum said to Falon.

"I think I've demonstrated the ability to take care of myself," Falon replied, allowing his horse to leap ahead of Darrum's before the old dwarf could contradict him.

Falon followed Erak and Uldane over the rise, with Shara and Darrum right behind him. Beyond the rise, the road dipped and then leveled out, and they could see a group engaged in battle about a half of a mile farther along the road. They were still a bit too far away to make out any details, but Falon noted that a few of the combatants were already sprawled across the ground and out of the fight.

"Bandits," Shara said, although Falon couldn't see what made her say that. He couldn't tell who was who among the chaos of the battle.

"Is that . . . yes, it is!" Uldane shouted with joy. "Look, Shara! A tiny dragon!"

"Stay focused," Erak said. He surveyed the situation for another moment, then said, "Let's go slay some bandits."

4 8 THE TRADE ROAD, DAY

Albanon saw that Roghar was struggling to rise. The fall from the horse must have knocked the wind out of him, but he didn't seem to have damaged anything. Of course, the four bandits moving in to surround him wanted to change that. Two of them had swords, one had a spiked club, and the fourth carried a spear. They moved with a practiced ease that indicated that they had used this tactic before. Roghar had his own sword in hand, but he hadn't had the opportunity to retrieve his shield from where it hung across his back. He'd have to fight without it.

Sylish Kreed, still atop his horse but with his sword in hand, circled around the four bandits who were closing in on Roghar. Albanon wanted to help the dragonborn, but he had to concentrate on his own situation. Two bandits were cautiously creeping toward him. They had dismounted and drawn their weapons. One, a grizzled human male with a jagged scar that ran down the left side of his face, wielded a spiked club. The other, a female who might have been a half-elf by the set of her eyes and the shape of her face, had a dagger in each hand. The young wizard also noticed that the two he had hit with his magic missiles were recovering and preparing to get back into the battle.

"Why don't you surrender," the female with the daggers suggested. "Save us all some sweat and bother."

"Let me think about that," Albanon replied, trying to keep his horse from bolting. The wolves were definitely making the animal nervous, and Albanon could relate. "No."

The female with the daggers smiled. "I always wanted to skin an eladrin." She started to bound toward him, ready to knock him from his saddle.

Albanon placed his hands side by side so that his thumbs touched. He spread his fingers wide and pointed them toward the two approaching bandits.

"Don't let him say . . . " the male with the spiked club began to shout, but Albanon said the words of power that released the energy of his spell. Flame burst from his outstretched fingers, sending a wave of heat and fire into the two bandits. The two bandits screamed. The male veered off, dropping his club and bringing his hands up to cover his face as the blast of fire rolled into him.

The female sprang back, avoiding much of the attack. But not all of it. Her long brown hair had caught fire. She started to scream, "Get it off! Get it off!" Then she started rolling around on the ground, trying to smother the flames.

Albanon left the two to their own devices so that he could check on Roghar. The paladin had already dropped one of the four bandits surrounding him, and the other three were trying to keep out of his reach as Kreed directed the wolves to move in and help. Luckily, Splendid was keeping the wolves busy. She darted in, slashed with her stinger, and flew out of reach over and over, occupying the wolves and making them more than a little crazy with her antics.

Albanon recovered his staff from where it hung through loops in the saddle and began calculating distances and burst radiuses in his head. He wanted to scare the bandits and drive them off, not kill any of them. At least, he hoped it wouldn't come to that. And he also didn't want to accidentally catch Roghar in the spell. An arrow whistled past his head. One of the archers was back in the fight, but he ignored him. He raised his staff, whispered a few words of power, and a globe of orange fire coalesced around the staff's tip. He motioned with the staff, and the ball of fire flew toward the spot that Albanon had selected. It hit the side of the road and exploded sending up a blossom of fire and smoke that knocked the remaining bandits off their feet. One archer and one of the bandits surrounding Roghar were caught in the blast, and fire and heat ravaged their bodies mercilessly. The wolves and Kreed had been far enough away that they weren't hurt by the explosion, but they all backed away warily and turned to look at Albanon.

"So you did learn a lesson or two these past seven years," Splendid said, landing atop Albanon's shoulder. "I would have been more impressed if you had actually hit a few more of them."

"I don't want to kill any more of them than I have to," Albanon retorted.

"Noble," Splendid said, "but foolish."

"Thanks for the vote of confidence."

Roghar backed away from the fallen bandits to stand beside Albanon. The eladrin wizard leaped down from his horse and put his back to Roghar's. "What do you have left in that staff of yours?" the dragonborn asked quietly.

Albanon decided that now was not the time to teach Roghar the intricacies of arcane magic. The staff was simply an implement, a focus, not the source of Albanon's power. "Not much," Albanon admitted, "I'm still pretty wiped out from lack of rest, and the fire ball spell was my heavy hitter. I was hoping it would convince the bandits to find easier prey elsewhere."

"Never leave your problems for someone else to deal with," Roghar said. "Would you rather these jackals go after someone weaker and less able to defend themselves than we are? There is no honor in that course of action."

Part of Albanon wanted to feel ashamed, wanted to humbly agree with Roghar's assessment. But another part didn't want to have to fight off nine bandits and two wolves with only a dragonborn paladin and a pseudodragon for company.

Kreed dismounted, gripped his large sword with both hands, and marched toward Albanon and Roghar. The two wolves padded along beside him, flanked to each side and growling menacingly. The rest of the bandits were scattered, but Albanon assumed they'd group up and be back in the battle in a moment or two.

"Congratulations," Kreed said as he approached, "you've managed to completely piss me off."

"My apologies, good sir," Roghar said, bringing his own sword back up into a defensive stance. "Our intent was to send you running with your proverbial tail between your legs. You can see how we could get the two attitudes confused in the heat of battle."

Kreed laughed. It was a deep, full sound that surprised Albanon. "I'm really going to hate killing the two of you. Would you care to surrender and become members of my band? It seems that at least two of my men won't be of much use when all of this is said and done, and I could use the replacements."

Roghar simply cocked his head to the side, a quizzical expression on his draconic face.

"No, I suppose that wouldn't work out well at all," Kreed said with evident disappointment. "Very well, let's get this over with."

The sound of approaching hoof beats suddenly filled the air, along with a number of shouts that Albanon imaged were the war cries of some crazed barbarian. He glanced back over his shoulder to see five riders coming on strong, bearing down on them with distinct purpose.

"Oh, what is it now?" Kreed asked in exasperation. "Can't a man work in peace on such a nice, pleasant day?"

A woman warrior riding atop a large horse was making all the noise, yelling at the top of her lungs as her horse pounded closer. Among the other approaching riders, Albanon noticed a dwarf and a halfling. If these were indeed friends, then the battle had suddenly gone from overwhelmingly in the bandits' favor to closer to even. And apparently Kreed wanted nothing to do with an even battle.

"Disperse, Wolf Runners!" Kreed called out to his associates. "We'll meet up back at camp!"

"Leaving so soon?" Roghar asked. "I was looking forward to seeing how well you swung that massive weapon."

"Another time, I'm sure," Kreed said with a smile. Then he did something that neither Roghar nor Albanon had expected. Kreed transformed right before their eyes. Bones and muscles snapped and reformed. Fur sprouted from flesh and clothing. Hands became paws, and teeth grew long and sharp as a muzzle extended from what was just a human face. Kreed had turned into a massive black wolf, easily twice as large as either of the gray wolves that flanked him. He fixed his bright yellow eyes on Roghar. Then the Kreed-wolf howled, turned, and ran into the brush beside the road.

The woman warrior and her companions arrived just as the last of the bandits that were capable of fleeing had mounted up and scattered to either side of the road. Three of the bandits remained on the ground. Whether they were dead or merely unconscious, Albanon didn't know, and frankly, he didn't care.

"Thanks for your timely appearance, friends," Roghar said to the woman and her companions. "We had those bandits right where we wanted them, and your arrival made them decide to retreat before another one or two of them fell to either my sword or my ally's spells."

"If that was the Wolf Runners," the woman warrior said, "then they won't take this insult lightly. Sylish Kreed hates to lose. Or so I've heard."

"Then perhaps we can ride together, if you're heading east, that is," Roghar suggested. "I think there are more than enough of us to give Kreed pause."

The woman warrior exchanged glances with the rider dressed all in leather. Albanon looked closer at the man and realized that he wasn't quite human. Or quite alive.

"The dragonborn speaks true," the revenant said. "Let's join forces, at least until we reach the mountain."

"Sounds like a plan," Roghar said.

A plan, yes, but Albanon couldn't help but wonder if it was a good plan. He had just seen a man transform into a werewolf, and now he was agreeing to team up with a party of apparent adventurers that included what had to be a revenant—a servant of the Raven Queen.

What had he and Roghar gotten themselves into?

49 THE TOWER OF SARUUN, DAY

Magroth had lost all track of time as he poured over the scrolls, loose sheets of parchment, and bound tomes that filled the library in the Tower of Saruun. The stone bastion, built into the side of the cavern, was almost completely deserted. If there were more than two or three mages within the structure, Magroth would eat his staff. No, the Mages of Saruun were few in number and protected more by their legend and reputation than by actual power. He could easily bring this entire building and the cavern beyond down without working up much of a sweat, and he was sure that there was no one among the vaunted Mages who could hinder him, let alone stop him. But that wasn't why he was here. If they wanted to pretend to be all-powerful and act mysterious, what did it matter to him? They had agreed to his terms, and he would honor that agreement.

Provided he found what he was looking for.

The Ordinator pointed out which shelves and stacks within the large tower room were likely to hold whatever information they possessed regarding the ancient site of Andok Sur. Then the wizard, still wearing his mask of gold and his black robes, floated out of the chamber and left Magroth alone to conduct his research. Now, after an hour or maybe five of unrolling scrolls and separating tomes that held promise from those that dealt with topics far removed from the concerns of the emperor, Magroth was ready to start reading in earnest.

It took time, as these kinds of tasks always do, but eventually Magroth found some of what he was looking for. The writings of Welsom Farwanderer, for example, spoke of Andok Sur and its location.

> The necropolis of Andok Sur was ancient when the kingdom of Bael Turath was merely a collection of loosely allied city-states that stretched across the middle of the continent. It lies to the far north, beyond the Mountain of Thunder and Lightning. Dedicated to the Demon Prince Orcus, the place was established by the warrior tribes of the Eastern Valley who interred their still-living enemies into the tombs and mausoleums that fill the necropolis as buildings fill a town. When I visited the site, it was truly a place of the dead. Roaming ghosts and even corporeal undead continued to haunt the streets of shattered tombs and crumbling mausoleums, but it was no longer the vibrant City of the Undead

that it had been under the rule of the vampire lord Zarguna.
I had come to discover secrets undreamed of, and all I found
was a place of sadness and decay.

Magroth read more, but descriptions of graveyards and statuary
soon bored him. Obviously, the ritual that Barana Strenk had
commanded him to perform was meant to revive this city of the
undead. Magroth could get behind that goal. He needed an army
and a site to establish as the capital of his new kingdom, and what
better location for a vampire-lich wizard than a necropolis full of
undead waiting to be awakened? All he needed to do was figure out
how to turn the loyalty of the necropolis' inhabitants from Orcus
to him. Perhaps he could alter the ritual in some subtle way? As he
continued to peruse Welsom's writings and consider how to best
rework the ritual he had been provided with, the Ordinator returned
to the chamber.

"I have found another volume that may interest you, Emperor
Magroth," the Ordinator said, holding forth a small book that
looked as though it might crumble to dust at any moment. "This is
from the century after your death. It concerns the prophecies of the
Felish Oracle, a seer who has accurately predicted many important
events of the past five hundred years, including the assassination of
the High Orator of Pelor and the fall of Nerath."

Magroth carefully took the small volume. It was written in Abyssal,
the language of demons. Fortunately, Magroth was fluent in Abyssal,
as well as seven other languages. "And why should the ramblings of
an insane mystic interest me?" he asked.

The Ordinator removed his gold mask, revealing an old human
male with a bald head and a short, gray beard. "Excuse me, my lord,
but you wouldn't believe how hot it gets inside that mask," he said
as he wiped perspiration from his brow. "In addition to predicting

the fall of Nerath almost to the exact day and time, the Felish Oracle went on to make a prediction about the remaining heirs to the Nerathi Empire. Examine stanza sixty-two, verses nine through thirteen."

Magroth turned to the appropriate page and found the passage the old wizard spoke of. He scanned the words. Then he read them again.

"This oracle suggests that one of my descendants, one of royal Nerathi blood, will disrupt the plans of Orcus and perhaps even set the stage for the Demon Prince's downfall," Magroth said as he checked the passage a third time.

"That is the popular interpretation of that particular prophecy," the Ordinator agreed.

So, this could be why Orcus's agent wanted all of my descendents destroyed, Magroth thought. *I would likely follow the same course, were I the Demon Prince.*

"One more thing, Emperor Magroth," the Ordinator said, apparently of the opinion that the more helpful he was, the less likely that Magroth would destroy the place as he was leaving. "There is a related prophecy that seems to be intermingled with the one concerning the Blood of Nerath."

"Well, spit it out," Magroth demanded, "I've spent too much time in this lightless hole as it is."

"Yes, of course. My apologies for being slow of tongue. The sixty-third stanza speaks of a Destroyer of Worlds, a demon of some sort, I believe, that is set loose by the actions of the Blood of Nerath."

"And what does this Destroyer of Worlds do? What grave prediction does the Oracle make concerning it?"

"Why, just what you'd expect, my lord. It begins the end times. A period that the Oracle calls 'the Abyssal Plague.' Of course, the few who make a study of the Felish Oracle can't agree on whether or not we're approaching this time, or even what the Abyssal Plague refers to. Still, since it mentions your descendents I thought it might interest you."

Magroth closed the small book and slipped it into a pocket within his robes. "You were correct to bring this to my attention," the emperor said as a hundred possibilities swam across his thoughts. "I believe that I shall enjoy reading through all of the Oracle's writings. Allow me a chance to catch up on all that I've missed."

The Ordinator looked shocked by the blatant theft of the book, but he recovered quickly. "Consider it a gift, my lord," he managed to blurt out before Magroth could react to the man's initial expression.

Magroth nodded and gathered up his staff. "I have what I need from this place," he said. "I believe that it is time for me to leave."

This time the Ordinator made no effort to hide his expression of relief as he turned to lead the emperor back to the teleportation circle.

50 THE LABYRINTH, TIME UNKNOWN

Nu Alin skulked through the mazelike corridors that were obviously fashioned for the use of creatures larger than the form he was currently wearing. Except for the unusual struggle that the female tiefling called Tempest had put up, a struggle that she almost won because of the pain that was wracking him as his previous vessel was literally falling apart around him. Now, however, he had firmly established his control and was using Tempest's form to sneak through the dark tunnels in near silence. It had been a long time since he had worn a form that was so fit, so strong, so skilled in ways that were close to his own innate abilities. He believed that he would enjoy this form for a long time, because he didn't think that it would succumb to the rigors of his presence quite as rapidly as had either the young boy or the female halfling.

There were creatures in the darkness, a variety of pitiful undead things that were neither a bother nor a threat. Nu Alin could avoid them easily enough, for the corridors and side chambers were built on a massive scale. There was plenty of room for a nimble tiefling to move through. There were a few things in the dark that were more powerful, but Nu Alin had no desire to test himself or his new form against any of them. He wanted to find the way out of this maze so that he could once again pick up the trail of the Voidharrow.

As he thought about the Voidharrow, a bolt of searing intensity ripped through his mind and sucked the breath out of him. Suddenly, the Voidharrow was once again within range of Nu Alin's senses, and the sensation of its presence flooded in when he wasn't prepared for its return. In his momentary disorientation, he could feel Tempest trying to exert her will. She was strong, stronger than any of the forms he had taken since he was set free. But he was Nu Alin, the Herald of the Voidharrow, and no form had ever denied his will. He pushed Tempest back into the shadows of her mind so that he could step forward and use all of her senses.

The Voidharrow was close, but not so close that he could reach out into the darkness and snatch it from the thief who carried it. It was somewhere above, somewhere higher up in this mountain that the Tempest creature referred to as "Thunderspire." As he strained the tiefling's ears to hear, a sound from nearby caught his attention. There was a side chamber off the corridor, some thirty feet from where he was standing. There was a faint light emanating from the side passage, which allowed the weak eyes to notice both the opening in the wall and chamber beyond that was evidently the origin point of the sound.

Nu Alin moved the body in graceful silence, reaching the opening without making the slightest sound. He peered around the corner, looking into the opening through Tempest's eyes. In the chamber beyond, which appeared to be another of the many burial chambers that filled this underground area, a luminescent moss grew across one wall and most of the ceiling. The moss was the source of the dim light, which revealed an armored minotaur who carried a battleaxe. The creature's face was sunken and its skin so dry as to be almost brittle, but its eyes glowed with a fierceness that Nu Alin respected. A name surfaced in Tempest's mind, and Nu Alin plucked it out to examine it. *Battle wight*. Some sort of intelligent undead creature. It seemed to be ordering two other minotaurs around, and these specimens were clearly undead, for there was gaping wounds that exposed organs and bones all over their emaciated bodies. *Zombies*, came another thought from Tempest's storehouse of knowledge.

While Tempest's thoughts indicated that the zombies weren't much of an issue, she had a clear level of respect and even fear when it came to the battle wight. Nu Alin decided to heed his vessel's opinion, and he began to slowly back away from the opening. Before he had taken more than a few steps, however, he heard something hit the ground beside him. The sound was almost deafening in the otherwise silent passageway.

Oops, came another thought from where Tempest was confined in the back of her mind. Nu Alin, furious, looked down to see that he had somehow dropped Tempest's warlock rod on to the stone floor. He reached down to retrieve the implement just as the two zombie minotaurs rushed into the corridor to see what was lurking in the shadows. They were followed a moment later by the armored battle wight.

Nu Alin couldn't yet call on Tempest's abilities as a warlock, but he could make use of her more mundane skills. He drew her matched daggers from the sheaths at her belt and prepared to deal with the undead creatures. *I hope they destroy us*, Tempest shouted from the recesses of her mind. Nu Alin had to admit that he was impressed with her ability to continue to have rational thoughts, not to mention how she had managed to alert the undead to their presence. But he was also furious at her for the time she was forcing him to waste, not to mention the risk of damage that any battle might pose to the form he wore. He wanted to keep this form for as long as possible, but its original owner was causing him all sorts of problems.

BILL SLAVICSEK

One thing at a time, Nu Alin decided. The first zombie shambled toward him, its decaying hands outstretched as though to grab him. He made Tempest's body dance out of reach so that the zombie stumbled, then he leaped back in and slashed out with both daggers. The zombie minotaur's head rolled off its shoulders as Nu Alin landed in a crouch. The zombie took another two steps, and then it collapsed to the ground.

The second zombie shuffled forward, swinging its massive fists as it came on. Nu Alin's first slash missed the zombie by a hair, and then it drove a powerful punch into the side of Nu Alin's head. Nu Alin could feel Tempest struggling with him for control, but he pushed her down and turned his attention back to the minotaurs. The battle wight was still watching from the open archway, content to take the measure of this foe before wading in to join the fight. The remaining zombie loomed over the fallen Nu Alin, raising its fists so that it could pound his borrowed form into the ground. Nu Alin exerted control of the form and rolled out of the way just as the zombie brought both of its fists down in a crushing blow. Then he tossed one of the daggers. His aim was true and it buried itself right between the undead minotaur's eyes. He leaped up, catching the handle of the dagger even as he brought the other one around and sliced through the zombie's throat. He pulled both blades free and jumped back as the zombie's body fell in a heap beside the first one.

"You have had your turn," the minotaur battle wight said, hefting its double-bladed axe. Dark energy crackled along the edges of the blades. "Now I shall have mine."

The battle wight charged toward Nu Alin, lowering its head to gore with its sharp horns. Nu Alin dove to the side. The horns barely missed as the undead minotaur rushed by. The creature surprised Nu Alin, however, as it was able to stop its motion with much more precision than Nu Alin had expected. It immediately swung its axe, using the long reach provided both by its size and the handle of the axe to strike Nu Alin with the flat of the axe head.

Necrotic energy flowed from the axe head into Nu Alin with the blow, even as the force of the impact hurled his vessel toward the far wall.

Tempest's body smashed into the wall of the corridor, momentarily rattling Nu Alin and Tempest alike. The body crumpled as it slid down the wall and came to rest on the cold stone floor.

"Another falls to my axe," the battle wight said as it moved to finish off the living creature that had dared to invade its lair.

The necrotic energy, clearly some sort of soul-draining attack, had scrambled Nu Alin's thoughts and allowed Tempest's mind to surge forward. She looked up to see the battle wight approaching in the dim light emanating from the side passage. Without thinking, a curse came to her lips and suddenly liquid fire was cascading down on the battle wight. The clinging flames burned with intense heat, and they continued to burn even after the rain of fire had ended.

Nu Alin reasserted control over Tempest then, shoving her consciousness back into the darkness. *You should have let the creature kill you*, he thought so that Tempest could hear him.

A mistake I won't make again, she thought back.

Nu Alin was up and dancing around the burning battle wight, striking over and over with the razor-sharp daggers. Before the fire had burned itself out, the minotaur fell.

Nu Alin looked at the three bodies. His borrowed form hadn't been seriously hurt in the exchange, and for that he was thankful. He would have to be more careful while he occupied this vessel. The tiefling was not going to make it easy for him.

You can say that again, Tempest thought, filling each word with as much hate and anger as she could manage.

5 1 THE SHINING ROAD, DAY

Kalaban walked briskly into the dark passage until the dim light of the Seven-Pillared Hall faded behind him. He allowed his natural darkvision to come to the fore and took a moment to get his bearings in the unyielding darkness. The twenty-foot-wide corridor must have been grand in its day, for the ornate arches that were spaced every forty feet or so along the walls and held the domed ceiling aloft were decorated in striking *bas relief* of dwarven design. Kalaban saw that there were still a number of disks of silver embedded down the center of the floor and ceiling. These disks would reflect the light of a torch if he had had one and had given this underground passage its name: the Shining Road.

The Shining Road cut through a maze of ruined chambers known as the Labyrinth before meeting up with the Avenue of Glory and eventually traveling north beneath the Old Hills. When the minotaurs of Saruun Khel ruled this underground kingdom, the place was magnificent, a wonder to behold. Now the entire complex was a haunted ruin, occupied by squatters such as the Mages and their merchant tenants, as well as by ancient memories of a time long past. Kalaban wondered again what had drawn him into the Labyrinth as his hand found the comforting shape of the glass vial within his belt pouch.

The knight-commander made his way down the wide passage, pausing every so often to examine an ornate pillar or a disk of silver set into the floor. He could hear movement in the corridors and chambers that led away from the Shining Road. There were things moving in some of the dark openings that he passed, but he ignored them. Whatever had drawn him away from the Seven-Pillared Hall wasn't in these side chambers. It was somewhere up ahead, beyond the terminus of the Shining Road.

Kalaban tried to get a sense of what he was searching for, but he couldn't put words to the compulsion that had drawn him in this direction. He lost track of time as his mind wandered, which was very unlike the knight-commander. He was not usually one who went in for introspection and deep thought. His gloved fingers caressed the glass vial absently as he finally registered the new sounds emerging from the darkness around him. He wasn't sure how long the new sounds had been building, but he was quite certain that he had allowed whatever was making the noises to completely surround him. Was he losing his edge? Had the centuries trapped within the stale dream of Darani somehow affected his mind? He had certainly seen the madness build in the emperor. Had Kalaban succumbed to the same affliction?

He reluctantly let go of the glass vial and tried to focus on what was happening around him. In addition to the sounds, Kalaban could smell a foul odor, and the smell was growing stronger. Now the knight-commander could make out shapes moving at the limit of his vision, circling around him as they filled the passage with their overpowering stench. If Kalaban were alive, the smell would have had him retching and gasping for air. Because he was undead, it just made the mood he was in even fouler. He drew his soulsword from its sheath.

"Let's determine how many of you I have to kill before you realize what a terrible mistake you've made this day," Kalaban said.

A stocky reptilian humanoid wearing robes cut from the hides of large beasts stepped forward. The creature carried a quarterstaff with a crystal tied to its top, and a cap fashioned from a horned skull sat atop its head. A troglodyte, Kalaban decided, although he had never actually had the opportunity to fight such creatures. Well, he thought, there's a first time for everything.

The troglodyte began to chant in a language that Kalaban didn't understand, and the crystal atop the creature's staff pulsed with a soft glow that mimicked the rhythms of the chant. The glow radiated away from the troglodyte in a burst, briefly illuminating the six other trogs and the large, four-legged lizard with a spiked frill framing its head. As the glow touched them, the chanter's allies began to move with supernatural speed. The trogs raced around him, still staying beyond the reach of his sword. The large lizard, meanwhile, which Kalaban decided was some kind of drake, scraped one clawed paw across the stone floor as though getting ready to charge.

The chanter spat out what could only be a curse of some sort, and a dark ball of crackling power rolled out of its staff and splattered across Kalaban's armor. The knight-commander almost laughed, because the chanter had used necrotic energy against him. It had no effect whatsoever.

"Necrotic powers don't work very well against the undead," Kalaban said, but it was evident that the troglodyte couldn't understand him any better than he understood the chanter. "My turn."

The knight-commander started to move toward the chanter. Before he had taken more than two steps, however, the drake exploded into motion. It moved almost blindingly fast and was on Kalaban before he had been able to prepare himself for the charge. It struck with both of its foreclaws, raking long gashes across the front of Kalaban's armor. The weight of the creature and the speed at which it plowed into Kalaban knocked the death knight back. He rolled and sprang up, his sword at the ready, just as the other trogs raced toward him.

Before Kalaban allowed the troglodytes to strike, he slashed his sword in a great arc. It cut through the two trogs that had gotten closest to him, spraying blood and coaxing cries of pain from the wounded creatures. A third trog was able to dodge to the left thanks to the supernatural speed the chanter provided. It avoided Kalaban's blade and countered by throwing a javelin at the knight-commander.

It tore through his shoulder and carried him back, pinning him to the wall.

The trogs regrouped around the chanter and marched toward Kalaban as a unit. The chanter controlled the drake, commanding it to stay behind with a click of its tongue and a hand motion. The group stopped about ten feet away from where Kalaban was pinned. The chanter took a few additional steps so that he could better study the death knight. Kalaban watched the chanter, waiting to see what the trog would command next. When the chanter raised its staff, the six troglodytes plodded forward, raising clubs and javelins as they prepared to finish off the knight-commander.

"When I fall," Kalaban said, even though he knew the troglodytes couldn't understand him, "it won't be to the likes of you." A burst of unholy flame exploded from Kalaban, catching the troglodytes in a combination of fire and necrotic energy. The creatures reeled back and howled in excruciating pain. The two that Kalaban had already wounded went down in flaming heaps, but the remaining five fell back and tried to escape the hungry fire.

Kalaban pulled himself along the shaft of the javelin and wretched his shoulder free, leaving the javelin sticking in the wall. His soulsword, its blade ignited by the unholy fire, slashed out two times, and two more of the foul-smelling creatures fell. He turned to deal with the chanter, whom he considered to be the real threat in this group, just in time to see the creature send out a burst of healing light that restored a small amount of vitality to the three remaining troglodytes. Their burns didn't completely disappear, but they had healed enough to keep them in the battle. Kalaban used his own power to close the wound in his shoulder, but he never took his eyes off the chanter.

The chanter, now obviously wary of the knight-commander, made a clicking sound and pointed its staff at Kalaban. The drake leaped forward at the command, positioning itself between Kalaban and the remaining troglodytes. The chanter said something else that Kalaban couldn't understand, and then the three troglodytes slipped back into the darkness beyond the limits of his vision. That left Kalaban and the drake alone in the passage. "I don't imagine that you'd be willing to call it a draw and be on your way?" Kalaban asked the drake without expecting an answer.

The drake roared, extending its spiked frill as far as it could to make itself appear to be even larger than it was.

"Yes, of course, to the death," Kalaban mused, bringing his souls-word up and preparing to deal with the drake's next charge.

The drake came on strong, its powerful jaw snapping open and closed as it tried to deliver a devastating bite to the knight-commander. Although the creature was powerful, it was no match for Kalaban. Kalaban's soulsword struck again and again while he easily evaded the drake's predictable attacks. It only took a few moments for Kalaban to deliver enough deep cuts and slashes to drive back the drake. Then, feeling a surprising sensation of mercy, he buried his blade into the creature's skull, ending its pain and misery with one swift stroke.

Kalaban quickly looked around, but it was apparent that the remaining troglodytes had fled, sacrificing the drake so that the chanter could escape. The knight-commander wiped the blood from his blade and returned his weapon to its scabbard. He no longer felt compelled to rush blindly into the darkness, but he needed to understand what was happening to him. What was out there in the Labyrinth? And why did he feel compelled to find it?

"I guess there's only one way to find out," Kalaban muttered. He knew that Magroth was going to be furious with him for abandoning his post, but he had to press on.

He had to.

5 2 THE MINOTAUR GATE, TWILIGHT

Falon and his companions rode through the pine forest along a steep cobbled path toward the base of Thunderspire Mountain. Gray, foreboding clouds crowned the upper portion of the mountain, hiding it behind a storm of blackness punctuated every so often by a flash of brilliant lightning. With each flash, a rumble of thunder reverberated among the rocky hills around them. It sounded like approaching doom.

Falon and Darrum, along with Erak, Shara, and Uldane, had joined up with Albanon and Roghar back on the Trade Road, and now they were all traveling together into the mountain. It felt crazy, but it also felt exhilarating, just like the stories that Falon's grandfather used to tell him. While young Falon wouldn't go so far as to say he felt like an adventurer, he did feel as though he was on an adventure. Now if he could only figure out why undead monsters were trying to kill him, he'd be better able to appreciate the new sights he was seeing since leaving the village of his birth.

The cobbled road rose through a valley of sparse vegetation, eventually leading to the base of the mountain. Water washed down from higher up the mountain, dressing the side of the cliffs in curtains of cascading liquid. As they drew closer, Falon saw that a fifty-foot-tall stone archway had been hewn into the mountainside. To each side of the opening, a towering colossus carved into the shape of a minotaur gazed down as if to welcome travelers. Or to warn them off, Falon thought more likely as he got a better look at the scowls carved on their faces.

"The grand entrance to the kingdom of the minotaurs, Saruun Khel," Darrum said as they approached the opening.

"I've been here a few times with my master," Albanon said, "and each time these statues made me feel small and insignificant."

"A lesson you'd do well to remember at other times," the pseudo-dragon Splendid said from her usual perch atop the eladrin wizard's shoulder.

The group had yet to exchange any meaningful information, except that they had all admitted that the mountain was their destination. Falon wondered what the dragonborn paladin and the eladrin wizard were up to. For that matter, he still wasn't completely sure why he and his companions were heading into the mountain, either. He just knew that Erak believed that this was where his mission was taking them, and he had agreed to trust the revenant—at least for the time being. Soon, however, he'd need to figure out what was going on and what he was going to do next, the revenant's visions notwithstanding. He would pray to Erathis for guidance before he fell asleep tonight, he decided. Erathis's light would guide him, just as it always had.

"I think that we need to decide on a course of action before we enter the mountain," Shara said as they made their way between the massive statues. She had grown unusually quiet the closer they had gotten to the mountain. In the distance, thunder boomed.

"The Road of Lanterns leads to the settlement known as the Seven-Pillared Hall," Albanon said. "Stay on the road and you shouldn't run into any trouble."

"And what about you?" Darrum asked suspiciously. "Aren't you going to the Seven-Pillared Hall?"

"No," Albanon admitted quietly. "We have another destination in mind."

Erak looked from Albanon to Roghar and then to his companions. He shook his head. "We need to stay together," he said. "What the Raven Queen has joined must not be parted."

"I respect the Lady of Fate," Roghar said gravely, "but I follow the path of Bahamut. We have our own quest to get back to, but we wish you good fortune with your own."

"Maybe," Uldane said quietly, speaking for the first time since they turned off the Trade Road, "it's time for us to share our tales. Then we can see just how similar or different our quests happen to be."

"Out of the mouths of halflings," Darrum chuckled.

Albanon exchanged a glance with Roghar, who nodded slightly.

"Very well," the eladrin wizard said. "Let's head for the Halfmoon Inn. We're probably better off reaching the Hall before full darkness."

"Isn't it always dark under the mountain?" Falon asked.

"You don't know the half of it," Shara said as the companions rode into the mountain.

53 THE SEVEN-PILLARED HALL, TWILIGHT

He went where?" Magroth asked, leaning against the stoneguard as he made sure he completely understood the ogre towering over him.

"Ran off," Brugg said again, clearly flustered by the undead wizard. "Headed right for da arch ta da Shinin' Road."

Magroth nodded appreciatively. "Ah, Kalaban, anticipating my needs. He must have gone to clear the path, since that happens to be where we're going next."

"Such capable help is so hard to find," said Barana Strenk, stepping out of the shadows around the base of the minotaur statue.

"The lovely Barana," Magroth said, bowing slightly to the death priest. "I might start to think that you don't trust me if you keep turning up like this."

"Trust is overrated, Emperor Magroth," Barana said. "I bring news that could aid you in your quest."

"As much as I enjoy our quiet moments alone, please get on with it. I have much work to do before my time in this world runs out."

Barana forced a smile on her hard, sharp face. "A new opponent has entered the arena. The Lady of Fate has decided to send one of her knights to disrupt your plans. She doesn't like to see my master succeed at anything."

"A revenant?" Magroth laughed. "Does the Raven Queen really think that a revenant can challenge me?"

"That's not all," Barana said, a twinkle suddenly lighting up her hard, dark eyes. "Your descendent travels with the revenant. They'll both arrive in this underground hovel before night falls on the world outside."

Magroth gave the death priest a respectful nod. "You really want me to deal with my descendent, don't you?"

Barana returned a slight nod. "I am just trying to help you complete the tasks that Lord Orcus has set before you."

"Lord Orcus?" the Ordinator Arcanis gasped, his gold mask once more hiding his face from those in the Hall. "I must protest, Emperor Magroth. You have brought things that do not concern the Mages of Saruun to our doorstep in the Seven-Pillared Hall. We want nothing to do with the struggles between Orcus and the Raven Queen."

"Neither do I," snapped Magroth, "but so few of us ever get what we truly want."

"I have given you the news," Barana said. "I shall leave you to deal with things as you see fit."

"Of course you will," Magroth said as Barana stepped back into the shadows and disappeared from the Hall. "Let's go find Kalaban," he said, tapping his knuckles on the stone golem.

"But Emperor Magroth," the Ordinator Arcanis said hastily, "what about the revenant?"

Magroth shrugged. "Tell him and my cursed descendent where I've gone. They can catch up with me if they so desire."

And then Magroth and his stone golem started toward the dark archway in the northern wall of the cavern.

54 THE SEVEN-PILLARED HALL, NIGHT

Uldane noticed that Shara had begun to trail the rest of the party as they reached the end of the Road of Lanterns. He always found their visits to the ruins of Saruun Khel to be extremely interesting. Borojon had led them into the Labyrinth on four separate occasions over the years, each time to deal with a problem for one of their patrons or to dig up some bit of historical curiosity for Valthrun the scholar back in Winterhaven. Uldane missed listening to the old scholar's stories.

Uldane had counted to make sure that all seventy-seven statues were still in place along the brick-vaulted length of the Road of Lanterns. Each statue depicted a different demon, and Uldane wished that he could linger and study each one to determine their similarities and differences. But no one ever let him linger. "You'll get into trouble, Uldane," they'd always say. They didn't understand. Trouble is what he wanted to get into! Well, not trouble exactly, but Uldane loved to discover new things and leap into new adventures. It was what he did! Borojon and Jarren had come closest to understanding that. He missed Borojon and Jarren. He even missed grumpy old Cliffside. A lot.

The Road of Lanterns got its name from the magical lanterns that hung along the length of the downward-sloping passage. Uldane had studied the copper lanterns at great length during one of their visits. The lanterns were spaced just far enough apart so that you could barely see the next one in the darkness ahead, but you had to move from the light into the darkness to reach the next dim pool of radiance. He thought that it would be useful to have one of these ever-glowing lanterns, but when he had pried one from the wall the magic immediately faded. Borojon yelled at him for that, he remembered gloomily. "That magic was for the use of all," Borojon had said, "not just for the amusement of a curious halfling!"

He let his horse slow so that he fell back into step with Shara. She looked miserable. The halfling knew what she was thinking. They were going to the Seven-Pillared Hall. To the Halfmoon Inn, in fact. That's where they first met Jarren. Poor Jarren. Uldane remembered the lucky coin that was in his pocket, the coin that he had borrowed from Jarren and had tried to return before the dragon attacked. Tears welled up in the halfling's eyes. Was Jarren's death his fault? Because he had the lucky coin and not Jarren during the dragon battle?

"Shara," Uldane began, but Shara shook her head.

"Not now, Uldane," she said. "Please, just leave me alone."

Uldane thought about telling Shara about the coin. He thought about giving her the coin so that she could have something of Jarren's. He thought about telling her how Jarren's death might have been his fault. He thought about all of these things and more in the space of a few seconds, and then he lowered his head.

"Sorry," was all that Uldane managed to say, but he continued to ride alongside his friend as they emerged from the passage into the Seven-Pillared Hall.

55 THE AVENUE OF GLORY, NIGHT

Nu Alin examined the wide passage through Tempest's eyes. Great statues lined the walls of the passage, each depicting a minotaur hero, a fearsome monster, or a terrible demon of some sort. One of the nearest statues, that of a minotaur with a wizard's staff and spell book, was cracked and broken. The horned head and a part of the spell book had broken off and were lying on the floor at the statue's base. For the moment, the wide passage was silent. No creatures that Nu Alin could detect were in the immediate vicinity.

Nu Alin had managed to push Tempest's consciousness back and had contained it, but she was incredibly strong willed. He would have to tread carefully with this vessel. She had the capacity to exert control if he let his concentration waver, and in the middle of a battle or other dangerous situation, that could cause his mission to end before he had recovered the Voidharrow and set it free. That he could not allow.

Nu Alin rummaged through Tempest's pack and found a length of rope, a hammer, and a few pitons. He wedged one of the pitons into a crack in the wall, setting it so that it was about the same distance above the floor as Tempest's knee. He tied one end of the rope around the piton, tugged it once to determine that it would hold, and then he turned and leaped the fifty feet to the other side of the passage. At the far wall, he repeated the process so that the rope stretched across the dark corridor.

Nu Alin reached out with his senses, seeking the presence of the Voidharrow. It was closer, but still not close enough to grasp. But it would come to him, exerting control over the thief that possessed it not unlike how he controlled the tiefling. Not the same, of course, but similar. All he had to do was wait and the thief would bring the Voidharrow to him. He climbed up behind the statue of a winged demon, using muscles that the vessel had honed so that he didn't have to put as much of his own power into the process as he had had to do with some of the other bodies he had worn. He wedged Tempest's body between the wall and the back of the statue, allowing the form to rest more or less comfortably in the darkness about ten feet above the floor of the wide passage.

Now we wait, thought Nu Alin.

In the darkness at the back of Tempest's mind, he could sense the tiefling's struggle.

You cannot break free, Nu Alin told Tempest.

That made the tiefling struggle even more vigorously.

Nu Alin forced the tiefling's lips into a smile. If he had to wait, he might as well enjoy himself. And Nu Alin began to feed on the fear that rippled through Tempest's deepest thoughts.

56 THE SEVEN-PILLARED HALL, NIGHT

Erak sat at the large, round table, his back against the wall. The rest of the companions were seated around the table, and food and drink had been brought by the halflings that ran the establishment. They were in the Halfmoon Inn, a large building built into the southern wall of the Seven-Pillared Hall, just to the west of the waterfall that fed the river that divided the Hall in two. The Halfmoon family owned and operated the inn, which included a taproom and a trading post, and Erak could see the resemblance on each of the many halfling faces that moved through the large room carrying trays and pitchers to the customers.

Shara sat to Erak's right, with Uldane beside her. Falon and Darrum were next around the table, and the old dwarf was already digging into a platter of roasted potatoes. Albanon and Roghar sat to Erak's left, while the pseudodragon Splendid crawled across the table, examining each bowl and platter in turn. "I prefer the food back in Moorin's tower," the pseudodragon sulked as she snatched a slice of baked fish from one of the platters.

"Let's get on with this," Darrum said, scooping more potatoes on to his plate.

"I'll start," Falon decided, speaking low so as not to let the rest of the room overhear their business. "A few days ago I was an apprentice cleric at a small shrine in the village of Nenlast. Several undead creatures attacked the shrine and tried to kill me. Darrum came to my rescue, and we've been on the run ever since."

"Why do the undead want to kill you?" Roghar asked.

Before Falon could answer, Darrum said, "Some kind of family matter. We're not exactly sure."

Falon gave the dwarf a strange look as he absently tugged the sleeve of his left arm down to his wrist. Erak was glad that the young cleric decided not to add any further details to Darrum's explanation. Better to keep Falon's true heritage a secret, at least until they got to know Albanon and Roghar a bit better.

"So why have you come to the Seven-Pillared Hall?" Albanon asked.

"That was at my request," Erak said. "Before we get to that part of the story, Shara should tell you about her and Uldane."

Shara gave Erak a hard look. She didn't want to talk about what had brought her to this location, didn't want to dredge up the memories that nevertheless haunted her. Erak placed his hand on hers. "Tell them," he said gently, and Shara nodded.

The woman warrior took a long pull on the tankard in front of her. She wiped her mouth on the back of her hand, a distant look creeping into her eyes. "We hunted the green dragon Vestapalk," she said, speaking more to herself than to any of the companions. "The foul creature had been terrorizing the land around Winterhaven, and we were the best there was in the area. But we weren't good enough. There were five of us, seasoned adventurers all. Borojon, my father, led the group. In addition to me and Uldane, we were accompanied by the paladin Cliffside and the fighter Jarren."

Shara took another long drink, tears glistening at the corners of her eyes.

"We hunted the dragon for five days, following its trail of destruction into the Cairngorm Peaks," Shara continued. "That's where we caught up with the dragon—or the dragon let us catch up with it. Vestapalk killed Cliffside and Borojon. It would have killed me if Uldane hadn't knocked the two of us out of the path of its poison breath and over a ledge into a fast-moving river far below. As we fell, I saw the dragon. . . . "

Shara's throat seized up and she couldn't find the words to continue. She stood up from the table and moved away, fighting to keep the tears at bay a little longer.

"Um," Uldane said hesitantly, looking from Shara to the companions at the table and back again. "Vestapalk killed Jarren, too," he said at last. "We're going to find the dragon, and we're going to kill it. That's the promise that Shara and I made after we pulled ourselves out of the river and returned to Winterhaven."

Roghar looked at the halfling rogue with obvious admiration, but he still had to ask the question that came to his mind. "The Seven-Pillared Hall seems a rather unlikely place to hunt for a green dragon that lairs in the mountains to the west."

"And so we come to my story," Erak said. "I awoke in a stone coffin, which was sealed within a stone mausoleum in the graveyard outside Winterhaven. I have few memories of the time before I awoke. I remember the voice of the woman, a woman I believe might be the Raven Queen, but I don't know that for certain. The voice told me to get up and get on with the work I was to do. The voice called me 'my champion,' for whatever that is worth, and I found these clothes and weapons wrapped and waiting for me within the mausoleum."

"I recognized you as a revenant when you first came to our aid," Albanon admitted. "I've studied lore concerning revenants and read a few accounts of revenant heroes in the histories of Andral the Sage."

"Then you probably know more about me and my kind than I do, friend eladrin, for my memories remain fragmented and incomplete. But I have felt a number of . . . compulsions since I awoke. I felt compelled to go to the aid of Shara and Uldane when kobolds ambushed them on the King's Road. I felt compelled to ask Falon and Darrum to join us when we encountered them at Fallcrest. I felt compelled to lead us all here, to Thunderspire Mountain, and along the way I felt compelled to help you drive off the Wolf Runners. I believe that whatever force has directed me back to this world, be it the Raven Queen or some other unknowable power, has brought us together for a purpose that I have yet to fully understand. But we need to stick together. We need to aid each other, for our quests are linked in a way that I feel will soon become clear."

Erak decided not to add that Shara believed that he was Jarren returned to life. Just as with Falon's heritage, there were secrets that it wasn't yet time to share. And, although he hadn't tried to dispel Shara's feelings, Erak didn't believe that her impressions were totally correct. Although he felt a strong connection to the warrior woman, he felt no such connection to the name or memory of Jarren.

"You've heard our tales," Darrum said, turning to look at Albanon and Roghar. "What's your story?"

Albanon swallowed hard, letting his eyes drop to stare at the table. The pseudodragon moved to the young wizard's side, rubbing up against his arm until the eladrin placed his hand on the creature's neck and began to pet her gently.

"I was apprenticed to the great wizard Moorin, who controlled the Glowing Tower in Fallcrest," Albanon said quietly. "I returned to the tower a few night's ago to find that the wards had been disabled. On the upper level of the tower, I found Moorin murdered, his bloody body among the wreckage of the room that suggested that a mighty battle had taken place."

"I saw it all," Splendid added. "An alien *thing*, not of this reality, wore the body of a female halfling as though it was a suit of ill-fitting clothing. It was looking for something, and it killed the Great Moorin without any sense of mercy or trepidation."

"Roghar and his companion Tempest agreed to accompany me to find the villain," Albanon explained. "We followed the halfling-thing south, across the Moon Hills to the ruins of Kalton Manor. It was a terrible creature, wearing the halfling much as Splendid said, although by this point the body had taken a considerable beating and strange, red liquid run through with streaks of silver and flecks of gold oozed from wounds that would have brought down a larger creature. It recognized that I was a wizard, but it seemed to have little understanding of the arcane arts. It demanded that I send it after 'the Voidharrow,' whatever that was. It seemed to believe that the magic circle in the ruins had been used to teleport someone to a distant location. I . . . tricked . . . the creature. I figured that if I sent it into the Labyrinth beneath Thunderspire, it would either get well and truly lost or be attacked and destroyed by the monsters that prowl the constant dark under the mountain."

When Albanon paused, Falon asked the question that was on everyone's mind. "Where's your companion? Where's Tempest?"

Albanon tried to speak, but no words came out of his open mouth. So Roghar picked up the narrative. "The halfling-thing leaped into the glowing portal that Albanon had opened," Roghar said, his voice distant and lacking emotion. "Unfortunately, it took Tempest with it when it left."

"We're going to try to find them," Albanon finally managed to say. "We're going to try to save Tempest before. . . . " He trailed off, and neither Roghar nor Splendid decided to finish the thought.

The others fiddled quietly with their tankards and plates of half-eaten food as Shara returned to her seat. She looked at Erak, who nodded. Then she said in a strong, clear voice, "Our quests may be connected or they may not be, but it is clear that Albanon and Roghar need our help. Whatever else we're here to do, surely we must have come together to track down this alien *thing* and save your friend Tempest. That's what I feel compelled to do. What about you, Erak?"

Erak smiled grimly. "Yes," he said, "I have a similar feeling concerning this."

Albanon looked at the companions gratefully, but before they could discuss the situation further, the door to the inn burst open. A large, well-dressed ogre pushed his bulky frame into the common room. A regal looking figure in black robes and wearing a gold mask followed a moment later.

"The Ordinator Arcanis," Albanon said with something like awe in his voice.

Erak moved to stand up, but the ogre used the back of its large hand to knock the revenant back into his seat.

"No need ta get up on our accounts," the ogre said. "Stay seated an' we'll get tru dis real quick."

The Ordinator glided to the companions' table, his stylized mask unreadable. A deep voice issued forth from beneath the gold mask. "I have been tasked with relaying a message to you, honorable revenant," the Ordinator said. "The Mages of Saruun have no desire to get between the agents of either the Raven Queen or Orcus, and we ask that you take your conflict out of the Seven-Pillared Hall."

"The message?" Erak prompted.

"His eminence, Emperor Magroth of Nerath, bids that I tell you that he has taken the Shining Road north, toward the Old Hills," the Ordinator said. "If you wish to catch up with him, you'll need to hurry."

"Emperor Magroth? He died well over five hundred years ago," Darrum said, a hint of fear breaking the dwarf's usual composure.

Erak knew that name, but his memories refused to cooperate and he couldn't put anything into context. Still, the name made him feel uneasy.

"I assure you, dwarf, it was the Mad Emperor who left this Hall merely an hour ago," the Ordinator said.

"Undead," the ogre muttered, a noticeable shiver in his voice.

"One of you must be related to Magroth in some way," the Ordinator continued. "He also bid you follow after him."

"To what purpose, mage?" Shara demanded.

"I don't know and I don't care," the Ordinator said wearily. "I have dispatched the task assigned to me, and now I would like all of you to leave the Seven-Pillared Hall. We want nothing more to do with the affairs of demon princes or gods of fate and death."

The Ordinator Arcanis departed the common room as he had entered. The ogre followed after him, but not before he gave the companions a stern look and pointed at them menacingly, each in turn. He wiggled through the door frame that was two sizes two small for his massive bulk, and then he reached back in to shut the door.

"Allow me," said Erra Halfmoon, the halfling matron of the inn, as she slammed the door behind the departing Ordinator and ogre. Then she turned to the companions. "Well? What are you waiting for? Take your trouble and kindly get out of my establishment. Please."

"The Shining Road," Albanon said, collecting his pack from where it was sitting on the floor beside the table.

"What about it?" asked Darrum.

"That's the fastest way to get from the Hall to where I sent the halfling-thing."

Erak stood, motioning for the others to follow.

"Then it seems our path is clear," he said, and he headed for the door.

57 THE SHINING ROAD, NIGHT

Magroth strolled along the eastern wall of the wide passage, humming and running his fingers along the cool stone. The stone-guard followed behind him, silent except for the heavy footfalls of its massive feet. Light gathered atop Magroth's staff and illuminated the path, and the emperor felt almost giddy with anticipation. Soon, he would reach the hidden necropolis of Andok Sur. There, he would use the blood of his descendent to corrupt Barana's ritual to his own purposes. And then Magroth would be free. Free of the curse that bound him to the Shadowfell. Free of the obligations he owed to Orcus. Free!

"Where is that impertinent knight-commander?" Magroth wondered.

Soon the vampire-lich came to the remains of a recent battle. He increased the intensity of the arcane light floating atop his staff so that he could study the area. He easily noticed the slain rage drake and the bodies of the four dead troglodytes. There was a circular scorch pattern that had to have been created by Kalaban's unholy flames. Magroth kicked one of the dead trogs. "Well done, my servant," he said, willing to compliment the knight-commander when he wasn't within earshot.

The Mad Emperor extended his senses, letting his arcane sensitivity search for anything that could either be useful or dangerous in the area. It didn't take long for Magroth to see the traps hidden all along the passage. He laughed as an idea sprang to his mind.

"I need to meet this descendant of mine, but the rest of his companions are of no interest to me," Magroth said to the stoneguard. "No, not even the revenant."

He placed his hand on to the wall and reached into the stone with his arcane senses. It didn't take that much effort to activate the trap mechanisms. He imagined that after all these centuries some of the mechanisms might not function. But some should still work. After all, I'm still working after all these years," he laughed, and even the stoneguard took a step away from the vampire-lich.

"Let's see if my descendant and his friends can make it past these ancient traps," Magroth said.

Then he began to hum again, and he started walking northeast, in the general direction of the Old Hills.

The stoneguard pounded after him as pressure plates and trip wires and other mechanisms clicked into operation in the passage behind them.

58 THE SHINING ROAD, NIGHT

Roghar and the others rode into the wide passage known as the Shining Road. They had to work to control their mounts, because the animals weren't keen to travel in the darkness under the mountain. Albanon had called forth arcane light, so it wasn't like they were traveling in complete darkness, but it certainly wasn't the same as riding under the open sky.

"I can't believe that I've been thrown out of the Seven-Pillared Hall," Roghar complained. "That's an all-time low."

Uldane took a sunrod from his pack and activated the minor magic item. He slid the sunrod through a loop at his shoulder so that he could keep his hands free while still benefiting from the item's light. "I'll scout ahead," the halfling said, and he urged his horse into a gallop.

"And I'll keep an eye on Uldane," Shara said, following behind the halfling. "If he sees something shiny, he might disappear down a side corridor and we'd never see him again."

Roghar and Erak rode side by side, with Albanon close behind them. Bringing up the rear were Falon and Darrum. The dragonborn paladin whispered quietly to the revenant. "Is it Shara or Falon? he asked.

"I'm sorry?" Erak questioned back, but Roghar got the sense that the revenant knew exactly what he was asking.

"The descendant of the Mad Emperor. Anyone with the slightest amount of schooling knows about the story of Magroth the Mad and how he was assassinated by one of his own guards. His descendant must be a human, so that means it's either Shara or Falon. Which one?"

Erak gave the paladin a hard look. "Is that really important right now?"

"I'd rather know now so that when it does become important I'm ready for it."

"Fair," Erak nodded. "It's Falon. Darrum is an Imperial Shield and Falon is the heir to the throne of Nerath."

"Great," said Albanon. "That and five silver pieces will get him a room at the Nentir Inn. It's not like there's a throne and a kingdom just sitting around waiting for him to claim it."

"No, but Orcus still seems to want him dead," Erak said, "which means that I want to do everything in my power to make sure that doesn't happen."

"I can get behind that course of action," Roghar agreed.

"Good. I may need to call on your skills before this is all said and done."

Roghar nodded. "As long as we find Tempest first," the paladin said. "Then I'll help you in whatever way I can."

"As will I," said Albanon.

"An honest-to-goodness member of the royal blood," Splendid cooed. "You meet the most interesting people when you're out adventuring."

Uldane and Shara had halted just up ahead. Roghar and Erak rode over to meet them.

"Trouble?" Erak asked.

"You could say that," Shara said. "Uldane has spotted something."

"Well, spit it out, halfling," Roghar said. "The suspense is killing us."

"Traps," Uldane said quietly. "The passage ahead is full of traps."

5 9 THE AVENUE OF GLORY, NIGHT

Kalaban strode boldly through the darkness until he came to a fork in the path. The Shining Road continued to the left, while a passage adorned with heroic and monstrous statues split off to the right. The knight-commander hesitated for only a moment before deciding that his path was through the statue-lined passage. He could see perfectly well in the dark, and the statues in the passage were magnificent and terrifying. Many depicted demons of various sorts, but intermingled among the demons were a variety of minotaurs in heroic poses. A gallery of demons and heroes, all worshiped in one form or another by the minotaurs of ancient Saruun Khel.

He continued along the wide underground avenue, thinking of some of the parades he had participated in when the heart in his chest still beat and his flesh was warm and supple. The lines of bystanders were never this monstrous or ugly, Kalaban thought as he studied one of the demonic statues to his right, even in the outer territories.

Kalaban passed a number of small passages and side chambers that led away from the broad avenue he traveled. Every so often, he heard a sound from one of these dark openings—a scrape of metal or bone on stone, a low growl, or even a caw or cry or roar. He ignored these sounds. Whatever had drawn him into the depths of the Labyrinth, it was ahead of him and not in one of these side passages. No matter what strange sound emerged from either side of the avenue, Kalaban never slowed, never paused to determine what had made the noise. If it was important or overtly hostile, he had no doubt that it would emerge to confront him. He would deal with it then. For now, he stayed focused on his task and walked straight ahead into the darkness.

As Kalaban approached a section where another wide passage intersected the avenue from the left, he slowed his pace, took a few more steps forward, and then halted to examine the area. An ornate archway of worked stone framed the intersecting passage. Carvings associated with the demon lord Baphomet, the traditional object of worship for the minotaurs, adorned the archway, suggesting to Kalaban that some sort of temple or shrine was located in that direction. Something else had attracted the knight-commander's attention.

however, and he was trying to determine what had suddenly suggested a looming danger.

"You carry the Voidharrow," said a voice out of the darkness. The sound echoed among the statues and the far walls, making it impossible for Kalaban to pinpoint the speaker's location.

Kalaban drew his sword. "Show yourself," he called back, trying to spot the speaker in the vastness of the passage.

"Give me the Voidharrow," the voice said. This time it sounded as though it was coming from somewhere above him. Was it flying? Climbing? Hidden on some invisible walkway above the avenue?

Kalaban proceeded forward, moving cautiously as he strained to hear or see where the attack—and there would be an attack, of that he was sure—would come from. A sound from behind him made him jerk around. Something had landed on the stone floor more than a dozen feet away. It appeared to be a female tiefling in leather armor. She held a rune-carved rod in one hand. A warlock, Kalaban decided. But there was something not quite right about this tiefling. She reminded Kalaban of the way the female halfling back at Kalton Manor had moved, more like a puppet on a string than a living thing. And there were cracks radiating out from the corners of her eyes, shallow wounds filled with a glowing red ooze. Just like the halfling-thing. She raised the rod and arcane energy began to crackle along its length.

"Give me the Voidharrow, thief," the tiefling said, pointing the rod at Kalaban. "Give me the Voidharrow, or you will die and I shall take it from your corpse."

"Death does not concern me, creature," Kalaban said, stepping back to dodge whatever curse the warlock was about to throw. He decided that this was the same creature they had encountered at Kalton Manor, only it had traded the battered body of the halfling for that of the tiefling standing before him.

Something was stretched across the avenue, and it caught Kalaban between his ankles and his knees. Not expecting the obstacle to be there, he tripped and fell backward as the backs of his legs tried to move past it and met resistance. He hit the stone floor hard, realizing that he had just tripped over a taut rope. This time, he managed to maintain his grip on his sword.

The tiefling didn't hesitate. As soon as Kalaban began to fall backward, the tiefling leaped. It was an amazing leap that carried the tiefling some twenty feet into the air and across the distance that separated them. One second, she was more than a dozen feet away. The next, she was standing over him, pointing the blazing rod directly into his face.

"The Voidharrow," the tiefling said, staring down at him with a strangely emotionless expression. "I sense its presence upon you. Give it to me. Now."

Kalaban thought about the glass vial in his belt pouch. Was that what this body thief was after? Rage welled up in the knight-commander. How dare this creature demand what was rightfully his! He brought the blade of his sword up and knocked the rod aside just as it unleashed a stream of hellish fire. The flames scorched the stone floor to the left of Kalaban's head, but all he felt was a sudden wave of intense heat. He kicked out with one mailed boot, catching the tiefling in the stomach and driving her back.

He rolled away from the fire that still burned on the floor and got to his feet even as the tiefling regained her own footing. She unleashed the power channeled through the rod and another gout of flame exploded toward Kalaban. He caught the fire on the blade of his soulsword, diverting the heat and energy before it could reach his body.

The jerky motions and momentary pauses before the tiefling acted made Kalaban overconfident. He assumed that the tiefling would continue to project her next course of action before she did anything, as she had been doing both in this form and in the halfling form he had met earlier. The tiefling surprised him, however, by suddenly launching herself directly at him. Before he could react, she hit him in his armored chest with the fist holding the arcane rod. Energy danced from the rod to his armor, and the unbelievably powerful force of the blow hurled him into one of the nearby statues. He heard the stone crack as he struck the statue and crumpled to the ground. Pieces of stone and dust rained down from the many cracks crisscrossing the legs of the minotaur hero depicted above him.

Kalaban remembered the sounds as the helmed horrors fell before this creature back at Kalton Manor. He tried to focus as the body thief moved again. She was on him before his head had cleared or he had gotten his limbs to fully function. She brought the rod down, hard, knocking the helmet from his head and driving him into the stone floor.

"I tried to do this another way," the tiefling said, each word emerging at a slightly delayed cadence. "But let's face it . . . " A strange smile spread across the tiefling's face, as though whoever controlled the body wasn't yet completely familiar with how the muscles worked.

" . . . I am so much more comfortable with this approach."

And the tiefling brought the rod down.

Again.

And again.

And again.

60 THE SHINING ROAD, NIGHT

Uldane climbed down from his horse and bent to examine the corridor ahead. In the light cast by the sunrod tied to a loop on his shoulder, Uldane could see the telltale signs of a perilous section of trapped corridor arrayed before him. Space between the tiles that paved the road indicated the potential for the stones to open. Whether these openings would reveal hidden compartments or deep pits, he was certain that they promised danger and destruction.

And excitement, too, although Shara wouldn't want to hear him say that.

He never could understand why his friends weren't quite as eager to open the next door or leap across the next chasm as he was. He found the simple act of discovery, of finding out what was behind the next curved corridor or inside the mysterious crate, to be extremely rewarding. It was why he had become an adventurer in the first place. But everyone was always asking him to think or take a deep breath or get behind the big fighter with the sword and shield. Where was the fun in that? Uldane wanted to be at the front of every encounter, the first to see into the next chamber or experience the thrill of meeting a new monster. That was exciting!

Erak moved to stand beside Uldane. He stood silently for a few moments, looking at the same stretch of corridor that Uldane was studying, and then he asked, "What do you think?"

Uldane's face lit up at the question. "I've found the trigger mechanism for this particular section of the trap," the halfling rogue said excitedly. "See there? That tile and that tile and that one over there? Those are pressure plates. Step on one of those, and it activates the trap."

"And what does the trap do?"

Uldane shrugged. "Got me," he said. "Could unleash a rolling boulder to crush us. Or maybe poison darts will shoot out of the wall. There's really only one way to find out."

Uldane drew his short sword and moved to within an arm's length of one of the tiles he had identified as a pressure plate. He raised his sword high, preparing to hit the pressure plate with its tip.

"Uldane?" Erak asked calmly.

"Yes?"

"Should we step back or move to the side or something?"

"Hmm? Oh, yeah. That'd probably be a good idea."

Erak waved the rest of the companions back, and they each took a position against one of the corridor walls. Uldane glanced back and waited for Erak to signal him. When Erak nodded, Uldane's face broke into a wide smile.

"Let's see what happens," Uldane said, and he poked the stone tile with his sword. "This simulates what would happen if one of us had accidentally stepped on the tile."

The stone tile sank slightly into the floor as Uldane poked it. He drew back the sword and the tile snapped back to its original position. At the same time, the carved face of a minotaur, set into the wall about twenty feet farther along the road from the pressure plate, began to glow. Specifically, the stone orbs that were its eyes glowed with a pale blue light. Other than that, nothing happened.

Uldane stepped back to look around. He seemed disappointed as he shrugged and said, "Well, that wasn't very exciting."

Suddenly, a number of loud clicks echoed from the corridor ahead. The tiles that Uldane had noticed earlier, the ones with the spaces between them, slid open, revealing three separate five-foot-wide holes in the floor. Puffs of dust billowed into the air as each hole was exposed. At the same time, two more carved minotaur faces lit up as their eyes flared with arcane energy.

And that was it.

"Well, that wasn't very exciting, either," Uldane said dryly. "I was expecting so much more out of a place built by minotaurs."

But what happened next, Uldane would agree later, was much more exciting than he had anticipated.

A tall metal construct slowly rose out of each of the three holes.

Each was cylindrical in shape, about six feet tall, and made of a coppery metal that reflected the light of Uldane's sunrod. As the metal cylinders rose out of the holes, metal arms unfolded from each cylindrical body. They were long and flat and appeared to be extremely sharp. Like blades set around a central spoke. And then the blades began to spin.

"Uldane," Shara said with a bit of annoyance in her tone, "you can turn those things off now."

"Right, right," Uldane said absently as he watched the twirling blades in utter fascination. "I'll get right on that."

"Now Uldane!" Shara commanded, drawing her greatsword as the three spinning blades started to move toward them.

Uldane saw that the blades spun like a child's top, although he couldn't see what was making them move. Probably magic, he decided, which he never found to be quite as interesting as a clockwork construct or a complicated system of gears and pulleys. Still, even magical traps had rules. All Uldane had to do was figure out what the rules of this particular trap were, and then he could find a way to disable it. Provided, of course, that the twirling blades didn't kill him or his friends before he figured it out.

The spinning blades closest to Uldane began to chart a zigzag course across the tiles toward the companions. The whirling metal arms were a blur of motion, no longer identifiable as separate components. Uldane was certain that if the whirling blades hit him, they'd cut through him like a hot knife through soft butter. The thought didn't actually frighten the halfling. Nothing ever did. But it suddenly made him feel a little peckish.

As the first of the spinning blades rotated toward him, Uldane tumbled to the side and rolled under the blur of coppery metal. The blades spun around the center spoke at a height of about three feet, so by staying low the halfling was able to avoid being hit by the sharp metal. He sprang to his feet, checking to see where the other two spinning contraptions were. They were moving in zigzag patterns, one on each side of the passage, about ten feet or so from the walls. As Uldane studied the spinning blades, he noticed that they were doing something new now. In addition to spinning around the central spoke, the blades were now climbing up and down the spoke as well, making it impossible to simply duck under them as Uldane had just done.

"Clever," the halfling said.

"Uldane!" Shara called as she stepped forward to meet the first of the whirling blades. "Less appreciation, more disabling!"

"Right, right," Uldane said, dodging toward one of the carved minotaur faces with the glowing eyes.

The halfling rogue examined the life-sized *bas relief* of the minotaur face. It was set into the wall, about seven feet above the floor. It was extremely lifelike, as though a minotaur had pushed its face into the stone from behind. Maybe that's how they made it, Uldane thought. He studied the jutting horns that extended from the proud forehead. He poked at the eyes that looked like half-orbs of stone but that glowed with pale blue light. He admired the bulging muzzle, the flaring nostrils, the powerful teeth. And then he noticed the metal ring clasped firmly within the minotaur's teeth. It was covered with runes that also glowed, but the light here was softer, etched into the lines of the runes, and almost imperceptible compared to the light cast by the eyes. Uldane leaned back and put his hand to his chin as he considered his options.

Shara tried to block the spinning blades as the first contraption bore down on her. Sparks flared on the blades and across the length of her greatsword, and then she was hurled back by the strength of the impact. Darrum leaped into the space between the oncoming blades and where Shara had fallen, spinning his twin hammers as if trying to match the speed of the whirling metal arms.

"Uldane, if you have a solution, now is the time to use it," Erak commanded as he prepared to deal with the second contraption. Roghar moved to stand beside the revenant, while Falon and Albanon moved around and looked for another way to help out.

"Yelling at me isn't going to make me go any faster," Uldane complained as he turned back to examine the carved face. He reached out and grasped the metal ring. It was comfortably warm to the touch. He lifted it, and was suddenly reminded of the knocker on the door of Lord Padraig's manor back in Winterhaven. He let the ring drop, but it didn't make a loud sound like a knocker.

"Halfling!" Roghar bellowed as the spinning blades scraped across the front of his shield. "Time is running out!"

Uldane, his face scrunched in deep concentration, grabbed the ring again. This time, he turned the ring. It took all of the halfling's strength, but he was able to twist it to the right until he heard a distinct click. The pale blue light in the eyes immediately winked out, and the contraption slicing toward Darrum and Shara stopped spinning. Its blade arms fell limp at its sides, and then, without any motion to balance it, the central spoke tipped over and crashed to the ground.

"Who's the best?" Uldane asked, turning to face his companions with a big smile across his face.

"Uldane!" Erak shouted. "There's still two more!"

One of the metal contraptions, the one that had just been weaving toward Albanon, was now spinning back down the passage, heading directly for Uldane.

And the other two glowing minotaur faces were across the width of the passage, set into the other wall.

Uldane wasn't afraid. Not exactly. But he also wasn't sure if he could reach the right carving before the spinning blades cut into him.

And that would certainly ruin the good time he was having.

61 THE SHINING ROAD, NIGHT

Falon's mood went from jubilation as the first of the whirling contraptions stopped spinning and fell over to extreme fear as the other two seemed to spin faster and move with more purpose. The contraption in front of Roghar and Erak pushed forward, forcing the dragonborn and the revenant to leap back to avoid the unrelenting sweep of the spinning blades. The third contraption, meanwhile, had reversed its course and was now bearing down on Uldane. The halfling was against the far wall, apparently trying to decide if he could run across the passage before the spinning blades reached him and tore into him. Falon didn't want to have to take that bet.

"Did you see what the halfling did?" Albanon asked as he raised his staff high.

"He turned the ring, I think," Falon replied.

"Do you think you can do the same?"

"Turn the ring? Sure."

"Then go!"

Falon moved as close to the wall as he could and began to run toward the remaining two carved faces with the glowing eyes. As he did so, he heard Albanon speak in a low voice as the eladrin began to cast a spell. A cloud of frosty air arced from Albanon's staff and hit the ground beside the spinning contraption that was almost on top of Uldane. When the cloud touched the stone floor, ice spread out in a burst pattern from the point of impact. Immediately, the spinning contraption slipped and slid along the ice, crashing into the wall beside Uldane and falling over.

The blades continued to spin, however, striking sparks along the stone and rocking itself almost upright as each blade scraped across the ground. Uldane didn't wait to see if it would right itself. He leaped over the patch of ice and ran toward the carved face with the glowing eyes on the far wall. Falon matched his speed and ran toward the closer carving. They reached their respective carvings at the same time, just as the whirling contraption regained its balance on the ice and began to spin toward them.

"Turn to the right," Uldane called.

Falon nodded, grasping the metal ring and turning with all of his might.

Both carvings let out resounding clicks at the same instant. As the glowing eyes in each carved face faded, the remaining two contraptions stopped spinning and crashed to the ground.

"Got it," called Uldane triumphantly.

Falon smiled at the halfling. He couldn't help it. The little rogue's mood was contagious.

"Maybe we should give you a medal," Shara muttered as she pulled herself back to her feet.

"A medal? You think so?" Uldane asked with wide eyes. "I think I'd like a medal."

"We'll get right on that," she said gruffly, but Falon thought he saw a smile in her deep blue eyes.

"Onward?" Falon asked.

"Onward," Erak agreed.

62 THE AVENUE OF GLORY, NIGHT

Magroth strolled the ancient Avenue of Glory, marveling at what the minotaurs had managed to raise up during the heyday of their underground kingdom. The stoneguard followed behind him, its great footfalls resounding in the large, open space beneath the mountain.

"I was never able to gather any of the real monstrous races under the Nerath banner," Magroth said out loud, talking to the stoneguard as though it could understand him. "Made the human and dwarf populations squeamish. Yes, I did subjugate the dragonborn and the tieflings, but no one really thinks of them as monstrous. Not like the minotaurs. Or the trolls. What I would have given to have had a couple of tribes of giants at my disposal!"

Magroth paused, stopping to listen to sounds up ahead. Something heavy and metallic clanged in the distance. As the echo began to recede, he heard the crackle and roar of fire. Then there was more clanging, as though something heavy was being struck against a metal shield over and over again.

"Come, golem," Magroth said, suddenly intrigued. "Let's see what's going on."

The Mad Emperor made no attempt to be stealthy. Even if he had wanted to, the resounding pounding of the golem's heavy foot-falls would have made it impossible. But Magroth had no need for stealth. He was confident in his abilities and unafraid of anything that might be loose beneath Thunderspire Mountain. He approached two figures locked in battled beneath a statue that had seen better days. It was cracked across the middle and appeared to be ready to fall apart. Neither of the combatants even bothered to look up, so stealth wouldn't have mattered in the least.

Magroth saw that one of the two figures was Kalaban, his knight-commander. The other was a female tiefling who was bashing Kalaban's head over and over again with a heavy metal rod. The Mad Emperor imagined that such a beating must have been quite painful, but he was reasonably sure that Kalaban, being a death knight, wouldn't be too damaged when the tiefling was finished. He studied the tiefling as he got closer, noticing the lack of expression on her face and the strange tilt to the way she held her head.

Not even bothering to use his staff, Magroth made a casual gesture with his open hand and muttered a word of power. Lightning streaked from his hand and crackled through the tiefling's body. The force of the attack repelled her from her position over Kalaban, and she slid across the stone floor, leaving behind skid marks of dancing lightning that showed her path before dissipating like mist.

"Get up, Kalaban," Magroth said, "this is no time to be lying about like the prize pig before the slaughter."

The tiefling sprang to her feet, showing remarkable recuperative abilities despite the devastating attack that Magroth had hit her with. He saw a fire deep within her eyes, an expression that hadn't been there when he first examined her. He also noticed that the hand that held the rod was torn and bloody, and a strange crimson substance that wasn't blood was also oozing from the wounds. Actually, it was expanding and contracting out of and back into the wounds, as though the substance was breathing.

"The thief will give me the Voidharrow," the tiefling said in clipped, emotionless words. "You will not interfere."

Magroth saw, from the corner of his eye, that Kalaban was struggling to his feet. He kept his gaze locked on the tiefling as he replied, "If I had more time, this could turn out to be a fascinating exchange. But I have places to go and rituals to perform. So, you'll have to excuse me if I don't trade villainous remarks with you. Another time, perhaps."

This time Magroth focused his will through his staff, unleashing a blast of blue-white power that bashed into the tiefling and then held her firmly in place. The tiefling's eyes went wide, and she began to struggle wildly to break free of the invisible grip surrounding her. Magroth, meanwhile, motioned at the cracked statue and whipped his hand in the direction of the immobilized tiefling. In response to his motions, the top half of the statue pulled away from the base, splitting along the length of the cracks with a terrible grinding sound. The upper portion of the minotaur statue flew at the tiefling. It barreled into her and then smashed into the wall, burying her beneath what remained of the stone form.

Magroth turned away from the scene without a second thought and addressed Kalaban. "If you're done fooling around, knight-commander," the Mad Emperor said, "we really need to get a move on. My accursed descendent should be right behind us, and I don't want to have to deal with him until we reach Andok Sur."

Kalaban recovered his battered helmet. The wounds to his head were already repairing themselves thanks to his undead nature. "That was the halfling-thing that followed us to Kalton Manor," the knight-commander said.

"Really?" Magroth asked, looking back at the pile of shattered rock. "My, her persistence is almost a match for her sudden growth spurt."

Then, his interest in the subject apparently abated, Magroth resumed his march to the northeast, in the direction of the Old Hills. Kalaban and the stoneguard began to follow him, but Magroth raised his hand.

"Not you, golem," Magroth said. "Stay here and make sure that only my descendent passes this point. The others traveling with him? I want you to destroy them."

Magroth resumed his stroll down the Avenue of Glory, and Kalaban followed, leaving the stoneguard alone in the dark passage. They walked for about a hundred feet in silence. Then Magroth spoke in a low, threatening voice.

"I don't appreciate secrets, knight-commander," Magroth said. "You will tell me about this Voidharrow, and then I will decide if your value to me is worth the pain of your deception."

63 THE OLD HILLS, NIGHT

Tiktag held on tight as Vestapalk banked right and began to circle back the way they had come. The cold night air made the wyrm-priest's teeth chatter, and he still couldn't look down without his vision swimming and his stomach tightening into a clenched ball. The green dragon dropped its right wing, tilting its entire body so that Tiktag had to dig in tighter to avoid sliding off. He thought he felt rumbling laughter beneath the dragon's rough emerald scales.

"The Old Hills," Vestapalk said, returning to level and drifting above the rolling hills that filled the land south of Lake Nen.

Tiktag had never been this far from the tribe's usual hunting grounds around Winterhaven. He wasn't sure he liked traveling so great a distance, and he certainly knew that he didn't enjoy flying. Still, he reminded himself of the honor that had been bestowed on him by the green dragon, and he tried to use that feeling of prestige to calm his racing heart.

"The Herald shall soon reach this area," Vestapalk said, letting his sharp eyes scan the landscape for some clue about where the Herald would appear.

It seemed to Tiktag, who had his eyes shut tight, that they had flown a hundred circles above the hills when the green dragon finally exhaled a grunt of satisfaction.

"There, wyrmpriest," Vestapalk said. "That oddly shaped hill is no hill."

Vestapalk began to descend. This made Tiktag happier than he had been in a long time, but it also raised a question.

"Why there, Great Vestapalk?" Tiktag asked.

"I have seen such places before," the green dragon explained. "When the places that the lesser races build grow old and become abandoned, the land around them moves back in to reclaim what once was untouched. Even as dirt and vegetation covers the worked stone, you can see the shape of construction still evident beneath it—if you have the proper perspective, that is."

Vestapalk certainly was impressed with himself, Tiktag thought. It was good to be a dragon, he supposed. No one ever showed any respect to kobolds, but to dragons? They were feared. Sometimes Tiktag wished that others feared him. It was true that other kobolds feared him. He was their wyrmpriest, after all. But other creatures? Humans? Dwarves? Kobolds were laughed at, not feared. Tiktag believed that his alliance with Vestapalk would change that. As would the coming of the Herald. Between the two, Tiktag would finally achieve the respect that he so desperately craved.

And power. Let's not forget the promise of power that the Elemental Eye had offered to them. Well, actually the offer was made to Vestapalk, but Tiktag was sure that he would share in the reward. It was his destiny.

The green dragon landed beside the strangely shaped hill. Now that Vestapalk had pointed it out, the wyrmpriest couldn't help but see the right angles and straight lines beneath the contours of the hill. Some kind of keep, perhaps? Or maybe the walls of a town? But it had to be a truly ancient place to have been so absorbed back into the land.

"Find an opening, wyrmpriest," Vestapalk commanded, lowering its head and neck so that Tiktag could more easily dismount.

The wyrmpriest looked dubious. He was a mystic, not a tracker or a dungeoneer. What did he know about finding entrances into underground lairs? More to the point, how was he going to find an opening large enough for the green dragon to use?

Under the watchful gaze of Vestapalk, Tiktag began to explore the circumference of the hill. He walked slowly and carefully, examining every crack and crevice, every depression, looking for—actually, the wyrmpriest had no idea what he was looking for. But he didn't feel comfortable expressing that fact to the green dragon.

Around the next turn, Tiktag's staff punched through a clump of tall grass and brambles. He moved the wooden staff back and forth, realizing that there was a large space behind the overgrown vegetation. He used the staff to push away the brambles so that he could peer into the darkness beyond. Darkness posed no problem to the kobold. His darkvision allowed him to see in the dark as other creatures could see in bright daylight. The depression was shallow, a small pocket within the dirt and stone that made up the hill. The walls of the shallow depression were covered with intricate symbols that the wyrmpriest recognized.

"Orcus," Tiktag said, reflexively making a sign of warding.

"Squeeze inside and tell Vestapalk what you see," the green dragon urged.

Reluctantly, Tiktag stepped through the space he made in the brambles and entered the shallow depression. In addition to the symbols that were carved into the walls and low ceiling, there was a small pedestal of black stone. A hollow space atop the pedestal looked like it was waiting for some sort of peg. Or a key. The place made Tiktag uncomfortable. This was a place of death, clearly dedicated to the Demon Prince of Undeath. The kobold wyrmpriest wanted nothing to do with this kind of magic. And there was magic here. Tiktag could feel it like an approaching storm hanging thick on the air.

"It's some sort of antechamber," Tiktag called out. "There's a pedestal with a hole, but I don't know what fits into it."

"The Elemental Eye has seen true," Vestapalk said solemnly. "The one that carries the key shall arrive soon."

The green dragon turned to find a spot where it could rest and still keep a watchful eye on the small cave. Tiktag watched the dragon walk away.

"How do you know that?" the wyrmpriest asked.

"This one does not know it," said Vestapalk. "This one simply has faith."

Tempest slowly came back to consciousness. It was like swimming up out of a dark pool. She blinked, but the darkness remained. And there was pain. A terrible, crushing pain. But the alien presence was gone. No, that wasn't quite right. The alien presence was . . . sleeping? Unconscious? She could still feel it inside her mind, but it was no longer active or in control. For the moment, at least, Tempest's body was her own.

Unfortunately, she couldn't move. Something heavy was on top of her. It felt like stone. A statue of some sort? Probably. There were certainly enough of them scattered throughout the Labyrinth. It was shattered and broken, but she was trapped beneath the heavy stone. She could move her right arm, and her head wasn't buried, but the rest of her was pinned. She hurt all over, too. She felt like one massive bruise from her neck down to her toes.

"Hello," she called out, but her voice sounded weak even to her own ears, and she didn't think there was anyone or anything nearby to hear her. She was totally alone.

In the dark.

Beneath Thunderspire Mountain.

With an alien presence that had crawled up her nose and taken control of her body the way she might shove her hands into a pair of silk gloves. She shuddered at the memory.

Time passed, but Tempest had no way of knowing how much time. The darkness was absolute, unchanging, and there were no sounds in the immediate vicinity to latch on to. She had nothing but pain to keep her company. Pain, and the growing sense of the alien presence inside her. Nu Alin. It referred to itself as Nu Alin. And it was . . . waking up? That was the only way she could describe the sensation. And that sense of it returning, of once again assuming control of her, that frightened her as nothing she had experienced ever had before.

Wrapped up in her fear and the growing sense of dread that was welling up inside her, for long minutes Tempest didn't recognize the approaching sounds as a change in the environment. When it dawned on her that something was making noise, that something was getting closer, she felt a moment of hope. But she quickly squelched that feeling. There was no hope for her. Not while the alien presence was inside her, and especially not when it was reaching a point where it could once again exert control over her. She didn't want that to happen again.

"You're right," she heard someone say. "I should have noticed the tripwire. Sorry about that."

"Sorry?" another voice, angry, deep. "That blade almost cut me in two!"

"Not even close," the first voice said. "Darrum, it easily missed you by almost a foot! Now, if you weren't a dwarf. . . ."

Tempest could see light now, faint but growing brighter as it danced closer through the darkness. There were seven figures approaching, each atop a horse and illuminated by two distinct sources of light. One radiated from the shoulder of a halfling. The other glowed at the top of a long staff. She recognized the figure with the staff. It was the wizard Albanon. And riding boldly beside him was Roghar.

"Roghar!" Tempest called, but her voice barely exceeded the volume of a whisper.

It was enough, however. She saw that Albanon had heard her. He was pointing excitedly, and he and Roghar were rushing toward her.

"No," she pleaded, "stay back. The halfling-thing. It's inside me."

Albanon and Roghar reached her side. The dragonborn got right to work, trying to lift the heavy stones.

Albanon bent down beside her, expressions of relief and concern that almost made Tempest laugh battled across his angular face. "I'm sorry," he said, taking her free hand in his.

"Albanon," she managed to say. "You have to do what I say. Before the creature takes control again."

Now the wizard looked confused, apprehensive.

"Kill me," Tempest pleaded. "Now, while you still can."

6 5 THE AVENUE OF GLORY, NIGHT

Falon listened to the brief exchange. Had he heard the tiefling woman correctly? Did she ask Albanon to kill her? He didn't quite understand what the halfling-thing that Albanon had described was, but it seemed that the tiefling believed that it was inside her now. How had she gotten trapped under the fallen statue? What had happened here? Falon felt completely unprepared for whatever they were next going to encounter under the mountain.

"Cleric," Albanon said to Falon, though his gaze never wavered from the tiefling. "Do you think we can drive this creature out of Tempest?"

Falon looked young and helpless. "I'm still an apprentice," he said softly. "I've never even heard of anything like this. Your guess is as good as mine at this point."

Roghar continued to struggle with the fallen rubble, trying to lift the heavy weight off of the tiefling. He wasn't getting very far. Shara and Darrum moved to help him as he said, "If we do as Tempest asks, can you bring her back?"

"From the dead?" Falon sputtered. "I can't perform that level of miracle. I only ever saw my master attempt such a feat once in my time with him, and he wasn't able to successfully complete the ritual. This is just crazy."

"Please," the tiefling said again, her voice barely a whisper in the dark passage. "I can feel it growing stronger. I don't have much time. You need to kill me now. While you still can."

Erak walked over to stand beside Albanon. Roghar, Shara, and Darrum continued to strain against the fallen statue, but so far they hadn't been able to budge it at all. The three positioned themselves to improve their grips on the stone.

"On the count of three," Roghar said. "Three!"

The three physically strong adventurers strained and lifted with all their might. They were able to raise the broken statue enough for Albanon to slide Tempest out from under the crushing weight. Falon could see how badly hurt she was. He wondered if his healing powers would be enough to save her from her wounds.

"Tempest's death is not something I wish to contemplate," Roghar said, "but I will not see her controlled by this foul invader, either. Perhaps divine magic can be used to cast it out. Both I and the young cleric have some aptitude in this regard."

"Albanon," Erak said gently, "you saw this creature in action. I did not. What is your estimation? Is it as powerful as the tiefling fears?"

Tears welled in the eladrin's eyes. The pseudodragon curled around his neck had remained surprisingly silent. Finally, Albanon said, "Yes. It killed the great wizard Moorin. It's as powerful as that and more."

Erak nodded, and in one swift motion that Falon could barely follow, the revenant drew his hellsteel blade and plunged it into the tiefling's midsection. Tempest opened her mouth and screamed. It was a sound that chilled Falon to the bone, because it seemed to be two screams being loosed simultaneously from the same set of vocal chords. The sound was unnerving.

"Falon, Roghar," Erak commanded, "prepare yourselves. When we see the creature's true form, use your magic against it. Then you must heal the tiefling as quickly as you can. And whatever you do, don't let the creature get near you."

Two things happened very quickly then. First, Falon saw a crystalline substance flow from the tiefling's open mouth and nose. It was translucent red in color, though it had strands of silver and flecks of gold floating within the thick liquid. As the substance poured forth from the tiefling's dying body, great echoes of heavy stone striking heavy stone resounded out of the darkness ahead. A large form, like a man in granite armor, barreled out of the darkness and plowed into Roghar and Shara, knocking them to the ground. Darrum had managed to leap out of the stone creature's path, and Uldane moved to help him against the monster.

Falon decided that the others would have to deal with the golem or whatever it was. He had to concentrate on the strange crimson substance that even now was flowing toward Albanon. "Erathis, aid your servant," Falon prayed, pointing the sword of Nerath at the fast-moving substance. A lance of radiant light flew from the tip of *Arante's* blade and burned into the crimson-silver substance. Smoke rose from the spot where the light struck, and the radiance rippled throughout the substance as a lingering afterglow. It never stopped moving, despite the wound, but it instantly changed direction. Like a thing alive, like a thing with a cruel and calculating intelligence, the substance flowed away from Albanon and directly toward Falon.

"That's it, cleric," Erak said as he leaped to join the battle against the golem, "you've got it right where you want it."

Falon gulped as the substance flowed closer. It was a fast-moving puddle, about the size of a large dog. Before it was on top of him, Falon began to recite a new prayer. But before he could bring the power of his calling to bear, a portion of the substance extended and struck Falon in the midsection with a surprisingly powerful blow. It knocked the air out of him and sent him stumbling backward. Even as he tried to recover, the substance was on him. It was flowing up his leg, extending crude crystalline appendages toward his face.

It meant to enter him, through his nose and mouth, the way it had the tiefling.

Falon tried to focus, to hold back his growing fear and revulsion.

And then the crimson substance was flowing up his neck and chin.

66 THE AVENUE OF GLORY, NIGHT

Shara heard the great lumbering creature approaching before she saw it. By the time it slammed into the circle of light around the companions, it was too late for Shara to do anything other than prepare herself for the inevitable crash when the fast-moving, massive stone figure met armor and human flesh. The thing was shaped like a man, but the proportions were exaggerated. Its arms were too long, its body too broad, its feet too wide, and its head too small for it to be a human in a suit of stone armor. It had to be some sort of golem, and that was Shara's last thought before the creature plowed into her and Roghar and sent the two companions flying.

Shara rolled as best she could, but she still had the breath knocked out of her and her head rattled by the impact. She tried to stand up, but when she put weight on her left leg it collapsed beneath her. Her ankle had been twisted and she could feel it swelling up inside her boot. She hoped that was all it was. She hated when she broke bones, or at least when she broke her own bones. The thought of it, her leg bones snapping, perhaps a jagged edge breaking through her skin, made her feel a little queasy.

Unable to stand on both feet, Shara glanced around to see what the rest of the companions were doing. Roghar was already rolling back to his feet and preparing to engage the stone golem. Darrum had somehow avoided the initial encounter, and his twin hammers were spinning quickly as he waded in to battle the strange construct. Uldane was beside the dwarf, short sword in hand but looking a bit unsure about where to strike the stone creature.

She looked back toward where Erak had just plunged his sword into the tiefling woman. Now Falon was backing away from something that reminded Shara of an ooze, except it was unlike any ooze she had previously encountered. Albanon was seemingly in shock, staring down at the tiefling, who Shara assumed was dead by the eladrin wizard's expression. Erak moved up to her and briefly examined her hurt leg.

"Don't try to move," the revenant said, "you might cause more damage."

"Did you have to kill her?" Shara asked, ignoring the revenant's advice as she struggled to put her back against one of the intact statues.

Erak looked at her with something akin to a pained expression. Had she hurt the revenant's feelings?

"I did what had to be done," he said simply. "The rest is up to Falon. Now, if you'll excuse me, I should help the others against the stoneguard."

"The what?" Shara asked, but Erak was already moving to engage the golem from behind.

Shara watched as Darrum's twin hammers struck the stone form over and over, driving it back as Uldane danced behind him and yelled words of encouragement such as "good shot," "nice backhand," and "wow, that had to hurt." Roghar and Erak, meanwhile, attacked from behind, flanking the golem and striking sparks off the hard stone with every swing of their blades. For its part, the golem seemed unimpressed. It pounded its massive fists into the ground, sending forth shock waves that rattled through the corridor and forced the companions back.

Suddenly, the golem's small head snapped up and the blackness within the visorlike carving on its expressionless face seemed to fix on Falon. Shara followed the golem's gaze and saw that the young cleric was struggling against the crimson ooze that was even now flowing up his body. Erak leaped at the golem, but the stone construct swung its massive fist and connected with the revenant in midair. Shara almost felt the impact of the blow from her position some fifteen feet distant, and she winced as Erak was sent sailing into the far wall of the wide passage.

With the way now clear, the golem turned and began running toward Falon, each thundering footfall shaking the passage. Shara tried again to put weight on her injured leg, but it was no use. She wouldn't be able to get back into this fight.

Falon was on his own.

67 THE AVENUE OF GLORY, NIGHT

Albanon had stepped back when the crimson substance began to flow out of Tempest's wounded body. He had done so more out of reflex than out of any real sense of self-preservation. He was numb inside. His actions, however well-intentioned, had resulted in the state that Tempest was now in. She was gravely wounded, perhaps already dead, and the thing that had taken her was now flowing toward Falon.

And Albanon didn't care. He was staring at Tempest, trying to determine whether or not she was beyond help. And if she wasn't, he was trying to decide what help he could offer. Arcane magic, the magic that he was trained in, provided nothing in the way of healing.

He bent down to examine the tiefling. The wound that Erak had inflicted was bleeding freely, but at least the blood was a normal shade of red. It looked just the way blood was supposed to look, without any strands of silver or a crystalline consistency. Tempest was still alive, but he didn't think she would remain in that state for much longer.

"You need to help Falon," Splendid said. The pseudodragon was still draped around Albanon's shoulders, even though the wizard had forgotten that she was there. "He can heal the tiefling, but only if he survives the next minute or so against the thing that killed the Great Moorin."

Albanon could see that the strange substance was flowing up Falon's body, working its way toward his head and the orifices that it could use to slip inside the cleric. Even without aid, however, Falon wasn't finished yet. The young cleric's sword gleamed with divine light, and he jammed the blade into and through a portion of the crystalline ooze. Wherever the radiant blade touched, the crimson liquid sizzled and dark smoke curled in ribbons from the wounds. The attack must have been some kind of healing strike, for a spark of the divine light flew into Tempest and the tiefling opened her eyes and gasped for breath.

"He did it," Albanon marveled. "He healed Tempest, at least a little bit."

While the attack had helped Tempest, it didn't seem to slow the crimson substance. It continued to flow up and over Falon's face, trying to force itself into his mouth, his nose, his eyes.

Albanon tried to select a spell that would do something, anything to harm the alien ooze, but nothing in his repertoire had the touch of the divine. Still, he had to try. He unleashed a volley of magic missiles, and the arcane darts peppered into the ooze with unerring accuracy. Before he could call on another spell, however, the rough stone hand of the golem pushed him aside as the massive form rumbled toward Falon and the body thief.

The golem grabbed a fistful of the crystalline substance and tried to pull it off of Falon. Albanon wasn't sure what the golem was up to, or why it was apparently attempting to help the young cleric, but its thick stone fingers pulled right through the liquid crystal. It was like trying to grab water. Falon was choking now, and at least part of the ooze was flowing into his mouth and nose. The rest of it, still outside the cleric's body, twirled into a ropelike strand and whipped at the golem. The relatively minor attack must have been loaded with power, for the stone golem was pushed back almost fifteen feet. The golem's massive feet left skid marks across the stone floor, and there was a terrible black scorch mark on its chest where the tendril of ooze had slashed.

Roghar moved into Albanon's field of vision then, stepping between the eladrin and the human cleric. The dragonborn held his shield forward, boldly displaying the holy symbol of Bahamut that adorned the front of the shield. Searing ribbons of radiance exploded from the shield, cutting through the ooze and eliciting a sound of pain that wasn't like anything that Albanon had ever heard before. Burned and smoking from the radiant light, the ooze puddled out of Falon and pooled around the young cleric's feet.

Falon, dazed and obviously disoriented by the creature's invasion, nonetheless acted swiftly. Still coughing and spitting, he raised his sword high and called down a column of sacred fire. It roasted the ooze with divine power, causing another alien scream to echo through the chamber.

As the sacred flames died out and Falon dropped to his knees, Albanon watched the ooze slither through a crack in the wall. He was sure that it was badly hurt. Perhaps it was even dying. But it managed to get away from them. At least it hadn't managed to claim another one of the companion's bodies.

Roghar knelt beside Tempest and whispered a prayer of healing. The holy words flowed through the tiefling, erasing her wounds with divine energy.

"Thanks," Tempest said, placing a hand on the dragonborn's arm. Roghar nodded, but he didn't say a word.

Albanon had almost forgotten about the golem when its resounding footfalls warned him of its approach. The wizard turned and barely called forth an arcane shield in time to absorb the deadly punch the golem had hurled his way. The shield held against the attack, but then it faded, even as the golem pulled back and prepared to strike again.

"No!" Falon screamed.

The golem stopped in mid-swing.

"How?" Albanon asked, looking to Falon for some kind of explanation.

"I have no idea," Falon said, seemingly as surprised as the rest of the companions that the golem had obeyed his order.

"Hmm," Darrum said as he moved to join them. "I think I might be able to explain this."

"Please," Albanon urged. "I'm all ears."

"All ears!" Uldane said, pointing at Albanon's swooped and pointed ears. "The eladrin. All ears!" And then the halfling began to laugh.

68 THE OLD HILLS, NIGHT

Kalaban and Magroth emerged from the Labyrinth into the Old Hills northeast of Thunderspire Mountain. Even in Kalaban's day, the Old Hills were considered ancient, and they were filled with a melancholy air that led to tales of haunted valleys and enchanted hilltops that few dared explore. If this was the location of Orcus's necropolis, then that would explain the feelings of dread and danger that the Old Hills had always inspired.

The two travelers had walked in silence since leaving the body thief and the stoneguard behind. Kalaban waited for the next outburst or the next question, but Magroth provided neither as they walked. The Mad Emperor drew forth the Necropolis Stone once they were out of the underground passages and on the moon-drenched path between the hills. Magroth studied the stone, tilting it at various angles to see how the moonlight played on its dark, flat surface.

"This way," Magroth said eventually, proceeding deeper into the depressions that crisscrossed the space between the hills.

Kalaban followed, casting his senses into the night to guard against any threats that might be present. He cleared his throat after a time, and the knight-commander said, "I am sorry, my lord. The Voidharrow, whatever it is, it intrigued me. I hadn't felt such an exhilarating sense of curiosity since . . . well since before we were drawn into the Shadowfell."

"Not now, Kalaban," Magroth commanded, a hint of anger in his voice. And was there something else there as well? Desperation, maybe?

Magroth led them to a dark depression in the side of one of the larger hills. Brambles blocked the small cave from casual observation, but once Magroth pointed out the spot, it was impossible for Kalaban not to see it.

"The way in," Magroth said, his voice still strained. "I need you to wait here, knight-commander."

"Your majesty," Kalaban protested, "I can't let you enter the Necropolis by yourself. I must. . . . "

"Enough!" Magroth screamed at him. Arcane energy crackled along the top of the Mad Emperor's staff. "You shall indeed accompany when I enter the ruins of Andok Sur. But that moment has not yet arrived. While there is still time before the sun rises, there is something I must do."

Kalaban suddenly understood what was bothering Magroth, and for once it had nothing to do with him.

"I am hungry, knight-commander," Magroth said in a low voice. "I must hunt. I must feed."

Kalaban could think of no response to this, so he simply nodded.

"Keep the path open and the way protected, Kalaban," Magroth said as he became mist and began to float away on a current of air.

Kalaban watched the mist swirl off into the darkness. Then the knight-commander got busy. With a few carefully placed slashes of his sword, he cleared the brambles from in front of the small cave. He stepped into the shallow chamber and examined the symbols that decorated the walls and ceiling. The marks clearly identified this as a place dedicated to the Demon Prince of Undeath.

"Your presence is strong in this place, Orcus," Kalaban whispered as he examined the pedestal of black stone set in the center of the small cave. There was an indentation on the top of the pedestal that appeared to be about the same size and shape as the Necropolis Stone. The dead glass. The knight-commander was sure that the stone was the key to opening the path into Andok Sur.

Kalaban continued to study the symbols and the carvings on the pedestal, unaware of the pair of eyes watching him from behind the next hill.

69 THE AVENUE OF GLORY, NIGHT

Darrum walked around the stone golem, examining it from every angle. For its part, the golem remained stock still; it didn't so much as twitch. Every so often Darrum reached out to touch different parts of the stonework body, obviously marveling at the construction. Uldane followed along behind the old dwarf, excited by the chance to study a magical construct while it wasn't trying to pound him into paste. The halfling had the good sense to keep quiet, however, though Darrum noticed him start to open his mouth when a question occurred to him and close it again quite a few times while he finished his inspection.

"So?" Falon finally asked. "You said you knew what this thing was and why it seems to obey my commands. Will you enlighten the rest of us?"

Shara cleared her throat. "I think Erak knows what it is, as well," she said, watching the revenant closely. "He called it a 'stoneguard.'"

Darrum looked from Shara to Erak, nodding. "Yes, that's what it's called," the dwarf said. "Though I haven't seen one since well before Nerath's collapse. These constructs were the guardians of the royal family, set with powerful enchantments to obey the commands of those of royal blood. This one specifically has the runes of an elite stoneguard. This construct will only obey the orders of the emperor of Nerath or one in line to inherit the throne."

"Someone like me," Falon said gloomily.

Erak stood. "It's time to move on," the revenant said. "Having a stoneguard on our side can only help when we face off against the Mad Emperor."

"Really?" Falon asked. "Obviously, my ancestor left this thing here to stop us. He either forgot or didn't care that I could control it. He probably thought I wouldn't figure it out until it had destroyed at least a few of you. What's to stop him from just reestablishing control of the golem when we catch up with him?"

"He might not be able to," Darrum offered. "Could be that living blood trumps undead blood when it comes to this kind of magic."

"That's a guess at best," Falon countered. "When was the last time that Nerath had an undead emperor on the throne?"

Darrum had no response to offer the young cleric.

"Tell us, Erak," Shara said. "How did you happen to know what the golem was?"

"I don't know," Erak said. "I saw it and I knew what it was. That's all. No other memories. No other flashes of inspiration. Just a name and an isolated packet of knowledge that immediately bubbled up out of the chaos of my mind."

"I can't stand this!" Falon shouted into the darkness. "Why does Orcus want me dead? Why has an ancestor I didn't even know I had want to kill me? Why me? Why now?" The young cleric stifled a sob, wiping at his eyes with the back of his hand.

Falon took a moment to collect himself, and then he offered his companions a wan smile. "Sorry about that. It's just not every day that you find out you're the heir to a throne that no longer exists and that a bunch of undead monsters are out to assassinate you."

Darrum returned the young cleric's smile. "Completely understandable," he said. "Let's do as Erak suggested and move on. The sooner we catch up with the creature claiming to be Magroth, the sooner we can end this threat to Falon."

"Can you make it move?" Uldane asked, pointing excitedly at the stoneguard.

Falon sighed. "Let's find out." He moved to stand directly in front of the golem and looked straight into the visorlike carving on its stone face. "Follow me."

As the companions headed out, the golem followed, remaining close to Falon as they traveled deeper into the Avenue of Glory toward the Old Hills.

70 THE OLD HILLS, NIGHT

Kalaban could see the first signs of the approaching dawn against the hills to the east. A faint brightening of the darkness in the sky signaled that the sun would soon be rising over the horizon. If Magroth hadn't returned before then, the Mad Emperor would be severely weakened by the full light of day. Now that his master was a vampire, or at least had some of the traits and powers of a vampire to go along with his lich abilities, the sun would be a deterrent as it had never been before.

Kalaban couldn't imagine what Magroth was going to find this far from any kind of settlement. Even the nearby Trade Road would be unused in the darkest hours before the dawn. The knight-commander remembered how disappointed Magroth had been with goblin blood. He couldn't imagine the foul mood he would be in when he returned.

Magroth was obsessed with power; Kalaban had seen that even when he was alive and serving the Mad Emperor. He took the Orcus medallion and freely placed it around his own neck, taking on the blood curse, specifically because of the power it offered. Magroth felt that he needed the extra power to overcome the deal he had brokered with Orcus, to break free of the hold that the Shadowfell had over them. Kalaban appreciated the effort that Magroth was going to in order to set them free, but he wished that there was another way. A lich and a death knight, that he had grown to accept over the centuries. But a blood curse? A craving for living blood that could never be sated? Kalaban wasn't sure if he could ever grow comfortable with the price his freedom seemed to be costing them.

So far, Kalaban had been unable to determine how they were going to gain entrance into the ruins of the necropolis that Magroth believed was beneath the Old Hills. The pedestal and the dead glass would play a part, but he could find no evidence of hidden doors or sliding panels in or around the shallow cave. With his work completed for the time being, Kalaban let his hand wander into the pouch that hung on his belt. Immediately, his fingers found the small glass vial nestled there. He could feel the substance within the vial moving responding to his touch. The Voidharrow, that was what the body thief had called the crystalline substance. It was clear to Kalaban that the body thief had a connection to the substance and even appeared to perhaps be composed of a similar crystalline ooze. It was a mystery, but one that Magroth was now aware of. Kalaban was certain that his time with the glass vial was drawing to a close.

A thick fog began to swirl around Kalaban's feet, rising up from the ground. At first, the knight-commander thought nothing of the mist. Then he noticed how it changed direction and moved against the gentle breeze blowing down the valley between the hills from the north. A moment later, the mist began to solidify, and then Magroth was standing beside him. The Mad Emperor appeared calm, sated, although he smacked his lips and stuck out his tongue like a child who had just been forced to eat something he didn't like.

"You wouldn't believe how awful giant spiders taste," Magroth complained. "It was all I could do to even find that in these gods' forsaken hills. No matter. My cursed descendent and his companions should be along any time now. Which reminds me."

Magroth pulled the chain that held the Necropolis Stone from around his neck. He held it up to inspect it briefly, then looked up to examine the sky.

"Daylight is coming," Magroth hissed. "Come, knight-commander, let us see what this key unlocks."

Kalaban followed Magroth into the shallow depression that contained the pedestal of stone. He watched as Magroth gently placed the dead glass into the carved slot atop the pedestal. Nothing happened. Magroth smiled at Kalaban's evident disappointment.

"One more thing to do," Magroth said, holding his hand above the black stone. He squeezed his fingers into his fist, letting the clawlike nails dig into his withered flesh until blood welled and dripped on to the dead glass.

Spider blood, Kalaban thought. Or whatever blood the spider ate before Magroth drew the precious liquid from it.

Three drops of the crimson liquid splashed on to the flat plane of the dead glass. Each one pooled into a brilliant dollop before being sucked into the stone. One drop, two drops, three. A loud click sounded from the stone pedestal or from something just beneath it. Then the hills began to rumble and the ground that they were standing on began to descend. The pedestal was part of some kind of platform that even now was lowering the two undead creatures into a great open space beneath the Old Hills.

As the platform continued to descend, leaving an opening above them, Magroth willed light to radiate from the top of his staff. The light revealed the sunken city of the dead that spread out to the north and east. It appeared that the place had once been above ground, but something had caused it to fall into the earth and become buried. An earthquake, perhaps, wondered Kalaban, or maybe the actions of an angry god? Parts of the necropolis rested at different levels beneath the hills, with some sections tilted at a steep angle to the right and others angled to the left. Very few sections were level or complete. The place was a literal ruin of mausoleums and vaults and temples dedicated to Orcus.

Finally, the platform came to rest some fifty feet beneath the surface. Magroth reclaimed the Necropolis Stone from the pedestal and stepped off to find the place where he had to perform the ritual that the death priest had given him. Kalaban started to follow, but Magroth raised his hand.

"This is where we part ways, knight-commander," Magroth said without turning to look at him. "At least for now. There is a green dragon in the hills above. It was waiting for us, watching us as we fiddled with the pedestal in the small cave. I have no idea what it wants, but it must not be allowed to interfere with the ritual I'm about to perform. Deal with it, Kalaban. Deal with it as you deal with everything I need you to."

"Yes, my lord," Kalaban said, drawing his soulsword and turning to face the opening above them.

"And whatever you do, knight-commander," Magroth added as he started to walk away, "make sure that my descendent is allowed to enter the necropolis. Don't let the dragon eat the young fool before I can use him as a sacrifice."

"Yes, my lord," Kalaban said again as he tried to think of a way to quickly defeat a green dragon.

Nothing brilliant immediately sprang to mind.

71 THE NECROPOLIS OF ANDOK SUR, THE DARK BEFORE THE DAWN

Tiktag watched in amazement as the hill and the land around it collapsed into the earth, leaving behind a jagged gash that opened into the ground.

"The way is opened," Vestapalk said. "The Herald must be below. That is why we were led here. That is why the very land itself has opened before us. The Elemental Eye sees these things, and it is well pleased."

Tiktag had to admit that the signs had surely brought them to this place. Something momentous was about to happen, the wyrmpriest was certain of that. The green dragon got up and moved from its hiding place. A few steps of the dragon's great stride and it was next to the opening in the earth. It peered down into the gaping hole, studying the terrain while Tiktag ran to catch up.

"Time to fly, wyrmpriest," Vestapalk said, lowering its head and neck so that the kobold could climb on. Tiktag was barely settled in when the dragon flapped its massive wings and leaped into the gaping hole.

Vestapalk soared into the darkness, carrying Tiktag on its back. They appeared to be flying down into a great cavern beneath the hills. Spread throughout the cavern were the ruins of a large town or a small city composed of cobbled streets and stone buildings. On further inspection, Tiktag could see that the buildings weren't homes or temples. They looked like the stone vaults where many of the races store their dead. He had seen examples of such things in Winterhaven, for example, but never so many or so ornate as the ones that filled this cavern.

But it was obvious to the kobold that the place wasn't built beneath the ground. It appeared to Tiktag that the entire city of the dead fell into the earth from above. Parts of it had settled on different levels of the cavern, and many of the sections were cantered at odd angles that gave the place an otherworldly feel. Moreover, the wyrmpriest saw many examples of Orcus worship. Statues, shrines, and carved symbols associated with the Demon Prince of Undeath were everywhere, covering the close-packed mausoleums, lining the cobbled paths, and filling every inch of worked stone.

"Why has the Elemental Eye led us to this place of death, wyrmpriest?" Vestapalk asked as he spiraled down toward a more or less level patch of ground below them.

"I don't know, mighty Vestapalk," Tiktag admitted, though he hated to not be able to provide the dragon with some kind of answer.

"And what is that thing waiting below us?"

Tiktag strained to see around the green dragon's wide neck. Standing beside the stone pedestal that had been in the shallow cave before the entire hillside had collapsed was a human-sized figure in fire-blackened plate armor. He carried a sword and shield, and Tiktag could see dark energy playing across the length of the blade. As they spiraled closer still, Tiktag saw the telltale signs of undeath about the figure: glowing red eyes and skin as pale as many of the stones around them.

"Something undead, Vestapalk," Tiktag warned. "Of that I am sure."

The green dragon decided to start the battle as it often did. It expelled a cloud of poison gas at the undead warrior. Then it prepared to dive at the creature and rip him apart with its claws.

Tiktag, trying to see from his unusual vantage point, noticed that the poison gas wasn't causing the undead warrior to gag or writhe in pain. In fact, it didn't appear to affect the undead warrior at all. "Master, beware!" Tiktag managed to shout, but the green dragon was already committed. It flew directly at the undead warrior, who calmly ducked low and raked his sword up in a deadly arc. Vestapalk howled in pain and suddenly lost control of its dive. Tiktag leaped just before the green dragon smashed into a small stone building. The structure shattered, revealing dozens of close-packed bodies that had been stored inside it.

The wyrmpriest rolled and managed to gain his feet. He leveled his fetish-decorated staff and launched an orb of green energy at the undead warrior. As with the cloud of gas, however, the poison orb seemed to have little or no effect on the creature. Fear gripped the kobold, who tightened his hands around his staff and danced back, away from the armored creature.

"Now I get to strike," said the undead warrior, striding forward without the least bit of hesitation.

Tiktag was certain that his time in this world was about to come to an end when Vestapalk roared a warning. The wyrmpriest dropped to the ground just as the green dragon's tail swept through the space above him and slammed into the undead warrior. The powerful blow sent the creature sailing back. He smashed into another of the stone mausoleums, but not as dramatically as the dragon had. The stone building held up to the undead warrior's much smaller bulk. Not so much as a crack appeared along the stoneworked surface. The impact was jarring to the creature, however, who connected with the hard stone and bounced off to crash loudly to the cobbled path before it.

"What are you and why do you challenge Vestapalk?" the green dragon demanded.

"I am Kalaban," the undead creature said as it lifted himself off the ground. "I am knight-commander of Nerath. I am a death knight. And I am your death, dragon."

The green dragon laughed. It was a sound that Tiktag would never get used to.

"Vestapalk has a destiny, little undead creature," the green dragon sneered. "You do not have the power to change that."

"We'll see," said the death knight, and he launched himself against mighty Vestapalk.

72 THE OLD HILLS, DAWN

Shara rode her mount out of the dark passage and into the cool air of the Old Hills. The sky was just beginning to brighten over the tops of the hills to the east, and the first rays of the sun would soon paint the sky in brilliant shades of gold and blue. Roghar had healed her injured leg, and she felt fit and ready for whatever happened next. The companions had all experienced the rumble and shaking that had rocked the passage a few minutes ago. None of them had any idea what was happening among the Old Hills, but Erak was certain that it had something to do with his mission.

Uldane rode beside her, as he always did. She saw the expression of wonder and excitement that the halfling wore, and she smiled. It was the first smile she could remember since that fateful day in the clearing high within the Cairngorm Peaks. It felt good to smile. It helped that Uldane was so full of joy and adventure, even after all that had happened to them. He couldn't wait to see where this quest took them next. And, whether she liked it or not, his mood was contagious. She had to get back to hunting the green dragon but for another day or so she was content to stay with this group and help Erak and Falon accomplish whatever it was that the gods seemed to demand of them.

Gods, Shara thought. She had little use for the strange and distant beings. All they ever seemed to do was make demands and engineer mysterious events that never appeared to serve any real purpose as far as she could tell. She certainly never complained when Cliffside or Roghar performed a healing or when Falon conjured up divine power to help defeat a foe. But beyond that, she had never been one to bend a knee or beg forgiveness. Faith could move mountains, she had heard a wandering cleric say once during an impromptu sermon in Winterhaven's town square. Be that as it may, Shara preferred to rely on her greatsword, her courage, and the commitment of her friends. As long as the gods didn't interfere in her affairs, she promised to stay out of theirs. That attitude had served her well until recently. And now? Here she was, riding into who knew what kind of danger to help a young cleric, who was apparently the heir to the long-gone throne of Nerath, and a revenant, who was the Raven Queen's champion. She had to admit, she could feel her old fire—her zest for life and battle—beginning to return.

Erak and Roghar led the way out of the underground Labyrinth and into the crisscrossing valleys of the Old Hills. Shara and Uldane followed behind them, with Falon, Darrum, and the golem next in line. Albanon brought up the rear, with Tempest riding in front of him on his horse. Her horse, actually, Shara had heard them say. Despite the long hours of travel and the number of battles they had endured since leaving Fallcrest, thanks to divine healing the companions were healthy and whole. Shara didn't think that Falon and Roghar had much more to give them in that regard, not without refreshing themselves with prayer and sleep. No one had said anything, but she figured they all knew that an opportunity for either wasn't in their immediate future.

"That's not something you see every day," Roghar said as he and Erak drew back on their reins and brought up their mounts. They had stopped beside a gaping hole in the earth, and Shara could see where a part of the hillside had collapsed into the ground. She dismounted and moved to stand beside the hole. It opened into a huge cavern. In the light of the steadily brightening sky, she could see the slanted structures that filled the hole.

"It's a sunken city!" Uldane exclaimed.

"A necropolis, actually," Erak said. "That's the lost necropolis of Andok Sur."

"And you know this how?" Shara said, unable to keep the annoyance out of her voice.

Erak simply looked at her. "Magroth must have opened this path," the revenant said. "This place is holy to the followers of Orcus. Whatever the Mad Emperor plans to do here, I have to find a way to stop him."

A great roar bellowed from the cavern beneath them, and Shara's skin went cold.

"Shara, did you hear that?" Uldane asked, obviously delighted by the sound. "That sounded like the green dragon!"

Momentary fear was quickly replaced by the hatred that Shara felt for the creature. She tightened her hand around the pommel of her sword.

"That's Vestapalk, the damned beast that killed my father and my friends," Shara said. "The rest of you can deal with Magroth. The green dragon is mine to kill."

"And mine," Uldane said, a note of seriousness creeping into his voice.

"Wizard," Shara said, addressing Albanon. "Can you get me into that hole in the ground quickly?"

Albanon examined the deep cavern, and then he said, "I can cast a spell on you that will allow you to fall like a feather to the bottom of the cavern. I can only use the spell once, however, so the rest of us will have to find another way down."

"Fine," Shara said, "do it."

Uldane moved to stand beside her. "I'm not very heavy," he said. "Shara can carry me."

"I don't know," Albanon frowned. "The spell's not meant to be used on multiple creatures."

"Don't cast it on multiple creatures," Shara said. "Just me. I'll carry Uldane. We'll be fine."

"But . . ."

"We'll. Be. Fine."

Albanon nodded and began to cast the spell. As he made gestures and whispered words of power, Shara took one last look at the companions. Erak nodded to her as he and Roghar tied lengths of rope together to use for their own descent into the ruins. Tempest and Falon were moving the horses back, away from the gaping hole. They would probably have to let the horses run free, because none of them were going to want to wait up here while the rest went into the ruins. Only Darrum stood apart, a look of troubled concentration on his face.

"Maybe Falon shouldn't go into the ruins," Darrum said, staring down into the deep darkness.

"What are you thinking, Shield?" Erak asked as he checked the knots in the ropes.

"Just that this Mad Emperor made it awfully easy for Falon to follow him. Maybe he wants Falon to catch up with him."

"I'm sure that's exactly what he wants," Erak said calmly.

"So we give this undead thing what it wants?"

"We end this," Erak stated. "And for that to happen, Falon must be there."

"He just knows it," Shara added, feeling the tingle of arcane energy play across her skin as Albanon finished casting his spell.

Falon walked over and put a hand on Darrum's shoulder. "I'm going, Darrum," the young cleric said. "I'm tired of running away. Besides, I've met so few members of my family. Seems like an opportunity that I just can't pass up."

"The spell is cast," Albanon said as another dragon roar issued from the darkness below.

"In addition to the green dragon," Erak warned, "the ruins are probably overrun with all kinds of undead. And few of them will probably be as friendly as I am."

"Good to know," Shara replied, another smile touching her lips. "You aren't Jarren, are you?"

"No," Erak admitted softly, "I don't believe that I was."

"May your battles end with you alive and your enemies dead," Shara called out. "All of you. And now, I have a green dragon to slay!"

Shara grabbed hold of Uldane, who was grinning like a child who had just been handed a sweet roll. She had the same feeling. Then she stepped into the open space above the cavern, and slowly began to fall.

73 THE OLD HILLS, DAY

As day exploded among the Old Hills, Falon saw that the cavern below was still shrouded in darkness like the night. Erak secured one end of the rope and tossed the other end into the hole. He tested the hold with a couple of hard pulls before nodding that it was ready for them to descend.

"I don't think your golem can climb down the rope," Darrum said.

Falon shrugged. "Yes, I already thought about that," he said. Then he pointed into the hole. "Stoneguard, jump!" Falon commanded.

Without hesitation, the stone golem stepped into the hole, much in the same manner as Shara had just moments before. Unlike Shara, the stone golem didn't simply drift slowly toward the cavern's bottom. It plummeted, immediately falling out of sight into the darkness below.

"Are Shara and Uldane going to be all right against a dragon?" Albanon asked.

Roghar began to climb down the rope.

"Once we get to the bottom," Erak said, "we'll determine our next course of action. Perhaps a few more of us may go to help Shara."

Erak pointed to the rest of the companions, determining the order of the climb. Tempest. Albanon. Falon. Darrum. Once everyone signaled understanding, the revenant scampered down the rope and disappeared into the hole. Falon watched as the others, one at a time, took their position and started to make their descent.

"Your turn," Darrum said.

Falon wasn't a natural climber, and he had rarely had to scamper up or down a knotted rope while growing up in Nenlast, but he was young and strong. He had little trouble making it down into the cavern. During the descent, however, there were moments when Falon was genuinely frightened. First, little light penetrated from the relatively small hole at ground level, so much of the cavern was in darkness. Second, the canted streets and oddly tilted stone buildings whose shapes he could just make out in the dim light loomed like some sort of mad landscape from another world. Even as Falon continued to climb, one hand at a time down the rope, he caught glimpses of movement at the edge of his vision. He was certain that he and his companions weren't alone down here.

Light blazed from below as Albanon cast a spell to provide them with some illumination. Falon saw ground that was more or less level beneath him and he leaped down into the circle of light. They were standing on a cobbled path that was cantered at about a fifteen degree angle, with weeds and grass growing out of the parts of the path that were cracked and broken. Around them, stone vaults crowded in from all sides. The vaults had heavy stone doors and were decorated with carved symbols related to Orcus and celebrating undeath in all its forms.

Falon shivered. Not only was it as cold as a grave within the cavern but the entire place seemed to be veiled in a cloak of evil unlike anything that the young cleric had ever experienced before. The place frightened him, but it also made him angry. It was anathema to everything he believed in, to the teachings of Erathis, who proclaimed that civilization and light would stand against all darkness. If there was a place that needed the light of Erathis, this was it.

The stoneguard lurched out of the darkness and into the light at the same moment that Darrum leaped down from the rope. Erak looked around to get his bearings, trying to decide which way to go in this place of insanely tilted streets and crazy-leaning mausoleums. Another roar, presumably the green dragon, sounded from somewhere nearby, although judging the actual direction was nearly impossible because of the way the sound bounced through the tumbled necropolis.

A bright flash of light appeared in the darkness, coming from somewhere much deeper within the ruins. All of the companions saw it. It blazed like an explosion before settling into a more subdued flicker. Like a signal fire. Or someone lighting a brazier.

"That's the way," Falon said, a feeling of certainty coming to him.

"I agree," said Erak. "It appears to be coming from the center of these ruins."

"So," said Tempest, who had been mostly quiet since both Roghar and Falon had used healing prayers to bring her back from the brink of death, "how are we going to handle this? Shara and Uldane are going to need help against a green dragon. At the same time, we have no idea about what kind of powers a century's old emperor might be wielding. What's the plan?"

The companions all turned to Erak, and Falon realized there was something natural about looking to the revenant for guidance in this city of the dead. Erak considered the question for only a moment. "Falon, Darrum, the golem, and I will look for the source of the light at the center of the necropolis," he decided. "Roghar, meanwhile, will lead Albanon and Tempest back that way, to help Shara bring down the dragon. Whichever group deals with its enemy first goes to meet up with the others. Any questions?"

"What about me?" Splendid asked. The pseudodragon was once again curled around Albanon's neck and shoulders.

"What about you, dragonkin?"

"I didn't hear my name called in the order of battle."

Erak smiled. "I meant no offense," he said with all seriousness. "I just assumed you'd want to stay with Albanon, to offer him your wisdom and guidance."

"Of course," the tiny dragon said, her chest swelling with pride and importance. "I just didn't want you lesser creatures taking me for granted."

"Never, oh wise and magnificent one," Erak said, bowing respectfully before the tiny dragon.

"You could learn a thing or two from this one, Albanon," Splendid said. "He's obviously been schooled in dealing with those of higher rank and privilege."

"Great, Erak," Albanon moaned. "Now you've made Splendid even more insufferable than she already was."

Erak grasped Roghar's hand. "Good luck," the revenant said.

"May Bahamut smile upon you," the dragonborn paladin returned.

Falon watched the three of them—Roghar, Tempest, and Albanon—head out, moving in the direction they had seen Shara and Uldane fall. Then he turned to follow Erak and Darrum, who were already climbing the angled path to the northeast.

"Come on," Falon said to the golem, wondering if they would ever see any of the other companions again.

74 ANDOK SUR, DAY

Shara held onto Uldane as the two of them drifted down into the darkness. Albanon had cast the spell of feather fall on to Shara, which made her the recipient of the spell's power. She was falling slower than she would have if she had simply jumped into the cavern from above, but she was drifting down faster than the spell dictated because of the added weight of carrying the halfling. She didn't think they were going to hit the ground hard enough to kill them, but it was going to hurt more than it was supposed to when using that particular spell.

"Get ready to bend and roll when we reach the ground," Shara said.

Suddenly a great form flew up out of the darkness. It was an emerald-scaled dragon, soaring and banking to make a run at something neither Shara nor Uldane could see in the darkness below. Shara studied the beast carefully, noting the marks that scarred its left fore leg. Twelve horizontal slashes, including three that appeared fresher than the others. There was no doubt in Shara's mind. This was the green dragon Vestapalk. The creature rolled in midair, then dove back down into the darkness. It roared a mighty challenge as it disappeared below them.

Uldane let go of his hold on Shara. "Uldane, what are you doing?" she asked worriedly as she tried to maintain her own grip on the halfling.

"Let go," Uldane said cheerfully. "I've got an idea."

Shara learned a long time ago to trust the halfling rogue. He was confident, fearless, and very good at everything he did, even if he often gave the impression of being childish and a tad too cheerful. She released her hold on Uldane. The halfling tucked his knees up to his chest and then pushed off of Shara, flipping back and somersaulting to reach a stone gargoyle that extended from the roof of a nearby mausoleum that had come to rest some twenty feet above the floor of the cavern. His sure hands found purchase, and he swung up on to the stone protrusion.

With the added weight of the halfling gone, Shara's descent slowed. She drifted on a gentle current of air, swaying toward the ground not unlike a bird's feather dropped from high above. She landed on her feet and drew the greatsword from the sheath slung across her back. The dragon was about thirty feet away, engaged in a frantic battle with a figure dressed in flame-blackened plate armor who defended himself with a long sword and shield. She saw the kobold wyrmpriest that had ambushed them back on the old King's Road skulking among a scattering of broken stones, looking for a chance to attack the armored warrior from hiding. Uldane did a spinning flip off the stone protrusion and landed silently beside her. He seemed to be having the time of his life, at least if she was correctly interpreting the wide smile that was plastered across his face.

He looked at her, and his expression turned serious for a moment. "Let's kill this thing for Jarren and Cliffside," Uldane said.

"And for Borojon," Shara added resolutely.

"And for Borojon," Uldane agreed.

Shara pointed toward the skulking wyrmpriest. Uldane nodded. Then the two of them began to move, Shara toward the dragon's exposed flank and Uldane toward the kobold.

Shara ran up a series of broken stone blocks, each one slightly higher than the last. There were five of the cracked blocks, the lowest about three feet high, the highest about fifteen feet above the level of the floor. As she reached the highest block, Shara repositioned her grip on her greatsword so that she could bring the blade down in an overhand arc. Without missing a step, she launched herself from the tall stone block and sailed through the air. This allowed her to come at the dragon—who was grounded and exchanging claw swipes and sword thrusts with the armored warrior—from above. The creature's back was wide open and exposed.

A cry of absolute rage and sorrow escaped from Shara as she flew toward the green dragon. Her boots hit the creature near where its wings attached to its body, and Shara brought her sword down like a spike, plunging the blade through scales and into soft flesh. Red blood spurted from the wound, and the green dragon let loose its own cry of pain and fury. It spun around, trying to determine what had attacked it, and Shara lost her balance on the fast-moving creature. It was like trying to maintain your balance on a log bobbing in a raging river. She turned the beginnings of a fall into a leap from the dragon's back, and she rolled across the ground to avoid a claw swipe or being stepped on by the massive creature.

"Vestapalk recognizes your scent, treacherous creature," the green dragon roared as its gaze fixed on Shara. "This one killed three of your clan and feasted on their flesh and blood. And now you come to Vestapalk, offering yourself as sacrifice and meal. This one is honored."

"Vestapalk will die!" Shara screamed at the dragon as she regained her footing and prepared to charge at the beast again.

"No, dragon," the armored warrior stated calmly from the dragon's other side, "we aren't finished yet."

Shara saw that the armored warrior's eyes glowed the color of fresh blood beneath the visor of his helmet, and his exposed skin, seen through places where a few of his armored plates were missing, was pale and dead.

"Vestapalk has enough power to deal with both of you lesser creatures," the green dragon responded, matching the undead warrior's calm, measured tone as it continued to stare at Shara. "You escaped this one, little female, but you have returned."

Shara, who had experience battling this particular monster, made sure that she remained on the opposite side of the dragon from where the undead warrior faced it so as not to provide it with an opportunity to catch both of them in its deadly breath. She took another step to the right, not able to draw her eyes away from the dragon's.

"Come to Vestapalk, little creature," the dragon said almost soothingly.

Shara, unable to help herself, began to walk directly toward the green dragon.

"Woman! Snap out of it!" the undead warrior shouted. "The dragon has placed a charm upon you!"

Shara heard his words, but she couldn't get her feet to stop moving. It took every ounce of willpower she possessed to bring her sword up into a defensive position just as Vestapalk slashed at her with its left foreclaw. The dagger-sized talons raked across the sword, saving her from bloody wounds, but the force of the strike knocked her back and to the ground.

"Vestapalk grows weary of this game," the green dragon said as it loomed over Shara. "The Herald arrives soon, and you lesser creatures are not worthy of standing in its presence."

"You never did make much sense," Shara shouted and swung her sword in a wide slash that scraped across the armored scales that covered the dragon's neck.

The undead warrior leaped over the dragon's whipping tail and delivered three quick jabs to the dragon's flank. Vestapalk whirled, catching the warrior in its large right claw and pinning him to the side of a half-sunken mausoleum.

"Which of you shall Vestapalk slay first?" the dragon mused aloud, blood trickling from its many wounds. Shara attempted to move in, but the green dragon held her at bay with a swipe of its tail. "The undead first? Yes. And then the female. Then the Herald's way shall be clear."

75 ANDOK SUR, DAY

It was day in the world above, but a deep and penetrating darkness continued to fill most of the ruins of Andok Sur. Magroth had reached what he supposed was the center of the city of the dead. A great brazier crafted from a metal that was so dark as to be almost black filled the open square that stretched before a structure that could only be a temple dedicated to the worship of Orcus. The brazier was fifteen feet across, and it was filled with humanoid bones—femurs, rib bones, skulls, and more were piled high within the bowl.

"The ritual begins here," Magroth said aloud. He raised his staff, whispered a word of power, and an unnatural fire burst to life within the brazier of bones. It gave off unholy light in the otherwise constant darkness in this part of the necropolis.

The Mad Emperor didn't need to refer to the scroll that the death priest of Orcus had provided him, or to the notes he had made while studying in the tower of the Mages of Saruun. He had memorized the ritual, as well as the changes he had made to the original, and he was ready to see if he could actually escape the conditions of the deal he had struck with Orcus.

Magroth removed a small pouch from the pockets of his robes. He untied the gold thread that held the pouch closed. Then, with a single motion and in time to the next series of words of power he had to recite, Magroth tossed the contents of the pouch into the unholy fire. What appeared to be fine dust was actually the ground bones of Magroth's enemies, collected and saved over many centuries of ongoing campaigns. The dust sparked as it hit the fire, and the flames flared brightly for long seconds as Magroth completed this portion of the ritual.

As the flames returned to their previous state, a great rumble began to echo throughout the entirety of the necropolis. It was as though the cavern itself had come alive. Then every vault and stone door shattered as the ritual did its work, breaking apart from the inside in rapid succession, starting with those closest to the burning brazier and radiating out in ever-widening circles.

"Come forth!" Magroth called out. "Arise, my army of undead!"

The Mad Emperor could hear the dead moving in the nearest mausoleums. Skeletons, zombies, and who knew what else that was resting and interred within the necropolis.

"The rebirth of Nerath begins this day," Magroth whispered as he surveyed the stirring graveyard around him. "Now I must have the living blood of a Nerath royal. Where is my misbegotten descendent when I need him?"

A sudden fire burned on his inner left arm. Magroth pulled up the sleeve of his robe to examine the mark that still adorned his withered flesh. The crown and stars—the birthmark of the royal house of Nerath—flared white-hot against his skin.

"Close," Magroth said, staring into the darkness beyond the light of the blazing brazier. "He's close and getting closer. Good. I can't wait to meet the hopeless whelp."

76 ANDOK SUR, DAY

Albanon followed Roghar through the mazelike necropolis toward the sounds of the dragon. Tempest was right behind him, but Albanon was worried that the tiefling wasn't recovered enough to help them in the coming battle. He kept gazing back at her, trying to assure himself that she was not only healed but that she was also herself and not some tiefling-thing getting ready to attack them from behind.

Splendid turned her head each time, matching Albanon's gaze whenever he turned back to look at Tempest. "She makes your skin crawl, too, huh?" the little dragon asked innocently.

Tempest scowled at both of them. "I'm fine," she said, more than a little angry at the two of them. "And I can still hear you. Get over it and prepare yourselves. We're about to battle a green dragon, and any mistake on your parts will get us all killed."

Roghar abruptly skidded to a halt as the entire cavern began to shake.

"Earthquake?" Albanon asked.

"We can only hope," Roghar said, his eyes sweeping the cavern around them for anything out of the ordinary.

The stone doors on the nearest mausoleums, which occupied a patch of ground that had fallen from above and come to rest at a forty-five degree angle to the left side of the cobbled path they were following, suddenly cracked open. Each stone door released a loud crack that was followed by a boom and a hiss of air as the door blew apart from the inside out. The three companions barely avoided being struck by pieces of flying stone.

"This can't be good," Tempest said, drawing her rod and preparing to hurl a curse at the first threat that revealed itself.

A single form stepped out of the nearest dark opening. It was still wrapped in its funeral linens, and it was more skeletal than decayed flesh. It appeared confused, unsure of where it was or what it was supposed to do. Then it opened its mouth to scream, but no sound issued from it. It stayed like that, silently screaming, until a wave of skeletons rushed out from behind it, knocking the first skeleton down and trampling it as the dozen or so others poured forth. And the same thing was happening at each of the mausoleums around them.

"That's a lot of skeletons," Albanon marveled.

Tempest began to unleash a series of dark, crackling bolts of energy into the nearest horde of undead. "A little help here," she managed to say between blasts.

Albanon stepped beside her and called down a vertical column of golden fire that exploded into the center of the skeletal mass. Skeletons and parts of skeletons flew in all directions, but the attack had barely made a dent in the swelling horde of undead.

"Come on," Roghar commanded. "There's too many of them. Let's try to reach Shara before they surround and overwhelm us."

"I like how you think," Tempest said with a grin.

"What am I missing?" Albanon asked, still trying to get in sync with the pair of adventurers who had worked together so long that they didn't even need to make plans during a battle.

"Nothing yet, friend elf," Roghar said. "And if we move now, you might not be missing anything when all is said and done. Come on! Run!"

Albanon hurled a couple of arcane bolts into the oncoming horde as he turned to run. He couldn't help but wonder how they were going to get away when it seemed like the entire necropolis was regurgitating its undead. Without finding any answers, he followed Roghar and Tempest along the twisted, cobble-stone path.

77 ANDOK SUR, DAY

Uldane moved silently between the cracked and slanted stones as he sneaked toward the kobold wyrmpriest. He owed the kobold for the last time they met, and this time he planned for a different outcome. The wyrmpriest was less than twenty feet ahead of him. It was concentrating completely on the battle between the green dragon and the armored warrior and Shara, obviously looking for an opening to launch its own attack against the dragon's foes.

Green energy began to coalesce around the head of the wyrmpriest's staff. Uldane planned to strike before the kobold had a chance to unleash the poison orb. The halfling didn't know who the armored warrior was, but anyone fighting against Vestapalk was a friend in the halfling's eyes. And friends don't let other friends get shot in the back by cowardly kobolds.

Uldane covered the last few feet as silently as he had the entire distance. He plunged his short sword into the kobold's back, inflicting a deep cut that continued to bleed even as he drew out his blade and leaped to the side in anticipation of the kobold's next move.

The wyrmpriest howled in pain, spinning and firing its orb of poison wildly into the space where Uldane had been standing just a moment before. It splattered harmlessly against the side of one of the pillars of cracked stone.

"Missed me," Uldane said, hurling a dagger at the kobold.

"You!" the kobold managed to say just before the dagger buried itself in the creature's right shoulder.

"Any last words, kobold?" Uldane asked as he tightened his grip on his sword.

The wyrmpriest, seriously wounded, widened its eyes in sudden fear. Uldane didn't expect that reaction. Even when he was winning a fight, few things ever appeared to be truly afraid of him. Something about his smile, he imagined. Or his size. But the kobold was clearly frightened about something.

"Undead," the kobold said, and it pointed behind the halfling.

"Oh, come on! I haven't used that old trick since I was a toddler. Do you really expect me to turn around and give you a chance to either run away or attack me while my back is turned?"

"I expect them to kill you while I flee, yes."

"Them?"

Uldane couldn't help it. Now he was curious. He turned to see a swarm of zombies climbing out of the nearest stone vaults and shambling toward him.

"Undead. Right." The halfling started to hack at the nearest zombie before it could grab him.

"Good luck," the wyrmpriest said as it slipped into the shadows.

Uldane couldn't even think of a clever retort as he weaved and dodged among the zombies, trying to hack them to pieces before they could grab him.

He didn't have high hopes that this was going to end well for him, but as always, Uldane gave it his best shot.

78 ANDOK SUR, DAY

Falon followed Erak and Darrum directly into the center of the necropolis. There didn't seem to be any reason to try to be stealthy, as the loud, plodding stoneguard accompanying them made the sneaky approach impossible to pull off. Getting to the open square in front of the Orcus temple was easy enough, despite the rumbling earthquake and the recently raised army of undead spilling into the cobbled paths around them. It was as though these newly risen undead, confused and disoriented, were simply allowing them to pass by. The light of the fire burning before the temple was like a beacon in the darkness, drawing the three companions and the golem directly toward its glow. The light cast by the flames was a sickly yellow seemingly ripe with what felt like evil to the young cleric of Erathis. That was the only word that came to mind when he gazed into those flickering flames.

The undead never ventured on to the path they were traveling. Instead, the hordes of skeletons and zombies, as well as the occasional pack of ghouls, spread out into the darkness, away from the spires of the temple that Falon could see peeking above the closer hills of burial vaults and oddly stacked mausoleums. Even though he expected it, none of the undead so much as glanced in their direction, let alone moved to try to stop them from approaching the sickly light and the looming temple.

It was as though they wanted them to pass, to reach the unholy fire and the doors to Orcus's temple.

"Does this feel like a trap to either of you?" Falon asked Erak and Darrum.

"Trap might be too harsh a word," Erak said, never slowing as he approached the light of the fire. "Invitation, more likely."

"That makes me feel so much better," Falon said, and then he cried out and clutched his left wrist.

"Falon?" Darrum asked, concern evident in his voice.

"The mark," Falon said through clenched teeth. "It burns."

"So does mine," called a voice from around the next set of stone vaults.

The companions turned the bend and entered an open square that was dominated by a huge brazier crafted from some kind of dark metal. In the pale glow of the fire that burned within the brazier, Falon saw a tall, gaunt man—the man from his dream. He was dressed in ornate robes and carried a wizard's staff. His hair, long wisps of white, framed a narrow face that revealed flesh that wasn't quite alive.

"The old adage must be true," the gaunt man laughed, "relatives can be a real pain."

Falon noticed that Erak had slipped into the shadows and literally disappeared. One moment he was there, and the next he was gone. He wasn't hiding, not the way the young cleric had observed Uldane use shadows to block himself from view. Erak seemed to step into the shadows and fade away. It was unsettling to think about.

In Erak's sudden absence, Darrum decided to take the lead. He stepped forward and addressed the gaunt man. "I am Darrum, an Imperial Shield of Nerath," the dwarf called out. "To whom do we have the pleasure of speaking with?"

The gaunt man laughed again. It was a chilling sound. "I'm not sure I'd call it a pleasure, but I am your emperor. I am Magroth the First, ruler of Nerath. Now step aside foolish dwarf and let me see my grandson—several generations removed."

Darrum hesitated and reached for the twin hammers that hung at his side. Before their civil conversation got out of hand, Falon approached the Mad Emperor. He stepped in front of Darrum and bowed before Magroth.

"I'm here," Falon said, rising out of the bow to stand straight and tall before his ancestor. "Shouldn't you be rotting away in some treasure-filled tomb somewhere?"

Magroth took a couple of steps away from the brazier and examined Falon from head to foot with a long, penetrating glance. "Eh," Magroth said, "I see the bloodline must have been corrupted somewhere along the way. You certainly don't look like the heir to the throne of Nerath."

"There is no throne, you old ghost," Falon said. "Nerath, like you, is long dead."

Magroth's insane smile twisted into a snarl. "And like me, boy, Nerath will soon return. And it will be stronger and more powerful than it ever was before!"

"Great," Falon replied, "if you say so. But why involve me? I don't want anything from you. I don't care about the throne."

"But I want something from you, boy. Something precious. Come closer and we can discuss just what you can do to help me."

The undead emperor tossed something into the fire, and the flames flared brightly for a moment as whatever was in the small black pouch was consumed. He was saying something as well, too softly for Falon to hear, but it reminded the young cleric of a chant or a prayer. A ritual! The undead emperor was performing some kind of ritual while carrying on a conversation with him.

"Falon, be careful," Darrum warned. He drew forth *Dawnfire* and *Nightstorm*, the magical warhammers that the dwarf wielded with such skill and prowess. "The stories I've heard about the Mad Emperor suggest that he's not to be trusted."

Magroth's milky-white eyes blazed with fury at Darrum's words. "Mad Emperor? Mad Emperor!?" Magroth screamed. "You dare insult Magroth the First? You dare?"

Lightning leaped from Magroth's long fingers and streaked toward the dwarf. Darrum barely managed to cross his warhammers in front of him, but the magical weapons caught the bolt of lightning and kept it from slamming into the dwarf.

Magroth waved his hand in disgust, casually dismissing the dwarf. "Kill him," he ordered, and a small army of skeletal warriors that were marching by changed course and rushed toward Darrum. Falon quickly calculated and determined that there were more of the undead than Darrum could handle. He signaled to the stoneguard that was standing right beside him.

"Help Darrum," Falon commanded. As soon as the golem began to move to engage the skeletal warriors, Falon turned his attention to his ancestor.

Emperor Magroth smiled. "Perhaps there's a little of me inside you after all, boy," Magroth said proudly. "Remind me to check after I complete the ritual."

Magroth gestured, reaching toward Falon and closing his fist as he whispered a word of power. As his fist closed, a giant hand of ice formed around the young cleric and slammed shut, wrapping him in its chilling fingers. Freezing pain seared through Falon as the icy hand grabbed him and lifted him into the air.

"Bring my descendent to me," Magroth said, slapping his closed fist to his chest. The icy hand duplicated the gesture, carrying Falon to where the Mad Emperor stood.

"Your blood, boy," Magroth said. "I wish you no ill, but I will have your blood."

Falon struggled within the icy grasp, but it seemed hopeless. He couldn't break free from the freezing-cold fist.

"With your blood, I may actually be able to end the curse and restore glory to Nerath," Magroth said, letting his insane smile stretch wider still. "Let's see if this works."

Falon could only watch as the Mad Emperor drew a wickedly sharp dagger from the folds of his robes.

79 THE OLD HILLS, DAY

The horses waiting at the top of the gaping hole that overlooked the cavern suddenly became nervous and agitated. They scattered in all directions, trying to put some distance between themselves and the approaching figure. Barana Strenk smiled. She had the same effect on most living creatures.

She stepped to the side of the gaping hole and looked into the darkness below. A blazing fire glowed near the center of the cavern, far down toward the rocky bottom of the great open space. The death priest nodded her approval. Magroth had begun the ritual. Soon, the way would be prepared for Orcus's army of undead. The Mad Emperor would have no choice but to lead the army, just as Orcus had willed it. Magroth was well on his way to completing the three tasks that Orcus had set before him. Before darkness fell, the Nentir Vale would be facing the worst threat since humans had settled the valley. Soon, Orcus would rule this land. And then the lands around it. And then the entire world.

Barana extended her senses, feeling for the life force of the one that was prophesied to disrupt the plans of Orcus and set the stage for the Demon Prince's downfall. There, near the blazing fire, she could feel the living blood of Magroth's descendent. He wasn't dead yet, and that momentarily troubled Barana. Then she thought about how powerful, how determined the Mad Emperor was, and all troubling thoughts left her.

The young cleric with the royal blood would be dead soon enough, and then nothing would be able to interfere with Orcus's grand plans for this world.

Nothing at all.

80 ANDOK SUR, DAY

Darrum swung *Dawnfire* and *Nightstorm* in great, sweeping arcs. Each swing shattered bones and momentarily cleared a section of space around the dwarf, but more skeletons immediately moved in to replace those that had fallen. Worse, even the skeletons that Darrum shattered with his magical warhammers weren't destroyed. He could see the bones drawing back together and repairing themselves even as he fought to take down more of the undead.

"I'm getting really tired of fighting things that are already dead," Darrum grumbled.

The stoneguard plowed through the mass of skeletons beside him, rolling over them like the great boulder of rock that it was. Falon had commanded it to help the dwarf, and that was just what it was doing. As strong as Darrum was, the stone golem was stronger. Each strike of the golem's massive fists pulverized the bones they hit. It would take a lot of time and effort for *those* skeletons to return to the battle.

"We should finish these things off in a matter of moments," Darrum said as he dropped another four skeletons with a swipe from *Dawnfire*.

The remaining skeletons clattered to the sides of the path, making room for a new combatant.

"This can't be good," Darrum muttered, trying to figure out how they could disengage from the skeletons and get back to help Falon.

The decrepit skeletons that remained positioned around them seemed to defer to the combatant striding forward. It was another skeleton, but it was slightly taller than the rest, and its bones were thick and solid. It had an extra pair of arms, positioned on an extra set of ball joints located in the pits of its first pair of arms. Each of its four hands held a wicked scimitar, and it twirled the blades in a way that suggested it knew how to use them. It crossed each pair of blades, letting the steel sing as it pulled each blade across the other. Obviously, the four-armed warrior was no ordinary skeleton.

"Right," Darrum said, realizing he wasn't going to be able to get back to Falon as soon as he had hoped.

31 ANDOK SUR, DAY

Shara remained just beyond the reach of Vestapalk's claws, but that also left her more than a few steps away from delivering sword strikes of her own against the dragon. The green dragon held the undead warrior in one taloned claw, and Shara could see that the talons had pierced the warrior's armor in three places. He had dropped his shield at some point in the battle, but he still maintained a grip on his long sword. Unfortunately, the sword and the hand that gripped it were trapped beneath the dragon's crushing talons.

Another rumble shook the cavern, opening steaming cracks along the floor and raining dust and small stones from above.

Shara wanted to scream in frustration! She was so close to her goal of killing Vestapalk, of avenging the deaths of all of the people the dragon had killed around Winterhaven, including her friends, her father, and her beloved Jarren, but she couldn't take down the dragon by herself. She wasn't that good or that powerful. She wasn't sure if anyone was. But part of her wanted to rush at the foul creature anyway, no matter how slim the odds.

"Face me, Vestapalk," Shara called. "Drop the undead and see if you can stand against my blade and my fury!"

The green dragon seemed to smile, though it didn't actually have the facial structure to accomplish such a gesture. It looked down at the weakly struggling creature it held tightly in one clawed fist.

"Vestapalk wonders what undead meat tastes like?" the green dragon said. "This one wonders if it tastes like carrion."

The dragon raised the undead warrior toward its tooth-filled maw, apparently intent on taking a bite. Shara tried to rush in and slash with her greatsword, but Vestapalk easily held her at bay with a swipe of its tail. The tail strike missed its mark, but it still made Shara dodge and back off to avoid a bone-crushing hit.

As soon as the dragon opened its mouth and started to bite, however, the undead warrior called forth a burst of black fire. The unholy flames spread out from the undead warrior's body, engulfing the dragon's arm, head, and part of its neck in the necrotic fire. Vestapalk roared in pain as the fire charred and blackened its emerald scales, but the dragon didn't let go of the undead warrior.

"Face me, you abomination!" Splendid roared as she flew straight toward Vestapalk's head.

The green dragon instinctively tried to bite the tiny dragon, but Splendid darted away from the snapping jaws.

Next, Albanon and Tempest rushed out of the darkness behind Shara to stand beside her, each taking a position to her left and right. They hurled arcane spells at Vestapalk, striking in unison with darts of force and eldritch blasts. These attacks further frustrated the green dragon, but they were little more than minor annoyances in the grand scheme of things.

Roghar appeared then, though he was facing back the way the

thers had come from. The dragonborn backed up until his armored shoulders were touching Shara's. "A lot of dead things are about to join us," Roghar said. "We're about to be trapped between the dragon and a horde of undead."

Worse than that, Shara realized. They were clumped too close together. The four of them made a perfect target for the dragon's gaseous breath. She looked into Vestapalk's emerald eyes and saw that it had realized the same thing. It prepared to breathe.

That was when another powerful rumble rolled through the cavern. Great monuments of stone, already slanted at dangerously unstable angles, began to topple over. One of the nearby mausoleums, its walls cracked by the same force that had opened its heavy doors, collapsed in a cloud of rising dust. At the same time, the ground the dragon was standing on split open and fell away. Vestapalk began to fall into the collapsing ground only to save itself by furiously flapping its powerful wings.

Shara stood at the edge of the newly opened chasm even as Albanon and Tempest threw themselves backward to avoid sliding in. The woman warrior held her greatsword at her side, its long blade parallel to the floor. She leaped at the dragon, bringing the blade around to open the creature's belly with one mighty strike. The dragon tried to defend itself, using the undead warrior's body as a shield. Shara's blade sliced through the undead warrior's belt pouch, narrowly missing cutting into the warrior himself. She briefly registered that her blade had ripped something free from the warrior's belt pouch. It was a small glass vial, full of a glowing red substance that was run through with veins of silver and flecks of gold. The chain attached to the metal cap that sealed the vial had caught on the edge of the blade, and it was now swinging on a collision course with the dragon.

As had happened whenever Shara felt the battle lust rise within her, everything around her slowed and came into precise focus. She was hurtling through the air in what she perceived to be slow motion, following through with a strike that she knew with certainty would be a death blow to the already heavily wounded dragon. She also saw the glass vial and its fascinating contents. Part of her was drawn to the strange, glowing substance in a way that she didn't understand. It was almost like the charm the dragon had used on her just moments before. Still, she was able to compartmentalize the sensation, to save it for later. If there was a later.

Shara's blade cut into Vestapalk's abdomen, drawing forth a great gush of blood and organs. The glass vial, meanwhile, swinging like a pendulum at the end of its chain, shattered against one of the dragon's torn scales. The glowing red substance, thick and viscous, splattered into the dragon's wound and on to Shara's sword. Vestapalk howled in terrible pain, finally releasing its grip on the undead warrior.

For Shara, everything seemed to stop. She could see the entire situation, and she knew that although she might have dealt Vestapalk a death blow, her own death was surely inevitable. The gravely wounded dragon was already falling, its wings refusing to work as it howled in pain. Shara was falling, too, with no hope of catching the crumbling edge of the newly opened chasm beneath them. At the same time, the undead warrior pushed aside the dragon's flailing talons and prepared to leap clear of the dying creature.

Shara couldn't help but look at the glowing red liquid with the streaks of silver and the specks of gold. It was flowing into the dragon's wound, mixing with the dying dragon's own blood. There seemed to be so much of the substance. How had it all fit within that small vial, she wondered? The portion of the substance still on Shara's blade was moving—flowing toward the sword's point and then somehow flinging itself through the air to join with the larger mass of the substance pooling around the dragon's torn scales and bleeding wound.

Shara saw all of this, and then she was falling. Something heavy slammed into her before she dropped into the chasm and knocked her back on to solid ground. She rolled once, bounced, and then hit the ground hard, coming to rest on her back. The undead warrior, rolling and bouncing alongside her, had somehow thrown himself from the dragon's opened paw and collided with her on his way to safety.

Her head reeling and the breath knocked out of her, Shara barely registered that Albanon and Tempest had moved back to the edge of the chasm and were hurling whatever offensive spells they had left after the falling dragon. The undead warrior, battered and beaten, grabbed her hand and helped her to her feet. Since he was already dead, she couldn't decide if he was badly hurt or not, but he didn't seem too worse for wear.

"Death knight," Roghar said, addressing the undead warrior as he recognized exactly what kind of creature it was.

"Paladin," the death knight said, nodding once with a mixture of wariness and respect in his tone and movements. "The dragon is gone. Truce?"

Roghar looked around. "Agreed," he said.

That was when Uldane leaped down from the top of a nearby stone vault. "Zombies!" the halfling cried exuberantly.

The death knight looked down into the chasm, an expression that Shara took as something like loss or regret passed over his skeletal face. Then he turned to Shara. "I thank you for the aid you offered me against the dragon," the death knight said. "I shall leave you to deal with the lesser undead on your own. Farewell." And with a slight bow, the death knight turned and started to run toward the fire burning at the center of the necropolis.

Shara sighed heavily. Then she smiled. "Looks like we have a bit more fighting to do," she said, and she hefted her greatsword and let out a battle cry that rocked the necropolis.

8 2 ANDOK SUR, DAY

Darrum met the charge of the four-armed skeleton, countering each scimitar strike with one of his twin warhammers. The stoneguard meanwhile, continued to make short work of the lesser skeletons smashing them apart with each swing of one of its massive fists.

The four-armed skeleton never spoke. Darrum wasn't even sure if it could. But the dwarf could feel the hatred and contempt that the powerful skeleton had for him. It was evident in the angry slashes of its scimitars and the casual way it blocked each of his own hammer strikes. Darrum glanced back to see what the golem was up to and noticed that it had defeated, at least for the moment, what was left of the horde of skeletons.

"Go," Darrum shouted at the golem, hoping the construct would understand him and follow the order. "Go help Falon!"

The dwarf ranger turned his attention back to the scimitar wielding skeleton just as one of its blades got through his defenses and slashed across his shoulder. He wasn't sure if the golem was following his command or not, but he could hear its powerful footfalls fading into the distance. It was heading back toward the flaming brazier. At least, Darrum hoped that that was where it was going.

Of course, that meant that Darrum was on his own against the powerful skeleton. He took a deep breath and prepared himself for one last push against the creature.

"All right, you monstrosity," Darrum said with conviction. "Let's see how you fare against the last of the Imperial Shields. For Nerath!"

8 3 ANDOK SUR, DAY

Falon struggled against the freezing-cold fingers of ice that were wrapped tightly around him, but he couldn't break free. He was held fast as Magroth brought the sharp dagger closer. If he didn't think of something quickly, he was going to feel the sting of that blade, and he didn't expect the Mad Emperor to stop with just a slight nick of his finger or cheek. He looked around, but Erak was still missing. Maybe he had deserted them, despite the pledge he made back in Fallcrest. And Darrum and the golem were fully engaged with a legion of skeletal warriors. He could expect no immediate help from that front, either.

"Why blood?" Falon asked, hoping to distract Magroth. "And why mine?"

"Why not?" the Mad Emperor cackled, resting the cold blade of the dagger against the side of Falon's face, its tip uncomfortably close to his right eye. "I jest, of course. You really don't deserve an explanation, but I do so love to hear myself talk."

Magroth moved closer, pressing his forehead against Falon's so that he could speak softly and still be heard above the clang of swords and the pounding of warhammers. Falon could smell dried blood in the Mad Emperor's mouth, and he couldn't help but notice the unusually sharp fangs that gleamed when he smiled.

"There's this prophecy, you see," Magroth explained, pressing the edge of the blade deeper into the side of Falon's face. The young cleric could feel the blade, ever so lightly, cut into his flesh. "It concerns the living blood of Nerath. You. This prophecy says that you will disrupt the grandiose plans that Orcus the Demon Prince has concocted for this era. I've been sent to remove you from the equation."

Falon swallowed hard, trying to maintain as calm an air as he could despite the circumstances he found himself in. "Why would you agree to help a demon prince? Why would you want to kill your own descendent?"

"You are nothing to me, boy," Magroth admitted. "A means to an end, nothing more. You see, Lord Orcus and I have a long relationship. Unfortunately, every deal I ever made with the Demon Prince has ended badly for me. I expect this current arrangement will wind up following that same weary path. So I've decided to change the deal. I'm performing the ritual he gave me, just as I was commanded to do. And I'm going to kill you, just as the deal demands. But I've made a few . . . improvements . . . to the spell. By using your blood, I can change the results of the ritual. Not only will this city of the undead bow before me, but I will also ensure, through the use of your blood, that Orcus is banished from this reality for a thousand years. With that done, I will be free from the curse that haunts me, free from the commands of the Demon Prince of Undeath and able to chart a new course for this world. Nerath shall rise again, and I shall be its emperor!"

"Deals? You made multiple deals with the demon prince?"

"Yes, boy, haven't you been listening?" Magroth almost shouted. "I wasn't much older than you are now when I first offered my soul to Orcus. What did I care? I wasn't really using it and I had an empire to win! Orcus gave me the power to turn Nerath into a great nation, and I was immune to harm from anything related to the natural world. So what if I had to pay a tithe in blood every ten years? That's what wars and backwater settlements are for, after all. But after I was killed—assassinated by one of my own trusted knights—I suspect that my descendents failed to honor the deal I had established. Really, I'm surprised Orcus allowed Nerath to last as long as he did after I died."

"Nerath was beholden to Orcus?" Falon couldn't believe what this terrible creature was telling him. "The great human empire? Built on blood sacrifices and deals with demons?"

"Don't sound so mortified," Magroth said. "After all, it worked for Bael Turath and the devils long before I thought of it."

"This mark on my arm is a curse," Falon shouted, "and that curse led to Nerath's destruction and all the pain this valley has undergone since the empire fell!"

"Enough!" Magroth commanded. "Lift your head so that I can make a clean cut along your throat."

"I shall not give up before the likes of you," Falon said, his voice clear and strong. "Erathis, drive this abomination before you with holy light!"

The symbol of Erathis, which decorated Falon's tabard as well as the hilt of his sword, glowed with a light that was pure and white. It expanded in a wave from Falon and burned into Magroth. The undead wizard screamed as the light seared him and pushed him away from the young cleric. The light continued to shine for another moment, and then it released its hold on the Mad Emperor.

"Parlor tricks?" Magroth said, turning the angry white orbs that were his eyes toward Falon. "You hope to defeat me with parlor tricks and uttered prayers to an insignificant god? And you do it with my own sword? I need you alive when I bleed you, boy, but just barely." The Mad Emperor began to cast a spell of his own, weaving arcane energy around the top of his staff.

Before Magroth could hurl the spell, however, the open square began to shake and rumble. The stoneguard charged Magroth, coming at him like an unstoppable avalanche. Magroth cursed and ordered the golem to stop. "Obey me," he shouted.

The golem didn't seem to hear him, or maybe Darrum was right and Falon's living blood was more potent than Magroth's undead blood when it came to commanding a stoneguard.

"You just can't count on good help these days," the Mad Emperor said. He turned the spell toward the golem. A serpent of lightning leaped from the tip of his staff and smashed into the golem, sending the stoneguard careening into a nearby mausoleum. The entire structure, already weakened, collapsed atop the golem.

Magroth turned back to address Falon. "Now, where were we boy? Oh yes, I was about to hurt you. Very, very badly."

84 IN SHADOW, WHERE TIME IS MEANINGLESS

Erak watched events unfold through the small opening he maintained between the natural world and Shadow. When he saw Magroth, when he heard the Mad Emperor's voice, a thousand disconnected images flashed through his mind. He was remembering something, and it was probably important, but he had yet to be able to sort through the cacophony of thoughts echoing behind his eyes. It was disconcerting, and he had to step out of the world for a moment so that he could deal with it.

Now, however, he realized that time was running out. He knew this undead wizard, knew him well. That much was evident in what he could fathom from the constantly shifting images. He knew him and he hated him. Was that a real memory? Or was it a memory planted by the Raven Queen to make sure that he did whatever it was she wanted him to do?

In the end, did it really matter? He had promised Falon that he would be his friend and protector, and right now he wasn't fulfilling either of those roles very well. He tried to calm his racing thoughts, to sweep aside the confusion and uncertainty. No matter who this creature was or what connection existed between them, Erak had only one course of action left open to him. His honor demanded it.

He had to return to the world and help Falon.

He had to save the heir of Nerath.

With that goal firmly in mind, serving as a fortress against the storm of raging memories, Erak stepped back into the world.

85 ANDOK SUR, DAY

Erak emerged from the shadows behind Magroth. He started to reach for the pommel of his hellsteel blade, when he noticed the dagger sticking out of the Mad Emperor's back. It was buried deep, all the way to the hilt. Erak remembered that weapon, like a distant memory slowly rising through the murk of centuries. At that moment, all thoughts of other weapons were pushed aside. At that moment, Erak knew that he had to use that dagger. He had to use it again.

Half a dozen silent steps brought Erak to within arm's reach of Magroth. The Mad Emperor was focused completely on Falon, and he had already hit the cleric with a scorching blast of fire that had partially melted the fingers of ice still firmly wrapped around the young man. Erak reached out, letting his fingers curl around the handle of the dagger. It felt good in his hand. It felt right.

And when his fingers closed around the grip, Erak remembered everything.

Krondor had not only grown disillusioned with Emperor Magroth, he had grown fearful of the man and what he was planning to do with the empire. Krondor had used his position and proximity to the emperor to uncover the secrets that others whispered about in the backrooms of taverns and the lower chambers of the many imperial palaces scattered throughout the land. He had discovered that Magroth secretly worshiped the Demon Prince Orcus, and the very thought of it made Krondor's blood run cold. This man, this empire that Krondor and his brother had pledged their lives to, they were built on blood sacrifices and unholy pacts with demons. That was why Magroth was untouchable. Why even grievous wounds did little more than inconvenience the man. He was protected by his dealings with the Demon Prince of Undeath.

It took many months, but eventually Krondor found the answer he was seeking. A wandering mystic devoted to the Raven Queen offered Krondor one way to end the nightmare he had found himself a part of. "If you pledge yourself to the Raven Queen and take on the aspects of Shadow," the mystic explained, "you will be able to overcome the foul protections that shield your emperor."

Seeing no other solution, Krondor agreed. Then, keeping his plan hidden from even his beloved brother, Kalaban, Krondor waited for the right moment, the right opportunity to strike. It would mean assassinating the emperor of Nerath, breaking every vow he had ever made. But Krondor believed that those vows had been made under false pretenses. His emperor had lied to him, deceived him, and had killed thousands of innocent people just to expand his own power. Krondor could no longer be a part of that. Moreover, he had to put a stop to it.

His honor demanded it.

On that fateful day in the city of Darani, on the steps of the imperial palace, Krondor listened as Magroth condemned hundreds of children to death. He could not allow that to come to pass. He would tolerate no more blood being spilled to sate the foul Orcus, not while he had a way to stop it. Krondor slipped his dagger from its sheath and plunged it once, twice, three times into Magroth's exposed back. As the Mad Emperor stepped away, Krondor let go of the blade's handle. It remained stuck in Magroth's back as he staggered down the steps.

"This . . . is . . . not . . . possible . . . " Magroth sputtered, spraying crimson droplets with every hard-fought word. "No natural power . . . can . . . harm me . . . "

"I am no longer natural," Krondor spat, "and your reign of evil ends today!"

Before Krondor could draw his sword, Kalaban's blade struck. It slipped between the plates of armor at his side, finding soft flesh and sinking deeply.

"Brother. . . . " Krondor tried to say, but the word never came out. He fell to the stone steps, and a deep and lasting darkness overtook him.

"I was Krondor," Erak said, drawing the dagger from Magroth's back with one swift motion. It emerged with a sound like a cork being pulled from a bottle.

Magroth turned, surprise evident on his sunken, skull-like face. "Krondor? You?"

Erak looked at the old wizard with a mixture of pity and contempt. "Now I am Erak, champion of the Raven Queen," the revenant stated simply.

Then he plunged the dagger into Magroth's heart.

The Mad Emperor's eyes grew wider still. "Not again," he said, and as his knees buckled underneath him, a dark and heavy mist swirled around him. The mist swallowed Magroth, drawing him back to whatever dark hole he had crawled out of that had set this entire situation in motion.

The icy fist holding Falon simply faded away as soon as Magroth disappeared. Falon fell to the ground, gasping. He looked up at Erak. "Thank you," he finally managed to say as he began to stand up.

"My liege," Erak said, bowing slightly. He turned to the brazier. "Now that Magroth is finished, we need to douse this unholy flame."

"Allow me," Falon said.

The young cleric drew forth *Arante* and held the holy sword high. "The way is clear, oh powerful and bright Erathis!" Falon prayed. "Extinguish this foul fire with your own holy flame!"

Sacred fire, white and pure, spilled out of the sky above and filled the dark-metal brazier. Erathis's fire was stronger, more potent than the flames dedicated to Orcus, and it was literally a case of fighting one kind of fire with another. As the sacred flames flared and died out, they took the sickly yellow fire with it.

"Krondor!" came a shout from the path leading into the square. An armored figure, his plate armor fire-black and terribly dented, strode out of the darkness. "Krondor, face me!"

86 ANDOK SUR, DAY

Kalaban couldn't believe his eyes. Although the body and form had changed, he knew, deep in his own dark soul, that the revenant who had just slain Magroth was his brother, Krondor, back from the dead. He watched in stunned silence as the dark mists of the Shadowfell reached out and pulled Magroth back, presumably to the dread domain of isolated Darani. He struggled to think of what to do next as the young cleric dosed the fire of Orcus with the power of Erathis's flames. Then, with a sinking conviction, he drew forth his soulsword and called out, "Krondor! Krondor, face me!"

The revenant turned and gave Kalaban a sad, forlorn look. He shook his head. "Krondor no longer exists," the revenant said. "And Erak has no desire to fight with you this day, Kalaban."

The revenant turned to the young cleric. He had to be Magroth's descendant, this age's heir to the throne of Nerath, because the thing that called itself Erak was bowing before him.

"If you ever need me again and I am able," the revenant said, "I will be at your side. Until then, walk tall and with honor, friend Falon, heir to Nerath."

And then, with only a single glance in Kalaban's direction, the revenant stepped into the shadows and disappeared.

Kalaban stood motionless for a long moment. He saw that the various undead that had been up and running around just minutes ago were either returning to their tombs or collapsing to the ground where they stood. Whatever foul plan Barana Strenk had set in motion was finished. At least for now. The Necropolis of Andok Sur was returning to its ancient sleep and would soon be just as they had found it. Silent. Dead.

He was sorry that he had lost the small glass vial and the strange substance inside it, but a part of him was also relieved that the thing was gone. He knew that it had cast some kind of spell on him, and it had been a spell that grew stronger with each passing day. Truth be told, Kalaban didn't think he could have tossed away the vial. It *wanted* him, and he had been very close to giving himself to the strange substance. Luckily, the woman warrior had taken the decision out of his hands. Now the captivating stuff was at the bottom of a crevasse with the body of the green dragon. Now that it was no longer in his possession, he felt no compulsion to go back and retrieve the stuff. He decided it was better this way.

The knight-commander looked from the young cleric to the dwarf ranger moving to stand beside him. He noticed that the stoneguard was also plodding over to take a protective position near the young man. Kalaban decided that that was good. He had enough of plots and battles to last several lifetimes, and for today at least, he was done. Without a word or a glance back, he walked into the darkness. He was free, and it was time to find his own place in this world.

87 THE OLD HILLS, DAY

Barana Strenk, death priest of Orcus, shrank back as the sky above suddenly flared with pure, white light. The holy radiance poured down into the cavern that held the ruins of the Necropolis of Andok Sur, momentarily driving back the shadows and disrupting the ritual that Magroth had been performing. Barana shielded her eyes from the blinding light and stretched out with her other senses to understand what was happening. It was always one god or another that decided to get in the way of her master's plans. Usually it was the agents of the Raven Queen who worked to undo their accomplishments, but this didn't feel like the work of the Lady of Fate and Winter. For one thing, it was much too bright.

"Erathis," Barana said the name as though it was a curse word. "The blood of Nerath still lives."

She crept back to the side of the chasm and peered down into the returning darkness as the light from above faded. She saw that the sickly yellow glow from the center of the necropolis had also been extinguished. The ritual had been stopped as easily as she could stamp out a burning ember. Magroth had failed. She had failed. There would be much to answer for in the days ahead. Much to endure as she begged and pleaded for her life.

No matter. Lord Orcus would not destroy her for this failure. Not while she still had something to offer the Demon Prince. Not while there was still a way for her to make amends for this momentary setback. She took comfort in that truth, even as she contemplated the torments that would be heaped on her before she was released to take up the next mission for her master.

Barana conjured up an image of the revenant, picturing the Raven Queen's creature that called itself Erak. He would pay for each scar inflicted on her, for each torment she was subjected to. The death priest swore to Orcus that there would be a reckoning with the Lady of Fate's champion, and she relished the thought of dealing with the creature personally.

Then she recalled the young and innocent face of Magroth's descendant, the cleric of Erathis named Falon. She burned the memory of the blood of Nerath into her mind, for she also promised to deal with him before he could cause more trouble for her master. She remembered the prophecy of the Felish Oracle. "The blood of Nerath shall grievously wound the Demon Prince of Undeath, perhaps even kill that which cannot die." That particular stanza had made Barana's blood run cold when she had first encountered it. She vowed that she would end the royal line of Nerath before she allowed such an event to come to pass.

But not today.

She heard the rattle of bones and flapping of wings that always signaled the presence of her master. Behind her, a swirling portal of shadow irised open, and a blast of stale, dead air blew past her. She turned and fell to one knee before the gaping hole in space.

Barana started to speak, to offer some sort of excuse, but she found no words that would justify the events of the day. So she simply said, "I have failed you, Lord Orcus."

A great taloned hand, its palm easily as wide as she was tall, reached out of the swirling blackness. It paused above her, as though deciding whether to slash her to ribbons or bash her into a bloody paste. Instead, the fingers curled around her and lifted her from the ground.

"I am ready, my master," Barana said.

The taloned fist, with Barana firmly in its grasp, slowly pulled back into the swirling blackness. For better or worse, Barana thought, she was going home.

8 8 THE OLD HILLS, LATE AFTERNOON

It took the companions hours to extract themselves from the ruin-filled cavern and make their way back to the safety of the Old Hills. Luckily, as soon as Falon had extinguished the sickly fire burning in the brazier before the temple of Orcus, the hordes of undead lost cohesion and their sense of purpose. Many collapsed right where they were standing, as though whatever dark magic had animated them had simply been snuffed out. The rest wandered away, returning to their tombs or finding other dark recesses in which to hide. What had started as a battle the companions couldn't win had become no battle at all. And for that, at least, Shara was grateful.

Sometime during the climb back to the surface, Erak had whispered a good-bye to Shara, and then he stepped into the shadows and disappeared. She was sorry to see him go.

"I'm not entirely sure what happened down there," Falon admitted. "Erak killed Magroth, but he seemed to have had some kind of history with the Mad Emperor."

"Perhaps he'll return one day and clear up all the mysteries," Darrum suggested.

"I know what happened," Uldane said, tossing a large gold coin into the air, catching it, and tossing it again.

"Please enlighten us, brave rogue," Tempest said, smiling at the halfling.

"It was my lucky coin," Uldane explained. "Actually, Jarren's lucky coin, but he gave it to me to hold on to. Anyway, as long as I had the coin, I knew nothing too bad was going to happen to us. It's magic."

"Well," Shara said, a smile playing across her lips, "Jarren always thought so. I think he'd be glad to know that it served you so well, my friend."

Shara looked over the group. Falon and Darrum stood together, checking to see if their horses were all right as the stone golem looked on. Uldane stood next to Albanon, gently petting the pseudodragon wrapped around the eladrin's arm. Roghar and Tempest, meanwhile, had rounded up the rest of the horses and were leading them back to the larger group.

"What now?" Falon asked.

Shara waited, but no one offered any suggestions. With Erak gone, she guessed it was up to her to lead this unlikely group. "Let's return to Fallcrest," she said at last. "We could all use a hot meal and a warm bed."

Albanon nodded. "I have some business to take care of in the town, anyway," he said softly. "I need to take care of Moorin's affairs, close up the tower."

"And prove your innocence," Roghar added gently.

"Yes," Albanon said, "that, too."

As they mounted up, Shara turned to Falon. "I'm not sure they'll appreciate you bringing a stone golem into the town walls."

"Hmm," the young cleric said, "probably not. But what do you think they can do about it?"

Darrum moaned. "I thought we had decided *not* to call any more attention to ourselves than necessary."

The companions laughed, and the sound was good.

Shara gave her mount a gentle kick, and she started to ride south, toward the Trade Road. The companions followed after her, glad to leave the necropolis behind them.

89 ANDOK SUR, NIGHT

Tiktag half-climbed, half-fell down the crumbling wall into the crevasse that had swallowed Vestapalk. He hurt all over. That damned halfling had wounded him, and the cuts in his back and shoulder burned as though they were on fire. He hated the halfling. But at the moment, all he could think about was reaching his master's side. If Tiktag was going to die, then he wanted to die beside the mighty Vestapalk.

The kobold wyrmpriest didn't need any light to see by. His darkvision allowed him to navigate the blackness of this pit without problem. Vestapalk was sprawled ahead of him, its limbs bent at unnatural angles and its neck twisted so badly that it made Tiktag hurt even more just thinking about it.

The wyrmpriest hobbled over to the green dragon and rested a tiny hand on one massive emerald scale. His poor master was cut even more terribly than he was, sliced by blades and scorched by magic. Its left forearm, head, and neck had been burned badly, and its blood, crimson with strands of silver and flecks of gold, covered its body.

Tiktag paused. Dragon blood didn't have strands of silver or flecks of gold in it. And it certainly didn't glow like the thick substance around Vestapalk's wounds was doing. What was this strange substance? Tiktag slowly poked at the thick ooze with a finger, and the stuff flowed away from his touch. The way it moved startled the kobold, and he stepped away from the dragon.

"Oh, mighty Vestapalk," the wyrmpriest moaned, "what have they done to you? Why has the Elemental Eye forsaken us? Where is the Herald we were promised? Oh, so many questions, and no answers for poor Tiktag."

Suddenly, strange veins of glowing crimson with silver undertones appeared around Vestapalk's closed eye. The veins spread out, covering the dragon's snout and working their way between the scales along its neck.

"What's going on?" the wyrmpriest asked, not really expecting any answer.

And that's when Vestapalk's eye snapped open and focused on him.

"Master?" Tiktag asked as he watched the veins of glowing crimson and silver continue to snake their way along the green dragon's massive form.

90 THE LABYRINTH, TIME UNKNOWN

Nu Alin flowed across the dark, stone floor. His entire being was wracked by terrible pain. He wasn't supposed to be exposed like this, outside of a vessel, and he could feel his liquid crystal substance beginning to lose cohesiveness and form. He was coming to the realization that he was going to die here, beneath Thunderspire Mountain, when he had finally gotten so close to recovering the Voidharrow.

Suddenly a flash of recognition rippled through his oozelike body. He hadn't felt such a sensation since the ritual they had performed so many centuries ago. Could it be? He stretched out his senses, trying to get a clearer feeling. Yes, yes! The Voidharrow was free!

Nu Alin felt a renewed sense of purpose. The Voidharrow needed him. He couldn't just die down here in the darkness. Not now. Not when the Voidharrow was finally free.

He flowed across the cold stone, moving faster as he sought any living thing that could serve as a vessel. He lost all track of time and distance, but eventually he felt the heat of a torch radiating from the passage ahead. Nu Alin flowed up the wall and across the ceiling, moving carefully as to avoid detection.

There, in the passage ahead, a single gnoll stood guard. The humanoid hyena stood beneath a dimly burning torch. It carried a longbow, one arrow nocked, while a hand axe hung at its side. The gnoll seemed bored, almost ready to doze off in this lonely section of the Labyrinth.

Yes, Nu Alin decided, *this form will do.*

EPILOGUE
IN SHADOW, TIME UNKNOWN

Erak flowed among the shadows, letting the quiet soothe his troubled thoughts. He didn't know how long he floated like that, or how long the presence had been with him. He just knew that at some point he wasn't alone any more.

The sound of a thousand fluttering wings suddenly surrounded him, wrapping him in peace and a feeling of total security. In addition to the sound of wings in the darkness, there was a chill in the air, like the approaching winter.

"Are we done now?" Erak asked, speaking to the darkness.

He waited, feeling the Lady's presence all around him. The feeling was good.

"Can I go back to the quiet and the peace? Can I return to the deep shadows?"

Not yet, my champion, the chill wind seemed to whisper, caressing him with its winter-cold touch.

Not yet. There is work to do.

The End . . .

ABOUT THE AUTHOR

Bill Slavicsek is the Director of R&D for Dungeons & Dragons and Book Publishing at Wizards of the Coast. He is the author or game designer of many titles, including *Dungeons & Dragons for Dummies*, *A Guide to the Star Wars Universe*, the D&D Eberron Campaign Setting, the *Castle Ravenloft* board game, and the D&D super adventure, *Revenge of the Giants*.

DUNGEONS & DRAGONS®

JAMES WYATT

THE GATES OF MADNESS

PART TWO

An exclusive five-part prelude to the worlds-spanning
DUNGEONS & DRAGONS® event

THE ABYSSAL PLAGUE

Bael Turath

"Flee," the Chained God whispered. "Now." He filled this thought with the image of the Living Gate, the tiny fragment of its substance that lay hidden in the ruins of Bael Turath, and sent those thoughts through the void, along the fragile connection between himself and his mortal servant. "Now!" he roared.

His voice echoed in the void, and the whispers of the Progenitor rose around him. "Now," it said, slithering in the utter darkness. "Free."

The Chained God gazed around at the red liquid crystal that swirled and undulated around him. "You will go before me to become the Living Gate," he said. "To open my way to freedom."

He formed a hand from the darkness of his substance and lifted a portion of the Progenitor's substance. Tiny droplets of the red liquid trailed from his hand, shimmering in their own light. The fluid in his hand coiled around him, seeking something it could infuse and transform, but the Chained God was not flesh or matter. He brought it close and whispered over it, his frozen breath forming patterns of crystals across its surface.

"They will drown in blood," he whispered, a familiar refrain.

All around him the Progenitor responded, "All will perish."

Miri walked with her axe clutched in both hands, its thick haft resting on her shoulder, ready to swing at anyone or anything that jumped out at them in the ruins. The jagged spires and crumbling walls of Bael Turath loomed around her like a nightmare landscape, devil faces leering at her from ancient columns. It wasn't so much the architecture and its grotesquerie that set her on edge, but a less tangible sense, an awareness of the evil history that brooded over the ruined city. It was within its walls, she knew, that the noble houses of the ancient empire that bore the city's name had struck their fateful bargain with the powers of the Nine Hells, infusing their blood with a diabolical taint that persisted in the descendants of those houses—no longer human, but a race unto themselves, the tieflings. Such monstrous corruption had left its mark on the city, or at least she imagined it had. It made her flesh crawl and set her nerves on edge.

"The sooner we find this thing, destroy it, and get out of here, the happier I'll be," she whispered.

"I know," Demas said, his voice as clear as a trumpet and almost as loud.

Miri flinched at his volume, afraid of what attention it might draw to their presence. She watched as he turned back away from her, his eyes searching the rubble ahead for any sign he might recognize from his strange and haunting dreams. She sighed. Not for the first time, she wished she understood him better, that she had even a taste of whatever it was that made him always so calm, so sure, so at peace. His walk with Ioun had made him more than human, rather like an angel given mortal form. His pale skin, marked with jagged patterns as red as blood, set him apart from more ordinary men, but the grace and calm that suffused his every word, his every movement, seemed like an image of the divine. When he was moved to wrath or compassion, and Ioun's power flowed through him to smite his foes or comfort and strengthen his allies, she imagined she could see the eyes of the goddess in his beautiful face, and he walked in the paths she laid out for him, confident and trusting.

He continued forward, following the visions Ioun had granted him, and she walked close behind. She wasn't sure how much his eyes saw of the ruins around them, and how much he was gazing into another world, so she would be his eyes, alert to danger.

His eyes and ears. She put a hand on his shoulder to stop him, and put a finger to her lips to silence the question that rose to his lips. In the stillness, she heard it again, more clearly: the clash of steel.

"There's a battle going on," she said.

Demas nodded. "Monstrous creatures haunt these ruins, and worse. Someone could be in trouble."

"Who? No one lives here any more, right?"

"Treasure hunters, perhaps, or fugitives using the ruins as a hiding place. But even such unsavory characters do not deserve the death that haunts this place."

Miri smiled at him. "I knew you'd say that." She started walking toward the sound, just to the right of the course they'd been on. "This way."

It felt good to lead the way, for a change, to know the right course and be able to guide him as he so often guided her. She had known nothing of battle before she met Demas, but now she was as comfortable with her axe as she'd been with her milk pail before, so long ago. Whatever dangers lay ahead, at least it was a threat she could understand, one she knew how to face. And with Demas behind her, his divine power filling the air around her, she felt ready to face any danger.

The sounds of combat grew louder—steel crashing against steel, the shouts of men, and growls and roars that came from no human throat. Miri hurried onward until she rounded a corner and the battle engulfed her.

A man lay on the ground at her feet, blood spilling from a wound in his throat that might never heal. Three others—two humans and one stout dwarf—stood in a tight ring, beset on all sides by creatures of nightmare. Six of the creatures looked almost like men, clad in armor of black iron plates, but their legs were bent like those of a beast, tipped with great scaled claws, and Miri realized with a start that the horns on their heads were not part of any helmet, but their own monstrous ornament. Reddish-brown tails lashed the air behind them as they closed in on the desperate defenders.

The other creature was a gaunt figure that towered over the others. Leathery skin stretched tight over its bones, from its claw-tipped feet to its strangely warped skull. A thin tail curled up behind it, and an enormous stinger like that of a scorpion hovered near its head, ready to stab downward at its foes.

Miri glanced back at Demas as he rounded the corner and took in the scene. He smiled at her, then bent to intone a prayer over the dying man. Miri had all the reassurance she needed. She charged the towering devil, running forward and putting all her strength and momentum into one great swing of her axe.

The blade bit deep into the creature's side and erupted in blinding white light—the product of Demas's blessing. The devil howled as it turned to face her, its flesh burning away from the wound as pale green ichor spilled out. As its eyes fell on her, Miri's confidence faltered. Fear surged in her chest, sending her heart hammering against her ribs and a chill into the pit of her stomach. Some part of her mind tried to assert that the fear was just a trick of the devil's magic, but the rest screamed at her to flee. One of the devil's enormous claws came swinging at her and she scrambled backward, just out of its reach. She wanted nothing more than to keep going, to turn around and run as fast as her legs would take her.

Then a column of white flame streamed down from the slate-gray sky and engulfed the battlefield. The radiant flames danced over the towering devils' body, licking at its leathery skin, and it howled in rage and agony. The smaller devils shrieked in pain as well, and three of them rolled to the ground in a desperate, futile attempt to stifle the holy fire before it consumed them. To Miri, though, the flames were soft and comforting, banishing her fear. She could feel the warmth of Demas's smile in the flames.

The three men looked bewildered as the flames washed down around them, searing their foes but leaving them untouched. Miri noticed that they did not seem to draw comfort from the divine power as she did, and she wondered briefly who they were and what business had brought them into the ruins of the tiefling capital.

Then the bony devil's stinger stabbed into her shoulder, and agony like nothing she had ever known coursed through her body.

Nowhere had dreamed of Bael Turath, especially in his childhood. In his dreams, though, he'd seen stately mansions and soaring towers, the city as he imagined it had stood at the height of its empire—proud, majestic, and deadly. In every dream, he walked unnoticed through bustling streets until he came to a certain manor house, dark and squat in contrast to the towering buildings around it. As soon as he opened the manor's door, the city fell into ruin and fiends of the Nine Hells assaulted him from every side, waking him from his dream in a surge of terror.

Echoes of that terror shook his resolve as he and his companions strode through the crumbled gates of the city. His eyes darted around, peering into every crevice and shadow, half-expecting some creature out of nightmare to leap out and attack. He could see tension in Brendis's shoulders and how tightly the paladin gripped his sword, and wondered whether Brendis were also haunted by old nightmares.

Sherinna, though, seemed completely undaunted by the ancient ruins—or completely unaware of them. She'd been holding the cultist's parchment inches from her nose for most of the journey, as if by sheer force of will she could command it to reveal the secrets hidden behind the words. She somehow managed to glide over the rubble with her customary grace, even with her eyes fixed on the parchment.

"Sherinna," Nowhere whispered, "what have you learned? Have you figured out what we're looking for?"

"Cultists," she said, not looking up from the parchment. "Or a fragment of the Living Gate."

"I thought maybe after all that reading you had picked up something more than what the big words said."

Sherinna shot him a withering glance before returning her gaze to the parchment. "You asked two questions. I chose to answer the second."

"Then you have learned more?"

"Nothing good." She sighed and lowered the parchment, looking around as if noticing for the first time that they had reached the ruins. "They're looking for a fragment of the Living Gate so they can use it in a ritual designed to pierce the barrier between worlds. The bulk of this writing is the formulas of the ritual. They intend to pierce the walls of the Elder Elemental Eye's prison so it can free itself."

"Will it work?" Brendis asked.

"That's just it. The ritual seems coherent, from what I can make out. But some of the components and formulas don't make sense if the place they're trying to reach is a primordial's prison somewhere in the Elemental Chaos."

"So maybe the ritual will work, but not as they plan," Nowhere said. "Maybe they'll bring something else through their portal, instead of the primordial they intend."

"Something else," Sherinna said. "Something worse."

"Worse?" Brendis said. "What could be worse than a primordial? The gods themselves joined in bands of three or five to bring down a single primordial in the Dawn War."

"Most primordials are much weakened since the Dawn War,"

Sherinna said. "And some forces are even stronger than the primordials were at the height of their power."

Nowhere frowned. "Get to the point, Sherinna. What are we facing?"

She glared at him. "The cultists plan to take this fragment of the Living Gate to Pandemonium and perform their ritual there. Pandemonium was the dominion of a god so evil and so powerful that all the other gods banded together to imprison him. I believe that can mean only one thing: These cultists hope to free the Chained God."

Brendis's eyes went wide. "That's madness."

"Of course it is," Nowhere said. "Just like the cultists serving the Fire Lord in Nera were mad. It just means we'd better make sure we stop them."

Miri stared up at the gaunt devil's leering face as the venom seared through her veins. Darkness closed around her vision until its visage was all she could see. It shifted, reaching one of its enormous claws toward her.

Brilliant light engulfed her and the devil, casting stark shadows across its angular face as it howled in pain. The fire in Miri's veins became a refreshing warmth washing through her, Demas's divine power repairing the damage the poison had caused.

She gripped her axe and swung with all her might at the devil's bony leg. The blade bit deep, spraying green ichor and splintering bone, knocking the creature's leg out from under it and sending it sprawling to the ground. She stepped clear of its flailing tail, glancing around to get a sense of the field.

Two of the smaller devils were circling around her, either moving in to attack from her flanks or trying to get past her to Demas. The other four lay dead on the ground. She saw no sign of the three men she'd been trying to rescue, and she frowned.

No time to worry about that now, she told herself. She threw herself in the path of one of the smaller devils, lashing out with a mighty swing of her axe. The blade glanced off the creature's heavy armor, but the force of the blow sent it staggering across the crumbling cobblestones and it crashed into its companion. Demas sent another burst of divine radiance to consume the devils, and they were gone.

The larger one gingerly got to its clawed feet, favoring the leg Miri had struck. Its tail weaved in the air behind it like a snake ready to strike, and it roared in pain and fury.

The devil's eyes were tiny points of yellow light sunk deep in gaping black sockets, and it fixed them on Demas. "Your god will not protect you where you are going, cleric," it called.

"Silence!" Demas answered, his voice charged with divine authority. "My god is the weaver of fate and the voice of prophecy. Do not think that your knowledge surpasses my own." He lifted his staff in both hands over his head, and the pure light of the sun washed out from him.

The devil recoiled, shielding its eyes from the divine light, and Miri rushed forward again. With one swing, she swept the devil's feet out from under it again. She spun with the momentum of her axe, then brought it down to cleave the monster's head from its bony neck.

"Well done, child," Demas said.

Miri's heart swelled with pride, even as tears pricked at her eyes. Why couldn't he see her as something more than a child?

"It appears that our rescue attempt was successful," the cleric continued. "Even the one who was dying—they all escaped."

Miri frowned. "Why did they take off like that?"

"You felt the fear the bone devil inspired," Demas said.

"True. Maybe they'll come back to thank us once the fear wears off."

"I wouldn't stand around waiting."

Miri sighed, irritated. "That thing could have killed me. I can still taste the poison."

"We did the right thing. They needed our help and we gave it. "

"Is it still the right thing even if they're ungrateful wretches?" Miri said.

Demas smiled, and her anger melted away. "Even then."

Gharik ran with his hand to his throat, as if he still couldn't believe that his head was still attached to his body. When he caught up with the others, Haver clapped him on the shoulder.

"I thought you were dead," Haver said.

"So did I," Gharik growled. He didn't meet Haver's gaze. "The cleric healed me."

"We're still half the number we were when we came to this wretched place," Albric said, glaring at his three acolytes. "The Elder Elemental Eye expects more from its servants."

All three bit their tongues and bowed their heads, though Albric caught a flash of anger in Fargrim's eyes. He would have to watch the dwarf—his stubborn pride would be an obstacle to his service of the Eye.

"While those bold and foolish heroes deal with the devils," Albric said, "the Eye will lead us to the object we seek." He reached beneath his heavy mantle and pulled out the golden spiral symbol he wore, his connection to the Elder Elemental Eye. His fingers tingled as he touched the warm metal, and his head swam at the edge of dream. Follow me wherever I lead, but be on your guard."

He closed his eyes and lost all connection to the world around him. The ruined city fell away, and he stood in a vast silver sea. Stars glimmered in the midst of a fine silvery mist that swirled around his legs. He turned around, looking for a path, and a stream of midnight blue formed from his feet, stretching off into the hazy distance.

He walked along the stream, letting its flow carry him as the silvery dream around him turned into a nightmare. The misty sea on either side fell away into a swirling maelstrom flashing with fire and lightning. The stream became a narrow bridge, and the reek of death wafted up from the abyss on either side, making him dizzy with nausea. He clutched the Eye's symbol to his chest and put one foot carefully in front of the other.

Shadows drifted up from the maelstroms alongside his path, and he heard, as if from a great distance, the shouts of his acolytes, sharp with terror. The shadows—great winged forms like demons or dragons—menaced but did not attack, and though he felt the acolytes draw in closer to him, they did not try to rouse him. One foot in front of the other, he followed the path the Elemental Eye set out for him.

The path began to descend, and darkness rose up around him on all sides. Some kind of obstacle stood before him, but he reached out a hand and felt the Elder Elemental Eye's power coursing down his arm, erupting in a spray of vitriol that washed the barrier away. He stepped through the broken remnants of the door or wall and saw a blinding glow, blood-red and cold as Stygia's icy sea. He threw his arms up to cover his eyes and woke from his dream.

Albric stood in a tiny alcove cluttered with ruined masonry. His three acolytes clustered behind him, wide eyes fixed on him in awe and terror. He allowed the hint of a smile to touch his lips. They should fear him and the power that flowed through him. He turned back to find the source of the glow that blinded him in his dream, the object of his quest.

A gnarled staff stood against the far wall of the small chamber supported by two wooden braces attached to the wall. The staff itself was unremarkable, nothing more than a length of yew branch worn smooth from the touch of many hands. At the heavy head, a lattice of gut strings held a long, slender shard of reddish crystal suspended in place—a shard of the Living Gate.

Albric seized the staff in triumph, and felt a surge of joy that was not entirely his own. The Elder Elemental Eye was pleased.

THE GATES OF
MADNESS

Continues in

CITY UNDER
THE SAND

JEFF MARIOTTE

OCTOBER 2010

WELCOME TO THE DESERT WORLD
OF ATHAS, A LAND RULED BY A HARSH
AND UNFORGIVING CLIMATE, A LAND
GOVERNED BY THE ANCIENT AND
TYRANNICAL SORCERER KINGS.
THIS IS THE LAND OF

CITY UNDER THE SAND
Jeff Mariotte
OCTOBER 2010

*Sometimes lost knowledge is
knowledge best left unknown.*

FIND OUT WHAT YOU'RE MISSING IN THIS
BRAND NEW DARK SUN® ADVENTURE BY
THE AUTHOR OF *COLD BLACK HEARTS*.

ALSO AVAILABLE AS AN E-BOOK!

THE PRISM PENTAD
Troy Denning's classic DARK SUN
series revisited! Check out the great new editions of
The Verdant Passage, *The Crimson Legion*,
The Amber Enchantress, *The Obsidian Oracle*,
and *The Cerulean Storm*.

DARK SUN, DUNGEONS & DRAGONS, WIZARDS OF THE COAST, and their
respective logos are trademarks of Wizards of the Coast LLC in
the U.S.A. and other countries. ©2010 Wizards.

RETURN TO A WORLD OF PERIL, DECEIT, AND INTRIGUE, A WORLD REBORN IN THE WAKE OF A GLOBAL WAR.

TIM WAGGONER'S
LADY RUIN

She dedicated her life to the nation of Karrnath.
With the war ended, and the army asleep—
waiting—in their crypts, Karrnath assigned her
to a new project: find a way to harness
the dark powers of the Plane of Madness.

REVEL IN THE RUIN
DECEMBER 2010

ALSO AVAILABLE AS AN E-BOOK!

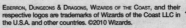
EBERRON, DUNGEONS & DRAGONS, WIZARDS OF THE COAST, and their
respective logos are trademarks of Wizards of the Coast LLC in
the U.S.A. and other countries. ©2010 Wizards.

RICHARD LEE BYERS

BROTHERHOOD OF THE GRIFFON

NOBODY DARED TO CROSS CHESSENTA . . .

BOOK I
THE CAPTIVE FLAME

BOOK II
WHISPER OF VENOM
NOVEMBER 2010

BOOK III
THE SPECTRAL BLAZE
JUNE 2011

. . . WHEN THE RED DRAGON WAS KING.

"This is Thay as it's never been shown before . . . Dark, sinister, foreboding and downright disturbing!"
—Alaundo, Candlekeep.com on Richard Byers's *Unclean*

ALSO AVAILABLE AS E-BOOKS!

FORGOTTEN REALMS, DUNGEONS & DRAGONS, WIZARDS OF THE COAST, and their respective logos are trademarks of Wizards of the Coast LLC in the U.S.A. and other countries. Other trademarks are property of their respective owners. ©2010 Wizards.